THE AFFAIR

Gill Paul lives in London, where she runs her own company producing books for publishers and has worked as an editor and researcher for some eminent historians. Her previous novels include *Women and Children First* (2012). She has written several non-fiction books, including *Titanic Love Stories* (2011), about the honeymoon couples on board the doomed ship, and *Civil War Love Stories* (2013), based on letters couples wrote to each other during the war. As a long-time Elizabeth Taylor fan, it was wonderful to go to Rome while researching *The Affair* and visit all the places she used to frequent. Gill also interviewed people who worked on the *Cleopatra* film set and heard from them first-hand about that extraordinary, life-changing time.

To find out more about Gill Paul please visit www.gillpaul.com

By the same author:
Women and Children First
Titanic Love Stories (Ivy Press)

THE AFFAIR

GILL PAUL

AVON

AVON
A division of HarperCollins*Publishers*
77–85 Fulham Palace Road,
London W6 8JB

www.harpercollins.co.uk

A Paperback Original 2013
1

A catalogue record for this book is available from the British Library

ISBN-13: 9780008277826

Set in Minion by Palimpsest Book Production Limited,
Falkirk, Stirlingshire

Printed and bound in the United States of America by LSC Communications

Find out more about HarperCollins and the environment at
www.harpercollins.co.uk/green

To Anne Nicholson, my lovely aunt,
who always encouraged me to write

Foreword

Ischia, June 1962

The sun hadn't yet risen but a glow was reflected in the eastern sky and the steely Mediterranean was beginning to lighten. An elderly fisherman sat on a wooden bench, struggling to knot frayed ends of a broken net. He liked the stillness of the hour before dawn. The air was uncannily quiet: no breeze, no birdsong, no hum of insects, just the regular shushing of waves.

Over a fence to his left, like a mirage, there were dozens of wooden boats from ancient times moored along a newly built jetty, to be used in a Hollywood movie. Banks of oars protruded from the sides of the vessels, and the sterns and prows curled ornately inwards. He'd heard they were to be destroyed in a mock sea battle and he shook his head at the extravagance. So much craftsmanship, all to be smashed to pieces – the world had gone mad.

He heard a murmur of voices before he saw two dark figures creeping down to the shore. There was a woman's laugh. They wouldn't see him where he sat with his back to a rock but he watched as she stuck a toe into the water and shrieked at the cold. Her companion said something indistinguishable; there was no doubt it was a man. They were

7

drinking from a bottle, and when it was drained the man threw it in the water. The fisherman let slip a tutting sound and the man turned in his direction as though he had heard.

Suddenly he grabbed the woman's arm and pulled her onto the sand. It won't be comfortable there, the fisherman thought, with small griping stones and the odd piece of sea glass. Sometimes stinging shellfish burrow under the surface; that would give her a start. Every second the air was lightening and now he could see that the man was lying on top of her. They're not married, the fisherman guessed. Who would choose to fornicate on a jagged shore instead of the comfort of the marriage bed? The thought briefly made him sigh for the memory of his wife, who'd passed four years ago, and for the vast comfort of her body.

Now the man was humping against the woman beneath him. Did he know there was a witness? Did that excite him? The fisherman took no pleasure in watching – there was no stirring in his loins – but all the same he didn't look away. When they finished, she stood to brush the stones from her back, and he could tell from the tone of her voice that she was laughingly complaining of small injuries. The man kissed her, and they spoke in lowered voices, but soon after he turned and walked back up the hill.

Instead of following, the woman began to stroll along the front, gazing out at the pink horizon, her shoes dangling from her hand. She crossed into the area where the fisherman's boat was hauled up on shore, and stood there for some time just watching.

Once the tip of the sun's brilliant-white dome had slid over the horizon and you could already feel the beginning of the day's heat, she spun around and began to walk up the shore path directly towards the fisherman. As she got close, he saw that she was a beauty, and a familiar one.

She was startled when she noticed him, but said '*Buongiorno*' in an American accent. She watched him, as if trying to gauge how much he had seen, and as she passed she gave him a wink.

He nodded briefly. She should put her shoes on, he thought. There were fish-hooks on the ground, easy to miss but hard to remove from the flesh. But he didn't know how to say that in English, so instead he carried on mending his net.

Some time later, the sun glinted on an object lying in the sand where the couple had been. The fisherman walked down to investigate and saw it was a piece of jewellery made of brilliant stones. He picked it up, surprised by the weight. He'd never seen diamonds before but had no doubt that's what they were. He considered for a minute, then slipped the object in the pocket of his oilskin trousers before going back to his net.

Chapter One

London, July 1961

'I have a telephone call from Los Angeles. In America. Just connecting you.'

'I think there's some mistake . . .' Diana protested – she didn't know anyone who lived in America – but her voice was lost in a succession of clicks and buzzes as the operator pushed plugs into a switchboard.

'I'm putting you through to Mr Wanger,' said a cheery American voice, and Diana raised her eyebrows in surprise. He was the producer of a film about Cleopatra they had been making at Pinewood Studios the previous winter but the plug had been pulled after its star, Elizabeth Taylor, suffered a bout of near-fatal pneumonia.

Walter came on the line, his voice sounding as though he was in a cave somewhere far off. She could hear her own voice echo disconcertingly, and kept pausing for the sound to subside.

'We need you in Rome,' Walter said. 'We start rolling at the end of September but come as soon as you can.'

'You need me? Whatever for?' She had spent one day at Pinewood giving him advice on their gaudy sets, and since she had basically told him they needed to start from scratch if they were aiming at historical accuracy, she'd never expected to hear from him again.

'You've got a PhD in Cleopatra from Oxford University, you're the British Museum's top expert, there's no one else who could bring such authority to the production. Frankly, without you it will only be half the movie it could be. You *must* come, Diana.'

'How long would you need me for?'

'Certainly no longer than six months,' he said. 'Perhaps a little less.'

She gasped. She'd been thinking it might be a week at most, but Walter explained that he wanted her on hand throughout the shooting. He was offering a salary that was almost double what she currently earned – even more than her husband Trevor earned as a university lecturer – and generous expenses as well. The studio would find her a room in a *pensione* and she'd be ferried around by a studio driver. Walter kept talking, mentioning all the perks she would enjoy, and the fact that there would even be a credit for her in the final movie. Diana hardly got a word in edgeways.

The possibility that she might turn down his offer didn't seem to enter his mind and Diana didn't voice her reservations because it all sounded so glamorous. She had never been to Rome; in fact, she had only been overseas once before on a student research trip to Egypt. If she were there while the film was being shot, she would surely get to watch the stars at work, which would be exciting. And she was flattered by Walter Wanger's faith in her.

But looking round their little sitting room after the long-distance call ended, Diana thought again. How could she leave Trevor? She'd miss him terribly and he'd be lost without her.

He was incapable of cooking a nutritious evening meal. Without her around he would probably live on toasted crumpets and cold baked beans straight from the can. He couldn't heat a tin of soup without burning it and he had shrunk all his clothes the one and only time he tried to operate the twin-tub washing machine. She was his wife. It was her duty to look after him.

Fortunately he'd never been one of those men who thought women should give up work on marriage. He'd always applauded the fact that she had a career and encouraged her to take her job seriously; so maybe he would agree to her taking up this opportunity. Six months wasn't so long in the great scheme of things.

Trevor got home late after a meeting of the Victorian Society, and Diana brought him a cup of tea and a plate of cold meat sandwiches for supper before telling him about the offer.

'You've got to be joking!' was his first reaction. 'How presumptuous of him to ask a married woman to leave her husband for months on end!'

'I know it seems a lot, darling, but there are expenses to cover trips back to London, and you could come over to Rome. We could probably spend every weekend together, either here or there. And we'd be able to save lots of money to help us get a bigger place for when . . .' Her voice trailed off.

They'd been trying for a baby ever since she finished her PhD but with no success to date. 'Maybe we're doing it wrong,' Trevor had quipped to hide his disappointment when her last period started. 'We obviously need more practice.' She'd felt guilty, as if it were her fault she wasn't falling pregnant. She'd read in a magazine that it was almost always something wrong with the woman.

'Neither of us is getting any younger,' Trevor reminded her now. 'I don't want to be too old and arthritic to teach my son to ride a bicycle. And your eggs might go rotten if they're left too long.'

'I don't think six months will make much difference,' she argued, but she knew it concerned him because he was eighteen years older than her and already well into his forties.

'Your head will be turned. Walter *Wanker* will ask you to advise on his next film and the one after that and before you know it you'll be swanning all over the world without ever needing to use your brain. Did you know he made *Invasion of the Bodysnatchers*? I'm beginning to feel that's what has happened to you. Aliens have come and replaced you with a substitute Diana who is a completely different person from the woman I married.' He smiled and rubbed her knee, trying to turn it into a joke, but she could tell he was upset.

'I'm still me,' she said, reaching out to hold his hand. 'I'm still your wife. I suppose I've just been feeling that I want a bit of excitement before I settle down to motherhood. I'll be tied to the home for twenty years or more once I'm bringing up our brood, and advising on the film would be a little adventure I could have first: something exciting to tell our children and grandchildren about one day.'

A hurt look clouded his eyes. 'So our life isn't exciting? What about all those thrilling departmental sherry evenings?'

She smiled at the sarcasm. 'I like our life, really I do. I even like the sherry evenings – but sometimes I feel trapped.' He took a sharp intake of breath so she continued quickly. 'It's as if my life is all mapped out for me and I have to stick precisely to the plan. I'd love it if you were transferred to Rome for six months – or anywhere foreign – and I could jet out to visit you at weekends. I'd love to travel more and explore foreign cities.'

'We can do all that some day, but you know that right now I have to build my reputation by publishing another book – if I can ever find the time. It would set me back months if I had to start doing laundry and housework on top of my course work because you were off gallivanting on a film set.'

'Bring your laundry to Rome at weekends and I'll do it for you there,' she quipped thoughtlessly.

'Now you're being silly,' he snapped, and there was a hint of anger in his tone, which he quickly disguised. 'Can you imagine me arriving in the Eternal City every weekend with a suitcase full of sweaty socks? If they decided to search my case at customs, they'd pass out from the fumes.'

'Perhaps I could use some of my salary to hire you a charlady.'

'Oh, it's *your* salary now, is it? I pay the rent on the flat here with *my* salary, and you get to make charitable offers with yours. Is that it?'

'I didn't mean it that way,' she whispered, annoyed with herself. Perhaps she shouldn't rub it in that she would be earning more than him. This was the closest they'd come to arguing for a long time and she knew she was handling it badly.

'Besides, I thought you wanted to apply for a junior lecturer's post as soon as something suitable comes up. What would the selection panel think of a six-month sabbatical spent on a Hollywood movie? It doesn't make you seem a very serious person.'

Diana was silent for a moment. She knew she would always have regrets if she backed down and didn't grab this opportunity.

'The truth is that I'm not as serious as you, Trevor. I'm bored with academia. I want a new challenge out there in the wider world instead of the dusty little part of it we're used to.'

Trevor was staring down at his lap. 'Can't you find a new challenge in London? I'd be miserable without you, darling.' When she didn't reply, he stood up. 'Anyway, I've got a full day tomorrow in boring old academia so I'd best go to bed now.' He kissed her quickly on the cheek as if to say 'no hard feelings'. 'You won't be long, will you?'

'I fancy another cup of tea. Warm the bed for me.'

In the kitchen, Diana sat at the red Formica kitchen table holding a piece of paper with Walter Wanger's phone numbers on it, scrutinising them as if the answer was hidden there in secret code. What was she playing at? She yearned to see Rome – but then she and Trevor could always go there on holiday. She was curious to see what life was like on a film set, but maybe Walter would let her go for a shorter period, perhaps just up to Christmas. Would Trevor accept that? She felt a pang, and knew that once she got involved in the film she wouldn't want to leave halfway through.

Was she being intolerably selfish? Yes, she knew she was. She was the wife, the homemaker, and it wouldn't be fair to leave Trevor in the lurch for so long. Her career should be secondary to looking after his needs. It's just that she'd thought she and Trevor were somehow more modern and progressive than other couples. That's one of the things she liked about their relationship.

Her head was swirling with thoughts and she couldn't make them quiet down. She knew she should go through to the bedroom, climb into bed beside him and whisper, 'Of course I won't go. I'm sorry for suggesting it.' He'd turn to kiss her and all would be well. That's what she must do, she decided, but she didn't stand up. There was a hard little nugget in her heart, a selfish nugget perhaps, but a stubborn one.

The clock on the mantelpiece struck midnight and then one o'clock and still Diana sat there, her head in her hands. Was there any argument she could use to persuade Trevor to let her go? The money would be useful, but every other reason sounded trivial. Women like her simply didn't do things like this. But she desperately wanted to. The more she thought about it, the more she knew she couldn't bear to let this opportunity slip through her fingers. She had to persuade him. Somehow she must.

At three a.m., she went through to the bedroom and crawled into bed. Trevor was in the depths of sleep and barely moving. She could feel the warmth emanating from his body but she felt bereft at the seemingly unbridgeable distance between them.

Chapter Two

Rome, July 1961

'*Un espresso, per favore,*' Scott Morgan called to a waiter, then sat down and folded his long legs under a pavement table. The air in the Piazza Navona was thick with petrol fumes and the sun was already fierce, exacerbating the pounding in his temples. He pressed his fingers into his eye sockets.

'*Hai avuto una bella sbornia sta'notte, eh?*' the waiter joked as he brought the coffee, then mimed glugging back a drink and staggering drunkenly. Some tourists at the next table sniggered.

'*Grazie Giovanni, non prendermi in giro!*' He managed a feeble grin.

The waiter was absolutely right, of course. He'd been out drinking with the foreign press pack the night before and, swept along by the camaraderie of shared anecdotes and enjoying the feeling of being a 'real journalist', he'd allowed himself to down several more whisky shots than was prudent. The others had egged him on, eager to see the youngest of their number pass out or throw up his supper all over the roof terrace of the Eden Hotel.

Scott sensed a certain jealousy from these raddled old hacks, who had worked their way up from junior copy-taking roles on local rags to reach the height of their careers as Italian correspondents for national papers back home. It was a posting they felt they had earned after long years of covering rodeos and manning the obituaries page, so it would hardly be surprising if they resented the fact that Scott had walked straight into the role from college, with only a Harvard degree in international relations and several pieces in the *Harvard Crimson* to recommend him. Granted, he wasn't working for *The New York Times* or the *Washington Post*. His paper, the *Midwest Daily*, was a respectable middle-market title, popular with farmers in the Bible Belt, but it was still a prestigious place to start his career. He didn't tell the others that the job had been offered after a phone call from his father, who owned a substantial stake in the business.

Scott had arrived in Rome in May and the first thing he did was buy himself a Vespa, a pair of Ray-Ban sunglasses and some black cotton turtlenecks. He wanted to be like the ultra-cool character played by Marcello Mastroianni in *La Dolce Vita*, seducing beautiful women all over town and fêted by the famous for the exposure he could get them, while at the same time filing serious, important stories that would win the admiration of his peers. So far the reality hadn't quite lived up to the image. In fact, he'd failed to get a single story in print since his arrival two months earlier, something the hacks hadn't hesitated to tease him about the previous evening.

'Had all your stories spiked, then? We should call you "Spike". What do you reckon, boys?'

They'd all joined in. 'Pass the ashtray, Spike.' 'Fancy another shot, Spike?'

When he read his compatriots' stories, about the strange allegiances between Italian political parties or impenetrable agriculture statistics from the south of the country, he had to suppress a yawn. Maybe that's what he should be doing, but he couldn't write stories like that because he didn't have the contacts. He'd expected to find a well-staffed office full of people who would set up interviews for him. All he'd have to do would be turn up, ask some insightful questions, and scribble off his piece. Instead, his only colleague was a middle-aged Italian woman who answered the phone and typed his correspondence. His predecessor, a journalist called Bradley Wyndham, had left without passing on any contact numbers or advice and it was entirely up to Scott to make his own way.

'Did any of you guys know Bradley Wyndham?' he asked the hacks, and they all said they'd met him but didn't know him well.

'Believe it or not, he was teetotal,' someone commented, incredulous. 'A journalist who doesn't drink is like a shark that doesn't swim. He wrote some decent stories but he wasn't one of us.'

'Maybe he had a health problem,' Scott suggested. 'Or maybe he was religious.' No one seemed to have any personal information about Bradley Wyndham or know why he had left Rome so abruptly.

One of the hacks, a man named Joe, started quoting his 'best friend' Truman Capote: 'Truman said "I don't care what anyone says about me, so long as it isn't true." Isn't that hilarious? When you're with Truman, you get the urge to take out your notebook and write down what he says because he comes out with the most amazing things from thin air.'

'Yeah, but then he repeats them to anyone who'll listen for the next ten years,' another hack drawled. 'He's never minded quoting himself.'

Scott was sceptical about Joe's friendship with Truman Capote. Surely the fêted New York writer would mix in more rarefied circles?

Sitting in the café the morning after their drinking session, Scott mused that maybe Rome wasn't the right posting for him. There simply wasn't anything he could write about. He wished he had been sent to Berlin, where a wall was being constructed to separate the Russian and American halves of the city and people were making daring last-minute dashes across before it was too late. Or the USSR, where Khrushchev was boasting of Soviet nuclear weaponry and the fact they'd taken the lead in the space race. Or Israel, where Adolf Eichmann was on trial for war crimes. Though at least he wasn't in Vietnam, where the CIA-backed Southern Vietnamese were being pushed back by the Viet Cong. That all sounded a bit hairy. He didn't fancy the danger and discomfort of a conflict zone.

At ten-thirty, the door of the building opposite opened and a stunning young Italian girl emerged, as she did every day at that time. It was the reason why Scott frequented that particular café, several streets away from his office. The girl had wave after wave of glossy-black hair and the prettiest face he'd ever seen: heart-shaped, with high cheekbones and melting chocolate eyes. She wore old-fashioned summer dresses in pale sherbet colours, tied with a sash round the waist and reaching modestly to well below her knees. Sometimes when the sun was behind her Scott could see the outline of her hips and legs through the fabric. Since he'd first set eyes on her, he'd been hopelessly smitten. His heart actually skipped a beat when she stepped out of her house each morning.

She was carrying a basket, and he knew that she was on her way to the market for provisions but that she would stop in a church to say mass. He'd followed her a few times and the routine was always the same.

She crossed the road and as she passed in front of the café, Scott called '*Buongiorno, signorina bella!*'

She nodded in his direction and gave a quick, nervous smile, without stopping.

He'd been greeting her most mornings for over a month now and was pleased that at least she now acknowledged him, although she hadn't yet returned the greeting. What were the chances that one day she might agree to go on a date? He fantasised about sitting across a candlelit table, wooing her in his best Italian, and then managing to kiss her in a dark side street as he walked her home. That was as far as the fantasy would stretch. You'd never get a girl like that into bed without marrying her and he wasn't prepared to go that far. But Scott liked a challenge and there was no doubt this girl presented a challenge.

He decided to make it his mission to get a date with her before the end of the summer. He was single. She wasn't wearing a wedding ring or any jewellery apart from a gold crucifix on a chain round her neck. What harm could it do? And if it came off, he'd have to get a photograph of the two of them to show his buddies back home; otherwise they'd never believe he could attract such a stunner.

Chapter Three

Diana arrived in Rome's Leonardo da Vinci airport on the 25th of September and collected her suitcase from a pile in the arrivals hall. She'd been told that someone would be there to meet her and that they'd be holding a card with her name on it, but she couldn't see any such person. It was a scorching day and she wished she hadn't worn her winter coat, but there hadn't been room for it in her suitcase. She took it off and folded it over her arm. Several taxi drivers approached, competing for her attention, but she waved them away. Her driver was probably stuck in traffic and running late.

As she waited, the arguments of the past few weeks echoed around her head. Trevor was right: she must be a very self-centred person. She knew she was being a bad wife. She knew she was letting him down. Their discussions had got increasingly bitter as each became entrenched in their positions. She couldn't contemplate turning down the opportunity to work on the film but Trevor had taken it personally, as if it meant she didn't love him enough. She tried every argument but he simply reiterated that he couldn't manage without her, that he'd miss her too much.

They had barely spoken since she booked her flight. He was so hurt he couldn't even look at her, and she was terrified that she might have damaged her marriage irrevocably. Surely

Trevor wouldn't divorce her? They didn't know any divorcees among their social set, or even at the university. What would she do if he decided to take that extraordinary step? She'd given up a secure, ordered life for the complete unknown, and it seemed emblematic of the chaos she could expect that no one had arrived to meet her at the airport. She stood amongst the taxi drivers in the bustling entrance hall wondering if she had just made the biggest mistake of her life.

After hanging around for half an hour, she changed some money at an exchange bureau. They told her she needed *gettoni* for the payphone so she purchased some and used them to call Walter Wanger's office, trying several times before she worked out which bits of the code had to be included when you dialled. The phone rang out but no one answered. Stilling her anxiety, she decided to take a taxi to Cinecittà film studios. What else could she do, since she didn't know the address of her *pensione*? She picked an older-looking driver, one who seemed less pushy than the others, and let him heft her suitcase into the trunk. Thank goodness she spoke passable Italian, learned on an extracurricular course she'd taken at university. She had always picked up languages easily while Trevor, despite his superior intellect, had no facility for them.

During the half-hour drive she wondered what could have gone wrong. Were they not expecting her that day? Had they changed their minds about hiring her? The driver pulled up outside the entrance to a single-storey peach-coloured building with the Cinecittà sign over the gate. Diana paid the driver and stood sweltering in the heat as an overweight guard in a dark suit telephoned Walter Wanger's office, then tried another number in the production block. Diana's stomach was in knots. What if this was all a huge mistake and they weren't expecting her at all? Had she jeopardised her marriage over a misunderstanding?

A pony-tailed girl in white Capri pants came running across the grass towards them. 'Diana?' she called. 'You must have thought we'd forgotten all about you. It's the first day of shooting and everybody was on set to watch, including the driver we had asked to pick you up. I swear, you can never rely on Italians.' She was American.

'It's fine,' Diana said. 'I'm here now.'

'Let's take your suitcase up to the production office and make everything official. You need to sign your contract and then I'll show you around. My name's Candy,' she added as an afterthought.

Diana followed her across a large grassy lawn. Dozens of people sprawled there, smoking cigarettes, catching the sun, reading magazines, chatting and laughing, and they glanced at Diana and her unwieldy suitcase with a flicker of curiosity before looking away again. The girls were all dressed in Capri pants or above-the-knee skirts with little blouses, and she suddenly felt old-fashioned in her longer, fifties-style skirt and jacket and her beige leather gloves. No one else was wearing gloves. Their legs were bare and bronzed while she wore American tan tights and she thought with envy how much cooler they must feel.

Candy led her to a group of buildings. 'These are the production offices,' she said. 'You can leave your suitcase here.'

She shook hands with several people sitting behind desks and signed her name as indicated. She was informed that she would receive her salary of 50,000 *lire* (about 28 British pounds), less local taxes, each Friday evening at the end of the working day, and that her permit to work in Italy would be arranged by the studio staff, although she would have to register with the police in the next few days.

As they left, she paused on the steps to watch as a man in a Roman toga came towards them, then did a double take when she realised it was Rex Harrison. She and Trevor had seen him in *My Fair Lady* at the Theatre Royal, Drury Lane, playing Professor Higgins, the man who teaches a Cockney flower girl to 'speak proper'. It had been a brilliant production and received a standing ovation, the audience clapping until their hands were numb. Rex Harrison passed without glancing in her direction, but she felt a bubble of excitement all the same.

'Have you met Walter?' Candy asked. Diana agreed that she had, during her one day at Pinewood. 'I'll take you over to say hi to Joe Mankiewicz, if we can catch a second of his time.'

'What does he do?' Diana asked, and Candy stared in amazement.

'He's the director. Didn't you know that?'

'I thought it was Rouben Mamoulian. I'm sure I read that somewhere.'

'Yeah, it was, but he got fired ages ago. The cast has all changed since we came to Italy. But we've still got Liz – for better or worse.'

'What do you mean?'

Candy rolled her eyes comically. 'You'll find out.'

Someone popped a head round the door. 'Candy, there's a problem with the elephants. They're being really aggressive and no one can get near them. Will you go and talk to the elephant guy, see what his explanation is?'

'Sure,' Candy agreed. 'Why don't you come with me, Diana? I'll get a chance to show you around. You can leave your coat and jacket. It's sweltering out there.' She glanced down at Diana's prim skirt and tights and seemed about to say something else but thought better of it.

They strolled up a shady avenue. Everywhere there were neatly mown grass verges and boulevards lined with stately rows of Roman pine trees and oleander bushes. Lots of people waved and called hello to Candy as she passed, and she called back but didn't make any move to introduce Diana.

'The commissary – that's canteen to you Brits – is down there and the bar's over that way.' She pointed to a separate block but walked straight past it. Diana was parched and could have used a cool drink but didn't want to cause any bother. 'I've reserved a room for you in the Pensione Splendid near Piazza Repubblica so it will only take you about twenty minutes to get here in the morning. A studio driver will pick you up around eight.' She chatted on about practicalities and Diana tried to remember everything while simultaneously getting her bearings in the vast studio complex, which seemed to stretch for miles in every direction.

They could hear and smell the elephants well before reaching the enclosure. Roaring, with trunks raised, and stamping their feet, they were terrifying the horses in the nearby stables. Diana couldn't count them all as some were inside a sandstone outbuilding, but four were pacing around outside. Candy approached a man who seemed to be in charge and had a conversation with him in Italian. He spread his arms and shrugged, telling her that it wasn't his fault they were restless; that's just how they were.

Diana looked at the poor creatures, each restrained with a heavy chain around one ankle. Their eyes seemed astonishingly human and knowing. The closest regarded her as one fellow creature to the other, requesting sympathy for its plight. Then she looked at its ears, which were small and drooping. She remembered her school biology teacher explaining that African elephants have large ears that fan back over their necks in the shape of Africa, while Indian ones have smaller ears that droop to a point, like a map of India.

She asked the trainer, '*Questi sono elefanti indiani?*'

'*Sì, certamente,*' he replied then spun off into a chain of complaints about his contract and the conditions under which he had to work.

'Is that a problem?' Candy asked Diana.

'It's just that Cleopatra would, of course, have had African elephants. Her kingdom was in Africa. Hardly any viewers will spot the difference, I'm sure.'

'Fantastic!' Candy exclaimed. 'You may just have given us a way to get out of our contract with this guy and his over-aggressive animals. Walter will be thrilled.'

'Oh, good. Should we go and find him?' Diana felt she would like to see a friendly face. Perhaps he would be able to explain what was expected of her.

'You can never find Walter when you're looking for him – only when you're not,' Candy said. 'We'll head back, and maybe stop for a drink? You look hot.'

Diana nodded gratefully. She had pale English skin that didn't take the sun well and she could feel her cheeks tingling after half an hour in the Roman sunshine. She asked the barman for some water, which came in a green glass bottle with a pretty label saying San Pellegrino. Why bother with bottled water, she wondered, when Rome was reputed to have the best tap water in the world, brought straight from mountain springs by their famous Roman aqueducts? It seemed crazy.

Candy had business in a back part of the studio and Diana tagged along, feeling completely lost. How would she ever find her way around this virtual metropolis? She was hot and tired and felt very grateful when at last Candy offered to call a driver to take Diana to her *pensione*.

She found she was on the second floor of an old building, in a large bright room with its own tiny balcony and a view towards the Baths of Diocletian. The room contained a double bed, a wardrobe, and a wash-basin, and it all looked neat and clean. On a side table there was a Cinzano ashtray with the familiar red, white and blue lettering. There was a shared bathroom down the hall and the first thing she did was undress and soak in some lukewarm water to wash away the grime of travel. She dressed in a cool cotton sundress, rubbed Pond's cold cream on her cheeks and went to ask the *padrona* if she might use her telephone.

'Sorry, it's out of order,' the woman told her. 'The nearest public phone is in the bar across the street but you will need some *gettoni*. You can buy them at the *tabaccaio* over towards Termini station.' She gestured vaguely.

Diana kicked herself for not buying more *gettoni* at the airport earlier. She knew the station was several streets away. She'd wanted to ring Trevor to let him know she'd arrived safely. Ideally she would have liked to tell him about seeing Rex Harrison, and about the Indian elephants, and all her other impressions of the set, but she knew she couldn't expect him to share her excitement. They were barely speaking to each other.

She felt a sharp pang of missing him. They normally told each other everything, in a long stream of conversation that they updated as soon as possible after spending any time apart.

It was hard to move from that intimacy to a life that was unshared, unwitnessed.

She hung up her clothes then sat on the bed looking out across the rooftops of the Eternal City as the sun gradually set, picking out individual windows to blaze fiery bright for a few minutes each, and casting a golden glow on domes and turrets. The smell of cooking wafted up from the kitchen of a *trattoria* next door and she decided she would eat there then come back for an early night. She'd call Trevor the following day. He hadn't even said goodbye properly so he had no right to expect her to ring on her first evening.

Chapter Four

'Hey, Scott, how's it going?' his editor's voice boomed down the phone. 'I've got a commission for you: fifteen hundred words on the Italian Communist Party. How does it differ from the style of Communism in the Soviet Bloc? What are its aims, and how much influence does it have in Italy? Think you can handle that?'

'Sure! When do you need it?'

'Is a week enough time? Or are you too busy chasing Italian chicks?' The editor saw Scott as an international playboy type and Scott didn't like to disillusion him by admitting he hadn't had so much as a kiss since he arrived in Europe.

'A week it is,' he replied. At last he could demonstrate what he was capable of. Those booze-sodden hacks in the Eden Hotel bar would have to take him more seriously once he'd had an intelligent opinion piece published.

He needed some direct quotes from Roman politicians so his secretary told him about a translator called Angelo who could set up the interviews and assist when his very basic Italian would not suffice. It would be his foot in the door of Italian politics, and it was just a shame that the first politicians he would meet were Communists. Scott knew very strongly how he felt about that. In fact he had begun to write the piece before meeting them.

Some trade unionists here in Rome condemned the brutal Soviet repression of the Hungarian uprising, but the party leadership kept quiet because they know where their bread is buttered, he wrote. *Moscow holds the purse strings on which their power base rests and even if they use more moderate language than Señor Fidel Castro, they still believe that the working classes should unite to overturn capitalism. Some 4 percent of Italian workers are members of the Communist Party but you can bet that these are not the forward-thinking textile workers who are making Milan such a modern center of clothing manufacture, and not the directors in charge of protecting the famous antiquities of Rome, Venice and Florence, because Communism would abandon those to dust. It is the politically ignorant peasant who believes all those fine words about sharing wealth, little realising that under Communism there would be no wealth, along with no freedom of speech or action.*

He interviewed the politicians but used their quotes in such a way as to make them sound naïve at best and self-serving at worst:

Corruption is a way of life in Italy, he opined, *and no one is exempt, but those of the far left with their moral posturing about the good of the many are by far the greatest hypocrites. Look how quickly Señor Castro rushed to abandon democratic elections in Cuba earlier this year. Given half a chance, Italian Communists would do so even faster.*

It was what his readers in the Midwest, smarting from American defeat in the Bay of Pigs just four months earlier, wanted to hear, and it happened to be what Scott believed. He and his classmates at Harvard had been aghast when the CIA-trained band of counter-revolutionaries were defeated by Castro's forces, with their Soviet-designed tank destroyers and fighter-bombers. Now it seemed Americans must resign themselves to Reds on the doorstep, just 90 miles across the water from the Florida Keys, unless John F. Kennedy had some other plan up his sleeve. Surely he must.

Scott's editor ran the piece across a double page, with photos of Italian workers in the fields alongside a textile loom in Milan, and Scott was thrilled when he got his copy by special courier. His byline was directly beneath the headline: 'by Scott Morgan, our Rome correspondent'.

A day later, though, he received a phone call from Angelo, the translator. 'I hope you never want to interview any Italian politicians again,' he said, 'because, to use an English phrase, you have burned all your boats.'

'Nobody will read it here in Rome, will they?' Scott asked. The thought simply hadn't occurred to him.

'Of course they will. They gave the interviews and their press advisors will have obtained copies to see how they were portrayed in your article. You can be sure they will not be pleased with your patronising attitude and lack of any attempt to understand the issues.'

'You're kidding. Why didn't you warn me?'

'My mistake. I gave you credit for a little intelligence.'

That evening, Scott went to the Eden Hotel to see what his compatriots thought, and he was greeted with much hooting and clapping on the back. 'Aw heck, you didn't want to be a political journalist anyway, did you, Spike?'

'You've all read it?'

'How could we miss your print debut, especially when it refers to Communist Party members as politically ignorant peasants?'

Joe bought him a large whisky and Scott downed it quickly.

'Shall I tell you *my* secret?' Joe slurred, his evening's drinking obviously well advanced. 'I read the Italian press and adapt stories from that. My editor never knows any better. Grab a dictionary and spend the morning going through *Corriere della Sera* and *La Stampa* and you'll do just fine here.'

The next morning, Scott decided to do just that, but the only stories of international interest were about Elizabeth Taylor and her entourage arriving in Rome to make a Cleopatra film at Cinecittà. There were descriptions of her seven-bedroom villa on Via Appia Antica, her children, her dogs, her recent near-death illness, and a rehash of the scandal when she 'stole' her current husband Eddie Fisher from her rival Debbie Reynolds. Scott was scornful of this kind of gutter-press journalism and determined not to lower himself. His heroes were Norman Mailer and Tom Wolfe, serious men who wrote in an innovative style that read like fiction but contained hard facts. Neither of them would sink so low as to comment on Elizabeth Taylor's dogs. He felt gloomy.

The clock read twenty past ten and he realised he just had time to catch his beautiful Italian girl leaving her house. She had begun smiling at him when he greeted her and once she had even returned his '*Buongiorno*' so he felt it was important to keep up the momentum.

He jumped on the Vespa and scooted through the traffic, arriving in Piazza Navona with minutes to spare. He popped into a tobacconist's to buy some Camels and through the window he saw her emerge from her house and cross the street. Throwing the money over the counter, he was able to step out of the shop straight into her path.

'Ah, *buongiorno, signorina bellissima*,' he grinned. 'We meet *finalmente!*'

She blushed and looked down modestly. He was directly in front of her so she couldn't walk on and there was a moment's hesitation while she tried to decide what to do.

'That's a pretty dress,' he said in Italian.

'*Grazie, signore,*' she said, then side-stepped neatly and continued down the road.

Scott stood and watched and when she reached the corner she turned back to see if he was still there.

'Thank you!' he whispered, and clenched his fists in delight.

Chapter Five

Next morning, Diana was picked up by a studio car just after eight and driven out to Cinecittà. The gate swung open and she felt very important as she showed her pass to the guard on duty and he waved her through with a '*Buongiorno, Signora Bailey*'.

When she opened the door of the production office, the first thing she noticed was a very attractive Italian man sitting on a desk, chatting to the girls in the office. He appraised Diana's figure, eyes sweeping up and down her body, then winked.

'Is she the one who's been causing all the problems? She looks so innocent.' He was teasing, his English fluent but heavily accented.

Annoyingly, Diana felt her cheeks flush scarlet and a blonde woman who looked as though she might be in her thirties took pity on her. She came over with an outstretched hand. 'I'm Hilary Armitage, and you must be Diana? This rogue here is Ernesto Balboni. He helps to procure things we need for the film.'

'You have been complaining about the elephants, I hear,' Ernesto challenged. 'What did the poor creatures ever do to you?'

Diana didn't know how to take him, so she answered seriously. 'I'm sorry, I didn't mean to cause trouble but Cleopatra wouldn't have had Indian elephants . . .'

'Clever you for actually knowing the difference,' Hilary interrupted. Her accent was English girls' boarding school, but she didn't seem toffee-nosed.

'They wanted elephants, I got them elephants,' Ernesto continued. 'It was a lot of trouble for me, and now you say, "I don't like these elephants." OK, I will fix it, but only if Diana will have lunch with me today.'

'I-I'm not sure. I may be busy.' Diana wasn't sure if he was simply being flirtatious or if it was part of her job to lunch with him.

'Leave the girl alone, Ernesto. She's just arrived and already you are trying to seduce her.'

He jumped down from the desk and Diana saw that he wasn't tall – only slightly taller than her – but he had a very good figure, with muscular arms under his open-necked, short-sleeved shirt. He reached out to shake Diana's hand and gripped it in warm fingers that held on much longer than they should have. 'We will have to see a lot of each other so I can choose props that are historically correct. If you can't manage lunch, maybe we should have dinner tonight?'

Fearing a misunderstanding, Diana held out her left hand to show her wedding ring. 'I'm married,' she said.

'Of course you are. You are far too beautiful to be single. I'll see you later. *Buongiorno, bella.*'

He glanced back and grinned at her on his way out the door. Did that mean he thought she had accepted the dinner invitation or not? She had no idea, but hoped that since they hadn't made a firm arrangement it didn't count.

Hilary rolled her eyes before showing Diana her desk and giving her a simple map of the studios to help her find her way around. She explained how to use the telephones and said to help herself if she wanted to phone home; she showed her where the stationery was kept, and the kettle and their office supply of English tea. She was friendly and efficient, but several times she glanced at her watch so Diana could tell she was impatient to get on.

'Do you have any idea what I am supposed to be doing today?' Diana asked. 'I haven't seen Mr Wanger yet to ask about my responsibilities.'

Hilary seemed surprised. 'I assumed he would have explained that to you. He won't be in till later because there was a PR disaster yesterday. A party of Congress wives turned up for a tour of the set hoping to meet Elizabeth Taylor but no one had told her and she doesn't like surprises so she wouldn't play ball. Walter will be tied up all day smoothing that one over. But they're filming a Temple of Isis scene on sound stage 5 so why not go down there and maybe you'll have a chance to introduce yourself to Joe.'

'The director?'

Hilary nodded. 'You'll find sound stage 5 on your map. Lunch is served in the commissary from twelve till three, and you can get snacks at the bar all day long.'

'Great, thanks.'

The office was empty so Diana made herself a cup of tea, then unclipped her right earring and lifted the phone to ask the operator to connect her with Trevor's office at City University. There was a lot of clicking and buzzing and a long period of silence before she heard the familiar voice of his secretary on the line.

'Hello, it's Diana calling from Rome. I don't suppose Trevor's around?'

The reply was so muffled she could hardly hear it, but it seemed he was in a meeting.

'Will you tell him I rang and that I've arrived safely? I'll try again soon.'

She was relieved not to have to deal with him being curt on the phone. At least he knew she was safe now. She finished her tea, picked up a notepad and pen plus her studio map, and headed out towards sound stage 5.

She walked around the lawn, then turned down a wide avenue with a row of pine trees planted along a central reservation. The sound stages looked like aeroplane hangars. When she got to number 5, she pushed open a heavy, padded door and was confronted by a huge dark cavern full of people. A beam of light illuminated an area where a scene was being prepared. There was a camera mounted on a small crane and behind it stood a portly middle-aged man in a crumpled Hawaiian shirt and a baseball cap, who was studying the scene with a dyspeptic expression. She wondered what his role was because, despite his scruffy appearance, others seemed to be taking orders from him.

It was hotter than outside, like working in an oven. A huge sign in both English and Italian read 'No Smoking' and there was a picture of a cigarette with an emphatic slash through it. Underneath it there was a bucket of sand and a sign saying 'Use in case of fire' but she noticed that it was being used as an ashtray and had dozens of cigarette butts in it.

'Are they filming?' she asked someone, and straight away fingers came up to lips and there was a chorus of shushing. Someone called '*Silenzio!*'

'Upstairs,' her nearest neighbour whispered, pointing to a staircase, so Diana crept off the set and up the stairs, not sure where she was heading. A handwritten sign on the landing at the top said 'Makeup, Dressing room 23'. There was a long corridor of closed doors, each carefully numbered. The only one open was number 23 and a bright light emanated from within. She glanced inside to see a pretty blonde girl doing her own makeup at a dressing-table mirror surrounded by dazzling lightbulbs. Some Italian women were sitting around chatting.

'Hello. Are you an actress?' Diana asked the blonde girl.

She gave a broad smile and answered in an English accent with a hint of Birmingham in it. 'No, I do the makeup along with these ladies. I'm just fixing myself up while we wait.'

'What are you waiting for?'

'Elizabeth Taylor's not here yet so they can't start filming. She's always late.'

'So they're not actually filming downstairs?' Diana was relieved. 'I thought I'd spoiled a shot because I asked a question and everyone told me to shut up.'

'They might have been doing fill-in shots. They're shooting live sound on this picture so they need dead quiet when the cameras are rolling. You're supposed to check whether the red light is on above the door before you go in. Don't worry, though – you'd know all about it if you'd spoiled a take!'

'Where is your accent from?' Diana asked, trying to place it.

'Leamington Spa. Near Warwick.'

'You're kidding! I was born in Leamington Spa and lived there till I was twelve!' Diana grinned, delighted to meet someone from home. It made her realise how lonely she'd been feeling.

The girl's name was Helen, she told Diana. They chatted about which part of town they came from and the schools they had attended. Diana asked how she came to be working on the film, and Helen said she had just graduated from a makeup course when she got the job at Pinewood and her school principal had negotiated a clause in her contract that meant they had to take her with them when the production moved to Rome. Most of the other makeup artists were Italian.

'It's a great place to work. I've met all the stars,' she said excitedly. 'Yesterday I was called down to assist Elizabeth Taylor's makeup artist, and Elizabeth actually asked my name. Wasn't that nice of her?'

'What was she like?'

'Oh my God, those eyes! I never believed it in the magazines when they said she has purple eyes but she really does: a kind of deep violet shade. It's almost like you can't breathe when you look directly at her. I asked her to sign my autograph book. Look!'

She showed Diana a book bound in pink fabric and opened it to a page with the signature 'Elizabeth T' followed by an 'X'.

'Lucky you,' Diana said. 'Who else's have you got?'

'Just crew really. I don't like to ask actors as it doesn't look professional. After all I'm here to do a job! Anyway, Rex Harrison is too scary to ask!'

Helen talked rapidly, full of awe at the surroundings she found herself in. She was probably in her early twenties, only a couple of years younger than Diana, but she had a childlike quality that was beguiling, and she was the first truly friendly person Diana had met there.

'There's no one about,' Helen pointed out. 'Shall we go and have a Coke? The bar's not far.'

Diana agreed. She knew she should be trying to find someone who could tell her what her job entailed, but perhaps it would be useful to hear a bit more about the personalities on the set. Helen told the Italian women she'd be back in half an hour and they nodded and carried on talking amongst themselves.

The bar had some tables on a broad outdoor terrace and Helen sat down at one of them, Diana beside her. They attracted appreciative glances from some Italian workmen on a coffee break. *They're interested in Helen*, Diana thought. *Not me.*

'I don't like coming here on my own,' Helen lowered her voice. 'It makes me self-conscious when they stare like that.'

They ordered two Cokes, and Diana explained how she came to be working on the film.

'Gosh, you're an intellectual. That's so groovy! Don't worry about not knowing what you're supposed to be doing. I don't think anyone does. We're all just muddling through, but we're getting paid to live in an amazing city and work with lots of famous people. It can't be bad, can it? Hey, a crowd of us are going out for a pizza tonight. Do you want to come?'

Diana agreed straight away. She would rather do that than go for dinner with Ernesto, which had all the potential to be compromising.

'Amazing! Give me the address of your *pensione* and I'll pick you up in a taxi about eight o'clock.' Suddenly she nudged

Diana and nodded towards a man walking down the avenue holding a small dog.

'Who's that?' Diana whispered.

'Eddie Fisher, Elizabeth Taylor's husband. The one she stole from Debbie Reynolds. He's handsome, isn't he?'

He was indeed, Diana thought, except for rather pitted skin where he must have suffered from acne in his teens. He was quite short as well. All the men seemed short. 'Is he working on the film?' she asked.

'He's got some job title or other but basically he runs around fetching drinks for Elizabeth and clearing up after the dogs.' Helen rolled her eyes.

Diana watched as he turned the corner and wondered what it must feel like to be married to the woman everyone said was the most beautiful in the world. You'd need to be quite a confident person. She'd heard Eddie Fisher was a singer but wasn't sure if she'd ever heard any of his songs.

Helen began to sing: 'Cindy, oh Cindy . . .' She had a sweet voice. 'You must remember that one? It was quite a hit a couple of years ago.'

Diana shook her head. She wasn't up to date with popular music: Trevor liked classical so that tended to be what they listened to. She felt so out of touch. She was only twenty-five but she might as well be forty because her life had become so middle-aged.

After they finished their drinks, they walked back to sound stage 5 and Helen scurried upstairs to the makeup room, while Diana walked back into the hangar-like set. The door was open and the red light was off. Round a corner she could see a huge cauldron made out of papier-mâché and surrounded by goblets and bronze statuettes of jackal-headed Anubis figures. She smiled, recognising the image they had used for reference, one that was now largely believed by historians to be a third-century fake. She took out her pad and began to scribble notes.

A young assistant was measuring the distance between the altar and the lens of the camera, which she saw was mounted on tracks. Some young women appeared in ancient Egyptian costume and she guessed they must be hand-maidens. The costumes weren't too bad, actually – someone had done their homework – but the hair and makeup were totally Hollywood.

There was a call of 'Quiet on the set' and people began to move towards the exit.

'Are you supposed to be here?' an American woman with a clipboard asked Diana.

'I'm a researcher. I don't know,' Diana said.

'Technical crew and actors only,' she ordered, pointing to the door, so Diana obeyed.

She wandered around for a while then decided to go for an early lunch and made her way to the commissary, following the little map Hilary had given her. It was already busy in there but she slipped into an unoccupied table in a corner. The waiter brought her a menu.

There was pasta to start – *fettuccine al ragù* or *agnolotti in brodo* – and the main courses were chicken *cacciatore* (the day's special) or *blanquette de veau* with peas, buttered baby carrots and creamed potatoes. The sweet was simple – a choice of ice cream or fresh fruit salad. It looked lovely, but much more than she normally ate at lunchtime.

'Do you have any sandwiches?' she asked the waiter when he came to take her order.

He took the menu from her without smiling. 'The bar serves sandwiches. We are a restaurant.'

She thanked him, got up and made her way out into the sunshine again. The bar where she had shared a Coke with Candy earlier was now packed with a lively, chattering crowd. Diana chose a couple of egg and tomato sandwiches, which she took to a shelf at one side.

A crowd of men came in, all of them handsome and bronzed like the ones in Lucky Strike adverts. They found chairs and dragged them together round a table and Diana noticed how muscular they were, like athletes. One of them took a chair from right beside her but didn't even glance her way, and no one spoke to her.

As soon as she had finished eating, she left the bar, planning to have a long walk round the studio and get her bearings. She peered into carpentry workshops, plasterers' studios full of statues, prop stores and vast warehouses with rail upon rail of costumes. Towards the rear of Cinecittà she could see rolling fields and she headed in that direction, thinking she could work her way back.

Suddenly, she noticed two men standing very close together in the shadows behind an abandoned set. They hadn't seen Diana and she gasped as she realised they were kissing. Shocked and embarrassed, she ducked out of sight and tiptoed away, only stopping for breath when she was sure they couldn't see her. Of course, she had assumed there would be homosexual men involved in the making of a film because she'd heard they tended to be creative types, but she hadn't expected them to be so open about it. It was illegal for them to have sexual relations in England and she assumed the law would be the same in a fiercely Catholic country like Italy. She was in a different world now and would have to get used to a lot of things she hadn't seen before. This was what she had wanted after all – a new experience.

The outdoor sets were constructed on the studio's back lot, and as soon as she got close she saw the replica of the Forum, which was if anything bigger than the one she had criticised in Pinewood. Walter hadn't listened to her at all. She took out her notebook and made copious notes on all the parts of buildings and frontages she could see, stepping over piles of building materials. She'd noticed a typewriter back in the production office and, when she finished, she decided to go and type up her notes.

She walked back around the other side of the lot. As she approached the offices, a small dog suddenly darted out of a building and across the lawn. A door opened just ten yards away and a figure in a bathrobe and a hairnet peered out. It was unmistakably Elizabeth Taylor.

'Here, baby,' she called in a husky but surprisingly high, childlike voice.

Diana was mesmerised. Miss Taylor was the most famous woman in the world at that time, after her near-death experience earlier in the year. She was more famous than Marilyn Monroe, Joan Crawford and Ava Gardner all put together – and there she was in a bathrobe and hairnet.

She glanced at Diana briefly, then retreated back into the building. Consulting her map, Diana saw that it was labelled 'Star's dressing-room suite'.

Seconds later the door opened again, and Eddie Fisher hurried out holding a dog's lead and whistling for the dog. Diana pointed to show him the direction it had disappeared in, and he grinned and called 'Thanks, honey!'

At school Diana had been an outsider, the bookish one with only a few equally serious friends, but now, for the first time in her life, she felt as if she was part of a charmed inner circle.

Chapter Six

At ten past eight that evening, a taxi beeped its horn in the street outside Diana's pensione and she rushed down the stairs. Helen was waving out of the back window. There was an Italian man sitting in the front and at first Diana assumed he was a friend of the driver's, but he turned round and spoke to Helen in English, telling her that he was going to Trastevere and they could drop him off at the next corner.

'Who's that?' Diana asked, after he'd got out and said goodnight.

'Just Luigi,' Helen said, without any further explanation. Diana assumed he worked on the film.

'We're going to Via Veneto, where all the stars hang out. Have you heard of it?' Helen asked. 'You must have seen it in *La Dolce Vita*?'

Diana had to admit she hadn't seen the film, which had come out the previous year, but she knew that the star, Anita Ekberg, famously danced in the Trevi Fountain. All the papers had shown her picture, buxom and blonde, with her strapless dress looking imminently likely to fall off.

'Here we are,' Helen announced, as the taxi pulled in to the kerb near the foot of an avenue curving up a hill. It was lined with bars and restaurants with outdoor tables, all of them thronged with customers.

Diana noticed a group of young men standing beside motor scooters, holding cameras and chatting amongst themselves. Suddenly someone shouted from further up the hill, and they all set off, running on foot like a pack of dogs.

'They're press photographers,' Helen explained. 'It probably means they've spotted someone famous up there – maybe it's Elizabeth and Eddie. Come on, we're meeting the others at a pizza place round the corner.'

Diana didn't have time to ask who the 'others' were before they swept into a noisy restaurant full of Italian families. Coloured lights were strung along the walls and a glow emanated from a big oven in the centre. Helen greeted a crowd of nine girls sitting at a circular table and introduced Diana to each one in turn.

'What do you do?' one of them asked, and they turned away without interest when they heard she was a researcher. Most of them were American actresses who had minor, non-speaking roles as maidservants to Cleopatra, and the talk was of the more famous actors and actresses: what they had said and done that day and, in particular, whether Elizabeth Taylor was likely to come out that evening.

Diana tried to engage the girl next to her in conversation, but could sense she wasn't interested. Perhaps it was because Diana's clothes looked so old-fashioned in comparison to theirs. They all wore evening clothes in Jackie Kennedy styles: colourful shift dresses that stopped at the knee, or white trousers with kaftan-style tops and bold jewellery. Diana had worn a favourite dress of red shiny material with little white dots that was belted round the waist and had a wide full skirt, but it looked completely wrong at that table. The skirt was far too long. None of the others were wearing white evening gloves. She didn't fit in.

The girls ordered pizzas. Diana had never tried one before so she ordered a Napoletana, same as Helen. A huge carafe of wine was brought and glasses poured for each of them. Diana took a sip and found it rather harsh. The pizza was divine, though, with chewy cheese melting down into a tomato sauce and something salty she couldn't identify. Helen went to the ladies' room and when she came back she fell into her seat, giggling inanely. Diana guessed she had downed her wine rather too fast and wondered whether she should urge her not to drink any more. She felt protective towards this girl from her hometown – but she had only known her a few hours so it wasn't her place to say anything. In fact, all the girls were giggling as they moved on to the second carafe of wine while Diana had barely touched her first glass.

The topic of discussion was which aspects of a star's life it was legitimate for photographers to take pictures of. The girls reckoned that they were only doing their job if they shot the actors as they walked into a party or nightclub all dressed up to the nines but that the *paparazzi* who hid in the trees round Elizabeth Taylor's villa and photographed her children in the swimming pool were going too far. Diana hadn't heard the term '*paparazzi*' before but realised it referred to the press pack she had seen outside.

'One of them offered me a hundred thousand *lire* for a shot of Elizabeth on the set,' a girl told them, and a couple of others concurred.

'Yeah, me too. But we'd get fired if we were found out so it's not worth it.'

50

When they'd finished eating, someone suggested they went to a piano bar and Diana tagged along, although she was beginning to feel tired. There were taxis cruising the street and she planned to pop into the bar for a few moments, to see what it was like, before coming out to hail one. They crowded into a small, dark hideaway with no name on the door, and just inside she spotted Ernesto standing at the bar. He kissed her on both cheeks and seemed genuinely delighted to see her.

'Diana, you must join me for a drink. I insist.'

'I was about to leave,' she began, but he didn't pay any attention, calling out to a waiter '*Due Belline.*'

'What's a Bellini?' she asked.

'Trust me. You'll like it,' he said, and she did. It was sweet, fruity and fizzy and it didn't taste alcoholic, although she suspected it probably was. The other girls had found a table, where they had been joined by some Italian boys, and she wondered whether she should sit with them.

'How did you become a Cleopatra expert?' Ernesto asked, and she explained about the subjects she had taken at Oxford and her fascination for the Egyptian queen who was an astute politician and military tactician. He seemed genuinely interested in her PhD research and asked questions about how Cleopatra held on to the throne for almost forty years. Diana enjoyed telling him her own theories about the clever ways Cleopatra won the support of the Egyptian people.

'Don't you think being involved with a Hollywood movie will undermine your credibility?' Ernesto asked.

'That's what my husband thinks,' Diana confessed. 'He didn't want me to come.'

'Of *course* he didn't. I am amazed that he allowed you! An Italian husband would have stopped you.'

Diana raised an eyebrow. 'In Britain in the 1960s, we women don't need our husband's permission to take a career opportunity.'

Ernesto shrugged. 'In Italy you would. But tell me, how was your first day on the set?'

Diana explained that she had no idea what to do. No one had explained what her responsibilities were and she hadn't met the director or caught up with the producer.

'Don't worry,' Ernesto patted her hand. 'Tomorrow morning, I will take you to the script meeting and you can meet everyone there. It's at ten o'clock.'

'You seem very well-connected. How did you get involved with the film?'

Ernesto explained that Cinecittà studios recommended him because he had worked on dozens of films there. He was good at finding locations, sourcing unusual items or materials that were needed, and striking deals with local businesses for supplies.

'I am a businessman, and I know a lot of people. That's all you require to do my job.'

'Your English is excellent. That must help.'

'I make deals with lots of English people and I need to be sure they are not cheating me,' he grinned. 'Many have tried.'

'What other films have you worked on?'

'Dozens! You know the opening shot of *La Dolce Vita* when a helicopter carries a plaster Christ over the rooftops? Who do you think hired the helicopter and oversaw the making of the statue?'

'I'm sorry, I haven't seen it.'

'But you *must*! I will take you some time. There must be a cinema somewhere that is still showing it and we will go together.'

Diana began to search her mind for an excuse, but he pre-empted her, holding up his hand.

'Don't worry. I know you are married. I am not a Casanova type. You and I are going to be good friends, that's all.'

She smiled. 'Excellent. I need some friends out here. I'm going back to my *pensione* now as I'm getting rather tired, but I'll see you tomorrow.'

'How are you getting home? Let me give you a lift.' He stood up and pulled a bunch of keys from his pocket.

'I was going to get a taxi. Don't worry. It's not far. I'm only in Piazza Repubblica.'

'I wouldn't dream of letting you take a taxi alone at night. Nice girls would never travel unaccompanied.'

'Oh my gosh!' Diana exclaimed. 'Well, in that case . . .'

She said her goodbyes to Helen and the other girls, then followed Ernesto out to the street. She'd been expecting a car and was taken aback when he climbed onto a Vespa motor scooter and gestured for her to get on behind. What option did she have, though?

'I don't know what to do. I've never been on one of these.'

'You just climb on and put your arms round my waist. It's easy.'

She gathered up her full skirts and straddled the scooter, wondering how on earth other girls managed in those tight short dresses. She placed her hands loosely on the sides of Ernesto's jacket, but when the scooter started to move, she gripped more firmly. Her skirt billowed out on one side and she tucked it under her thighs. The breeze blew her hair back off her face and she closed her eyes, enjoying the sensation. When she opened them, they were going past a beautiful church.

She was in Rome, in 1961, riding home on the back of a Vespa. The life she had been waiting to lead felt as though it had finally begun.

Chapter Seven

Ernesto came to the production office to collect Diana at five to ten the following morning to take her to the script meeting.

'Are you absolutely sure I'm supposed to come along?' she asked.

'Of course. You must be there. You can actually make a difference at this stage.'

The director's office was in a building opposite the main gate. A dozen people were sitting smoking and drinking coffee, among them Walter Wanger, who leapt to his feet and rushed over to embrace Diana.

'Sweetheart, you made it! It's terrific to see you. Let me introduce you to everybody.' He went round the room, pointing out John De Cuir, the set designer; Hilary Armitage, the woman she already knew from the production office; Leon Shamroy, the director of photography, whom she recognised as the man in the Hawaiian shirt she had seen on set; as well as some production managers, continuity girls, and various others. Diana desperately tried to remember their names. The door opened and in walked a man with an open, friendly face that seemed familiar. He was smoking a pipe.

'Joe, meet Diana, our new historical advisor,' Walter called. 'I asked her along today to see how she can be of use to you.'

This was a lie, of course; Walter hadn't asked her at all. 'Diana, this is Joe Mankiewicz.'

She shook hands with the director and realised she had read an interview with him in the *Sunday Times*; she recalled him from the photograph. He'd struck both her and Trevor as being very bright and articulate.

'Welcome on board,' Joe said, then sat on the edge of his desk and held out a sheaf of typewritten pages to a girl called Rosemary Matthews, who began to distribute them. 'Give Diana a copy as well,' he instructed.

She liked the smell of his pipe tobacco, which was like new-mown hay compared to the stale harshness of cigarette smoke. Everyone smoked here, male and female – she had yet to meet anyone who didn't.

'Joe rewrites the script every night,' Walter explained. 'We weren't happy with the last draft. As soon as you get your copy in the morning you should read it through and tell Hilary if you can see any major problems. You'll have to be quick, though, because we start rehearsing right after this meeting and we start shooting about noon.'

'On the script you've just written?'

Joe nodded. 'Yeah, it's crazy but I've known crazier things to happen on movies. You'll get used to it.'

They began to discuss a scene they wanted to shoot the following week down on the Anzio coast, in which Cleopatra is encamped facing Ptolemy's troops and trying to work out how to reach Caesar to ask for his help. Joe asked Diana about the way the troops would have been positioned and she was relieved that she knew the answer and could draw a sketch for him on the back of one of the sheets of script.

He nodded, pleased. 'OK, we can use the natural curve of the bay for that bit and have the cameras here.' He pointed to a spot on the paper and all heads bent to look.

'Any dialogue?'

'I'll keep it short,' Joe said.

Ernesto leaned over and told her in a whisper that they avoided dialogue on exterior shots as much as possible because they would have to dub it later, which could be hit-and-miss.

'Does anyone know if Miss Taylor is coming in today?' someone asked.

'Nobody called to say she isn't,' Walter told them.

'Have you checked the calendar? Is it a red-letter day?' another voice called, and there were snorts round the room, which Diana didn't understand. She'd have to ask someone later.

They ran through the parts of the script they'd been given and Diana attempted to skim read but it was hard to comment without knowing the context. No one had any criticisms. They just talked about camera angles. It seemed more of a technical meeting than anything else.

Joe got up to leave, but turned for a word with Diana on the way out. 'Will you leave a message at the production office to say where you're going to be every night? In case I need to call you about something while I'm writing.'

Diana agreed that she would do, and glowed with importance. The director was going to consult *her* while he was writing the script! She would be on call, like a doctor.

Brimming with pride, she made her way over to Walter to ask about her other responsibilities. How did he see her role?

'I want you to have a look at all John's wonderful sets and discuss with him if there are any little details that could make them just a tiny bit more authentic.'

John De Cuir scowled, making it obvious he didn't want any interference.

'Introduce yourself in the props and costume departments and see if they want any advice,' Walter continued. 'Talk to people in makeup and hair. You're the lynchpin, communicating with people across the set and raising the intellectual level of the movie.'

'I've already written some notes on the outdoor sets I saw yesterday,' she volunteered. She'd brought them with her in her handbag and started to open it.

'Wonderful!' Walter clasped his hands behind his back. 'Give them to Hilary and she'll make sure the right people see them. It's great that you've got off to a flying start. Is your *pensione* comfortable?'

'Charming, thank you.'

'Good, good. Well, I better get going, but I'm really glad you are with us.'

Ernesto appeared by her side again. 'They have some stills here from the scene that was shot of Miss Taylor at the altar of Isis. Do you want to have a look?'

Diana went over to a table by the window where the photographer had laid them out. They showed Elizabeth Taylor's Cleopatra in front of the cauldron that Diana had seen in sound stage 5. Her appearance was completely wrong; Trevor would snort with derision if he could see it. She was wearing a low-cut evening gown, whereas Cleopatra would have worn a long high-necked tunic with coiled ropes of pearls round her neck. In that era, pearls would have been the most desirable jewel, their equivalent to diamonds, and it was known that Cleopatra was especially partial to them. Her hairstyle was wrong as well, with a fringed bob style, as was the heavy black eye makeup that curved outwards at the corners. Ancient Egyptians had used black kohl on their eyelids to protect their eyes from the sun's rays, but it wouldn't have been stylised like that.

'It's all wrong,' she whispered to Ernesto.

He grinned. 'You're welcome to tell Irene Sharaff your views but take a suit of armour! She has a reputation for not welcoming criticism.'

'Everyone keeps telling me to give my honest opinion and then they proceed to disregard it. I've no idea why I'm here. What am I to do for the next six months?'

He rubbed her arm sympathetically. 'You could relax and let me show you around Rome. Or you could talk to the key people with some tact and see if you can persuade them to make minor changes to their designs. Personally, I recommend you do both.'

Before leaving the meeting, she took her notes from the previous day over to Hilary. 'Walter said to give these to you.'

Hilary glanced at them and seemed puzzled. 'Did he? OK. Thanks.' She tucked them under her arm.

Ernesto hurried off and Diana returned to the office to read the script properly, but it was invented dialogue without any facts she could correct. When she finished, she decided to walk out to the back lot, where she'd been the day before, and work her way along an avenue that was marked on the map as having several workshops. The first ones she came to contained huge pieces of scenery, most of them in white marble with gold leaf decoration. There were some enormous unguent jars that looked fine from a distance but close up she could see they were papier-mâché and liable to topple over if the wind blew. She saw gold-painted cat-goddess statues but from the wrong period so she took out her notebook and made a note. There was no one around to discuss them with.

In the next workshop, a couple of Italian men were making Roman standards and she stopped to watch. They'd got the eagle's feet curling over the SPQR lettering, and they'd inserted full stops between the initials, which was incorrect. She drew a quick sketch in her book to show them the authentic style and held it towards them.

'It should be like this,' she said in Italian. 'The eagle's feet here, and SPQR down there.' She pointed with the tip of her pen.

'*Chi diavolo sei?*' one of them responded – 'Who the hell are you?' – in a manner that definitely wasn't friendly.

'I'm the historical advisor. From the British Museum, in London. I've just arrived.'

It was only then she noticed that they had already completed around fifty of the standards, which were all propped up to dry, each with the incorrect design.

'Why don't you fuck off back to London?' one of the men said in accented English. He dipped his brush into a pot of gold paint and carried on with his work.

She held up her hands defensively and backed out of the workshop.

Chapter Eight

When Diana got back to the production office, it was empty. She decided she ought to try to reach Trevor again so she called the operator and gave the number. While she was waiting for the call to be put through, Hilary came in and nodded as she sat down at her desk. Diana considered hanging up and trying again later but at that moment she heard the ringing sound and Trevor's secretary answered the phone.

'You're in luck. I'll just put you through,' she said.

'Hello, it's me. How are you?' Diana asked once Trevor was on the line.

'Surviving,' he said, and there was a long pause in which neither spoke.

'Have you thought about whether you could come out here one weekend soon? The weather's fantastic and it would be nice to go round the sites with you.'

'I'm too busy,' came the reply. 'I've been asked to tutor several more students who enrolled at the last minute and I'm up to my ears in assessments.'

Diana sighed. 'I'm not sure when I'll be able to come back to London because it seems we have to work on Saturdays. I do wish you would come out, Trevor.'

'It's a long way and a lot of money just to spend a Sunday with you.'

She knew she was asking a lot, but she desperately wanted to see him and make things alright between them. 'If you could come on Friday night and stay till Sunday night, or even first thing Monday morning, it would be worth the trip.'

'I wouldn't like to cramp your style. My colleagues are warning me that you'll run off to Hollywood with a movie star and the first I'll hear of it will be a headline in the *Daily Mail*.'

She knew he meant it as a joke, but it came across as an accusation. Diana's eyes filled with tears. 'That's silly. I would *never* leave you.' She kept her voice low, acutely conscious of Hilary's presence.

He spoke sadly: 'Well, that's what I always thought – and yet it appears you have.'

A tear spilled over and trickled down her cheek. She smeared it with the back of her hand. 'I'm working, Trevor. I miss you terribly but this was something I had to do. I wish you would try to understand.'

'I *am* trying to understand. It's difficult to get over the fact that you attached no weight to my feelings on the matter. Honestly, Diana, you can't have it all ways. I wish you hadn't gone. I'm too busy to visit you. Just let me know when you are coming back. Now, I have some students arriving for a tutorial so I will have to hang up on you.' He paused then added: 'Take care of yourself, darling. Goodbye.'

'Goodbye, Trevor,' she said, but he had already replaced the receiver and she could no longer hold back the tears. She covered her face with her hands.

Hilary hurried over to put a hand on her shoulder and placed a packet of tissues on the desk. 'You poor thing. I couldn't help overhearing. Was that your husband?'

Diana nodded.

'He didn't want you to come out here? I imagine there aren't many men who would want their wives in a place like this unless they were around to supervise. Don't cry, dear. He'll come round. How long have you been married?'

Diana blew her nose. 'Two years.'

'Were you a couple for long before that?'

'Yes, ages. He was my tutor at Oxford and we fell in love, but we kept it secret for a while because the university authorities wouldn't have approved. It was only after I graduated and started work on my PhD that we told people.'

Hilary perched on the desk, her hand on Diana's shoulder. 'Is he very serious and academic? I imagine he must be older than you.'

'He's eighteen years older, and he's fiercely clever, of course, but he's funny as well. He can always make me laugh.' She paused. 'Well, usually.'

'Tell me his bad points,' Hilary asked. 'Does he try to control you?'

'No, not really. I suppose we've never disagreed about anything before. Not anything major. His worst fault is that he is very slovenly to live with. He puts down cups of tea wherever he happens to be at the time and I spend my life clearing up his dirty socks and tattered old history magazines.' She smiled fondly. He was always losing things because of his untidiness and she would find them in the most ridiculous places. His chequebook once turned up in a windowbox outside the sitting-room window after he'd been watering the plants. 'Are you married?' she asked Hilary, glancing down to see that her ring finger was bare.

'I couldn't be under any man's thumb,' she said. 'I like my freedom too much so I doubt I'll ever marry. I feel lucky to have been born in an era when women can earn a good salary doing an interesting job and they don't need a man to look after them. Throughout history, women have never enjoyed as much freedom as now, have they?'

'Actually, they were pretty free in Egypt in Cleopatra's day,' Diana told her. 'Women could own properties and businesses. They were educated to as high a standard as men and could choose their own husbands. But if you cross the water to Rome in the same era, the women were the chattels of their fathers and husbands.'

'Maybe that's why you were attracted to Cleopatra?' Hilary suggested. 'Because you're an independent sort? Anyway, that husband of yours will have to buck up his ideas. It's hard on the phone, especially when the line can be so crackly. Why not write him a letter explaining why you had to take this opportunity and asking him to please try to understand? Tell him you love him but this is something you need to do. If he loves you, he'll come round in the end.'

Diana nodded. 'That's a good idea. I'll do that.'

'Don't make the mistake of putting it in an Italian post box, though – they hardly ever empty them. We've got a courier service that goes daily to London and you can stick a letter in there. Ask Candy about it.'

Diana handed back the pack of tissues. 'Thank you for your advice. It sounds very wise.'

She sat down at the typewriter and focused on typing up her notes for the day, then decided to go back to the sound stages and see what was being shot. On the way there, she noticed Helen on the grass swigging a bottle of Coke.

'Are you having a break?' she asked, sitting down.

'They're not filming today,' Helen told her. 'Elizabeth Taylor has her monthly and it's written into her contract that she doesn't have to work for the first three days of it.'

'But that's ridiculous!' Diana exclaimed.

'They keep a calendar where they mark the days so they can try to predict the next one.'

Diana remembered someone at the script meeting asking if it was a red-letter day and guessed that's what they had been referring to. 'What if all the women on set did that?' she asked. 'I'd love three days off when I have my monthlies.'

Helen nodded agreement. 'Me too! The idea is that she has to look perfect on camera and she doesn't believe she looks good enough at that time of the month. What does she think makeup is for? Between ourselves, it's a running joke that her periods don't follow a calendar month but seem to coincide with the morning after she's been out partying.'

'That's so unprofessional! I'm amazed she gets away with it.' Diana remembered that Helen herself had been the worse for wear the previous evening. 'It was fun last night. Thank you so much for inviting me. I hope you are feeling alright today?'

'Yeah!' Helen grinned. 'I had a great time. We met a bunch of Italian men and were dancing with them. Don't you just love the way they're so flirtatious? They're much more fun than British men.'

Diana thought of Ernesto and agreed. She was getting used to the way his eyes lingered on her figure and he touched her arm and chatted in an intimate fashion, as though they had known each other for ages. It was innocent flirtation and she rather enjoyed it.

'Do you have a boyfriend?' she asked Helen.

'No, but I'd love to find one. There are so many handsome men working here, I don't know where to start. I wish I spoke better Italian because they are the cutest, but there's an American cameraman I like, and one of the lighting guys.' She sighed. 'If only they'd hurry up and ask me out.'

'I'm sure it won't take long,' Diana assured her. 'You're lovely and they won't be able to resist you.'

When she left Cinecittà that evening to go back to her *pensione*, there was a lone photographer hanging around at the gates.

'*Liz Taylor è lì oggi?*' he called through the open window of her studio car – 'Is Liz Taylor there today?'

Diana told him she wasn't.

'*E domani?*'

'*Non lo so.*'

On the drive into town, she thought what a boring job these men had, waiting around for the few moments in the day when Elizabeth Taylor was driven out of the studio gates, or walked from her car to a restaurant to eat dinner. What was it Helen had called them? *Paparazzi*. Strange word. It was similar to *papatacci*, a term Italians used to mean a small mosquito. Perhaps that's where it came from. They buzzed

66

around on their motor scooters trying to catch the rich and famous in the glare of the flashbulb, like a sting. It didn't seem a particularly rewarding way of earning a living, but good luck to them.

Chapter Nine

The next time Scott contrived to bump into the beautiful Italian girl, he asked her name.

'Gina,' she said quickly, then blushed and tried to hurry past.

Scott turned to walk alongside her, as if he were going in the same direction and it was the most natural thing in the world. She bowed her head, trying to stop anyone seeing her talking to this American boy. Instead of hitting on her directly, he chatted in a friendly fashion. He told her that he had only been in Rome for three months and didn't know many people so he spent most evenings at home alone. He mentioned that he was a recent college graduate and that he had been a champion athlete. High jump was his best; he could high jump over five feet. Did she want him to demonstrate by jumping over a parked Vespa?

'No, no,' she giggled. '*non è necessario.*'

He asked if she liked music, and when she said '*Sì, certamente,*' he sang a short burst of an Elvis song that had just been released back home – 'Can't Help Falling in Love'. He could tell she was interested in him because she was laughing, despite her nervousness. Scott liked girls and had long ago realised that if you could make them laugh, you were halfway there. He'd watched other friends hitting on them too obviously and being brushed off or crushed by bitchy put-downs, and that's when he decided that a slightly clownish approach would work best, by putting girls at their ease.

He wasn't bad-looking, in his own opinion. One ex-girlfriend had told him that he looked like a younger, handsomer version of John F. Kennedy. Unfortunately, that girl later dumped him for one of his best friends from the athletics team, but at least he still had the compliment to cherish. He'd been hurt at the time, but hadn't been in love with her so it was more to do with pride than heartbreak.

'Every day I see you go to the church and then the market,' he told Gina in Italian, and he guessed he must have used an awkward sentence structure or got a word wrong because she giggled. 'What do you do in the afternoon and at night?'

'I cook for my family,' she replied. 'Lunch and dinner. I help my sister with her babies.' She began to describe how cute the babies were and how one of them had recently said his first word.

'You're going to make a very good mother some day,' Scott told her and she clutched her face in embarrassment. He noted that she seemed more relaxed with him now that they were a few streets away from her home. Was it time to make his move?

'I'm glad we got a chance to talk at last. I've been watching you for ages now, every morning at the same time. You're so beautiful I can't help looking at you.'

She bowed her head and kept walking.

'Can I take you out one evening? We could have dinner, or coffee, or go for a walk in the Villa Borghese gardens?'

'No, it's not possible.' Her tone sounded regretful so Scott persevered.

'If you like, I could come and meet your family so they can see I only have respect for you.' He touched her arm lightly and gazed at her with pleading eyes. '*Per favore*?'

'I'm sorry, but it would never work. My father is an important businessman around here and he will never accept his daughter dating a foreigner. Never.'

'What's his name?'

'Don Ghianciamina. You have heard of him?' She watched his face, but he just shrugged. No, he hadn't. 'Well, if you ask around, you will find out that he is a very traditional father. I really can't talk to you any more.'

She began to walk off and Scott caught hold of her arm. 'Please don't go.'

Suddenly she screamed and pushed Scott away. 'Go now! Run! It's my brother.'

He turned to see a young Italian man charging up the street towards them. Scott decided to stand his ground and try to talk to him. If the worst came to the worst, he was taller and reckoned he could take him.

The man grabbed Gina by the elbow, shouting at her in Italian so rapid that Scott couldn't make it out. He opened his mouth to say 'Leave her alone' and too late he saw a left hook curving towards his nose. The force of the blow caught him off balance and he fell to the pavement. As he tried to get up, a boot struck him in the ribs, then he was kicked from the other side and that's when he realised there was more than one attacker. Fists and boots came at him from all directions in a relentless rhythm. There must be at least three of them and they were taking turns. He curled into a ball to protect his head and tried to crawl back towards a doorway behind him but still the blows rained down.

Christ, they're going to kill me, Scott thought.

Out of the corner of his eye, he could see passersby scurrying past and called out '*Aiuto!*' but no one stopped. Cars were driving by. It was mid-morning and no one was prepared to intervene. His attackers didn't say anything but didn't appear to be planning to stop the barrage any time soon. Somehow Scott managed to haul himself through the doorway and tried to push the door shut, and at last, with one final kick, the men disappeared.

Scott closed the door and lay still for a while, cataloguing his injuries. Everywhere hurt: his face, his ribs, his stomach, his kidneys. He threw up, mostly bile, then wiped his mouth with the back of his hand. He'd heard the clichés about protective Italian men but this was out of all proportion. He could have died.

He raised his head and saw he was in some kind of courtyard with a little fountain in the middle. He called out for help again, but there was no response and no one in sight. Surely one of the passersby would have called the police at least? He listened for sirens but there was no sound except the tinkling of the fountain and the hum of the traffic outside. He needed to get to a hospital but his knees gave way beneath him when he tried to stand up.

Cautiously, he opened the door a crack and peered out to make sure the men had definitely gone. He crawled on all fours to the roadside then leant on a car to pull himself to an upright position. Further up the hill there was a taxi with its light on. He waited until it was almost alongside then stepped out into the road so it was forced to stop. He staggered round, wrenched open the nearest door and fell in.

'*All'ospedale*,' he told the driver. '*Presto.*'

Chapter Ten

Diana decided to make the acquaintance of Irene Sharaff, who was designing the costumes for Elizabeth Taylor, but, following Candy's advice, she first made an appointment through Miss Sharaff's secretary. By all accounts, she wasn't a woman you wanted to rub up the wrong way.

Once in the costume department, she was directed to a cavernous room full of vibrant colour. Gowns in jewel shades were pinned around white-faced tailors' dummies and swathes of glittering fabric covered tables and chairs. Irene Sharaff was instantly recognisable from magazine pictures, her strong features and odd hooked nose emphasised by the fact that her dark hair was scraped back in a tight bun.

'So you're a historical advisor?' She gave a little snort. 'How are you finding everything, my dear?'

Diana decided to be honest. 'No one seems particularly keen to have my advice. Still, I promised Walter that I would offer it all the same.'

'And you're here today to give me your advice?' In a sharp glance Irene took in the flared yellow skirt and white blouse Diana was wearing.

'I wouldn't presume, Miss Sharaff. I'm a huge fan of yours. I loved *West Side Story*. The girls' dresses were wonderful. And

I loved *Guys and Dolls*, and *Meet Me in St Louis* . . . You bring so much panache to all your productions.' She'd memorised this speech beforehand, so nervous was she about meeting the great woman.

'Someone obviously told you to butter me up. Good job!' She smiled. 'Now I already know what you're going to say about Cleopatra's costumes. In the first century BC they wouldn't have been low-cut and they wouldn't have been caught in at the waist; they would have been a straight tunic style, maybe with a belt. Is that what you were going to tell me?'

'I was sure you would know that already,' Diana said hurriedly. 'I just wanted to ask about the decisions you've made.'

'It's obvious. The reason why they wanted me on this movie is because I know how to dress Elizabeth Taylor, and that's no laughing matter. Those renowned mammaries have to be on display; if it's not actually written into her contract it might as well be, because the last film she made without thrusting them at the audience was *Lassie Come Home*.'

Diana grinned, feeling more at ease.

'I have to choose styles that don't show off the fact that Miss Taylor is, to be blunt, chubby. And I have to be able to adjust the costumes from day to day because her weight goes up and down like a yo-yo. I swear she can gain an inch on her hips overnight! A straight tunic would never work for her, especially when she is standing beside all these skinny hand-maidens. She'd look like a sack of flour.'

Diana could see what she meant. 'You've done well in researching the colours. Just fifty years earlier they wouldn't have had all those dyes, but you've captured the blues, greens and terracotta shades they used in Alexandria in 40 BC.'

'Do you know what Walter's instructions to me were? Make sure Elizabeth stands out in front of all that fancy scenery so it's her the audience are looking at whenever she's on screen. She's costing a million bucks and he wants his money's worth.' She snorted. 'You'll be pretty lucky if you manage to convince him to change anything for the sake of historical accuracy. He won't sanction any change that costs one cent more than the alternative.'

'So I'm beginning to realise.'

Irene stood up and led Diana round the room, showing her some costumes that were to be used later in the shoot. They got more and more ornate, with one made out of gold-plated chain-mail that would never have been used in the first century BC, but Diana didn't point that out.

'Feel it,' Irene instructed, placing it across Diana's arms, and she gasped at the weight. It had to be at least twenty pounds. How would Elizabeth walk around in it?

'She'll be sitting down in that scene,' Irene explained with a grin.

They talked about the iconography on the headdresses and Diana sketched a starburst symbol that might have appeared. They discussed the costumes worn by other characters, which were being made by different departments, and Diana showed Irene a picture of the jewelled sandals Cleopatra would have worn.

She laughed. 'Elizabeth would never wear flat shoes. She's got chubby feet, and she needs a good three-inch heel or Caesar would tower over her. It's not ancient Alexandria; it's Hollywood on the Tiber, honey.'

Before Diana left, Irene looked at her outfit again. 'Can I make a suggestion? You've got slim hips but no one would know it in that skirt. Let me see your legs.'

Embarrassed, Diana hesitated before lifting the hem of her skirt to knee level.

'I thought so. You boyish-figured English girls all have great legs. You need to get yourself some knee-length skirts and dresses that fit you on the hips. Pick pastel shades for your skin tone. You'd look great in Capri pants as well. If you don't mind me being honest, you look a bit gauche in that swing skirt, like some backing singer in a rockabilly band.' She smiled. 'No offence.'

'None taken,' Diana replied, although she was taken aback by the directness.

As she walked back towards her office, she decided she would take the hint. It came from one of the world's top costume designers, after all! She realised she had no idea where the women's clothing shops were in Rome – she hadn't seen anything but bars and *trattorie* on the drive to and from the studio – but Helen would know.

She made her way to the sound stages and followed the handwritten sign to the dressing room that was being used for makeup that day. Helen was flicking through a copy of a women's magazine called *Honey*.

'Thank goodness you came by,' she exclaimed, throwing down the magazine. 'I'm bored to tears. There's nothing to do and it's not warm enough to sunbathe.'

'No actors to make up?'

'I did a few handmaidens and centurions this morning and now I'm not needed.'

'You are by me,' Diana told her, before asking if she knew any decent, affordable clothes shops in Rome where she could update her wardrobe.

Straight away, Helen suggested La Rinascente on Via del Corso. 'I've only been here a few weeks and I've bought tons of things there. Why don't we go this afternoon? We could slip off at five and they stay open till seven-thirty. I'll give you a second opinion. I love shopping with my girlfriends.'

Diana readily agreed because she wasn't a confident shopper, and when they arrived at the store she was glad she had taken Helen along because the choice was overwhelming. Faced with such endless racks of clothes stretching into the distance around the store's elegant columns and balconies, she would have given up and headed home.

Helen ferreted out some lovely garments and brought them to the plush changing rooms, where all Diana had to do was slip into them. She knew there was plenty of money in the bank account from a travelling allowance she'd been paid in advance by the film company, so she splashed out on four shift dresses in the style Irene Sharaff had recommended, one lilac evening gown, a pair of white Capri pants, some kaftan tops and a lightweight coat, because she could tell her heavy woollen one wasn't going to get much use in Rome.

Helen tried on a pretty black and white sweater with a geometric pattern but put it back on the rack.

'Why don't you get it?' Diana asked. 'It suits you.'

'I'm broke until payday. Going out every night is costing me an arm and a leg.'

'Let me treat you,' Diana said. 'I insist. It's a gift to thank you for being so helpful today. I'd have walked out without finding anything if you hadn't been here.'

Helen protested but Diana simply picked up the sweater and added it to her pile on the cashier's desk. As she wrote a travellers' cheque to cover the bill, she felt a twinge of guilt about Trevor. Of course, this wasn't just her money – it was his as well. He was paying all the bills at home. She would write to him that evening, as Hilary suggested.

Back at the Pensione Splendid, she sat on the bed and poured out her feelings on paper. She told Trevor first and foremost how much she missed talking to him. She hadn't yet been to see the Forum or the Colosseum because he was the one person she would want to see them with. She told him she knew it was shallow and frivolous to work on a Hollywood movie but that it was an education of a different sort – an education in human nature. She described Joe Mankiewicz and the way he was writing the script for each scene the night before they shot it. She wrote about Irene Sharaff and the criteria she used to design Elizabeth Taylor's costumes, such as displaying the 'renowned mammaries'. She told him about the Indian elephants and the fact that the circus owner who supplied them was now suing Twentieth Century Fox for 'insulting his elephants'. The letter spilled over many pages. It made her feel close to him to be able to express everything that was on her mind and she prayed that he would read it and try to understand.

At the end, she begged him to write back soon, using the studio's courier service, or to telephone her at the office, and if she wasn't there someone would take a message and she would call back. And then she couldn't think of anything more to say so she signed off with all her love and lots of Xs underneath. There was a pain in her chest, in exactly the same place as her heart.

Chapter Eleven

Scott spent two days in a morphine fug, while doctors and nurses came and went, occasionally stopping to perform some unpleasant procedure. His nose had been broken and there were strips of plaster across it and great wads of cotton wool stuffed inside so that he could only breathe through his mouth. His ribs were strapped up and his left wrist was also broken and in plaster. He vaguely recalled one of the men stamping on it. He had a catheter and he knew there was blood in his urine from all the kidney punches and kicks he'd taken, but the doctor assured him the 'trauma' would heal in time.

As well as bruising and swelling, there were many contusions on his face and body, and a nurse said they must have used a *pugno di ferro*. He'd never heard the term, but from her mime he realised she meant a knuckleduster. What kind of person carried one of those around on a normal weekday morning? That suggestion shook him, but when he examined a cut above his forehead, he could see the indentations of metal knuckles, so it must be true.

Two *carabinieri* came and he told his story slowly and carefully, remembering every detail of his conversation with the girl and giving a precise description of her brother. He hadn't seen the other two attackers clearly but thought they had been wearing leather jackets. But when he mentioned the name Ghianciamina, and the fact that they lived in Piazza Navona, the *carabinieri* glanced at each other.

'I think you must have misheard, sir. There is a family of that name but they are a very prominent family of good character.'

'I can show you the exact house where they live,' Scott insisted. 'Take me there and I'll identify the man who did this.'

One of the policemen produced a loose-leaf folder. 'There's no need, sir. We've brought pictures of all the violent criminals in the city and you can go through and point to the men who hurt you without getting out of your bed.'

Scott began to flick through. They were rough-looking, dark-skinned young men, aged between fifteen and twenty-five, all of them scowling out of police mugshots. 'My attacker was dressed smarter and his skin was paler than these men,' he said, but continued to work through the folder until he reached the end. 'Nope, none of them. Can we go to Piazza Navona now?'

'The doctors say you can't be moved. Don't worry, because we are asking shopkeepers and bartenders in the street and we hope there will be witnesses. You're sure your wallet was not taken? Often, there is robbery involved.'

'My wallet is here,' Scott said, pointing to the cabinet by his bed. 'I wasn't being robbed. It was because I was talking to the girl, Gina.' He was frustrated that he had given them a name and an address and was not being taken seriously. 'For crying out loud, don't you guys want to catch him? What's the problem? Are you going to wait till he does this to somebody else?'

'At least you are alive,' one of them said quietly. 'Your bones will heal.'

Scott stared at him, too surprised to respond.

The nurses had asked if he wanted a family member to be contacted but he decided it would cause too big a furore to call his mother and father in the States. They'd fly over and make a huge fuss and want to stay on for weeks while he recuperated. Scott knew this because he had been beaten up once before. A local gang attacked him on the way home from school and he'd fought back, which meant he'd come off worse than his friend who'd run away after the first punch was thrown. His mother had reacted with hysteria and insisted on collecting Scott from school in the automobile for the rest of the semester, not letting him go out with friends in the evenings either. Getting beaten up was just one of those things that happened to guys from time to time – hopefully not too often.

Still, he shuddered every time he thought of the knuckle-duster, and the fact that it had been three against one. They had wanted to inflict serious harm and hadn't cared whether he lived or died, and that was chilling.

One young nurse, Rosalia, seemed especially concerned that he didn't have any visitors and began to linger by his bed to chat with him while she was on duty. She was a little plump around the hips but had sexy dimples in her cheeks so he began to flirt.

'Rosalia, do you think I will ever get a girl again? I'll look horrible with all my scars and a crooked nose. Will I have to check myself into a monastery?'

'You'll do fine,' she replied. 'It's personality that counts.'

'OK then, I'm doomed,' he said. 'I've never had a personality. I always relied on my gorgeous face to get the girls.'

'Maybe you will be a nicer person now,' she suggested. 'You'll have to be very sweet to girls, buy them presents and be a gentleman.'

'I'm going to be real lonely when I get out of here. I'll be stuck in my little apartment recuperating all on my own. I'll miss our talks. I don't suppose . . .'

It didn't take much to persuade her to have dinner with him after he was discharged. It would be handy to have a nurse around, he thought, just in case he needed more painkillers. Surely she'd be able to get spares from the hospital dispensary? Meanwhile, flirting with her helped to pass the time.

His secretary came to visit, bringing some paperwork he had to sign. He explained about his frustration that the police wouldn't act over the attack but when he mentioned the name Ghianciamina, she was visibly startled.

'Scott, you must listen to me. They are Mafia, from Sicily, and you must not try to press charges against them because the police will not be able to protect you. Come back to work, forget what happened and stay well away from them. Otherwise, you will have to leave Rome.'

'You're joking! So they get away with it? No way.'

'Yes, that is exactly what I mean.'

'What kind of a country *is* this?'

Scott knew they had Mafia back home in New York and Chicago because occasionally the details of some internecine war hit the headlines, but the American police did their best to lock away the worst offenders. Here in Italy they seemed happy to let them roam the streets. It was outrageous.

He lay back against his pillows. No way could he let them off the hook. Somehow, he had to get revenge, but he'd have to think of a way of achieving it that didn't compromise his own safety. He decided he'd sleep on it.

Chapter Twelve

On the 14th of October, Walter Wanger dropped by the production office to invite Diana to a party hosted by Kirk Douglas to celebrate the anniversary of the release of *Spartacus*. 'He said to bring our top people. Elizabeth is coming, of course. See you later, my dear.'

Diana felt shy about going, but Helen offered to come round to her *pensione* to do her hair and makeup so she would look her best. She sat in a chair by the window as Helen smoothed a creamy base all over her skin and chattered nonstop about the stars who might be there.

'You know Roddy McDowall, who plays Octavian?' she giggled. 'I had an embarrassing encounter with him when we first arrived in Rome. There was a welcome party and I got a bit tipsy. They tried to find a studio car to take me home but the only one available was already booked to take Roddy back to his villa. Anyway, he offered to drop me off and in my drunken state I got the impression that he must like me so just before we reached my place, I leant over and tried to kiss him.' She cringed at the memory.

'What did he do?' Diana mouthed in sympathy.

'He was very sweet. He put his hands on my shoulders, like this . . .' she demonstrated. 'And he said with a twinkle, "I should tell you that I dance on the other side of the ballroom, darling." Of course, I didn't know what it meant exactly but the next day someone told me that he is here with his boyfriend John Valva. He got him a part in the film, as a centurion.'

'Has he said anything to you since? Do you ever have to do his makeup?'

'I haven't, no, thank God. But next day I bumped into him in the corridor and he gave me a huge wink.' Helen laughed. 'That's how I know he's a nice person. He's virtually Elizabeth Taylor's closest friend in the world. And to think I nearly kissed him!'

'What a shame he's not interested in girls. Otherwise I'm sure he would have pounced on you!'

'Everyone here is already taken.' Helen began ticking them off. 'You know about Elizabeth Taylor, of course: on her fourth marriage and she's not even thirty! Rex Harrison is here with Rachel Roberts, the actress. Do you know her?' Diana shook her head. 'You'd recognise her if you saw her. She's an alcoholic, they say. Anyway, they're engaged and getting married soon, even though it's only two years since Kay Kendall died. She was supposed to be the love of his life, everyone said at the time, but I suppose he must have got over her. Richard Burton is here with his wife Sybil; they've been married for twelve years. You know about Walter Wanger, don't you?' Diana shook her head. 'He's married to Joan Bennett, the actress, but he found out she had a lover and shot him in the privates. He went to jail for a while, but not long. They haven't divorced but I haven't seen her here in Rome. I can't imagine all is well in that marriage.'

'Good grief!' Diana tried to assimilate this information with the very suave elderly gentleman she had met. 'How about Joe Mankiewicz? Is he married?'

'Not at the moment. He's too old for me, though. Hey, when is your husband coming out? I'd love to meet him. Is he very dishy?'

Diana laughed. 'He's not at all what you would call "dishy". He's a very nice man, though . . .' She hesitated, wondering whether to confide about her marriage problems but decided against it. Helen was too loose-tongued and she didn't want everyone knowing her business. 'He's very busy at work but I hope he'll be able to come out before long.'

Diana hardly recognised herself in the mirror after Helen had finished. There was mauve eyeshadow smeared on her eyelids and up towards her brows, in a tone that complimented her new lilac dress, and somehow it brought out the greeny-hazel of her eyes. Her shoulder-length brown hair was stacked high on her head and fixed in position with masses of sticky lacquer. She worried that it might act like flypaper, but Helen assured her that never happened. They caught a taxi together to the Grand Hotel on Via del Corso, then Helen continued on to a *pizzeria* where she was meeting some American actresses from the set, the same crowd Diana had met before.

'Break a leg,' she called as Diana climbed out of the taxi onto a red carpet leading up to the hotel entrance.

Photographers snapped some shots of her, in a reflex action, and the flashes were startling, but then they stopped and looked at each other in puzzlement as if to ask 'Who is she?' No doubt they would destroy those shots in the darkroom when they realised she wasn't famous.

She was ushered into an ostentatious ballroom with gold cornice-work, pillared arcades, stained-glass skylights and inset murals of painted cherubs on the ceiling. A band were tuning their instruments on a stage at one end and groups of expensively dressed men and women were standing round the edges of the room, but there was no one she recognised. A tower of glasses was balanced at the end of a table and, as she watched, a waiter popped the cork of a bottle of champagne and poured deftly into the top glass, so that it overflowed down the sides and into the glasses below. She'd never seen anything quite so extravagant.

'Some champagne, madame?' a waiter asked her in English, and she accepted with pleasure. She'd had Babycham at her wedding but had never tasted the real thing before. The first sip was a little bitter for her palate, but it was very smooth on the tongue, like stroking suede.

Clutching her glass, she began to wander self-consciously round the room hoping to spot someone – anyone – she recognised from the film set. Roddy McDowall was sitting with a group of friends but they didn't glance up as she passed. She wondered which one was his lover. Surely Hilary should be there? And when would Walter arrive? She took a seat behind a pillar from where she could watch the proceedings without sticking out like a sore thumb.

Suddenly Ernesto appeared by her side. 'Ah, Diana, you look amazing!' He kissed her on both cheeks and gave her shoulders a brief squeeze. 'That dress is beautiful on you. And the hair.' He held out his hands in appreciation. '*Bellissima!*'

She hoped he would sit with her so she was no longer quite so obviously the lone friendless female. 'I'm glad to see you. I wish I'd known you'd been invited.'

'I'm not,' he whispered. 'I'm gate-crashing. That's the phrase you use in English, isn't it?' He grinned at her shocked expression. 'I said I was a guest of Walter Wanger and they let me in.'

'You've got a nerve!' she smiled.

He sat down beside her and began pointing out the celebrities: 'That's Tony Curtis. Did you see him dressed as a woman in *Some Like it Hot*? And that's Jean Simmons. She's English. Have you met her?'

Diana shook her head, amused that Ernesto would think she might know an actress simply because they were both English. He recognised everyone, knew everything about them, and was very entertaining company.

The room filled out and Hilary came over to say hello although she didn't stop for long before rushing to join a group with Joe Mankiewicz at its centre. Walter was there but surrounded by dignitaries all evening so Diana couldn't get close enough to thank him for the invitation. The dancing began and Ernesto urged her to get up with him.

'I can't dance. I don't know what to do,' she protested.

'Don't worry. I'll do everything,' he insisted. 'You just follow.' He wouldn't take no for an answer, pulling her by the arm to the dance floor then guiding her with a hand on the small of her back. 'Just relax,' he whispered, and she found that if she stopped trying to keep up, his legs and the hand on her back guided her around the floor. She almost felt elegant. No one was watching them so there was no need to be self-conscious.

Just after ten o'clock, a flurry of whispers passed around the room and a wave of heads turned to the door. Women adjusted their hair while men straightened their jackets and ties as Elizabeth Taylor and Eddie Fisher walked in. She was wearing a clinging silvery-white gown trimmed with long white ostrich feathers and very high heels that made her walk in tiny hobbling steps. Even at a distance, Diana could see that she emanated a kind of effortless star quality. It was hard to quantify or describe but she instantly became the centre of the room, like a sun around which all the planets revolved. She accepted a glass of champagne from a waiter then sat down at the head of a large table. Instantly the most famous party guests rushed over to pay court – Tony Curtis, Kirk Douglas, Jean Simmons, Walter Wanger, Rex Harrison and Rachel Roberts – all keen to be seen in her presence. Eddie beamed benignly and chatted to those on the edges of the throng.

Ernesto excused himself for a moment, so Diana sat on her own watching the spectacle. She couldn't help wondering what Trevor would make of all the fuss. This woman might be beautiful but so were lots of other women, and truth be told she wasn't a particularly good actress. No one reported her as being especially clever. She was simply famous for her marriages, famous for the fact that her third husband died in a plane crash and she stole her fourth from Debbie Reynolds, America's sweetheart. Yes, it was her love life Elizabeth Taylor was famous for rather than her acting talent. What a strange career.

Suddenly she noticed Ernesto hiding behind a pillar at the back of the room and speaking into a walkie-talkie. It seemed odd that he would have one, so when he rejoined her, she asked what he had been doing.

'I was making some security arrangements for when they leave,' he said.

She thought it was bizarre that he was involved in security for an event to which he hadn't been invited but didn't get a chance to question him further as just then the band struck up a rumba and Joe Mankiewicz led Elizabeth Taylor to the dance floor. She tottered like a skittle on her stiletto heels and when she wiggled those well-fleshed hips, the tight white dress threatened to split at the seams. Now, wouldn't that be a story! All eyes were upon her but Elizabeth's eyes were fixed on Joe, and Diana had to admit that she was extremely sexy. What man could resist her magnetism? It must feel like being sucked into a vortex.

The dance brought them close to Diana's table for a moment and her attention was caught by a varicose vein on Elizabeth's ankle, like a fat little worm resting on her skin. It was re-assuring to see she wasn't perfect, that she was real flesh and blood.

Diana heard a scream before she saw a flash of light, then there was a thump as one of the Italian musicians dropped his cello and leapt off the stage. He ran towards Elizabeth and began to pat her legs and bottom, while Joe stood to one side looking bemused. There was a faint smell of smoke now. Elizabeth turned to peer over her shoulder at her own backside and let out a whoop of laughter.

'I'm on fire,' she said. 'Damned ostrich feathers. Someone must have dropped a cigarette.'

'*Scusi, signora,*' the musician bowed, having extinguished the flames. She held out her hand to him and he touched those famous fingers to his lips.

'My hero,' she said warmly. 'Thank you for saving me.'

No one else had reacted in time to deal with the emergency. Few people seemed to realise what had happened, as the musician leapt back onto the stage and began to play again. The rest of the band had continued without him.

'It seems you Italians never miss a chance to touch a girl's bottom,' Diana whispered to Ernesto, and he beamed proudly.

'Who knows? Perhaps he even arranged the fire himself.'

Elizabeth reached down to brush the charred edges of her ostrich feathers, as Joe solicitously took her elbow and guided her back to her table. Eddie hadn't seen the incident and he leapt to his feet in alarm when someone told him about it but Elizabeth appeared to think it was all a huge joke. They could hear her raucous laughter from the other side of the room.

At least I've got a story to tell Helen tomorrow, Diana thought. *She'll love hearing about this.*

Soon afterwards, Elizabeth and Eddie decided to leave, and they were followed by a crowd of hangers-on, still warming themselves around the glow of her fame. Diana wondered if Elizabeth liked being fawned over in that way. She didn't seem to mind.

As soon as they had gone, the party began to thin out. Even though the band was still playing and the champagne was still flowing, the consensus seemed to be that the evening was over and there was no point in staying any longer.

Chapter Thirteen

When Scott told the American hacks who drank in the Eden Hotel bar that he'd been beaten up by Don Ghianciamina's son after flirting with his daughter, they almost fell off their barstools.

Joe gave a long low whistle. 'Jesus, you had a narrow escape. Look at your nose, pal. What a mess!'

There was a knuckle-shaped groove across the bridge of Scott's nose and the tip now veered off to the left. What was worse was that his left nostril kept dripping, meaning that he had to sniff or wipe it on a handkerchief every minute or so. The doctors had said that might improve over time – or it might not. They didn't seem sure. That's what bothered him most. He'd been dating Rosalia, the nurse, since getting out of hospital but he couldn't kiss her properly because of his dripping nostril. He suffered from thick, poisonous headaches as well, and was popping painkillers several times a day.

'What do you know about Ghianciamina?' Scott asked. 'What's he involved in?'

'Drugs. Probably heroin, because that's where the money is. But I'm sure he's also involved in money laundering, prostitution, all the usual stuff. He's a big cheese.'

'Why don't the police do something about it? I told them exactly who beat me up, and gave them a full description and his address but they refused to go to the house and question him. It's incredible!'

'I'll bet they did. They probably have families. Seriously, you're lucky to be walking around and I would keep your head down. Stay away from Italian girls, Spike. You won't get anywhere without putting a ring on their finger.'

'Is that so?' Scott couldn't resist boasting about the nurse, with whom he'd had sex three times. She was sweet but not really his type. In fact, she seemed rather keen and he wasn't sure how he was going to extricate himself. As she left his apartment a couple of mornings previously, she had clung to him and asked plaintively when she would see him again. He said he had a lot of work on and would telephone when he had a moment, and she seemed upset. Warning bells were sounding. But the hacks were suitably impressed.

'Bring her to meet us. Maybe she's got a friend. I've always had a thing about nurses.'

'He wouldn't bring her here,' Joe said. 'He's scared she'd run off with me.'

They all hooted. Joe was an ugly big guy with buck teeth and one blind eye that stared off to the side. All the men in that crowd were at least twenty years older than Scott, with middle-aged paunches, thinning hair and bulbous red noses that signposted their love affair with booze.

'Where is the drugs scene in town?' Scott asked. 'Where would I go to buy stuff if I was that kind of guy? Which I'm not, of course.'

'The Via Margutta, and the area around there. That's where the arty types hang out. I hear there are bars where you can buy marijuana or LSD over the counter if the bartender knows you.'

'They have LSD parties where everybody's tripping. I don't know where you get heroin, though. You probably need to know the right people but I'm pretty sure it's not hard.' Joe peered at Scott. 'You haven't got any stupid ideas about writing some kind of story, have you, Spike?'

'Course not,' Scott lied. That was exactly what he had been thinking. He hadn't yet figured out how but he knew he wanted to get revenge on his attackers and the best way would be to write an article exposing their crimes. It would have to include information so damning that the police would have no option but to arrest them. It would take a lot of research – but didn't someone once say that revenge was a dish best served cold?

'I filed my first Liz Taylor story today,' Joe told them. 'Her feather boa caught fire at a party last night and one of the guests had to throw her to the ground and roll on top of her to put out the flames – or so he said. Nice excuse.'

'Was she hurt?' someone asked.

'Naw, just shaken up.'

'Where were they?' Scott asked. 'Has anyone interviewed the guy who put out the fire?'

'It was in the Grand Hotel but I have no idea who he was. Who cares? People just want to read about Liz. Any excuse to put a picture of her on the front cover and my editor's happy.'

Scott pondered this. His own editor had phoned before he left the office to ask when he might start filing stories again, but it was hard to get anything substantial to write about since no politicians or their aides would talk to him. He abhorred the idea of writing about people simply because they were famous, but maybe he could compose a quirky little story about flammable fashions. He'd have to move quickly though, before it became old news.

He made his excuses and scooted back through the streets to his office. That day's Italian newspapers had been thrown out but the wastebin hadn't yet been emptied by the cleaner. He pulled them out and located some stop-press items that mentioned the incident with the dress, then composed a snappy little piece about the vagaries of designers who don't consider that their creations are going to be in close proximity to cigarettes. It was almost midnight in Rome but only four in the afternoon back home, leaving plenty of time to get a piece in the next day's paper. He picked up the phone and rang to dictate his story to a copy-taker.

Job done, he drove down to the Via Margutta for a look around. Rock 'n' roll music was blaring from some windows above a large art gallery. He saw an entrance round the side and when he walked up the steps, no one gave him a second glance, even though his sandy hair clearly signalled he wasn't Italian. Some guests were swaying to the music in a world of their own. Others sat dazed and saucer-eyed, staring into space. Yet more chatted with high animation and screeched with laughter. Scott hadn't ever tried drugs and didn't know anyone who had, but he'd read enough on the subject, especially in Norman Mailer's articles, to realise this was the kind of behaviour you might expect. He was pretty sure he'd be able to get some of these people to talk, and the best thing was they'd be unlikely to remember the conversations next morning.

That's what he would do. He would start investigating the Ghianciaminas, slowly and carefully building up a dossier of information until he was ready to publish. After it was in print, he'd have to leave the city and seek a posting elsewhere, probably with another paper. In the meantime, if he could keep his editor happy with a few stories about Elizabeth Taylor, that was all to the good.

'*Vorresti LSD?*' a tall, slender girl offered.

'Sure, why not?' he replied, thinking he might as well get to know what it was like. She gave him a sugar cube and told him to let it dissolve on his tongue. After just a moment's hesitation, he popped it in his mouth. He hadn't expected to notice much difference but half an hour later he realised he felt immensely content with the world. Everyone at the party seemed extraordinarily good-looking and the music was the best he'd ever heard. He wandered round without talking to anyone, simply soaking in the vibe.

So this is it! he thought in a moment of self-awareness. *It's good stuff. Well, I'll be damned.*

Chapter Fourteen

In October, the temperature in Rome dropped by ten degrees and cold blustery rain set in. Instead of lounging on the grass inside Cinecittà's main entrance, people sprinted from one building to another with coats held over their heads to protect their ancient Egyptian makeup and hairstyles. Huge puddles formed in the uneven pathways and girls shrieked as they stepped on loose paving stones, causing muddy water to splash up their bare legs.

Diana was invited to watch what Hilary called the 'dailies' – footage that had already been shot – in a screening room. She wasn't sure why they wanted her there but Walter explained that if there were any dreadful mistakes they could fix them in editing.

'In the worst-case scenario we can reshoot scenes but I'm hoping that won't be necessary. On most films you can watch dailies at the end of the day they were shot – hence the name – but we have to courier the film stock back to LA for processing. We pack up the cans every night and send them off then it's a week before the so-called "dailies" get back to us, by which time the sets have been taken down. So if something hasn't worked out, it's a complete pain in the proverbial.' He smiled as he spoke, and Diana wondered if anything on set ever rattled his composure. She'd only ever seen him in good humour but he obviously had a dark side if Helen was right about him shooting his wife's lover.

They took their seats, the lights were switched off and the projector cast a big white circle onto the screen, then diminishing numbers flashed up . . . 3, 2, 1. She saw the clapperboard slowly closing and a big cross appeared, before an image of Elizabeth Taylor and Rex Harrison. The sound had been synched on but there was no background music or sound effects so their voices seemed curiously flat. They watched one short sequence in which Cleopatra argued with Caesar, then the clapperboard came up again and they were in an entirely different and non-sequential scene.

Diana found it hard to follow the short snatches of action but she was impressed by Rex Harrison's acting. He was easily plausible as Caesar, a man struggling to hold together the vast Roman empire but facing insurmountable problems due to the geographical distances and implacable enemies. Elizabeth Taylor, on the other hand, was simply playing Elizabeth Taylor. With her curious Anglo-American accent and modern looks, she bore no resemblance to the first century BC queen Diana had studied. Her extraordinary beauty and sexually charged acting were pure Hollywood.

The film was going to be a love story, not a historical documentary. Would cinemagoers have been interested in watching the true Cleopatra story of the woman who married her brother, ordered the deaths of her rivals, defeated foes in battle and bribed the Egyptian people to win their loyalty? To Diana's way of thinking, the fact that, far from being beautiful, she had been hook-nosed, strong-jawed and stick-thin yet extremely quick-witted, made for a more entertaining story. But as it was, she could see that this was going to be a sentimental movie designed to showcase its star. There was nothing she could do to change that.

When the projector was switched off and the lights came on, they sat discussing what they'd seen, and Joe Mankiewicz suggested a couple of fill-in shots. The cameraman agreed and someone wrote it down. No one asked Diana's opinion.

'Great work, everybody,' Walter beamed, and the group dispersed. Sheltering under a studio umbrella, Diana hurried back to the production office, wondering whether there was any point in her attending the dailies. They would never reshoot anything based on her opinion; that much was clear.

'I've just been booking a trip for you,' Hilary told her as she walked in and threw her wet brolly into a rack. 'Joe wants you to check the sets they're building in Ischia. I thought I'd ask Ernesto to go with you because he knows the people there. You OK to leave tomorrow?'

'Yes, that would be fine.' She sat down at her desk, racking her brains as she tried to remember where Ischia might be. 'How long will I be away?'

'Depends what you find, but no more than a week I'd say. Just long enough to tell the set builders what they're doing wrong.'

Diana glanced over towards Hilary's desk. It would feel odd to leave Rome without letting Trevor know where she was going. 'Did the courier arrive from London?'

Hilary pursed her lips sympathetically. 'Nothing for you. Hasn't he replied yet?'

Diana shook her head.

'Call him. Go on, I'll make sure no one disturbs you.' She got up and gave Diana a quick pat on the shoulder. 'Stick to your guns but tell him you miss him. And good luck!'

Diana looked at the clock. Trevor was probably sitting at his desk over lunch. She placed the call through the operator and, almost as soon as it rang, she heard her husband's voice on the end of the line. His secretary must have gone out.

'Hello, it's me. How are you?'

'I'm fine.'

'I wrote to you. Did you get the letter?'

'Yes, I got it.'

'Why haven't you replied?' Diana asked.

'I don't know what you want me to say. Of course I miss you, but this wasn't my decision.' His tone chilled her. Suddenly she felt cross with him for being so unsupportive but she knew that nothing would be resolved if she lost her temper.

'I'm going to Ischia tomorrow to check the outdoor sets. They're building boats for the sea battle of Actium.'

'No doubt that will be educational,' he commented drily, then added 'I'm sorry, but it's hard for me to get excited about it from back here in rainy London.'

There was a long pause, then they both began to speak at once – him to say he had a tutorial to prepare and her pleading 'Don't shut me out, Trevor. Please come over to Rome, or at least write to me.'

'Diana, it's only a few weeks till Christmas. We can talk then. I don't see any point in coming out beforehand to sit on my thumbs while you prance around with the stars.'

He was immovable. She had no choice but to agree that they would talk on her return. When she came off the phone, she sat for several minutes with her head in her hands. She knew him well enough to sense that, behind the curt tone, he was depressed and lonely. It had been selfish of her to leave him. She couldn't blame him for his attitude but wished that he would at least support her now she was there. She was having the time of her life, and didn't for one moment regret the decision she'd made.

Chapter Fifteen

Scott's editor was pleased with the ostrich feather story but next time, he said, he wanted a picture of Elizabeth Taylor in the dress, and preferably while it was on fire.

'Rome is crawling with photographers. Surely that's not too hard to organise?'

Scott went to visit Jacopo Jacopozzi, the amiable chief of Associated Press in Rome. The walls of his office were covered in pictures of popes and presidents, movie stars and politicians.

'You want it, we got it,' Jacopozzi told him. 'I've got people covering Elizabeth Taylor from the moment she steps onto her verandah for breakfast until her car takes her home from a restaurant at night. I can get shots from inside the film set, or whichever nightclub she happens to be in. Just say the word.'

'Did you get the ostrich feather dress?' Scott asked.

'Sure,' he shrugged. He flicked through some files on the desk in front of him and pulled out one that showed Elizabeth Taylor leaving the Grand Hotel in a white dress, with Eddie Fisher by her side. 'Tazio Secchiaroli himself got this one. You've heard of him? He's our best man. He's getting more famous than the stars themselves, but he's not cheap.'

'How much to use that photo, for example?'

They discussed the rights needed, the print run, the size at which it would be used, and when Jacopozzi was finally pinned down to a price, Scott whistled in astonishment.

'That much? I've got a budget less than a tenth of that.' He named his figure.

'It can't be done, my friend. My photographers are bleeding me dry and I have a family to feed.' The expensive clothes and swanky office belied his penury.

'Yeah, yeah.' Scott tried to negotiate an affordable price but it was obvious they weren't going to agree. Jacopozzi had plenty of business and no need to compromise, so they shook hands and Scott retreated to think of another plan.

That evening he sat outside a café on the Via Veneto watching the *paparazzi* at work. There was a lookout at either end of the street checking inside approaching cars and calling up or down the hill to alert colleagues to celebrities. Scooters were parked in the road, ready for a quick take-off. Scott watched as Richard Burton and his wife Sybil emerged from one car and walked into the Café de Paris.

'Who are you planning to fuck on *Cleopatra*, Richard?' one of the photographers yelled at him in English.

Another darted in front of them and a flashbulb exploded right in their faces.

Burton looked tight-lipped but didn't rise to the bait. It made a photo much more valuable if the subject was yelling or shaking their fist and he knew better than to give them that prize.

Scott noticed that one photographer was standing apart from the crowd on a set of steps further up the street. He took several shots of the Burtons and Scott guessed they would work well from that angle. Draining his beer, he left some money on the café table and approached the man.

'I'm Scott Morgan of *Midwest Daily* in the States. And you?'

'Gianni Fortelesa.'

'I'm looking for a photographer. Would you be interested in coming to the office tomorrow to show me some of your work?'

He realised straight away that he'd chosen well because Gianni's face lit up. It was a competitive world out there on the street and he seemed keen and hungry. What's more, he spoke good English.

'I can't pay Associated Press prices, but I can give you a retainer and a fee per picture. Bring the shots of the Burtons you took tonight and I'm sure I can use one of them.'

Next day the deal was struck and Scott wrote a quick story about Richard Burton to accompany Gianni's best photo. He wrote that Burton had only got the role after Stephen Boyd dropped out and neither Marlon Brando or Peter O'Toole were available. The producers had to buy him out of the Broadway show *Camelot*, where he was playing King Arthur to Julie Andrews' Guinevere. He was a renowned womaniser who was said to have had affairs with Claire Bloom, Lana Turner, Angie Dickinson and Jean Simmons (while she had been married to his friend Stewart Granger). Sybil, his wife of twelve years, normally turned a blind eye.

'In fact,' Scott finished, 'rumour has it that the only one of his leading ladies he hasn't had an affair with was Julie Andrews – because he was already shacked up with an exotic dancer called Pat Tunder.'

Cheap it certainly was, but Scott found this kind of journalism couldn't be simpler to write, and Gianni promised to give him tip-offs about any stories from the film set doing the rounds in Rome. It would buy him time to pursue his own story – the one he was determined to write about the Ghianciaminas, the family who appeared to be above the law.

Chapter Sixteen

Ernesto proved an entertaining companion on the trip to Ischia, pointing out landmarks they passed on the train to Naples and then on the hydrofoil across the bay. It was evening when they arrived, but early next morning they drove to the boatyard where the battleships were being constructed and Diana leapt out of the car in her eagerness to have a look. Brilliant sunshine lit the bay, where rocky cliffs descended to coarse bronze sand. Working fishermen plied their trade just along from the set on which a fleet of ancient craft had been constructed. Some were converted fishing boats that would sail on the water, while others were one-sided, to be held in place for camera.

'*Buongiorno, che piacere vederla,*' one of the boatbuilders said – 'nice to see you' – and they all came over to shake her hand. She soon realised these were proud, perfectionist craftsmen who were keen to hear her views on their work, and when she suggested a slight change in the decorative carvings at the prows, they assured her it would be done. They demonstrated how the barrage of stones and blazing javelins would be fired during the sea battle, showed her the spikes that would protrude from the front of the ships and mimed the way they would ram each other.

Next she went to see Cleopatra's barge, the *Antonia*, which would be filmed arriving at Tarsus, where she went to meet Mark Antony. The interior scenes would be shot in the studio at Cinecittà but there was a spectacular outdoor scene planned as the barge pulled up in Tarsus with Cleopatra watching from beneath a gold canopy. The basic hull of the ship was ready, and its huge size and curved shape were accurately reproduced. Diana drew a sketch of the rigging, and told them that the sails should be purple, and they nodded, because they already knew. It was an exciting day, when she felt useful and appreciated.

At dinner that evening, Ernesto ordered a bottle of wine and as she finished her first glass, Diana realised she was more relaxed than she had been for a while – certainly since arriving in Italy. The rift with Trevor was on her mind, and towards the bottom of her second glass she found herself telling Ernesto about it. She felt disloyal but he proved a good listener.

'Do your family like Trevor?' he asked.

'I don't really have a family,' she told him. 'My mother died of cancer when I was three, so I only remember her through photos. Then my dad died of a heart attack when I was nineteen.' There was an unexpected catch in her throat as she said the words. 'I've got an aunt and uncle in Scotland, and a couple of young cousins, but I don't see much of them. Trevor's my family now.'

'What age were you when you met Trevor?'

'Nineteen. He was one of my college tutors when my dad died. He was really supportive, then gradually we fell in love.'

'He is older than you?'

'Yes, eighteen years . . .' She could see how it must look to him: as if Trevor had become a father substitute. She'd wondered about that herself sometimes. Certainly, she'd felt very scared and isolated when she was orphaned, and Trevor made her feel safe and connected to the world again. That might have been part of the attraction but it wasn't by any means the whole story. They'd become good friends as well as lovers. They discussed everything. That's why the current lack of communication felt so horrible, as though a part of her had been amputated.

Ernesto put a comforting hand on her knee. 'I'm sorry you're lonely,' he said, his eyes full of kindness.

She moved her knee so he had to shift his hand. 'What about you? You haven't mentioned your family. I presume you are married?'

'No,' he shook his head sadly. 'But I have a huge family, with so many cousins that I can never remember all their names.'

'I'm surprised!' she said. 'Surely most Italian men are married by your age? I don't mean . . .' In her wine-befuddled head, she realised that sounded rude.

'I'm not yet thirty,' he told her. 'But I am very cautious with women. There was a girl I was in love with for many years. We were at school together, we became girlfriend and boyfriend in our twenties and I always thought we would be married, until I found she had been betraying me.'

'Oh no! How did you find out?'

'One day she told me she was marrying someone else, a man who is much wealthier than me. They even invited me to the wedding but I didn't go. My heart was broken in pieces.' He held his hands over the spot.

'Was that recently?'

'Four years ago, but since then . . . I don't know. I am a cynic. I think I need to work hard and make lots of money and then I can choose the woman I want and she will say yes.'

'We're not all motivated by money,' Diana protested. 'You've just had bad luck.'

'I think I am too soft when I give my heart. I should have realised what was going on with my girlfriend but every time she cancelled a date I forgave her. I never suspected a thing. I don't think I will ever fall in love like that again.'

'I'm sure you will,' Diana smiled. 'We humans always heal eventually.' But then she thought of Cleopatra, the queen who gambled everything she possessed, and Mark Antony, the man who lost the sea battle of Actium and eventually his life because of his liaison with her. There had been no healing there.

They talked of affairs on the set and Diana asked, 'Did you hear some of the extras have complained to Hilary about men groping them?'

Ernesto twinkled. 'What do they expect when they are wearing next to nothing? We Italian men are very red-blooded.'

'I'm insulted!' Diana exclaimed in mock protest. 'I've been in Rome for two months and I haven't so much as had my bottom pinched. Maybe I am too old for those lotharios. They prefer the lithe young actresses.' She meant it as a joke, but it reflected her feeling that she was less attractive, less hip than the other girls on the film.

Later that evening, as they walked up to their rooms, Ernesto grabbed her bottom in both hands and squeezed hard. She jumped in surprise and turned to rebuke him, but he gave her a broad wink. 'Does that make you feel better?' he asked.

Over the next few days the colour flooded her cheeks every time she thought of it.

Chapter Seventeen

When Diana arrived at the production office on her first day back from Ischia, she could hear an altercation inside. She opened the door to see the actor Richard Burton shouting at Candy. She recognised him straight away as she and Trevor had seen him in the film *Look Back in Anger* but he was much shorter than she'd imagined and his skin was as cratered as a piece of pumice stone. The eyes were piercing and the voice was magnificent but on the whole she didn't think him very attractive.

'Can I help?' she asked Candy, wondering if she needed moral support.

'No, it's OK. Hilary's on her way.' She looked like a cornered animal.

Richard Burton glanced at Diana briefly then returned to the attack. 'If it were the first time or even the second, I'd think it was just one of those bouts of inefficiency that every film set is prone to, but a fourth cock-up is rather too much, don't you think? Was your silly blonde head too preoccupied with the Italian lads in carpentry?'

'I was just doing what I was told, Mr Burton.'

Diana decided she didn't like him. No matter what Candy had done, it was arrogant of him to speak to her in that way.

Hilary burst in, bringing an instant air of calm, and Diana stepped outside the office to let them resolve the dispute in peace. A woman with a pretty, young-looking face and back-combed silver-grey hair was standing smoking by the window.

'I don't suppose there's anywhere to get a cup of tea round here, is there?' she asked in a strong Welsh accent. 'I'm fed up with this Italian coffee. It's like swallowing bloody tar. I'm not sure how long I'll be stuck here while my other half does his nut in there.'

Diana realised this must be Sybil Burton. 'We keep a stock of tea in the office,' she said. 'Typhoo suit you?'

'Bless you, love. Milk and two, please.'

As Diana made the tea she wondered at the physical differences between the Burtons. Sybil's prematurely greyed hair made her look older than him, although her skin was smooth and wrinkle-free while his face looked decidedly lived-in. What must it be like to live with a man who had a temper like that? Diana also knew that he was notorious for having affairs. Was Sybil a doormat?

'You've saved my life,' she said gratefully when Diana took the tea out. 'It's so early we didn't have time for any breakfast. Rich was told he had to be in makeup at nine but when we turned up there wasn't a soul here. I think we even wakened the guard at the gate.'

'I wonder how that happened?' Diana was puzzled.

'Seems they don't need him today after all. No harm done, though. We might go and look around the Colosseum and the Forum. Have you been yet?'

'I haven't had time,' Diana admitted. 'I'm looking forward to it.'

'Course I've seen the one they've got here. It's more than twice the size of the real thing, I heard. That's bloody Hollywood for you.' Frowning slightly, she glanced through the window of the production office. 'They like everything larger than life.' She dropped her cigarette and ground it under a stiletto heel. 'So what's your role on the film?'

Diana explained and Sybil's eyes widened. 'You must meet Rich. He's been doing a lot of background reading and I'm sure he'd love to have a chat with you. Maybe not today, though.' She glanced inside again. 'What's your name, love?' Diana told her. 'I'll mention you. Don't worry. He's not as fierce as he looks!' She grinned in a way that seemed genuinely friendly and Diana warmed to her.

After they left, Diana entered the office to find Candy dabbing her eyes with a handkerchief while Hilary comforted her. 'It was a simple misunderstanding. He's got no right to be so rude to you.' She raised her eyebrows at Diana. 'Don't upset yourself now.'

Half an hour later as they walked to the script meeting together, Hilary confided in Diana that the mistaken call had been entirely Candy's fault and that she really wasn't on top of the job. This was just one in a string of mishaps. Diana remembered that it was Candy who'd been supposed to arrange the car to pick her up from the airport – the car that never materialised.

'Will she be sacked?'

'No, but I'll ask everyone in the office to try and watch her back from now on. Anyway, how was Ischia?'

'Wonderful!' Diana enthused. 'They're doing a great job down there. I'll type up my notes later.'

'And Ernesto behaved himself?'

'Of course! He was the perfect gentleman.' She caught a knowing look in Hilary's eyes. 'Honestly!'

She had lunch with Helen, who had been missing her, and relayed all the details of her encounter with the Burtons.

'Did you know about their daughter?' Helen asked. 'They don't know what's wrong with her yet but she's three years old and she can't speak or walk; she just rocks back and forwards. I read an article about it.'

'That's awful! Poor Sybil. I wonder how she copes?'

'They've got an older girl who's fine, but it must be a worry.'

Diana considered Sybil with fresh respect. She must be a resilient woman to cope with that and put up with her husband's philandering as well.

Helen seemed depressed so she asked what was wrong.

'I really want a boyfriend and nothing ever works out. I was chatting to Antonio from the set department all yesterday evening but when I asked him if we could go out some time he said no, that I wasn't his type.' She sniffed. 'It was so hurtful. I don't know what's wrong with me.'

Diana put a hand on her shoulder. 'He sounds like a cruel piece of work. It's as well you found out sooner rather than later that he's not the one for you.' She considered suggesting that Helen let the man make the move next time – men liked to be the hunters, all the magazines said so – but decided not to be so personal. What did she know anyway?

'My sister Claire's got a lovely boyfriend. Did I tell you that she works for *Vogue* magazine in London? She's glamorous and clever and her boyfriend is a stockbroker so they'll probably be rich and have a big house and lots of children. My mum and dad are really proud of her.'

'I'll bet they're even prouder of you,' Diana told her, 'and I bet Claire's jealous. You're working on the movie of the century with some of the world's most famous stars. After this, you'll be able to hand-pick the jobs you want anywhere in the world. You'll never look back.'

'You seem very cheerful,' Helen said, looking at her curiously. 'At least one of us is.'

'I think we're lucky to be here and we should make the most of it. Why don't you and I go out tonight, Helen? I'll treat you to dinner somewhere nice.'

'OK,' Helen agreed, with a brave attempt at a smile. 'I'd like that.'

After they finished eating, she asked the waitress for a glass of milk. 'Want to see something cute?' she asked.

Diana followed her out of the bar and over towards the far wall of the studio where, under a large bush, there was a heaving mass of grey and white furry bodies. A cat lay full length, her eyes closed to slits, as half a dozen wriggling, mewling kittens scrambled over her and fought to attach themselves to her nipples.

'They're only a week old.' Helen poured the milk into an old saucer lying by the wall and slid it towards the mother, who immediately began to lap at it with a delicate pink tongue. She bent to pick up a kitten and it was dwarfed by her hands.

'They're lovely,' Diana said.

'Aren't they? I pop out here to watch them playing whenever I can find a moment.'

She was mesmerised by them, like a child, and Diana was glad she had found something to lift her low mood. It occurred to her that feral cats might well have fleas but she didn't want to spoil Helen's fun. With her face lit up and her blue eyes sparkling, she had a fresh, natural beauty to rival that of any movie star – even Liz Taylor herself.

Chapter Eighteen

Scott took Gianni out for lunch at Chechino's, an old-fashioned restaurant that had been recommended by the foreign press hacks. 'Order the *coda alla vaccinara*,' they urged him, and there it was on the menu. He asked Gianni what it was and for once he was stumped for the English word, but began to wave his arm behind his lower back, repeating '*La coda, la coda*'. Eventually Scott worked out that it was oxtail and gave it a wide berth. He ordered a bottle of Chianti, though, and when they finished it he got another.

Gianni's language skills were superior to Scott's and so they conversed almost solely in English. The man was in his mid-twenties and had a wife and two children – one of two years old and the other a baby, he said, rocking his arms to demonstrate.

'Doesn't your wife mind you going out every night?' Scott asked.

Gianni rubbed his fingers and thumb together. 'We need the money.'

Talk turned to the Cleopatra film being made at Cinecittà and Gianni told him that two months into shooting it was already the most expensive film ever made. Elizabeth Taylor's million-dollar fee was one cause, but tales of excess spending kept filtering out of Cinecittà. Almost the entire cast and crew were on full pay for the duration even though only a fraction of them were being used at any given time, so most were sitting around with nothing to do. They'd spent quarter of a million dollars on a special kind of mineral water for the bar, but there was a sign there telling them not to be wasteful with plastic cups – as if that would make all the difference.

'Have you been inside?' Scott asked.

'Yes, there is a side entrance. I got thrown out but not before I'd had a look around. Unfortunately the security guard took the film from my camera.' He rolled his eyes. It was a hazard of his trade.

'Any stories about the stars making unreasonable demands?' That's the kind of thing that would make a printable story.

'Of course!' Gianni told him. 'I hear they flew in some chilli for Signora Taylor from her favourite restaurant in Hollywood.'

'Which restaurant was it?'

Gianni screwed up his eyes trying to remember. 'They have Oscar parties there sometimes and it is famous for its chilli.'

'Chasen's?' Scott guessed.

'That's the one. So they spend with one hand, but with the other they try to save money. Just yesterday Rex Harrison was told he no longer had a personal driver but had to share one with other actors. I hear he was so angry that he said he was going to . . . *fare sciopero*. How do you say? To stop work. Everyone clapped and cheered and he got his driver back.'

'That's great, Gianni. Cool. I'll do a story on that. Could you get me a picture of Rex Harrison in his car, with his chauffeur?'

'No problem,' he shrugged. Scott noticed that he had polished off some pasta and a meat dish and was mopping up the sauce with a piece of bread, as if he were still hungry.

'Want anything else?' Scott asked. 'Dessert? Company's paying.'

Gianni began to peruse the menu, reading the main course section. He looked as though he wanted to ask something but was embarrassed. 'Could I have another *secondo*?' he asked, blushing.

'Of course you can.'

Gianni ordered another helping of the hefty meat dish he'd had for his main course, while Scott drained his glass of wine. The dish arrived and Gianni dipped his fork into it but didn't start eating. After a while Scott got up to go to the gents' and when he came back the meat dish had disappeared.

'All finished?' he asked, surprised. 'Should I get the check?'

'*Molte grazie*,' Gianni said, looking somehow bashful.

Scott paid and still couldn't put his finger on what the man might be embarrassed about until they walked out of the restaurant and each headed towards their own scooter. It was the careful way Gianni placed his camera bag in a back compartment of the scooter that gave the game away. Scott guessed he had asked them to put that meat dish in a carton and he was taking it home for his family. They must be really hard up. He resolved to get him as much work as he could in future, to try and help out.

The day after *Midwest Daily* ran the Rex Harrison story Scott took a call from someone very grumpy at the Twentieth Century Fox press office.

'Who the hell are you? Some college kid straight out of diapers? Did nobody tell you that we're happy to help the press so long as you don't fuck with us? Well, now you've fucked with us and I'm going to make sure you don't get any press releases from the film set, no interviews, no invitations to special screenings, no nothing. Not on this or any other Twentieth Century Fox movie ever. You happy now, college kid?'

The phone was slammed down and Scott stared at it, grinning. He guessed it was the sign of a successful story if it got them so riled. Gianni's photo of a glowering Rex Harrison had complemented it perfectly.

Meanwhile, there was another photograph Scott wanted. He considered asking Gianni to take it but decided that he couldn't put him at risk. This was his hometown and he had family here, so Scott would have to get this one himself. He bought one of the new Kodak Colorsnap cameras that had just been launched and a couple of rolls of film, then he drove to Piazza Navona and parked round the corner. His heart was pounding and he wrapped his scarf around his face, as if against the cold.

Just across the square from the building where the Ghianciaminas lived there was a stairwell connecting some offices. Scott had never seen anyone there when he drove past. The entrance was through a gated courtyard but the gate was slightly ajar. He walked in unchallenged and made his way upstairs to the spot where there was an open-air walkway. He crouched on his heels and got the camera ready, then he lit a Camel. If he heard anyone coming, he would quickly stand up and walk down the steps as if leaving after an appointment.

He sat on his heels and waited and watched the entrance to the Ghianciaminas' home. At the usual time, Gina emerged with her basket and his heart did a little flip to see her, even at that distance. She walked up the road towards the market. If only Rosalia, the nurse, had her innocent freshness. There was something about Rosalia that felt burdensome. She needed so much from him: kisses, compliments, reassurance – no matter how much he gave, she needed more. He should have broken up with her long before because he knew she wasn't for him, but he was being a coward about the tears and recriminations he knew would follow. Instead, he was making the gaps between their dates slightly longer, which only had the effect of making her more anxious when they were together.

The door of the Ghianciaminas' home opened again and a group of men emerged and walked down the street. Their backs were to him so he couldn't see if Gina's brother was among them. This was useless. They continued to the far corner of the square and then suddenly one of them turned back, as if he had forgotten something. As he got closer, Scott saw that it was his attacker. He ducked his head below the parapet, pointed his camera in the general direction and pressed the shutter. He wound on the film then pressed again, then a third time. His heart was beating so hard he felt it would leap out of his chest as he listened for footsteps on the stairs below.

After several minutes of silence he raised his head again. All the men had gone and the street was empty. He hurried down the steps, jumped onto his bike and drove all the way across town, past the Colosseum, past the meat market, as far as he could go before the buildings began to thin out and he could see countryside beyond. Only then did he stop and finish off his film with some shots of a goat tethered by the roadside. He put the film into the cardboard envelope that had come with it, then looped round past an industrial estate in Ostiense until he found a tiny pharmacy with a Kodak sign above the door. He handed over his film, took a receipt and agreed to pick up the prints the following week.

Chapter Nineteen

Arriving at the studio on the 13th of December, Diana could sense the heightened atmosphere on the *Cleopatra* set. Actors and technicians had turned up at Cinecittà even though they hadn't been called and were sitting around in the commissary or the bar, whispering and watching. Outside the *paparazzi* had got wind that something was up. Everyone coming into the studios was offered money to take photos that day: five hundred dollars, a thousand dollars, or millions of *lire*. Little did they realise that only a select handful of people would be permitted onto the sound stage to watch the filming, and even they would be searched on the way in, because Elizabeth Taylor had a nude scene in which Cleopatra would be massaged by her handmaidens.

Security had been tight around the set since a girl had been caught the previous week with a camera hidden in her bouffant hairdo. Diana knew there was no chance she would be allowed into the sound stage – she'd only seen three scenes being shot in two and a half months. Like everyone else, she was curious that day and she joined Helen in the bar from where they could watch the comings and goings.

Eddie Fisher hurried between his wife's dressing room and the sound stage, head down, as if on some vitally important mission, but, as Helen whispered to Diana, he was probably just making sure her special chair was set up in the right place. When Elizabeth finally appeared in full Cleopatra hair and makeup with a bathrobe wrapped around her, Eddie was glued to her side, part of a little entourage of assistants fussing over her. When she saw the crowd watching from the terrace outside the bar, Elizabeth waved and called 'Hi there!' before disappearing into the building.

'When are you going back for Christmas?' Helen asked. 'I hope you'll be here for the Christmas party at Bricktop's. Isn't it amazing that we're all invited, and not just the stars? I can't wait.'

'Of course I'm staying for it,' Diana told her. 'Irene Sharaff has offered to lend me a dress. I'm sure she'll lend you one as well if I ask. She's got dozens.'

'Fab!' Helen said. 'You're a brick. I haven't bought anything new in ages.'

Some time later, a door opened and a technician came out for a cigarette. He whispered to a friend and soon there was a buzz going round the bar that Richard Burton had made a rude comment about Elizabeth Taylor's figure. Seemingly he had said that it changed shape after being massaged.

'Isn't that mean?' Helen exclaimed. 'He sounds horrid.'

Diana wasn't surprised. She'd already formed a low opinion of him. She wondered if the film would be given an X certificate. Surely it would have to be if there was nudity? Helen didn't know any more than she did.

They went to visit the kittens, who were growing bigger and noisier by the day. Helen had livid scratches on her arms from their claws but still she loved to pick them up and cuddle them, nestling them against her cheek. Afterwards, Diana wandered back to the production office and was about to phone Trevor to tell him the time of her flight home on Christmas Eve when the door burst open.

'Hi! We haven't been introduced. I'm Eddie Fisher.' He had a friendly smile and very white teeth.

'Diana Bailey.'

'I need your help. Do you know where I could find some sanitary napkins and belts? I figured one of you girls might have a supply. It's kinda urgent.'

'We've got some in our bathroom cupboard.' Diana jumped to her feet. 'How many do you need?'

'Just two or three will do until we get home. Thanks a million, sweetheart.'

Diana fetched the towels, all the time wondering how Elizabeth could be doing a nude scene if she was menstruating. Wasn't she supposed to take three days off when she had her monthlies?

As she handed them over, Eddie grinned again. 'They're not for Elizabeth, if that's what you're thinking. They're for our dog, Baby. She's bleeding all over the dressing room, the messy bitch.'

Diana snorted with laughter. 'Are you sure these will fit? I don't know how much the belt will tighten.'

'All I can do is try. Nice to meet you, Diana. I'll see you around.'

After that first encounter, he always stopped to have a friendly word whenever they passed on set. He remembered her name and asked her how things were going, commented on the weather or made some remark about the scenes being filmed that day. She found him very unaffected and natural, which seemed odd considering the woman to whom he was

125

married. Maybe that's why Elizabeth loved him. Perhaps his genuine niceness was rare in her world.

On the 23rd of December, Diana and Helen got ready together and caught a taxi to Bricktop's basement piano bar for the *Cleopatra* Christmas party. When they walked down the steps it was already thronged, with a four-piece band playing in the corner. Helen headed straight for the dance floor and Diana watched with admiration, because she seemed to know all the latest dance moves and undulated with effortless, unselfconscious rhythm.

'She's good,' Ernesto said in her ear. He handed her a drink. 'And you look amazing. I almost didn't recognise you.'

She glanced down at the tight-fitting turquoise shift dress that stopped just above her knees. 'It's not really me but one has to make an effort.' She smiled. 'How are you?'

They found a corner table to sit and chat and Diana was delighted he was there because she barely saw Helen for the rest of the evening. If it hadn't been for Ernesto she would have been utterly on her own. He told her he was spending Christmas with his family and that he would be forced to eat industrial quantities of his mama's food. She told him that she and Trevor always spent Christmas Day together before going to visit his relatives on Boxing Day.

'Are you looking forward to seeing him?' Ernesto asked and she replied 'Yes, of course.' It was true. She couldn't wait.

Rex Harrison and Rachel Roberts got up to dance and Diana saw that she was obviously inebriated and hanging on to him to keep her balance. Her face was flushed and she couldn't stick to the beat. Suddenly she reached down and tried to open the fly of Rex's trousers and he batted her hand away in an angry gesture that made her hoot with laughter. Rex charged off the dance floor back towards their table, and Rachel flung her arms round an Italian boy standing nearby, making his friends roar and wolf whistle.

'I hate women who drink too much,' Ernesto confided, watching the scene.

'And yet you ply me with alcohol wherever we go,' Diana teased.

'Yes, you are another case entirely. You need to be loosened up. This is my strategy.' Their faces were close and he looked directly into her eyes.

Diana raised an eyebrow. 'Your strategy indeed! Perhaps you had better rethink it or you will turn me into one of the drunk women you hate.'

Ernesto was staring at her. 'I love the way you can make one of your eyebrows lift but not the other. I practised in the mirror at home but I can't do it. I think I have the wrong sort of eyebrows.'

'It's only the right one,' she told him. 'I can't do it with the left.' They both tried for a while, twitching their faces comically.

There was the usual hush as Elizabeth and Eddie arrived at the party. 'They won't stay long,' Ernesto told her. 'It's a guest appearance because Walter asked them to come. They don't usually mix with the common people.'

'How do you know all this?'

'I know many things, my little Diana. You just ask me and I will tell you them.'

Rachel Roberts was trying to open the Italian boy's fly now and Diana thought someone should stop her but Rex was

127

nowhere to be seen. When the boy began to grope her breasts and she didn't make an attempt to remove his hand, Diana leapt to her feet.

'Excuse me, Miss Roberts,' she said, taking Rachel's arm and pulling her away. 'You are needed in the ladies' room.'

The boy released her without a murmur, aware he'd been pushing his luck. Rachel came like a lamb, leaning hard on Diana's arm even though they'd never met.

'Where's Rexy?' she asked.

'I'm not sure, but if you sit here I'll go and find him for you.' There was a comfortable armchair in the corner and she lowered Rachel into it.

'Will you get me a drinkie-poo?'

Diana agreed she would, although she had no intention of doing so. She hurried back out into the club and pushed through crowds looking for Rex Harrison.

'Are you OK?' Eddie Fisher asked when she passed their table, but in response to her query he said he hadn't seen Rex all night.

Diana found Hilary sitting in a corner with Rosemary Matthews and Joe Mankiewicz and asked what she should do about Rachel. Immediately, Hilary leapt to her feet.

'I bet Rex has gone home without her again. Let's get her into a car.'

By the time they arrived back at the ladies' room, Rachel had fallen asleep but, with one of them on either side, they managed to pull her to her feet and guide her out the main door to where the Twentieth Century Fox drivers were waiting. A few flashbulbs popped, but a drunken Rachel Roberts wasn't the picture the *paparazzi* were hoping for that night.

'Is she often like that?' Diana asked as the car pulled away.

'I'm afraid so. She and Rex have rather a volatile relationship and she drowns her sorrows. They're planning to marry early in the New Year and perhaps things will settle down after that.' Hilary didn't sound too convinced.

When they got back inside, Diana went to find Ernesto again. As she sat down, she noticed an odd sight: Elizabeth Taylor dancing cheek to cheek with Richard Burton. Diana was amazed: she'd assumed that they wouldn't get on with each other, that the two oversized egos were bound to clash. They looked good together, though. Even in heels, she made him look tall and his muscular physique was in stark contrast to her voluptuous curves. The number finished and they parted, laughing, to go back to their respective spouses.

Diana turned to Ernesto, a question in her head that she hardly liked to put into words. 'Surely not?'

'Yes, I think maybe it will be so.' Ernesto was deep in thought, almost talking to himself. 'I think Eddie Fisher is not a man who will keep her interest for much longer.'

Diana thought of the affable guy who had come to borrow a sanitary belt for a dog and felt concern for him.

Chapter Twenty

Scott's editor wanted him to stay in Rome over Christmas and New Year so his parents said they would fly over from the States to spend the holidays with him. He booked them a suite at the Intercontinental Hotel and arranged for a driver to pick them up at the airport, all the while bracing himself for the moment when his mother walked into the lobby and saw his broken nose. She'd be hysterical.

However, on the 23rd of December, the day they were due to arrive, there was a horrific train crash in Calabria and Scott's editor sent him to cover the story. The train had been crossing a viaduct when it derailed and carriages plunged 130 feet into a river below. Scott sped south in a hire car and spent some time at the crash site talking to investigators, in the hospital talking to survivors, and at a nearby shrine created by relatives of the seventy-one passengers who lost their lives. It was the first time he'd covered a major tragedy and he felt very moved by it and unsure how to talk to the traumatised survivors. As he shaved in his hotel room that evening, he found tears rolling down his cheeks.

He drove back to Rome late on Christmas Eve, amidst the clamour of church bells announcing midnight mass. When he got to his apartment, he found a long letter had been slipped under the door and he ripped it open and started to read. It was from Rosalia. She had been hoping to spend Christmas with him and his parents; she'd arranged her hospital shifts so she would be free on Christmas Day, but he hadn't been in touch. What was she to think?

Scott hadn't invited her to meet his parents, hadn't even hinted at the possibility – that was all in her head – but at the same time he knew he had behaved badly towards her. As soon as Christmas was past he'd have to let her down as gently as possible.

The following morning, he telephoned a subdued Rosalia and lied to her, saying that he had been delayed down south covering the rail crash and didn't know when he would be back. She couldn't argue with that but he knew he had ruined her Christmas and felt very guilty. He dressed in a suit and tie for the first time since arriving in Rome, and jumped on his Vespa to drive to the Intercontinental. As he walked in, Rosalia was still on his mind so at first he couldn't work out why his mother screamed when she saw him.

'Sweet Jesus, what happened to you?'

His nose. Of course. 'A man attacked me in a bar. It was a case of mistaken identity. He was arrested. Don't worry, Mom, I'm fine.'

'But your nose is broken. Couldn't they fix it up better than that? It's a mess.'

'It's OK, Mom.'

She turned to Scott's father. 'We should take him back to the States for plastic surgery with that colleague of yours. What's his name?'

'He doesn't do cosmetic work,' Scott's father replied gruffly. 'If the boy says he's fine, he's fine.'

They drank Martinis in the lounge before going into the

grand dining room for Christmas dinner, and throughout Scott's mother wouldn't stop asking questions about the attack and worrying that he wasn't safe in Rome. Maybe he shouldn't go out after dark. Certainly he should stop going to bars. Every time he had to wipe a drip from his nose, her face wore an anguished expression.

Eventually his father changed the subject. 'I haven't seen any Pulitzer Prize candidates in the articles you've been writing. What's with all this movie star nonsense?'

Scott shrugged. 'I have to do what the editor asks.'

His father snorted. 'You're in Europe in the middle of the Cold War. Why haven't you interviewed Italian politicians about their views on the East–West divide? How does post-Mussolini society view the Reds?'

'I did write a piece on the Italian Communist Party. And I'm working on something important, but it's taking a lot of research.'

'You don't want to get a reputation as a shoddy gossip columnist. You're not exactly using your brain, are you?'

Scott felt wounded. His father had always been critical: his high-school marks were never quite good enough; he didn't try out for the football team, preferring athletics, to his father's grave disappointment; and he hadn't got into the most prestigious fraternity at Harvard. Ridiculous that it still affected him, but he couldn't help it. It was partly to get away from the pressure his father subjected him to that he had sought a foreign posting in the first place.

The meal stretched on interminably, from an antipasti dish of cold meats to a pasta course and then roast turkey. There had been an option of stuffed pigs' trotters, which the waiter assured them was a great delicacy, but the Morgans all opted for a traditional turkey dinner. Of course, it didn't come with all the trimmings they'd expect in the US – no cranberry sauce, no stuffing even – but it was moist and tasty.

'Have you heard anything from Susanna?' his mother asked, and Scott sighed. She was the college girlfriend who'd left him. His mother had frequently intimated that he'd been crazy to let her 'slip through his fingers', as if there was something he could have done differently, some way he could have stopped her choosing his team-mate instead.

'Not since I've been here,' he said. 'I don't think she has the address.'

'She could find you if she tried. She could always call me. Never say never,' his mom said, trying to sound upbeat.

They exchanged presents after the meal. Scott's parents had bought him some binoculars and a new pair of chinos. What on earth was he supposed to do with binoculars, he wondered. Take up birdwatching? He gave his mother a silk scarf and his father a cigarette lighter with the Colosseum engraved on it. Everyone remarked on how well-chosen the gifts were and self-consciously tidied them back into their boxes, then they went for a walk round the nearby streets. Scott pointed out some landmarks but everything was closed and there was a chill in the air so before long they went back to the hotel for a coffee. He tried to stop looking at his watch, but time dragged as his mother chatted about friends of theirs from home and his father scowled, bored to distraction.

In the early evening, Scott pretended he had to go to his office for an hour or so to check in with the newsdesk, but it was an excuse to get away. His parents were staying in Rome for another three days and they stretched in front of him like a jail sentence.

'I'm not sure that motorcycle is safe,' his mother called as he mounted his Vespa. 'Why don't we buy you a car instead?'

He pretended he hadn't heard, struck his foot hard on the pedal and accelerated up the street as noisily as he possibly could.

Chapter Twenty-One

During the flight home and the train journey from Heathrow, Diana was excited about seeing Trevor. She yearned to feel his arms around her and smell the woody scent of pipe tobacco from his clothes, to sit down and ask him about his work and tell him the edited highlights of her three months away. So much had happened that it seemed much longer since she'd seen him. She missed his pithy insights, but most of all she wanted to feel as though he had forgiven her and that they were going to be fine.

She caught a bus from the station and alighted just past the zoo, then hurried down the frosty street to their rented flat in a Nash terraced house in Primrose Hill. It was only three in the afternoon of Christmas Eve, but already getting dark.

She knocked on the door first because it felt strange simply to barge in after so long away, even though it was her home. She'd just taken out her keys to unlock the door when Trevor pulled it open.

'Oh!' she exclaimed. 'Hello!'

Straight away she saw that he looked terrible. His pallor was grey in the harsh electric light of the hall and he seemed very thin. 'You've lost weight,' she said with concern, giving him a hug.

'Perhaps a bit,' he said. As he picked up her bag and carried it in, she noticed that there were holes in the elbows of his sweater and one shoe was flapping off his foot because the shoelace was broken. She had a stock of shoelaces in one of the kitchen drawers but he obviously hadn't found them.

She'd expected the flat to be uncared for but when they entered the kitchen, she saw that the sink was clear of dishes and the floor looked as though it had been recently mopped.

'Did you get a charlady after all?' she asked.

'No, I did it myself. It's not exactly hard, is it?'

'Oh good. Thank you,' she said. It felt strange that he had usurped her role, but she couldn't complain. She should be delighted.

'You've got new clothes,' he commented. 'And you've done something different with your hair.'

'It's backcombing,' she said. 'Seemingly it's *all* the rage!' She meant this to sound ironic, but Trevor looked surprised.

'It's nice,' he said. 'Very modern.'

While drinking her tea, she checked the larder, expecting to have to rush out and buy provisions for Christmas dinner, but there was a turkey on the shelf, much larger than they would need. He'd also bought potatoes, vegetables, mince pies and a round Christmas pudding in a wrapper with holly printed on top. She was touched that he'd gone to so much trouble.

'When did you manage to shop? That was thoughtful of you.'

'I've had to learn how to manage,' he said. 'It's a tricky business. Did you know that all the shops have half-day closing on a Tuesday, except the butchers, which for some reason is Wednesday? Sheer cussedness.'

'I'm sorry, I should have warned you about that.' She felt guilty. All this should have been her job.

'I hope you don't mind but I've invited an American student, Chad, for Christmas dinner. He was going to be on his own. I told him to come at two-thirty, in time for a sherry before the Queen's Speech.'

'That was nice of you.' As if the atmosphere wasn't already awkward enough, now they had a young American to entertain.

She turned to check the shelves, listing all the parts of the dinner in her head, and realised there were a couple of items they still needed: Paxo stuffing ('Christmas wouldn't be Christmas without the Paxo') and some orangeade to go with the bottle of gin she'd brought back. Trevor liked gin. 'I just need to pop out for a couple of odds and ends,' she told him. 'I won't be long.'

She pulled her coat back on and rushed down to catch the shops in Camden before they closed for the holidays, feeling somehow wrong-footed by Trevor's preparations.

On her return he was in his study marking student essays so she took a duster round the flat, noticing that he had dusted around ornaments without lifting them. Still, she should count herself lucky. Women's magazines sometimes gave tips on how to get your husband to take out the rubbish, or empty the Hoover bag, but none expected them to cook and clean.

Over supper that evening, the conversation between them felt strained. Every time she mentioned something about the film, there was an awkward silence before Trevor changed the subject. He simply didn't want to know. Instead he talked at length about a paper published by a university colleague that he felt was based on an incorrect premise. He tried to get her to understand some small distinction but it seemed fairly trivial to her.

'Wasn't it peer-reviewed?' she asked.

'Yes, by an imbecile! I can't imagine what he was thinking.' It had really got under his skin, and she sensed he felt threatened by this colleague, who had equal rank to Trevor but was known to have set his sights on the departmental chair when the present incumbent retired.

During a brief pause, Diana tried to tell him about the extraordinary craftsmanship of the boats at Ischia, but she could tell he didn't want to hear about them. He didn't ask any questions. 'I wish you would come out to visit some time,' she said wistfully. 'My room has such a lovely view over the rooftops and spires, and I still haven't had a chance to explore the city properly. I'm saving it for when you come.'

'Well, don't hold your breath,' Trevor said. 'I hardly dare leave the department just now for fear of what I'll find on my return.'

She felt irritable that he wouldn't even consider it. 'In what way? Is all this worry because of one article by a colleague you don't agree with? Surely it would be better to direct your energies into writing your own articles rather than criticising his?'

'Is that a dig?' Trevor's voice rose. 'I hope not, because the reason I've had less time to write up my research over the last three months is because I've had to rush out and buy food after lectures and come home to cook and clean. The chequebook ran out and its replacement got lost in the post so I had to find time to go to the bank when I needed money. I'm managing – don't get me wrong – but you should be aware that while you were swanning around Rome's hot spots, I wasn't exactly sitting here with my feet up.'

Diana felt another stab of guilt but brushed it aside. 'Trevor, you managed before we were married. You're very capable.'

'I just want you to understand why I'm not further ahead with my research. Life has been a juggling act and compromises have had to be made.' He turned away, seeming close to tears.

Diana's cheeks burned. 'I'm sorry,' she whispered.

The words hung in the air between them, until Trevor stood up and scraped back his chair. 'I think I'll go to my study and mark some more essays,' he said. 'If I catch up tonight, I'll be able to take more time off later in the holidays.'

Diana rose to start the washing-up, feeling aggrieved. Why couldn't he take time off the night she arrived back from three months away? How long was she to be punished for accepting a job that made her happier than she had ever been in her life? If he truly loved her, shouldn't he be pleased for her?

At nine o'clock, she made a cup of tea and took it to the study. 'I'm sorry we quarrelled,' she said. 'I think that sherry before dinner must have gone to my head. I didn't mean what I said. I'm sorry things have been so hard for you.'

'Thanks,' he said. 'I'm sorry too.' He didn't specify what for.

She was first to go to bed later and she listened to the familiar sounds of Trevor's bathroom rituals – the vigorous tooth-brushing, the spitting, a last wee. When he came to bed, he put his arm round her and let her rest her head on his chest, as they always did, but neither attempted to initiate sex. The distance between them seemed too great. After a while, he said 'I'm rolling over' and turned onto his side, the position in which he liked to sleep.

Diana lay awake, wondering how she could make things better. She loved him and couldn't face losing him. Without Trevor she would be entirely alone in the world. He was her

139

anchor and, until recently, her best friend. Why couldn't he show an interest in her new experiences? She was dying to share them but he'd erected a barrier that it was impossible to breach.

'Trevor?' she whispered.

There was no reply, but she was pretty sure from his breathing that he was only pretending to be asleep.

'Merry Christmas,' she whispered into the distance between them. *Tomorrow*, she thought. *Tomorrow I'll make things right, no matter what it takes.*

Chapter Twenty-Two

On Christmas morning, as soon as she could sense he was awake, Diana began to stroke Trevor's back through his flannelette pyjamas. He lay still, facing away from her. She began to rub his shoulders, which was one of their precursors to sex. Normally he would roll over and kiss her, but there seemed to be something wrong. When she reached her hand around, his penis hung completely limp between his legs. She kissed behind his ear and began to stroke him, trying to encourage an erection.

Suddenly Trevor pulled away. 'I'm afraid I have rather an upset stomach,' he mumbled. 'Excuse me.'

He swung his legs out of bed, grabbed his dressing gown and went to the bathroom, where he locked the door. Diana lay, listening for a sign that he would return but there was silence. She wondered if the upset stomach was genuine or if he was still too upset with her to make love. He had never rejected her advances before.

After a while, when it became obvious he wasn't coming back, she got up and went to the kitchen to make tea, her spirits heavy. She heard the bathroom door being unlocked, then he followed her down the passageway.

'Merry Christmas, darling,' he said, and they hugged, awkwardly, without letting any erogenous parts touch.

'Let me get your presents,' she said brightly. She'd wrapped them already: a new pipe and some special tobacco, a light blue sweater from Rinascente department store, his favourite type of marmalade and a box of Black Magic chocolates. He sat at the kitchen table and opened the parcels, making appreciative comments.

Diana had bought a present for herself, as she always did, because Trevor claimed he didn't want to waste money on the wrong thing. She produced the parcel, and smiled. 'This is what you're giving to me. Just the one present because it was rather expensive.' She opened the paper and pulled out a black fur-trimmed crocodile-skin jacket, with a tie belt. It wasn't her normal style but it looked so chic she hadn't been able to resist.

Trevor was surprised. 'That's unusual,' he said doubtfully. 'I thought black wasn't your colour. But so long as you like it. In fact, I got you something myself.' He pulled a paper package with a C&A logo from his dressing-gown pocket. She opened it and found a pair of soft leather gloves, cream in colour, similar to a pair she had left on a bus earlier that year. It was thoughtful of him to remember. In fact, she had stopped wearing gloves in Rome because no one else did. They now seemed as old-fashioned to her as swing skirts and headscarves. But how could Trevor have known that? She was touched he'd got her anything at all and resolved to wear them while in London.

They kissed, said 'Happy Christmas' to each other and then she started preparing the turkey for the oven.

Chad arrived at two-thirty and his presence provided a welcome distraction. He was big and lanky, with chestnut hair and a broad freckled face. He and Trevor had a playful relationship in which they teased each other about the differences between Britain and America.

'Do you know, Chad thought his name was an original American one? I had to disabuse him and direct him to read about the seventh-century Anglo-Saxon bishop Chad of Mercia.'

Chad grinned. 'Is Mer-see-a another of those strange English places with misspelled names, like Gl-ow-cess-ter and Eddin-burra?' He pronounced them phonetically. 'Why don't you just try to get the spellings right in the first place? Maybe you should invite an American over to correct them for you.'

This was fuel to the fire and they had a lively debate which culminated in Trevor suggesting that Britain should recolonise the United States in order to teach them how to speak the English language correctly and how to understand irony. Chad retorted that England was a defunct colonialist power, and Trevor snorted at the fact that Americans mistakenly used the term 'England' rather than 'United Kingdom'.

Chad ate three helpings of Christmas dinner and Diana could tell he was having a good time. 'Why don't you stay over?' she suggested when she heard he would have to walk several miles to his lodgings since the buses weren't running. Having a third person there made it easier because there was no chance of uncomfortable topics being raised.

They listened to a rather good play on the radio that evening and drank gin and orange, then Diana made up a bed for Chad and lent him a toothbrush.

When she and Trevor got to bed, neither attempted to initiate sex. Diana felt hesitant about making the approach after her rejection that morning and was waiting for a sign from him that he felt up to it. It would be good to make love;

it would make things feel normal again. But Trevor didn't make any advances. Perhaps he felt inhibited with Chad next door. Instead they cuddled and chatted quietly about their plans for the following day. No mention was made of Diana's imminent return to Rome, or Trevor's colleague's paper, or any subject that might threaten the equilibrium. They both wanted things to be fine and by striving to make it so, created an atmosphere that felt artificial and forced.

On Boxing Day, after driving Chad back to his student accommodation, they visited Trevor's parents. His sister was there with her three young children, and Trevor instantly became the fun uncle they could climb all over. Diana had a lump in her throat as she watched him 'skin the rabbit' with the littlest one by pulling her hands through her legs until she twirled round in a backwards somersault. He wanted children so badly and he'd be a great father; there was no question about it. It wasn't fair of her to make him wait. As soon as she got back from Rome, they should begin trying again. Unfortunately, her period started while they were at the house and Trevor's sister had to lend her a sanitary towel and belt. Diana told her the story of Liz Taylor's dog needing one, and they both had a chuckle.

For the rest of the holiday, Trevor and Diana steered clear of controversial topics. They visited friends for supper one evening, at which Diana carefully played down all mention of Rome, and on another evening they attended a recital at the Royal Academy of Music. Diana mended Trevor's clothes and bought him some new ones in the post-Christmas sales. They were affectionate, and often held hands as they listened to the radio in the evening or cuddled up in bed, but her period precluded any love-making. Diana was glad, because when she looked at Trevor she didn't feel desire. She enjoyed his company, but it still felt odd that he wouldn't let her tell him anything about her role on the film set and this exciting new chapter in her life. Was this how their marriage would be from now on? Is that what marriage was like for other people: companionship without passion?

The atmosphere became chillier as her departure date, the 4th of January, approached. Trevor shut himself in his study when she began to pack her case. She tried asking once more if he would join her for a weekend – or longer, if he could be spared – but he claimed it was entirely out of the question given his workload.

On the morning of her departure, they stood with their arms around each other in the hall, her head on his shoulder, absorbing each other's body warmth and inhaling the scent. She knew he felt sad and resentful that she was holding him back in his work, but she was hurt that he showed no interest in something that meant so much to her. Was that the behaviour of someone who loved her? Or had Trevor only cared about her when she was being the wife he wanted her to be? It felt like the end of an era.

Chapter Twenty-Three

Diana started crying as soon as the plane lifted off British soil and tears kept rolling down her cheeks throughout the flight. An air hostess brought her some paper handkerchiefs and a glass of water but that just made her cry more. Being so distant from Trevor was a form of bereavement. There were three more months before she would return home and she had no hope that he would relent and join her. He barely spoke when she telephoned him from Cinecittà. Once she got back to London, the distance between them would be even greater and she began to question how they would ever overcome it.

It's not over yet, she told herself. *You can still save your marriage if you try your hardest.*

But she had been trying her hardest all Christmas and it had been a terrible strain. How could she stay with Trevor if he wouldn't let her be herself and talk about the subjects she was interested in? How could she stay with him when she was no longer attracted to him? She wished there were someone wise she could discuss it with. If only her mother were alive; that's what mothers were for. She had women friends in London, of course, but none of them knew there was the slightest question mark over her marriage and it would seem disloyal to say so. Many were married to friends of Trevor's and she couldn't risk word getting back to him. Maybe she would confide in Hilary if the moment arose, but Hilary was always frightfully busy.

The flight landed at Leonardo da Vinci airport at four in the afternoon and she made her way through to arrivals, expecting to see one of the studio drivers. Instead, there was Ernesto, standing with a cheeky grin and holding a card with her name on it.

'Mrs Bailey? Your car is waiting,' he said in a mock-formal voice.

'What are you doing here?' she laughed.

He noted her red swollen eyes and pulled her in for a hug. 'I was trying to make up for the fact that no one met you last time you arrived, but now I have a second mission. I am going to take you for some Bellinis to cheer you up. No arguments now.'

'I wasn't going to argue. I'd *love* a drink,' she said.

He drove her to Trastevere, a district of narrow twisting streets and pretty church squares that she hadn't visited before. The bar he pulled up in front of wasn't grand. Empty beer casks served as tables, with small leather stools to sit on, and every inch of wall space was covered in drawings, many of them nudes.

'Artists swap them for a drink when they run out of money,' Ernesto explained. 'It's an old European tradition.'

She gulped thirstily at her first Bellini and Ernesto raised his finger to order another round. By halfway down the second glass, Diana found herself telling him about her Christmas. She was careful not to exaggerate the difficulties and grateful that Ernesto let her talk rather than leaping in with his own opinions, but when she had finished he simply said 'Your husband sounds like a fool.'

His words made Diana start to cry. 'But I love him,' she sobbed. 'I do.'

Ernesto put his arm around her and pulled her head to his shoulder. 'You deserve someone who loves you with passion, someone who will do whatever it takes to make you happy. I think you will find that person if you just allow yourself to look.'

'I can't think about finding someone else when I'm married. Why is everything so complicated?'

The barman brought them each a bowl of pasta, with forks rolled in serviettes, and Diana was surprised because she hadn't thought it was a restaurant.

'It's not,' Ernesto told her. 'This is what his wife has made for the family this evening and they are sharing it with us. It's why I like Trastevere. This is the food everyone should eat in Rome.'

The pasta was simply coated in butter and Parmesan cheese and it melted in the mouth. Soon after they finished eating, the third round of Bellinis arrived and Diana could feel the alcohol taking the edge off her despair and making her light-headed.

'How was Christmas with your family?' she asked. 'Was it as busy and chaotic as you predicted?'

'I was sad,' Ernesto told her. 'I missed someone.'

'Do you mean that girlfriend you told me about who married a richer man?' She frowned. Hadn't he said that happened years earlier?

He leaned towards her. 'No, someone closer to me.' He whispered in her ear. 'I missed *you*, Diana.'

The words took her completely by surprise, but when Ernesto took her chin between his fingers and placed his lips on hers, she didn't resist. The kiss was just a touch at first but soon grew more intense, and at the same time he stroked her head, running his hand back over her hair again and again, as if petting a kitten. For a moment she allowed herself to surrender to the sensations, ignoring the voice in the back of her head that said *I'm married. I should stop this now*, but then guilt overcame her and she pulled away.

'You mustn't do this.'

Ernesto stroked her cheek. 'You're so beautiful, Diana. You have the kind of face that doesn't need makeup or artifice. I'd like to look at you first thing in the morning, with sleepy eyes and a crease on your cheek from the pillow.'

Her lips were still tingling from his kisses but she managed to find some reserves of willpower. 'Please take me home. I'm a little tipsy or I would never have let you kiss me. I do hope I didn't mislead you.'

'As you wish,' he whispered and raised his hand to signal for the bill.

Driving back in the car, he stroked her kneecap with a firm, sensual touch, and she didn't try to stop him. It felt lovely. Outside her *pensione*, Ernesto pulled her close for another hug but she resisted when he tried to kiss her on the lips.

'Thank you for picking me up,' she said, pulling away, 'and for the drinks and supper, but I must go now.'

He jumped out of the car to carry her suitcase up the stairs to her landing. At the doorway, she took it from him and began to say goodnight but he reached out to embrace her.

'One goodnight kiss. Only a little one,' he insisted, and she surrendered to the luxury of his lips before pulling away.

'I must go inside,' she insisted, with a firmness she didn't feel.

'I shall dream of you,' he said, looking at her intensely before turning to walk down the stairs.

She shut the door and threw herself onto her bed, feeling more aroused – and more confused – than she had ever been in her life.

Chapter Twenty-Four

Scott took Rosalia for dinner early in the New Year. She'd bought him a shirt as a Christmas present and he didn't have anything for her, so that was the first awkward moment.

'You shouldn't have,' he told her. 'Really, it's too much.'

The evening became more and more difficult, with long silences and tears obviously not far off, and he regretted that he hadn't simply suggested a coffee instead. He could have done the deed and been on the way home by now, instead of which he was forced to make small talk about his parents, his work and her family.

'It looks like this year is going to be very busy,' he began, after the main course had been cleared. 'The editor wants me to travel more and I don't know when I'm going to be in Rome. Under the circumstances, it doesn't seem fair to ask you to wait for me.' *Coward*, he thought to himself. *Why can't you just be honest?*

'But of course I'll wait!' she exclaimed.

'The thing is, I don't want you to. I don't want to feel like I have an obligation or anything. I need to put my work first to get my career established and I can't have any ties.' It sounded plausible; he was starting to believe it himself.

'What are you saying?' She seemed to be rather slow getting the message. Perhaps it was the language barrier.

Scott lowered his voice. 'I'm saying that I think you should date other guys. I can't offer you anything. You're a great girl and you deserve someone better than me.'

She looked puzzled and insisted she only wanted him. It was when he was brutally honest – 'I'm sorry, but I don't want to see you any more' – that the tears began to flow and he felt like a complete bastard.

He walked her back to the nurses' home, feeling accusation in the eyes of everyone they passed as she sobbed and blew her nose into his handkerchief while leaning woodenly on his arm. There was a prolonged hug in her doorway and then finally – at long last – he was free.

Scott jogged down the street and the jog turned into a run as he tried to create distance between them in case Rosalia decided to pursue him. He fancied the idea of getting high so he headed up towards Via Margutta and walked along the street until he could hear a party underway. He climbed the stairs to a large open room and entered unchallenged. A girl with brownish-blonde hair that hung down below her bottom approached. She spoke English with a Northern European accent.

'Do you want to smoke some pot?' she asked, swaying so that it was obvious she was already high.

'Sure!' he grinned. 'Have you got some?'

She pulled a joint from her pocket and motioned him to follow her out to a balcony, where she sat down cross-legged on the floor. The soles of her feet were black with grime. Scott joined her and, as they smoked, he took the opportunity to ask her some questions.

'There's loads of gear around here. Do you know where it all comes from?'

She nodded, with a dreamy look. 'Yeah. Of course. Those young guys with their flashy cars bring it up from the south. I know a few of them. It's cheapest if you buy direct from them rather than the dealers.'

'Where do you find them?' He was getting a buzz after just a few tokes on the joint. It must be strong stuff.

'You don't find them. They find you. They're always hanging around these parties . . .' She swivelled to look inside the room. 'There's one by the door, wearing the sunglasses.'

Scott turned to look.

'Hey, what happened to your nose?' the girl asked. 'You're kind of funny looking.'

'I got trampled by a herd of elephants,' he told her. 'I'm lucky to be alive.'

'Oh my God, that's amazing! Did you really? You're a funny guy.' She leaned over and touched his nose, running her fingers over the scars, and he closed his eyes and enjoyed her touch. At least it put the difficult early part of the evening with Rosalia out of his head.

When he opened his eyes, the girl had gone, so he got up and went over to talk to the youth in the sunglasses.

'I heard you know something about how drugs get to the city. I'll pay good money if you tell me what you know.'

'Why would you do that?' the man asked, and Scott had to focus hard to comprehend his thick southern Italian accent.

'I'm a journalist. I want to write about it. Your name would never be mentioned and I won't give away any details that could get you identified. But I could pay you . . .' He named a price, and the youth took his sunglasses off and stared hard at him.

'How do I know if I can trust you?'

153

'I don't even need to know your name,' Scott told him. 'Make up a name. Just answer a few questions and I'll hand over the cash.'

The man considered this. 'OK, but not here. There's a bar in Testaccio . . .' He gave the address. 'I'll be there on Tuesday at seven, but only for half an hour.'

'I'll see you there,' Scott promised. 'What should I call you?'

He shrugged. 'Enzo. Why not Enzo?'

Scott put out his hand to shake on it, but 'Enzo' turned and walked off down the stairs. He went to find the girl with the long hair to say goodbye and thank her for the smoke.

'Are you going? I'll come with you,' she offered. She linked her arm through his and at first he imagined she wanted him to walk her to a taxi, or to her apartment, but when they reached the street she asked where he lived, and it seemed she had decided to come home with him.

Scott noticed her feet were still bare. 'Where are your shoes?'

'I lost them somewhere,' she said airily. 'Never mind.'

'It's freezing! You can't go out with bare feet in January.' Scott pulled off his own shoes and let her walk in those, her feet slopping around in them, while he stepped carefully along in socks. It was chilly but at least it wasn't raining and his scooter wasn't far.

As soon as they got to his place, the girl pulled off her dress and began to unfasten Scott's trousers. *Wow!* he thought. *This is something else.* She was flat-chested but he liked the blanket of dark blonde hair and her long skinny legs. What would his friends think when he told them?

They had sex, then Scott fell into a deep, drug-induced sleep. When he awoke next morning, he offered to buy break-fast for the girl but she refused, simply pulling on her dress and heading shoeless out onto the street. She didn't even ask whether she would see him again and he was rather pleased by the convenience of it all. It felt very modern and sexy.

When he got into the office, his secretary handed him his messages. It was only ten a.m. but Rosalia had already called twice asking if she could see him one more time. He decided not to reply.

Chapter Twenty-Five

All the way to Cinecittà next morning, Diana hugged herself, feeling overwhelmed by the events of the night before. As she walked into the production office, she felt she must look different somehow, but everyone called 'Happy New Year' and 'How was your Christmas?' and no one rebuked her for being a scarlet woman who had kissed a man who wasn't her husband.

She went to the script meeting with Hilary, and when she returned there was a parcel on her desk, wrapped in a napkin, alongside a little note saying 'In case you are hungry'. It was a *cornetto* with chocolate inside. Ernesto had introduced her to them during their trip to Ischia, so this must be from him. She felt a rush of blood to her face. She would have to talk to him and explain that their kisses could never happen again. As soon as he came by, she would take him outside for a chat and apologise for her behaviour.

She didn't encounter Ernesto that morning, so at lunchtime she went to find Helen, who was delighted to see her.

'I've missed you *so much*,' she announced dramatically, giving her a tight squeeze. 'Look, I've brought you a present.' She fished it from her handbag.

Diana opened the neatly wrapped parcel to find a black kohl eyeliner and some pale pink lipstick. 'They're lovely. Thank you.' She had given Helen a Christmas present of a gold chain-link necklace before leaving for London. 'How was it back home?'

Helen screwed up her nose. 'My sister was showing off her boyfriend and flashing all her fancy new clothes. She's so stuck up.'

'I'm sure she doesn't mean to . . .'

'Yes, she does. It was like that all through our childhoods. Oh well, at least I don't have to live in the same house as her any more.'

'Have you been to see your kittens yet?' Diana asked, to change the subject.

Helen's face fell. 'I can't find them. I went to look yesterday and the mother was there but all her babies have gone. I tried to ask a gardener, using sign language, and I think he said they've found homes for them but I'm not sure what he meant. Maybe you could translate?'

Diana saw a gardener pushing a wheelbarrow and rushed over to ask but he told her the kittens had been bundled into a sack and drowned in a river. They had managed to get into the framework beneath a sound stage from where their mewling had disrupted filming one morning so he lured them out with bits of liver and dispatched them pronto.

Diana didn't usually lie but on this occasion she made an exception: 'They've all gone to local families,' she told Helen, who seemed reassured.

'What a shame. I wanted to keep one, but I suppose I wouldn't have been able to take it home with me when filming is over. It's best this way.'

Over lunch, Diana nagged Helen to eat a sandwich instead of just swigging Coke. 'Your New Year resolution should be to eat more,' she suggested.

Quick as a flash, Helen said, 'No, my resolution is to find a boyfriend!' She asked if Diana would offer advice: 'You must help me to spot the decent ones and not waste my time on rotters.'

'I think you over-estimate my abilities. I'm not very experienced with men.' She blushed as she spoke, thinking of the previous night. It was never far from her thoughts. In the ladies' room later, she leaned her body against the cool tiles, feeling overwhelmed as she remembered the effects of those kisses – kisses that must never happen again, she told herself firmly.

That afternoon she steeled herself before phoning Trevor to say she had arrived safely. There was an awkward silence on the end of the line and she worried that he could read her thoughts somehow.

After a long pause, he said, 'I miss you already, Diana.' She felt so guilty she could barely reply and her hands were trembling when she hung up.

She was delayed at the end of the day by a late request from Joe Mankiewicz for information on Cleopatra's visit to Rome, and it was almost seven by the time she had typed up her notes. She hoped there would still be a driver to take her home and walked out to ask the guard at the gate. A horn parped and she glanced into the car to see Ernesto beckoning her.

'*Ciao, bellissima!*' he grinned. 'I waited to give you a ride. Get in!'

She felt flustered by her conflicting emotions: flattered that he had been so thoughtful; lustful at the mere sight of him; and yet guilty, so guilty.

'I bought you something,' he said, as she climbed into the passenger seat, and handed her a single white rose, long-stemmed and perfect.

'You mustn't do this.' She shook her head. 'I'm not going to have an affair with you. I can't. We can be friends but that's all.' She sniffed the rose and picked up a faint sweetness.

Ernesto grinned as he started the car. 'OK, friend! There's a restaurant I really want to take you to. Let's go there now, as *friends*.'

He chatted naturally about events on the film set that day, but his hand crept onto her knee and after a brief hesitation she lifted it away.

The restaurant he took her to was tiny, dark and cramped, so that they were crushed up against each other at a corner table, his thigh pressing against hers, and she guessed that's why he had chosen it. She could feel the warmth of his leg through her skirt. He held a leaf of artichoke to her lips, and she blushed as she tasted it. She realised she had been achingly lonely ever since she first came to Rome, but with Ernesto she could talk about whatever she wanted, and he listened and responded. Suddenly she wasn't alone any more.

In the car outside her *pensione*, he put his arms round her and kissed her, as she had known he would. She wanted him to. When she asked him to stop, he pulled away, looked at her face and, reading the desire in her expression, he carried on. This time the back of his hand brushed her breast, making her jump.

He whispered in her ear: 'If you would let me come inside, we could lie on your bed and kiss some more then I would leave whenever you asked me to.'

'I can't,' she sighed, feeling a tug deep in her belly. He stroked her stomach, almost as if he knew.

'You can. But I won't push you, little Diana. I've fallen for you but I will hold back until you decide you don't want me to any more.'

As he kissed her, she was consumed with intense lust. The foreignness of his accent; the golden colour of his cheek against the jet black of his hair; the incredible gentleness of his touch – she had never felt attraction like this in her life.

'Until', he had said. Not 'unless' but 'until'. Did he think it was inevitable? It mustn't be. She couldn't do this. She had to stop it now.

When she dragged herself away to climb the stairs to her room, her knees felt shaky and her lips were raw. Lying in bed, she tried to picture Trevor's face. She imagined how distraught he would be at the thought of her kissing another man. She tried to remember the comfort of lying in his arms in their marital bed, but all that came into her head was Ernesto's face and his smell and his touch.

What if I had an affair? she allowed herself to think. *It would be over in three months when filming ended. Would it really be so wrong?*

But she knew it would. How could she go back to a passionless marriage after what she knew would be a wildly passionate affair? How could she accept a lifetime of routine sex with Trevor once she had images of Ernesto in her head?

Maybe if I had a glorious sexual affair with Ernesto, I would learn some new techniques and be more confident about seducing Trevor once I'm back?

But then Trevor would wonder where she had learned them. He would know.

Is there a way to have an affair without anyone finding out about it? These were dangerous thoughts, but once in her head they took root and she found it hard to think about anything else.

She and Ernesto slipped into a routine of having dinner together every night and always they sat in the car and kissed passionately afterwards. At work, they tried to behave as before but Diana's cheeks burned and her legs turned to jelly when he walked into the production office. If they were on their own, he would pin her to the chair for a clandestine kiss. Hilary almost caught them once and Diana wasn't sure if she had seen anything but assumed not when she didn't comment.

Meanwhile, the shooting of the film was progressing, but in every corner of Cinecittà there was gossip about Elizabeth Taylor. Over Christmas, she and Eddie Fisher had finalised their adoption of a one-year-old German girl, an orphan they named Maria. She'd been unable to come to Rome with them, though, because she had problems with her hip that would require many operations by specialist surgeons. At the same time, renowned Hollywood gossip columnist Louella Parsons had published a front-page story claiming that Elizabeth and Eddie were about to get divorced, hinting she'd heard it from 'Italian sources'.

'It's ridiculous!' Helen exclaimed. 'Why would they adopt a child if they were getting divorced? I don't believe it for a second. Liz is passionate about her children. She never goes anywhere without them.'

Diana agreed. 'We know for a fact that journalists make things up. Truth means nothing to them. Think of all the stories that have appeared about the filming here that we know are completely wrong.'

Eddie came into the office later to check some details of the week's schedule and seemed his usual happy-go-lucky self.

'Was Santa good to you?' he asked Diana, then admired the crocodile-skin jacket she held up.

'How about you?' Diana asked.

He grinned. 'A Rolls-Royce. Good old Santa!' He kissed his fingertips. 'You girls have a great day now!'

A Rome newspaper printed a story that purported to come from Elizabeth Taylor's housekeeper, saying that she treated Eddie like a servant. That certainly seemed plausible, Diana thought. What Elizabeth wanted, Elizabeth got. If she fancied a few shots of vodka poured into her Coke to drink while her makeup was applied, Helen or one of the other makeup girls would rush to the bar to fetch some. If she wanted shooting to stop early because she had a party to get ready for, Joe Mankiewicz would do as she wished. And you would often hear a shrill cry – 'Eddie, where are my shoes?' 'Get my robe!' – as you passed her dressing room. She'd been brought up surrounded by people who indulged her every whim but that didn't make her a bad person. She simply couldn't remember a time when she wasn't famous. This was all she knew.

At least, that's how Diana thought until the 22nd of January, just over two weeks after her return to Rome. It was the first day that Elizabeth was due to film a scene with Richard Burton. Diana had read the script that morning and knew it called for them to meet in Caesar's villa, a meeting at which they were both attracted to each other although she remained Caesar's mistress. It was a pivotal scene in the film. Of course, it was completely historically inaccurate. Caesar would never have invited the Egyptian queen to such a critical meeting with his young general and various senators – if indeed it ever took place. Diana mentioned this at the script meeting but Joe Mankiewicz shrugged and drawled, 'Artistic licence, honey.'

The filming had gone well, everyone said, despite the fact that Richard appeared hungover and Elizabeth seemed tipsy. Word was they had 'chemistry', which was good for the movie. *I suppose that's what I've got with Ernesto*, Diana thought. *Chemistry.* She'd never had it with Trevor. Not like this, anyway.

After they wrapped on sound stage 11, Diana went looking for Joe Mankiewicz because she had some information he'd requested about the port city of Tarsus. He wasn't in his office so she traced his route towards the sound stages, wondering if he might have stopped to chat with someone along the way. And that's when she saw Elizabeth and Richard standing very close to each other in the gap between a trailer and an office block, not far from her dressing room. They were still in costume. His arms were pressed against the wall on either side of her, so she couldn't escape. Her head was tilted back as she gazed up at him.

Diana leapt back instantly. She didn't want to be seen witnessing the encounter. Her heart beating, she retraced her steps to take another route, but seconds later she looked over her shoulder and saw Elizabeth hurrying into her dressing-room suite.

If they wanted to talk, why do so in such an out-of-the-way spot? There was no question in Diana's mind that they were flirting but maybe it was just the heat of the moment. She wondered if pretending attraction in front of the cameras made actors feel it, just for that fleeting moment. She hoped that was all it was, for Eddie's sake. He was so nice, she'd hate for him to be hurt.

That evening, she couldn't resist mentioning what she had seen to Ernesto, and he tapped his nose. 'Didn't I tell you this would happen? I knew it months ago, not from anything they did or said but from the way Eddie acted around her. The man is a patsy.'

'In that case, they'll have to be extremely careful,' Diana said. 'If I saw them, goodness knows who else might have.'

'They won't be able to hide. You can't hide anything on a film set,' Ernesto told her.

'I hope we can hide our friendship.' She felt suddenly anxious. 'I don't want everyone gossiping about me. That would be horrible.'

He kissed her neck, making her shiver with lust. 'You are beautiful, Diana, but I am glad to say that you are not the world's most notorious *femme fatale*. Our friendship is private and I understand why we must keep it that way. It's against my nature because I want to boast to everyone: "Look at this beautiful woman who lets me kiss her! What did I ever do to deserve such joy?"'

He covered every inch of her face with kisses and she rested her head back on the car seat feeling as though she would melt with desire. When she was with him, it all felt so right. But afterwards, as she lay in bed reliving every caress, she thought of Trevor and felt like an absolute heel.

Chapter Twenty-Six

───────•◆•───────

Scott went to the Testaccio bar at the time suggested by the man who called himself Enzo and found him already sitting in a dark corner with a cup of coffee in front of him.

'Money first,' he insisted as Scott sat down. Scott handed over an envelope with the requisite number of *lire* enclosed. Enzo glanced at it quickly then tucked it inside his jacket pocket.

'*Allora*, what did you want to know?'

'I was told that the drugs in Rome are driven up from the south. Is that right? And if it is, why don't the police try to stop them?'

Enzo gave a wry smile. 'You think they are sitting on the passenger seat with a big notice on top? No, of course not. They are in suitcases with false bottoms, in secret panels in the car doors, inside tennis balls or medicine bottles. I know someone who transports heroin inside a statue of the Virgin Mary, which I think is sacrilegious, but what can you do?'

Scott had to ask him to repeat some unfamiliar phrases until his ear became attuned to the thick accent, with stresses on different vowels. He came from Naples, Enzo told him, making an effort to slow down and speak more clearly.

'What happens after they get to Rome? Where do you take them?'

Enzo glanced over his shoulder. 'I'm not saying I do anything myself,' he cautioned, 'but I've heard there is a garage in the Via Spagna where cars are taken in for servicing. When they are picked up the next day, or two days later, they are empty. *Capisce?*'

Scott was suspicious. 'Why are you telling me this? Aren't you taking a risk by meeting me?'

'Not as much as you are, my friend,' Enzo said, spreading his hands. 'You don't know me, you don't know where I live. I could be telling you a pack of lies – but as it happens, I'm not. I want this trade to end. I want out but they won't let me stop. Once you are involved, you can never leave.'

'They? Who do you mean by "they"?'

'Now that I can't tell you.'

Scott pulled out his photograph of Gina Ghianciamina's brother, the man who had attacked him. It was blurred but the figure was recognisable. 'Do you know him?'

Enzo nodded straight away. 'Of course I do. Everyone does.'

'What's his name?'

'Alessandro Ghianciamina.'

Scott narrowed his eyes. Alessandro, was it? 'Is he involved in the drugs trade?'

'This is common knowledge,' Enzo told him. 'Everyone knows he is.'

'Why don't the police do something?'

Enzo rubbed his fingertips together. 'The police, the judges, the politicians: everyone turns a blind eye to protect that family. No one will take them on.'

'Can you think of any way I can prove it conclusively, so the police would have to take action?'

Enzo laughed out loud, shaking his head in amusement.

166

'You are so young, my friend, but you will not last long in Rome if you keep asking such questions. You are lucky you chose me. I am cheating you because I am taking your money in return for telling you things that you could hear for free on any street corner. None of this is a secret. But if you go around asking people you meet at parties for evidence against the Ghianciaminas, you will be a cadaver before the summer comes.' He pushed his chair back. 'I think there is nothing more I can tell you.'

Scott stood to shake his hand. 'It's OK. You told me I'm on the right track, and that's a good start. Can I get in touch again if I need to?'

'Certainly not. You were stupid to trust me. You mustn't do this again because next time you will pick the wrong person and they'll go straight to the Ghianciaminas.'

Scott shrugged. 'I guess if you were going to double-cross me you wouldn't have come alone today. Maybe I'm wrong.'

All the same, as he drove back to the office, he kept glancing over his shoulder. Every time a bike revved its engine or a child shrieked, he jumped. Once in the office, he noted down all he could remember about the conversation, trying to capture Enzo's exact words. He would describe the meeting as if in fiction, using the new techniques that Norman Mailer had perfected. He'd describe the bar, the man with a false name, and all the dramatic pauses and glancing over shoulders as they talked. Already he had begun to write it in his head, although of course he still needed much more information.

The telephone rang and he picked it up.

'Scott?' It was his editor. 'How come you're the only fucking journalist in Rome who hasn't filed a story on Taylor and Burton?'

'I'm on the case, boss,' he said straight away. The rumours of their affair were all over that morning's Italian press.

Scott zoomed down to Via Veneto to find Gianni. 'What can you tell me?' he asked. 'Is there anything nobody else has printed?'

Gianni chuckled. 'I have a friend who has a friend who works in the men's makeup trailer at Cinecittà. He says that when Richard Burton came in to be made up this morning he announced with a triumphant clench of his fist' – Gianni demonstrated – 'that last night he "nailed" Elizabeth Taylor.'

'Did he say where they did the dirty deed?' Scott asked.

Gianni snorted with laughter. 'In the back seat of Burton's Cadillac.'

Scott returned to the office and filed the story.

Chapter Twenty-Seven

The crunch came towards the end of January. Diana phoned Trevor during the afternoon and found him in a foul mood about some imagined slight by the colleague he seemed so jealous of. On the phone he sounded petulant, like a sibling vying for his parents' favour. As she hung up, she allowed herself to think, *Sometimes I don't even like him any more.* She used to admire his great wide-ranging intellect but when it came to women – when it came to her – he was blind, deaf and dumb. How could he not realise that his behaviour was driving her away?

Over dinner with Ernesto that night, a subconscious devil-may-care attitude took hold and she let him refill her wine glass two or three times – she lost count. It loosened her, made her more daring. When he pulled up outside her *pensione* later, she reached across to initiate the kissing, and was surprised when he held back.

'It's cold tonight, little one,' he said. 'Too cold to sit in a car.'

She didn't hesitate. 'Let's go upstairs then.'

In her head, she remembered him suggesting they could lie on the bed and kiss and that he would leave when she asked him to. That's what she was imagining would happen as they climbed the stairs, and that's certainly how it began. He kissed her mouth thoroughly, with tender, lingering kisses, then rolled her onto her front and stroked her, with a long firm movement from her bottom right up to the top of her head. Next he turned her on her back and began to stroke more and she craned her neck upwards, gasping for his kisses. It must have been at least an hour before he started slowly taking her clothes off, and another half hour as he caressed her naked body, and then at last he made love to her and it was a complete revelation. She had never known, never remotely guessed, that it was possible for her to react in that way. The sensations were unfamiliar and totally overpowering.

Afterwards, she lay in his arms in a haze of sensuality and sheer astonishment. Trevor had been her only other lover and sex had never been anything like this. He must be unaware that it was possible to please a woman in this way. How did Ernesto know? She didn't want to think about that. He had fallen asleep and she examined his face in the moonlight, mentally rewriting her entire future. Who was this amazing man? Could he possibly turn out to be the person with whom she would spend the rest of her life?

When Diana opened her eyes the following morning, Ernesto was breathing gently by her side. She was overcome with lust, remembering the delicious sensations of the night before, but then she thought of Trevor and knew that she had done something momentous from which there could be no turning back. Before this, he'd been the only man she'd ever slept with; now he would never be that again. She felt a lurch of anxiety. He would be devastated if he found out.

'*Buongiorno, bellissima*,' Ernesto murmured. He pulled her close for a hug that soon turned into more irresistible love-making, so that she had to rush to get ready and had no time for breakfast before the studio car arrived.

'Be careful the *padrona* doesn't see you,' she cautioned on the way down the stairs. 'She might be cross that I have an overnight guest.'

'Film companies often use Pensione Splendid. You'll find the *padrona* is used to people staying in each other's rooms.'

'I don't want anyone at the studio to know about this,' she told him. 'It wouldn't be fair on Trevor.'

'I understand,' he smiled, touching her cheek. 'But can I see you tonight?'

'Yes, oh yes please,' she breathed, and they both laughed at her eagerness. A final thought occurred to her and she moved close to whisper in his ear. 'You'll make sure I don't get in the family way, won't you? I can't risk that.'

He laughed at her shyness. 'Didn't you see those rubbers in the bin? Calm down, Diana. I will look after you. I'm not some fly-by-night monster who will let you come to any harm.'

'I know you're not,' she blushed. 'Thank you.'

He hung back inside the doorway as she got into the studio car so the driver wouldn't see them together.

I suppose this is what love feels like, she thought. *I could have gone through my entire life without experiencing this feeling. It would have been a life unlived.*

It was wrong to sleep with another man while still married – of course it was – but it was far too late to back out now.

During the course of the morning, she got no work done at all. Her heart was beating fast as she pondered all the options in front of her. She had never contemplated divorce before but now it seemed possible, maybe even desirable. Surely there could be no going back after her night of passion? Trevor took her for granted, whereas Ernesto seemed to cherish everything about her. She tried to compose the words she would use when she told Trevor she had a lover, but she couldn't bear to imagine the hurt on his face.

At last she decided there was no need to think about it for now. She would phone Trevor from work every few days, just to make contact, and the rest of the time she would shut him out of her head while she saw how things developed with Ernesto. Already he was talking about the future: sights he wanted to show her when spring came, places they should eat, parks where they could walk. He assumed they were an item, and so did she.

The guilt always surfaced when she saw Eddie Fisher on the lot, though. His appearance pricked her conscience.

'What do you think of this glorious weather!' he called in passing, and Diana felt embarrassed as she agreed it was wonderful. Should she tell him that she had seen his wife in intimate conversation with her co-star? No, of course she shouldn't.

Only a few days later, while having lunch with Helen, she heard some assistant cameramen cracking a lewd joke in Italian about Burton and Taylor 'making the beast with two backs'. She glanced at Helen to see if she had understood, but found her lost in thought.

'You're still not eating,' Diana chided. 'You don't want to lose any more weight or you'll get knocked off your feet when the wind blows.' It was something her father used to say to her when she was a picky eater as a child.

Helen was startled. 'I was miles away,' she said, shaking herself. 'I'm not hungry today. I'll just have a Coke.'

'Do you think it's true what they're saying about Elizabeth Taylor and Richard Burton?' Diana asked. 'You know how people exaggerate round here.'

Helen wrinkled her nose. 'It's true alright. I've seen them loads of times. They're always sneaking off together. She was in makeup one day when he popped his head round the door and asked if she fancied a cocktail in his trailer and she was off like a shot. She came back forty-five minutes later with her makeup so messed up they had to take it all off and start from scratch. Mr Mankiewicz kept sending messengers up from the sound stage to ask what was keeping her.'

'It must be strange being famous. She's being watched the entire time so they can't keep anything secret.'

'Eddie and Sybil are bound to have read the news reports by now. Imagine what it's like for them. How humiliating to have the world knowing that you're being cheated on! I don't know how you could do that to someone you're supposed to love.'

Helen spoke so vehemently that Diana was surprised. She looked at her closely. She was very pale, her blue eyes seeming huge in her pretty birdlike face. Under the table her foot was tapping. 'Are you OK?' Diana asked.

Helen shook her shoulders. 'You know me. I'm just cross that everyone else has a boyfriend except me. Liz and Richard have a spouse and a lover each!' She laughed, unconvincingly. 'I suppose I won't be so bothered when I find someone myself.'

'Any new candidates?' Diana asked, then lost concentration as Helen launched into a long list of men she liked on the set and what this one had said to her, and why she preferred another. It all seemed so childish. But even still, Diana was surprised that Helen hadn't found a boyfriend yet. She was

173

extremely pretty, with great fashion sense; she was a fantastic dancer and went out every night; and there was a naïve honesty about her that was endearing. Possibly she was too honest and gave too much away about herself. Maybe that's what put men off. That, and the fact that she drank too much.

Diana resolved to tell Ernesto that she wanted to spend an evening with Helen some time soon. She felt protective towards her. Maybe she would be able to help her in some small way.

Chapter Twenty-Eight

Scott took Gianni for a beer in a piano bar near the Via Veneto. They both ordered Peronis and stood looking round the buzzing room. Every table was crowded with fashionably dressed men and women, most of them foreigners and, according to Gianni, lots of them from the *Cleopatra* film set. In the corner, a pianist was playing but Scott could barely hear a note over the chatter in the room. The doors to the terrace were closed because it was a cold, rainy night, but he could see the lights of the city blurred by raindrops on the glass.

'Does Elizabeth Taylor ever come here?' Scott asked, and Gianni shook his head.

'It's too public. She will only go to private parties, or to restaurants that will give her a quiet table away from the public view. And you can be sure she won't go anywhere with Mr Burton because every photojournalist in Rome is on their tail. The first picture of them together will be worth millions. I'll do my best, boss,' he grinned, 'but don't hold your breath.'

'Shame.'

He asked Gianni about his sources on the set and whether any of them might be able to get photographs but was told that it was impossible now. Security had been tightened and everyone knew they would be sacked if they were caught with a camera at Cinecittà.

Scott kept an eye on the people from the film set. One group of girls appeared to be drinking heavily, as carafe after carafe of wine was ordered and slurped back. If he could get talking to them perhaps he could pump them for information, but approaching the table as a whole wouldn't work. He'd have to try and catch one on her own. A blonde girl seemed particularly the worse for wear. She was resting her head on her hands with half-closed eyes when her elbow slipped off the table, making her jerk awake. Scott kept an eye on her and managed to intercept her on the way back from the ladies' room.

'Excuse me,' he grinned. 'I was just saying to my friend here how attractive you are and he bet that you wouldn't let me buy you a drink. Will you help me win the bet?'

She hesitated, and Scott cursed his broken nose. He'd never had trouble picking up girls before but his face looked less trustworthy now.

'You want to buy me a drink?' she slurred, slow on the uptake.

'Sure! What can I get you?'

'A Prosecco would be lovely.'

Scott immediately called the bartender and ordered the drink. 'Will you stay and talk to me or do you need to get back to your friends?'

'I could stay for a little bit,' she said. 'They're not really friends. I just go out with them.'

'You all work on *Cleopatra*, don't you? That must be fun.'

She was pretty but she could barely stand up. She kept wobbling in her shoes, which had high heels like pins, and he worried that her skinny ankles would snap. Her blue eyes were unfocused and her speech thick and slow.

'It's OK, I suppose.'

'It must be pretty glamorous seeing the stars up close. Which ones do you like the best?'

Helen considered this. 'I used to like Elizabeth Taylor, because she's kind. She gave me her autograph on the very first day we were filming. Once I scratched her eyelid when I was sticking on one of the spangle things in her makeup and she was so nice about it. She told everyone it was her own fault for moving.'

'That was nice. It's not the impression you get from the newspapers, is it?'

'No, they're all mean about her.' The drink arrived and the girl picked it up greedily and took a slurp then the glass slipped through her fingers. It splashed the front of her dress as it fell then shattered into pieces on the wooden floor.

'Oops!' She looked down in dismay.

The barman passed them a pile of napkins and Scott began to mop at her front, while someone appeared with a dustpan and brush to sweep up the fragments.

'You seem tired, sweetheart,' he said tactfully. 'Why don't you let me take you home so you can get out of your wet dress?'

The girl looked wistfully at the glass. She obviously wanted another drink but Scott realised he'd get nothing useful out of her if she drank any more.

'OK,' she said. 'I'll just tell my friends.'

Gianni raised his glass to clink against Scott's, impressed at his successful technique. 'See you tomorrow, boss. Don't do anything I wouldn't do.'

Outside the hotel, Scott decided to hail a taxi. Although the rain had stopped he was worried the girl might fall off if he took her on his Vespa and, besides, sitting in the back of a cab

177

would give them more chance to talk. She gave an address close by and as soon as they drove off, Scott began to pump her with questions.

'What do you think of Richard Burton? You said Elizabeth Taylor was nice. Is he nice too?'

'He doesn't talk to me,' she slurred. 'No one talks to me except Diana.'

'Have you seen him with Elizabeth Taylor? Or do they keep their affair a secret?'

'It's disgusting,' she said. 'I think it's wrong. Too many people, all getting hurt.'

Her head rolled onto Scott's shoulder. He sighed. She wasn't going to be much use to him tonight. He tried another tack. 'Could I take you for dinner some time?' he asked. 'Maybe later in the week? You're very pretty.'

'You don't even know my name,' she said. 'It's Helen.'

'I'm Scott. So how about it, Helen? Can I buy you dinner?'

The taxi pulled up in front of the address she had given and he went round to open the door and help her out but motioned for the driver to wait.

'How about I pick you up on Friday at seven?'

'Do you mean like a date?' Helen asked, wide-eyed.

'Sure.' Scott grimaced. Was this going to be another situation that would become difficult to extricate himself from?

'But what will I do tonight?' she asked, frowning.

'You should probably go to bed and get some rest. It's past eleven.'

'No, it's not that.' She whispered conspiratorially: 'I don't suppose you've got anything, have you?'

'What kind of thing?' She was rubbing her nose as if it were itchy, then she began to scratch her bare arm.

178

'Oh . . . you know. To get high.'

He was shocked because she looked so young, but appearances could be deceptive. 'Sorry, I don't.'

She sighed and turned into the courtyard of her *pensione*.

'See you Friday,' he called after her but wasn't sure if she'd heard because she didn't turn round.

Chapter Twenty-Nine

Diana arrived at the script meeting on the 17th of February to find an atmosphere of alarm in the room. Joe was on the phone, the film's publicists were on separate phones trailing long extension leads and Walter was nowhere to be seen. Diana sat down and waited as they all spoke urgently in separate conversations.

'Where is she now? Where's he?'

'Has anyone said anything?'

'I've just spoken to the hospital. She's still there.'

'Who's in hospital?' Diana whispered to the continuity girl sitting next to her.

'Elizabeth. She took an overdose last night.'

'She did *what*?' Diana got goosebumps.

'Richard broke up with her and first she tried to walk through a glass door and then she took some pills.' The girl was enjoying her role as news-breaker. 'It's because Eddie Fisher went to see Sybil and told her in no uncertain terms that the rumours were true, and that his wife was being tupped by her husband. Sybil told Richard he had to drop Elizabeth – and lo and behold he did.'

'But she seriously tried to kill herself over an affair that's only lasted a few weeks? Are you sure?' Diana was incredulous.

'Well, she's in hospital.'

Diana was alarmed by the news. She was falling more deeply in love with Ernesto every day that passed but if they broke up she would never consider killing herself. It seemed obsessive, insecure behaviour. How could the most famous woman in the world be insecure? Was it just that Elizabeth was used to getting whatever she wanted and couldn't bear to be thwarted? Or was it a ploy to make Richard feel guilty and win him back?

'OK, people,' Joe announced, raising his hand for silence. 'Obviously we're not filming today. We'll probably need a few days off but I want you all on set. Walter is with Elizabeth and he says Eddie just arrived. The story is food poisoning and we must stamp out any rumours that say different. Got it?' There was a murmur of assent. 'That's all for now.'

Diana wandered out of the office, feeling shell-shocked. Up till now, bystanders at Cinecittà had treated the Burton–Taylor affair as an entertainment, a movie within a movie. Now it became apparent that real people's feelings were involved and that genuine damage was being done. Far from it being an observer sport, Diana realised how close she was to causing the same kind of hurt and damage herself. She couldn't picture any of the protagonists in her own love triangle taking an overdose but people could surprise you. It was a warning and she knew she should heed it.

A few days later, Elizabeth was back at work and the drama seemed set to blow over, apart from the fact that the owners of the restaurant where she had eaten on the night of the overdose were suing for damages, claiming she could not possibly have been poisoned by their food. Diana assumed some appeasement money would change hands. The last thing anyone needed was a lawsuit about the events of that evening.

Richard was in Paris doing some work on another film, so all was peaceful for a while. His press agent made a vague, woolly statement not quite denying the rumours of the affair, but saying that Richard would never do anything to hurt Elizabeth Taylor, either personally or professionally.

'Of course he doesn't deny it,' Ernesto said cynically. 'It is the best thing that ever happened to his career. Sleeping with a household name means you become a household name yourself, and can increase your fees to match your new status. Stardom rubs off.'

Diana's distaste for Richard increased. Could he possibly have planned it this way from the start? She hoped that when he got back to Cinecittà they were both professional enough to carry on working together as before.

A few days later Richard arrived back on set with a leggy blonde beauty several inches taller than him. Everyone gawped as they walked arm in arm from his trailer to the sound stage.

'Her name's Pat Tunder,' Candy told Diana. 'She's a dancer in the Copacabana club in New York. He had an affair with her when he was doing *Camelot* on Broadway.'

All eyes turned to Elizabeth to see how she would react to this new arrival and the gossips didn't have long to wait. That afternoon, a fierce argument between Elizabeth and Richard spilled out onto the avenue outside the sound stages while Diana was having an espresso with Helen.

'You sonofabitch!' Elizabeth shrieked. 'I know more about movie acting than you ever will with your poncy theatrical ways. Don't dare tell me how to play a scene again or I'll have you sacked from this movie.'

Richard looked round at the watching crowd with amuse-ment. 'Your bosom is a better actress than you are. At least it's not wooden and shrill like your dialogue. Go ahead: try and have me sacked. The lawyers need the work.'

'Fuck you, you arrogant, malevolent Welsh *dwarf*.' She strode off in the direction of her dressing room, head held high, in full Cleopatra makeup and wearing a purply-blue décolleté gown that swept along the muddy ground. Richard charged past Diana and Helen into the bar and they heard him ordering a double whisky. The leggy blonde tottered over to join him, looking unsure of herself.

'How horrible that passion can turn to hatred in the snap of your fingers,' Diana said to Helen under her breath. She couldn't imagine how such a thing could be possible, but she assumed the Burton–Taylor affair must have been all about sex. They hadn't had time to get to know each other the way she was doing with Ernesto. They couldn't enjoy the luxury of long, relaxed dinners in restaurants, talking about their lives, their hopes and fears, and the things they loved. They weren't able to sleep curled up in each other's arms and waken in the morning to see the other's sleeping face. Diana loved looking at Ernesto while he slept: she could examine his earlobe, the curve of his Adam's apple, the tiny flecks of grey in his hair that he plucked out furiously when he spotted them. She liked listening to his breathing and feeling the warmth emanating from his golden skin. Their relationship was still very sexual – that side just got better and better – but there was a genuine meeting of the minds as well. The more she got to know him, the deeper she fell in love.

Helen was staring down into her glass, her thoughts miles away.

'Are you OK?' Diana asked, with a flicker of concern. 'I'm going to have a pastry. Shall I get you one?'

'No, I ate earlier. Thanks anyway.'

'Are you free to go out one night this week? We haven't had a pizza in ages.'

'I'm trying not to eat out because I'm flat broke. Actually . . .' She hesitated, and screwed up her face. 'I don't suppose you could lend me some money till payday, could you? I'm really strapped this month.'

'Of course I will. How much do you need?' Diana opened her purse and had a look. 'I've got forty thousand *lire* with me. Would that help?'

Helen was terribly embarrassed. 'Are you sure that won't leave you short? I couldn't . . . I'll pay you back as soon as . . .'

'It's not a problem. And don't be silly, there's no rush to pay it back.'

As she walked to the production office, she worried about Helen. Her salary was decent and she should have been able to live on it, but she obviously wasn't very good at budgeting. Hopefully she would start being more careful.

Hilary was in the office, smoking a cigarette and having a cup of tea. 'Did you hear about the fight outside the sound stage today?' Diana asked. 'Elizabeth and Richard were going at it hammer and tongs.'

Hilary snorted. 'That's nothing compared to what they're like on set. She's wild with jealousy about the New York dolly bird. She's either screaming at him or frostily ignoring him, one or the other. He just seems amused by it all.'

'How does Joe manage to direct them? I'd hate to be in his position.'

Hilary grinned. 'He says that when you are in a cage with tigers, you must never let them know you are afraid of them.'

Diana laughed. It seemed very apposite. That evening as

she lay in bed with Ernesto in the languorous after-glow of sex, she repeated Joe's comment. He laughed heartily, and she was pleased because she loved to make him laugh.

He rolled over to kiss her once more. 'I think I'll just pop out for a cigarette. Won't be a moment.'

She liked the fact that he didn't smoke in her room but went to sit on the front step. She had never asked him to; he did it as a matter of common courtesy. Of course, she was used to people smoking around her at work and in restaurants but it was nice to keep the smell out of the room where she slept at night.

After a few moments, she decided to go out and keep him company. She pulled on a dress and cardigan, slipped on a pair of shoes and tiptoed down the stairs so as not to waken the *padrona*, who went to bed early. When she opened the front door she couldn't see Ernesto on the step, so she looked up and down the street. There was a bar diagonally opposite and through the window she saw Ernesto making a phone call, his back half turned. Who could he be phoning at that time of night? His mother perhaps?

Diana wandered over and as she walked into the bar, she heard him repeating the cage of tigers story in Italian. She stopped, puzzled. Ernesto hadn't seen her yet. Why would he tell anyone that story? Next, he said that Burton and Tunder were going to be at Harry's Bar later and that Paolo should try to catch them there.

'Who's Paolo?' she asked when he hung up the receiver, and he jumped and turned round, guilt etched all over his face.

'Diana!'

'Who's Paolo?' she asked again.

'Sit down and have a drink. I will explain.' He motioned towards a table at the back of the bar. 'Would you like a Bellini?'

185

'No, I want to know who Paolo is. Why not tell me now, to put my mind at rest?'

Ernesto shrugged. 'He's a photographer. Sometimes I give him a tip-off when I know where people are going to be, and if he gets a photograph I get a little money. That's all.'

She frowned. 'But who were you speaking to?'

'A journalist. Someone I work with from time to time.'

Diana was livid. 'You just told a journalist a story that Hilary told me in strictest confidence? If it's printed in the newspapers, she'll think it was me who blabbed to the press. I can't believe you would do that.'

Ernesto was defensive. 'You didn't tell me it was a confidence.'

'I assumed I didn't have to. Does everything I ever tell you go straight to the Italian media? Don't you care how bad that will make me look?'

'Calm down, Diana.' He tried to put an arm round her shoulder to lead her to the vacant table at the back of the bar but she shrugged him away.

'These people have feelings. Sybil Burton reads these stories. Eddie Fisher reads them. It's horrible to think you don't see anything wrong in being a source. It makes me wonder about your morality, to be quite frank.'

Ernesto looked her in the eye. 'Are you sure you should be talking to me about morality? Aren't you the one who's having an affair behind your husband's back?'

Diana flinched and Ernesto immediately tried to backtrack. 'I'm sorry, *cara mia*. Forgive me.'

She turned and fled across the street to her *pensione* and up the stairs to her room, Ernesto following right behind her. She lay face down on the bed and he sat beside her. 'I'm so sorry. I should not have said that. I can't bear to hurt you. I love you, Diana.' He put his arm around her and kissed her cheek. 'You mean the world to me.'

She remained face down and he began to stroke her back, just as he had done on the first night they slept together, and spoke to her quietly. 'I told you how important it is to me that I can earn enough money to support my family. This is just one source of income. I only tell my contact things that are trivial and I didn't think the tigers story could hurt anyone. I was wrong and I'm sorry.'

She didn't say anything but let him undress her and make love to her. Afterwards she lay awake for a long time. It was their first argument and also the first time Ernesto had said he loved her. She wished it had been in different circumstances but still the words glowed inside.

She was disappointed to hear he spied on set and passed information to a journalist. She knew there must be lots of people doing it because the rewards were there but she found it sleazy. Yet, she admired him for supporting his extended family and if he needed a little bit extra on top of his Cinecittà salary, that was one way of getting it. Besides, who was she to take the moral high ground? Ernesto was right; she was in no position to judge anyone else.

Chapter Thirty

Scott went to pick Helen up for dinner the following Friday but the *padrona* said she hadn't come back from work. He drove to the piano bar where he'd met her but she was nowhere to be seen. There was nothing more he could do but keep an eye out for her. He had a feeling she would be a useful source of gossip from Cinecittà once she was no longer under the influence of alcohol or drugs or whatever the heck it was she took.

Next time he saw her was a couple of weeks later and she was sitting in a dingy bar behind the Galleria Nazionale d'Arte Antica with an Italian man. Scott went in and ordered a beer but Helen didn't show any sign of recognising him. She looked terrible, with lank hair, dark shadows under her eyes, and a miserable expression. She was pleading with the man and he was refusing whatever it was she wanted, but Scott wasn't close enough to hear the details. Suddenly the man stood up, scraping his chair along the ground, and walked out. Helen laid her head on her arms and began to sob. Her shoulderblades were sharp through the fabric of her dress, like the wings of a little bird.

'Helen, what's the matter?' Scott asked, hurrying over to join her. 'Please don't cry.'

She looked up, all tears and mascara.

'Don't you remember me? Scott. I took you home in a taxi a couple of weeks ago. We were going to have dinner.'

He could see a vague recognition dawning on her.

'Scott!' she said. 'Of course. I don't suppose you could lend me some money? I really need some.' Tears began to roll down her cheeks again. 'I'm in such trouble and I don't know what to do.' She opened her handbag and fumbled for a tissue with shaking hands.

Scott pulled out his own cloth hankie, fortunately clean, and handed it over. 'Tell me the problem and I'll see how I can help. Do you want a drink first?'

'Oh God, yes. Prosecco please.'

He ordered the drink and got himself another beer. When he sat down Helen seemed more composed, but her hands were trembling as she lifted the glass.

'So what's up?' he asked.

'I've been such a fool,' she said, the tears springing to her eyes again. 'I just wanted to fit in. Everyone else was taking drugs so I did too, but they seem to be able to take it or leave it and I can't. At first it was OK but when I don't have any now, I feel really ill and can't work. I can't do makeup because my hands are shaking too badly and I can't eat anything or I get terrible stomach cramps. But I've run out of money till payday and Luigi won't give me any more stuff.'

'Was that Luigi I saw you with?'

She nodded, and Scott tucked the information away.

'What kind of drugs have you been taking?'

'It's called *eroina*. You smoke it in a little pipe.' She opened her bag to show him but he frowned and put out a hand to stop her bringing it out on display.

'Heroin.' He pursed his lips. 'I know a bit about that, and none of it's good. You need to get off it straight away. I'll ask around about the best way to do it.' He had heard about the 'cold turkey' heroin addicts experienced during withdrawal and wondered if there was a clinic in Rome where Helen could get help. Maybe Gianni would know.

'I don't want anyone at Cinecittà to find out.' She looked scared. 'They'd sack me for sure.'

'It will be our secret,' Scott assured her.

'Can you find someone tonight? I need to get to work in the morning and I don't know how I'll manage.' Her fingers clutched his wrist and she peered at him beseechingly.

'You poor kid,' Scott frowned. 'Look at you! You're too young to have got yourself into such a mess. I have a friend who may be able to help. He's probably on the Via Veneto but if we can't find him tonight, you could always phone the set and say you've got flu.'

She sighed. 'I've done that so many times already, I don't think I'd get away with it again.'

'Tell me a little about you,' he asked as they finished their drinks, and it all came out – the middle-class English upbringing and the sister who was more glamorous and better at everything. Helen was the human face of an ugly trade, the poor innocent who was lonely and vulnerable in a strange city. She told him she was twenty-one, but she looked as though she could still be in high school.

When she finished her Prosecco, he paid and led her outside to his Vespa.

'Think you can hang on?' he asked, and she nodded, but she was shivering in her light wool coat so Scott gallantly offered his leather jacket.

He drove carefully round to Via Veneto and cruised up the hill until he spotted Gianni near the Hotel Imperiale. 'You wait here,' he told Helen and hurried over to explain the problem.

Gianni said his brother-in-law worked as a hospital technician and might know someone who could help, so they slipped into a bar while he made a phone call. He was given one number, then another, and finally he got through to a doctor who said yes, he treated such problems. He used vitamin injections to help heroin addicts come down without side effects.

The doctor spoke English so Gianni passed the phone to Scott.

'Are you saying there's no cold turkey?' Scott asked. 'How does that work?'

'It's a special mixture of vitamins that counteracts withdrawal symptoms. I have been using this formula for three years now and it's worked every time, so long as the patient really wants to get clean.'

'She does,' Scott said. 'She's desperate. When could you see her?'

'I live above my surgery so if it is an emergency you could come tonight. In about an hour?'

'How much is it?' Scott asked, and winced at the price. Helen could never afford it, but he decided he would pay. She was so sweet and fragile. In other circumstances he might have been attracted to her, but instead he felt protective.

'We'll be there,' he said.

After hanging up, he asked Gianni, 'Are you sure this guy's OK?'

Gianni shrugged. 'He's a friend of a colleague of my brother-in-law, and it's a good address. Why not?'

Helen jumped up and down and clapped her hands when Scott told her. 'Oh, that's so great. You're my hero! Yes please, let's do it!'

The doctor's house was in the north of the city near Parco di Villa Glori. Scott was chilled to the bone by the time they arrived because Helen was still wearing his jacket, leaving him to freeze in a skinny-rib pullover. She clung on around his waist, and he could hear her sniffing, either from the cold or because she was crying – he wasn't sure which.

'You OK?' he asked as they got off the bike.

'I'm scared,' she whispered. 'Will you come in with me?'

'Of course I will. I'm not going to abandon you here. I'll be beside you the whole time.'

The doctor was grey-haired and rotund, wearing black-rimmed spectacles, he spoke English. It was just as well because Helen spoke hardly any Italian. First, he asked what drugs she was taking. She brought out her little pipe to show him and he examined it then threw it in his wastebasket. He asked how often she was using, and she said that it had increased from once or twice a week to every day because she found she couldn't work without it. The doctor noted down the withdrawal symptoms she was experiencing, then asked about her general health. She'd had all the usual childhood illnesses but no operations. He took her blood pressure and listened to her heartbeat through his stethoscope, then glanced at Scott and asked if they were using contraception. Scott explained that he was a friend, not a boyfriend. Helen said she didn't have any boyfriends. Her voice was trembling with nerves, and Scott gave her hand a squeeze.

'I am going to give you a powerful injection of *moolti-vitamins*,' the doctor explained. 'This will counteract the effects

192

of your withdrawal from *eroina*. It will last a few days and if you need another shot after that, you can come back to me. Once the drug is completely out of your system, you will be well again.'

'How quickly does it work?' Helen asked. She scratched an itch on her leg.

'You will notice a difference within an hour, if not sooner. Don't eat anything tonight but drink plenty of water and take it easy. You need to rest.'

'OK,' she agreed.

'Who is paying?' the doctor asked, and Scott counted out the cash from his wallet, noting the reassuring-looking medical certificates on the wall. The doctor disappeared into a side room and came back with a syringe filled with a golden liquid. Helen gave a little murmur of fear.

'Don't watch,' Scott suggested. 'Hold my hand and look at me.'

The doctor took her other hand, tapped to find a vein in her elbow, then plunged in the needle. Helen's grip on Scott's hand tightened but she didn't cry out as the liquid disappeared into her vein. The doctor removed the needle, put on a small Elastoplast, then wished her luck and told her to be strong.

Scott led her out of the surgery and they got on the Vespa to drive home.

'I know you can't eat but do you want to go somewhere for a drink?' he asked when they pulled up by her *pensione*.

'I think I should probably have an early night,' she blinked, 'But thanks, Scott. You've been amazing.'

Scott gave her a hug, and under the streetlight he could see that her complexion was healthier already, while her eyes seemed more alert and focused.

'I'll come by tomorrow night to check you're OK,' he promised, and gave her a quick kiss on the forehead.

She touched the spot as if surprised then gave him a cute smile, like a child.

Chapter Thirty-One

Diana's contract with Twentieth Century Fox was scheduled to end at Easter, which was less than two months away, and she had no idea what she was going to do after that. She couldn't contemplate leaving Ernesto but how could she stay in Rome without an income? She didn't mention it to him, because it seemed too early in the relationship to put him under any pressure, but it preyed on her mind. And what would she say to Trevor? Whichever decision she made, it was going to be horrid.

When she looked at the constantly changing schedules that Candy typed up in the office, Diana realised that shooting would continue for several months beyond April. The big outdoor crowd scenes, such as Cleopatra's entrance into Rome, the arrival of her barge at Tarsus, the sea battle of Actium and the grand finale in Alexandria, were all being shot after Easter. Maybe Walter reckoned Diana would have told them all they needed to know by then and her services wouldn't be required any more. She mentioned it to Hilary.

'Am I right in thinking I won't be needed for the outdoor scenes? My contract ends in mid-April.'

'God, is that right? We'll have to do something about that. I'm absolutely positive Walter and Joe want you here till the bitter end. In fact, I heard them talking about taking you to Egypt in the summer for the battle in the desert.'

'Really?' Diana's heart leapt. That would mean maybe another six months working on the film, and another six months with Ernesto. But what would Trevor say?

Word came back that Walter very much wanted her to stay until the film wrapped, which was currently scheduled to be the end of June, and then to fly out to Egypt with a much-reduced crew in August.

'Can you do it?' Hilary asked, with a knowing look. 'Same terms.'

'I'd love to!' Diana beamed. 'That's fantastic news.'

She couldn't face telling Trevor on the phone and having him pour cold water on her excitement so she wrote a letter that night, explaining that everything was running behind schedule, partly because of the Burton–Taylor romance but also because it simply took longer than expected to get the film made. She said she would feel she was letting them down if she walked out before the job was done, and that she was sorry for the inconvenience it would cause him but that she felt she had to stay for as long as they wanted her.

Trevor had never replied to the letter she wrote to him the previous September, and he wasn't very communicative during their twice-weekly phone calls, so Diana was astonished when she received a letter from him just two days later, via the courier from London. She sat at her desk and opened it to find a devastatingly honest love letter. The blood drained from her face.

I'm an idiot. I've been hurt and depressed beyond measure that you were able to leave me for so many months but I realise

196

I haven't expressed those feelings to you. Maybe you think I am quite content in your absence, but I believed you would understand how miserable I am when you saw me at Christmas. I miss you more than I would ever have thought possible. I find our telephone calls excruciating because I hear your voice sounding cheerful and excited and then you are gone again and I am alone. Do you know, you never say you miss me? I don't believe you do. The only thing that's kept me going has been counting the weeks till Easter when we can be together again. I still want all the things we planned before: I love you and want you to be the mother of our children. I want to live with you by my side and for us to grow old together. Please tell me you still want this too.

We've been apart too long, Diana, and I feel you slipping further and further away. Let me come out to Rome for the Easter holidays and we can spend time together, touring the sights and remembering why we got married in the first place. Please let us do that with open hearts. I want my wonderful wife back.

Diana couldn't move. Her hands shook as she stared in anguish at the pages covered in his familiar handwriting.

'Bad news?' Hilary asked.

Diana bit her lip. 'Trevor wants to come out here for Easter,' she whispered.

'But I thought you two must have separated? I . . . forgive me, but I saw you with Ernesto and assumed you must have ended your marriage when you were back at Christmas.'

Diana blushed scarlet. 'No, I'm afraid I've got myself into rather a mess. How can I stop Trevor coming? What reason could I give? I simply don't know what to do.' What had she expected? That he would accept the extra months' delay

197

without complaint? Him coming to Rome would be a disaster on all counts.

'You'll have to tell Ernesto to stand aside. He'll understand.' She caught the fear in Diana's expression. 'You haven't fallen for him, have you? It's all happened at lightning speed. You must take care, my dear.' She frowned as she patted Diana on the shoulder. 'Affairs on film sets never last.'

Diana turned her head away. That might be true of actors and actresses but Hilary didn't know how much she and Ernesto were in love. How could she?

She was working at her desk that day checking through requisition forms and trying to resolve oddities such as why thirty-six dark blue nuns' wimples had been ordered for the Nubian slaves. The words and figures swam in front of her eyes as she imagined Trevor and Ernesto coming face to face. She felt sure Ernesto would give the game away. Somehow she had to keep them apart. Oh, it was all such a mess. Previously she had considered herself a decent person, but now she would be forced to hurt the two men she loved most in the world.

That evening Diana was invited to a party to celebrate Elizabeth Taylor's thirtieth birthday. Eddie Fisher had popped in to ask everyone in the production office, smiling from ear to ear and obviously jubilant. He'd won the competition; his rival had been vanquished.

Elizabeth was said to be furious with him for confronting Sybil Burton about the affair but she hadn't thrown him out and now he was planning to give her the best birthday party ever. It would show the world they were still united, still in love.

Diana would have to wear her lilac dress again because she didn't have anything else that was suitably dressy. She asked Helen for help with her makeup but Helen claimed to have another engagement.

'Is it a date?' Diana smiled, and Helen shook her head.

'No, nothing like that, just a friend.' She didn't volunteer any more information.

'You're looking much better. Have you got your appetite back?'

'Yeah, I'm fine. Hey, I'm sorry I haven't been able to pay you back yet. I'm still sorting out my debts.'

'Just forget about it,' Diana told her. 'Consider it a gift.'

'Thanks,' Helen beamed. 'That will help a lot. Have a good time tonight.'

She felt guilty that she couldn't invite Helen to the party. Eddie had said they could each bring a partner, so she was taking Ernesto but she knew Helen would have loved to attend and hoped she wasn't hurt not to be invited.

They took a taxi to the Hostaria del Orso, a fourteenth-century building between the Piazza Navona and the Tiber. The party was being held in an enclosed loggia, the so-called Borgia Room, beyond which you could see stone columns with Corinthian capitals. She told Ernesto that Corinthian was the most ornate type of order, with fluted acanthus leaves and scroll decorations, and he gazed at her in admiration.

'I love it that you know these things.'

'You're not spying tonight, are you?' she asked. 'I'm not going to be left alone while you rush off to report on proceedings to your journalist friend or to call Paolo?'

'Of course not.' He sounded hurt, but she could tell from a flicker of the eyes that's exactly what he had been planning.

She was learning to read him. Now he would have to think of a convincing excuse if he wanted to slip away and she would do her best to detain him.

They were offered glasses of Dom Pérignon champagne and led to a table on the far side of the room. Everyone chatted, listened to the music drifting through from the nightclub where they would dance later, and waited for Elizabeth and Eddie to arrive. She was late, of course, but she looked stunning in a white fur jacket over an ice-blue satin dress, her hair piled high in an elaborate style. She sat beside Rex Harrison and Rachel Roberts, with Joe and Walter opposite. There was no sign of the Burtons. Eddie clapped his hands and asked for silence while he presented his birthday gifts.

First, there was an antique mirror set with emeralds, and Elizabeth exclaimed with pleasure when she unwrapped it.

'I just love presents, but this is rather big,' she announced theatrically. 'Don't you have anything smaller, dear?'

Eddie grinned and produced a jewellery box from his top pocket. He opened it, presented it to his wife, and she gasped and put it on her finger. It was a huge diamond ring that caught the light of the Murano glass chandeliers, producing beams that shot around the room.

'She's acting,' Diana whispered to Ernesto. 'What a peculiar scene. It looks as though they rehearsed it. Why didn't he give her such a special present in private?'

'You know a lot of things, my treasure,' Ernesto took her hand, 'but you don't yet understand the ways of the rich and famous. This is all about making a statement. Eddie is trying to tell the world that he's back in his place as the husband of the most famous woman in the world.'

'I don't understand. Why does he need the world to know? Isn't it enough that they have each other without such embarrassing public pronouncements?'

'Ah, but the point is that it is not actually true. He knows it, she knows it and most people here know it. You are the rare exception. I love your naïvety.'

Diana was slow to catch his meaning. 'Are you implying it's not true?'

'Yeah, she's back with Richard again. I saw them myself. She had a shawl over her head as she hurried into his trailer this afternoon and minutes later the entire vehicle was rocking on its wheels. They're addicted. They can't give up now.'

'Oh no, poor Eddie.' Diana glanced over to where he was toasting his wife with raised glass. *And poor Trevor*, she thought to herself. *Poor old Trevor.*

Chapter Thirty-Two

It was Diana's birthday just a couple of weeks after Elizabeth Taylor's but she planned to keep it as quiet as possible. Twenty-six wasn't an age to celebrate. She felt ancient compared to all the gorgeous young actresses and makeup artists and assistants working at Cinecittà. Ernesto wasn't about to let it pass without marking the day, though, and when she awoke in the morning she found he had slipped out to buy some flowers – yellow roses surrounded by white baby's breath – and one of the chocolate-filled *cornetti* she especially liked.

'This is just the start. I will bring your real present later, when we have dinner,' he promised, as she kissed him in thanks.

Her second surprise of the day came with the arrival of the courier from London. There was a large brown envelope addressed to her and she recognised Trevor's handwriting. What on earth could it be? She sat down at her desk to open it and pulled out a book – *Pale Fire*, by Vladimir Nabokov, a Russian author who had written a scandalous novel called *Lolita* seven years earlier. Diana and Trevor had both admired it as a fine piece of writing and talked scornfully of reviewers who didn't seem to understand the concept of the unreliable narrator and thought that Nabokov was advocating sexual relations with a minor. She was keen to read this next book, which had just been published.

There was something else in the envelope: a jewellery box. She opened it with trepidation, and was touched beyond measure when she recognised a charm bracelet that had belonged to her mother, one of those ones on which you hang mementoes from places you visit. There was a tiny shield with the national badge of Switzerland, a pixie from Cornwall, a Pictish symbol from the island of Skye, and so forth. The catch had broken long ago and Diana stored it as a keepsake only, but when she looked she saw that Trevor had had it mended, good as new.

'*I thought you might like to have this,*' he wrote in a little flowered card, '*and perhaps you can add a Roman charm. Happy birthday to my wonderful wife.*'

Apart from the gloves he bought her at Christmas, she couldn't remember the last time Trevor had chosen a present for her himself, apart from books – they often bought each other books. Repairing her mother's bracelet was extremely thoughtful. She fastened it on her wrist and Hilary came over to admire it.

'Is it your birthday?' she asked, spotting the card. 'Goodness, you should have said. I'd have got you something. Why don't we all go for a drink later?'

'I think Ernesto has plans.' Diana frowned, realising she'd either have to remove the charm bracelet or explain it to him.

Eddie Fisher appeared in the doorway.

'Guess what? It's Diana's birthday!' Hilary called.

'Congratulations!' he smiled, and came over to give her a hug. 'Eighteen again, are you? Wish I could stay to help you celebrate but I came in to say goodbye because I'm off to New York on business.'

'That's a shame,' Diana said, meaning it. 'Will you be gone for long?'

He shrugged. 'You just have to see how these things go.' There was an odd look on his face. Perhaps he meant that he would have to see how his marriage went, rather than his business meetings.

His arm was still draped around Diana's shoulders as the door opened and Ernesto walked in carrying a pink and white birthday cake. He glowered at them.

'Oh, look!' Hilary cried. 'Lovely Ernesto has brought cake. Don't you have any candles for it? In England we light candles on our birthday cakes.'

Diana stepped away from Eddie. 'It's perfect as it is. What a glorious idea. Shall we all have a slice?'

'I have a plane to catch,' Eddie said, sounding melancholy. 'But many happy returns, Diana.'

Diana didn't have time to think about him further as Candy made tea and Hilary cut the cake. After they'd eaten, Ernesto asked if he could have a word with her in private, so she stepped outside onto the lawn with him.

As soon as they were out of earshot, he demanded: 'What were you doing sucking up to Eddie like that?'

She was astonished. 'Don't be ridiculous! He hugged me because Hilary told him it was my birthday. You're not jealous, are you?'

Ernesto seemed somewhat mollified. 'Well, he is a single man now. For all I know he might have been trying to seduce you.'

'Wait a moment. What do you mean he's single?'

'Richard turned up drunk at their villa last night and insisted that Elizabeth choose between them – and she chose Richard. That's why Eddie is skulking off to New York.'

'How do you know all this? You have spies inside her villa, do you?' She narrowed her eyes in distaste.

Ernesto shook his head. 'She was having a dinner party at the time and the scene was witnessed by many guests. Everyone is talking about it on the set today, not just me.'

'Oh poor Eddie. That's horrible.' Her heart went out to him. It was bad enough being rejected without being publicly humiliated.

Suddenly Ernesto's eyes were on her wrist. 'Where did you get that bracelet? Was it from him?'

'Eddie? Of course not! Silly boy!' She touched his cheek. 'It used to be my mother's. I don't wear it very often.' She turned away so he couldn't see her cheeks flush with the almost-lie. 'I must go to sound stage 7 now. Joe wanted me to have a look at the sunken bath.'

It was interesting to learn that Ernesto had a jealous streak. She rather liked it because it proved how much he cared about her but she would have to be careful not to give him any reason to be jealous. She dreaded to think how he would respond to the news that Trevor was coming out at Easter. He was going to be terribly hurt. She would have to choose the moment to tell him with great care.

At dinner that evening, Ernesto presented her with another birthday present – a silver cross on a chain. It was pretty but she was puzzled that he would buy her a traditionally Catholic item.

'I thought you could wear it when I introduce you to my family,' he said. 'When my mother sees it, she will assume you are Catholic and the meeting will go much better.'

Diana's pulse quickened. 'You want me to meet your family?'

'Of course I do. You're my girl.' He reached over the table to squeeze her hand. 'Sadly, my mother is unwell just now, with something we call *fuoco di San Antonio*, but when she is better . . .'

It wasn't a term she had come across but Diana questioned him about the symptoms of the illness and realised it must be shingles. 'I'll look forward to meeting her whenever she's ready.'

She felt very moved that he was taking steps to make their relationship official. He genuinely seemed to want to make it work. With a jolt she realised that if he asked to marry her she would have to convert to Catholicism. Did they accept divorcees? She wasn't sure.

When they made love that night, there was a special intensity about it and Diana felt as though she had fallen just a little bit further in love with him. But while he slept she lay awake racked with guilt about Trevor, who had made such an effort to choose thoughtful gifts for her. It felt wicked to be betraying him. He'd done nothing to deserve this.

She tried to picture what she would have done if she had been in Elizabeth Taylor's position. What if she had been having a dinner party in the home she shared with Trevor, with all their friends there, when Ernesto burst in, insisting that she should choose between them? She simply couldn't picture the two of them in the same room, but she knew she wouldn't have humiliated Trevor publicly. It was as well that they lived in different countries, hundreds of miles apart, but she went cold with panic when she thought about Easter. She couldn't tell Trevor not to come, and she still hadn't told Ernesto about it, although the visit was only a month away. She was being a coward, and it was tearing her apart.

At least Elizabeth had made a choice and taken action. Perhaps she was just braver than Diana. She must have nerves of steel. But then why had she taken an overdose back in February when Richard broke off the affair? Maybe she had set her heart on the prize and was determined to get it. Diana shook herself. How could the likes of her attempt to get inside the mind of such an extraordinary star? They had nothing in common except dull marriages and exciting lovers but she felt a kinship with Elizabeth as they coped with their men in their own individual ways.

Just ten days later, Diana got an insight into Elizabeth's state of mind that made her think about the woman quite differently. Every day there were minor dramas at Cinecittà but the drama became a crisis on the 26th of March when a *paparazzo* managed to sneak a long-lens photograph of Elizabeth and Richard kissing outside her dressing room, wearing bathrobes over their costumes. It was the first proof positive of the affair for the outside world and the picture instantly went global. The furore was such that next morning Diana's studio car couldn't get through the entrance gates for all the *paparazzi* outside and the driver had to take her round to slip in via the commissary.

Copies of *Gente*, the Italian newspaper that had splashed the fuzzy picture on its front cover, were all over the set, surreptitiously folded into jacket pockets or handbags so as to avoid causing offence to the protagonists. In the bar at lunchtime, word buzzed from table to table that Richard had released a statement to the press accepting what everyone knew to be the truth about his affair – but he added that he would never leave his wife Sybil. How would Elizabeth react?

By one of those extraordinary coincidences that often seemed to happen at Cinecittà, that very afternoon Elizabeth was to film a scene of jealous rage. Cleopatra hears the news that Mark Antony, her lover, has married Octavian's sister back in Rome. The marriage is obviously one of political expedience but still Cleopatra flies into a frenzy. In the script, she is called upon to slash Antony's possessions to ribbons with a sword. Diana had read the pages that morning and couldn't believe how clearly the film mirrored real life at that precise moment.

Now that her face was known, she occasionally managed to step in to the sound stages and watch the filming and she decided to try that afternoon. She felt almost protective of Elizabeth, although that was ridiculous. The woman didn't even know her name.

The centrepiece of the set was a large bed circled by gold gauze curtains. Diana stood in the shadows by a back wall and kept very still as Elizabeth emerged and Joe went over for a word with her.

'Quiet on set. Going for a take,' called the assistant director, then there was the familiar sequence: 'Roll sound', 'Rolling', 'Roll camera', 'Speed'. The clapperboard operator called 'Slate 57, Take 1' and slapped the wooden boards together. 'And action,' Joe called.

Elizabeth began to slash at Antony's clothes with a Roman sword, a deranged expression on her face. 'Cut!' Joe called, then asked for another take. When that scene was in the bag, Elizabeth had to sweep the ornaments from a dressing table, and this took several takes, with continuity girls hard pressed to replace them in exactly the same positions between times. In the last scene, Elizabeth leapt onto the bed and began to stab it with the sword so that the stuffing spilled out. She went utterly berserk, sobbing and stabbing the mattress and pillows over and over again. Joe failed to call 'Cut'. Everyone was mesmerised.

Finally, someone said 'She's hurt herself' and Diana realised there was blood on the sheets. Joe rushed onto the set to put an arm round Elizabeth as she wept uncontrollably, then led her quickly out towards her dressing room. There was silence until the door closed behind them, then a script girl remarked, 'I hope we don't need to retake any of that.'

'Are you OK?' a voice next to Diana asked. It was only then she realised that she was crying herself.

Chapter Thirty-Three

Scott called round at Helen's *pensione* the evening after her vitamin shot and found her looking cheerful and full of beans.

'It's wonderful. I wish I'd known about this doctor months ago. Thank you so much, Scott.' She threw her arms around his neck.

'Wanna come out for dinner? My bike is round the corner.'

'I'm not hungry but we could have a drink if you like.'

Scott looked at her skinny arms. 'You need to eat, sweetheart. You're all skin and bone.'

'I know. None of my clothes fit any more. I'm sure my appetite will come back soon.' She laughed. 'Tell you what. Could we get an ice cream? I love ice cream.'

'Sure can. I know a place not far from here.' He'd noticed it because it reminded him of an American soda fountain with high stools on which you sat at a counter. There were no other customers. They chose stools with a view into the street and perused the menu.

'Could I have one of those?' Helen pointed to a picture on the wall of an ice cream sundae with three different scoops of ice cream – vanilla, strawberry and chocolate – and some pink syrup and sprinkles on top. 'It looks divine.'

Scott laughed and ordered her one, requesting just a coffee for himself.

'What's your job?' she asked. 'Did you tell me and I've forgotten? I'm famous for that.'

Scott decided not to mention that he was a journalist. The press had a bad name at Cinecittá and he didn't want her jumping to the conclusion he was only befriending her to get information about Taylor and Burton. 'I'm a writer. A struggling writer.'

'How romantic!' Helen licked a spoonful of ice cream. 'Do you write love stories?'

'Not exactly. I write crime stories and sometimes there's love involved. Gangsters and their girlfriends. Say, I was wondering if you and Luigi were ever an item?'

Helen shuddered and shook her head, but she wouldn't meet his eye. 'He's *disgusting*,' she exclaimed with feeling. 'I really *hate* him.' The question seemed to have upset her and he regretted asking it because she stopped eating and simply toyed with her ice cream as it melted into puddles in the dish.

'I hope he'll leave you alone now, but tell me if you have any trouble and I'll deal with him. OK?'

She nodded, but a dampener had been put on her mood. 'Do you have a girlfriend?' she asked, and Scott found himself telling her about Rosalia, who still called the office from time to time.

'I don't understand why she doesn't have more pride,' he complained.

Helen had a distant look in her eyes. 'If she could only get you back, she could pretend the rejection never happened and that it was all a misunderstanding. Then she could stop thinking of herself as the kind of girl men always leave.'

'Is there such a thing as the kind of girl men always leave?'

'I think so,' Helen frowned. 'Don't you?'

'No, I think they just need to meet the right person. And maybe stop trying so hard.'

All of a sudden Helen leaned her head in her hands and seemed exhausted. 'I need an early night, Scott. Sorry I'm not much company.'

'Hey! I'm just glad you're on the mend. Let's go out again in a few days when you've got your appetite back. Why don't you give me your number?'

Helen scribbled the phone number of her *pensione* on the cover of a matchbook. 'I won't hold my breath since you've already admitted you're the kind of guy who doesn't return girls' phone calls.'

'Idiot!' he grinned. 'Of course I'll call. We're friends. It's the girls who try to force me down the aisle on the second date I tend to dodge.'

When he dropped her off, he put his arms round her and hugged her tight, then kissed her forehead. She looked very vulnerable as he drove off, and he decided that he would definitely try to see her again soon. Perhaps he would find out more about this Luigi character as well, so he could protect Helen from him.

Every evening Scott had a few beers in one of the bars round the Via Veneto or Via Margutta, where he kept his eyes open and watched the comings and goings, especially the furtive deals in which money was palmed from one person to another and small paper packages given in return. It wasn't long before he noticed Luigi, the dealer he'd seen with Helen, but this time he was talking to an actor Scott vaguely recognised. They disappeared to the men's toilet, then the actor left first, glancing around self-consciously, before Luigi sauntered out and stood near Scott at the bar.

'*Bella serata*,' Scott ventured in Italian, and Luigi looked up at him. 'Do you speak English?'

'When I feel like it.'

'The town is full of actors at the moment. Must be good for business.' Luigi shrugged and Scott continued. 'I hear they're all alcoholics or drug addicts. They pretend to be someone else at work during the day then use mind-altering chemicals at night so that they never have to face up to who they really are.'

'That's profound,' Luigi replied. 'Are you a philosopher?'

'No, just a businessman,' Scott lied. 'Look, I know this is a long shot and I'm sorry if I'm way off target but I saw you going to the gents' with that guy and I wondered if by any chance you know where I could buy some cocaine? I heard it's easy to find drugs in Rome. Someone told me that certain bartenders will even supply you from under the counter if they know you, but I haven't been able to find any like that.'

'If that was the case, the quality would not be good,' Luigi scoffed. 'Every time it changes hands I expect it will be cut with *farina*. You need to buy from a dealer if you want it to be pure.'

'You sound like a guy who knows what he's talking about. Can I buy you a drink?'

'Sure.' Luigi made a face as if it was neither here nor there to him and ordered a coffee and a Jack Daniel's.

'So how does it work when famous people want to buy drugs?' Scott asked. 'Let's say Elizabeth Taylor fancied a couple of tabs of LSD for a party. How would she get them?'

Luigi gave a sly smile. 'I imagine she has trusted people she would send out to make enquiries. For all I know, you could be one of them.'

'Well, maybe I am,' Scott grinned. 'So does that mean a dealer could be supplying lots of famous people without even knowing it?'

'Some, perhaps. Other dealers have more personal relationships with their clients. They know the precise type of product the client prefers, the exact strength and purity, and make sure they supply what is wanted. The client will pay a premium for guaranteed quality.'

'I bet you know a lot of famous people yourself,' Scott hinted. 'Who are your favourites?'

That was the tipping point. Luigi couldn't resist boasting about the international stars he had dealt with. The names tripped off his tongue in a libellous stream. He said they always sought him out when they were in Rome and he never let them down. Many of them were household names across continents.

'The Via Veneto is my patch. Anyone who wants to buy anything round here has to go through me.'

Scott took mental notes but knew he could never print any of this information when the only evidence he had was the word of a shady Italian dealer.

'I'd be honoured if you would sell me a little something,' Scott said. 'Just so I can enter their illustrious company. How does it work?'

Luigi glanced round but the barman was serving someone at the other end of the bar. 'You want cocaine?' He named an extortionate price for a paperfold of the stuff.

Scott sensed it was several times the market rate and that Luigi saw him as a patsy, but he nodded agreement. He had just enough cash on him. 'Shall I go to the gents'?' he asked.

'Cup the money in your palm and we will shake hands. You must leave the bar immediately afterwards.'

The deal was done, and Scott said goodbye. As he walked down the street, he wondered what to do with the cocaine. He'd never taken it before and was curious to see what it was like but he didn't want to do it on his own. He'd heard it intensified the sensations during sex and wished he had a telephone number for that long-haired, barefooted girl. He climbed on his Vespa and drove round to the building on the Via Margutta where he had met her but the lights were out and nothing was happening. He couldn't even ask after her because he'd never discovered her name. It was a shame. She would have been the ideal person for a cocaine experiment.

He stuck the paperfold in his back pocket and drove home to write notes on his conversation with Luigi, for a new section of his journalism article. Shame he couldn't name all the celebrity drug users Luigi had mentioned. You couldn't have everything . . .

Chapter Thirty-Four

'That's that, then,' Candy remarked when Diana arrived at the production office on the morning of the 3rd of April. She threw across a copy of a newspaper with the headline 'Elizabeth and Eddie Say They Will Get Divorce'.

Diana was shocked that it was all proceeding so fast. She sat down hard in her chair and quickly read the story. It appeared that Eddie had phoned Elizabeth from New York with some reporters in the room and tried to get her to say she still loved him, but she humiliated him by refusing. Next, he was informed by letter that Elizabeth was issuing a statement announcing the end of their three-year marriage 'by mutual consent'.

'What about the baby they adopted in January? Maria, wasn't it?'

'Neither of them have seen her much because she's too sick to come to Rome, so I don't think the poor little mite will even come into the equation.' Candy folded her arms. 'But Liz's other children must get mixed up about who to call "pop". Look.' She picked up another paper, an Italian one this time, and showed Diana a blurred photograph of Richard Burton joining Elizabeth and her children for a picnic.

'So is he leaving Sybil?'

'Who knows? Sybil is back in London with their girls and she's keeping quiet about it all.'

Diana realised with a start that it was Eddie she'd been feeling most sorry for, because she liked him, but of course Sybil must be suffering as well. Why did she put up with it? She'd seemed a no-nonsense type so surely she should either come back to Rome and fight for her marriage, or throw Richard out for good?

Without either of their spouses around, Elizabeth and Richard came out of hiding. Almost every night they were photographed going for dinner and then on to a nightclub. At Cinecittà, they sat holding hands and kissing in the bar, or threw cocktail parties in her dressing-room suite or his trailer. When one of Richard's scenes was being shot, Elizabeth sat on the sidelines watching silently. If Diana passed her on her way to the sound stages she beamed and called 'Hi there!' She was almost skipping, as vivacious and happy as a lark. They were in love and wanted the world to know.

Is it really so easy? Diana wondered. *If I told Trevor that I wanted a divorce, would I be equally happy?* She thought not. She knew she would be racked with guilt. If only it were possible to follow her heart without anyone else being hurt in the process. She hated herself for being an adulteress.

When Trevor rang to say he'd booked his flight and was arriving on the 15th of April, only a week hence, Diana knew she had to act. That evening she told Ernesto, pretending she had only just found out herself, and predictably he flew into a wild rage.

'Where will he stay? Are you going to sleep with him? It's disgusting. How can you do this to me?'

'I'll sleep in the same bed but I promise we won't make love. We never do.'

'What about my clothes? My shaving things?' Ernesto kept everything he needed at her place so he didn't have to nip back to his mother's before work.

'I'm sorry but it would be best if you move them out, just while he is here. I don't want him to divorce me on grounds of adultery.'

'What would the grounds of your divorce matter? You *are* an adulterer, are you not? Why not tell him, and then we can be together without deception?'

Eventually, he calmed down after Diana promised to ask Trevor for a divorce. She agreed for the sake of peace, but the more she thought about it, the fairer it seemed. It was kinder to tell him the worst rather than let him live in hope. Ernesto tried to insist that she should bring it up on the first evening then book him a hotel room, but she refused.

'I love you, Ernesto,' she said softly. 'It's you I want to be with. You just have to let me handle this in my own way, causing as little hurt to Trevor as possible so that I can live with myself afterwards.'

Finally he was appeased, but she felt deeply troubled. She'd been coasting along trying not to confront the situation but now she would have no choice. The emotions she felt when she considered a separation from Trevor were very raw. He was her family, her only security in the world. That was no reason to prolong an unhappy marriage but she was terrified about what would become of her. Where would she live when filming ended? How would she earn her living? Ernesto was always protesting his love for her but he hadn't asked to marry her. She understood that he couldn't propose while she was still married to another man, but he must realise that Diana didn't have Elizabeth Taylor's wealth and had to consider how she would put a roof over her head.

Having lots of money must make everything easier, Diana decided, as she read in the newspapers that Richard had bought Elizabeth a hundred and fifty thousand dollar emerald and diamond necklace from Bulgari's. It could cushion you from many problems – but it brought others at the same time. On the 12th of April, Elizabeth was confronted with a situation created by her fame and one that was difficult to laugh off.

Diana had been expecting to have lunch with Helen but there was no sign of her in the bar so she wandered up to the sound stages. She followed the arrows to the makeup room and was surprised to find Elizabeth sitting with several hair and makeup girls clustered around, including Helen.

'Hi!' Elizabeth welcomed Diana, narrowing her eyes slightly as if she recognised her but couldn't put a name to her. 'Have you heard the latest? I've been condemned by the Vatican. The Pope has declared me an outcast from polite society. What was the exact phrase?' She picked up a dog-eared newsletter, which Diana saw was *L'Osservatore Della Domenica*, and slapped it on the arm of the chair. 'Someone translated it for me earlier. It says I'm an erotic vagrant.' She gave a throaty little laugh. 'What a joke! Is there anyone in this room who is *not* an erotic vagrant?'

They looked at each other and assured her they were all vagrants as well. Helen quipped dolefully, 'Chance would be a fine thing!'

'Bloody Catholic Church! Who wants their opinion anyway? A load of celibate old men in dresses telling me I'm not doing

219

a good job of bringing up my children. Fuck the lot of them!' Elizabeth spoke with bravado but Diana could see from a tightness round her eyes and hear from a wavering in her voice that it had really disturbed her.

She picked up the newspaper to look for herself. It was a letter, clearly addressed to Elizabeth, that began: '*Dear Madam, When a short time ago you said that your marriage (the fourth to be exact) would last a lifetime there were those who shook their heads in a rather sceptical way.*'

By the end of the first paragraph it was implying that her children didn't seem to count for her, as she focused solely on satisfying her libidinous urges while trailing them around behind her. Diana skipped to the end, where it suggested that her children should be given to a farmer's wife with a clear conscience rather than left in the care of a capricious princess.

'*These children need an honoured name more than a famous name, a serious mother more than a beautiful mother, a stable father rather than a newcomer who can be dismissed at any time.*' She sucked in her breath, hoping no one had translated that bit for Elizabeth.

The dark eyes were upon her. 'We haven't been introduced, have we?' Elizabeth said.

'I'm Diana Bailey, historical advisor to the film.' She reached out her hand and Elizabeth shook it, meeting her eyes with warmth.

'And tell me, Diana, how is your love life?'

'It's complicated,' Diana said quietly.

'Aren't they all, honey?' Elizabeth drawled. 'Good luck with your complications. I hope the Vatican doesn't condemn *you* as well.'

Diana decided that she genuinely liked this woman. She was vulnerable, confessional and, once you got over being dazzled by her fame and beauty, quite human.

'I wouldn't pay too much attention to *L'Osservatore*. It's not written by the Pope himself – just a few opinionated cardinals – so it doesn't necessarily represent official Vatican policy.'

'Well, I guess that's something to be thankful for,' Liz laughed. 'Maybe they won't be sending an exorcist to drive the demon spirit from within me quite yet.' She clasped her hands to her magnificent bosom.

'It's very nice to meet you properly,' Diana said, 'but I was just picking up Helen for lunch.'

Helen stood reluctantly. She wanted to spend as long as possible bathed in the glow of celebrity, but Diana was ravenous.

'Bye, girls,' Elizabeth called after them.

'You're looking great.' Diana put an arm round Helen and hugged her as soon as they were out in the corridor. 'I'm sorry we hardly ever catch up just now but it's been all go. My husband is arriving at the weekend.'

She waited to see if Helen would comment but she didn't seem to be aware of Diana's affair with Ernesto. Diana hoped that Hilary was the only person on the set who'd realised. Helen had never asked any questions, which seemed to imply that word hadn't spread beyond the production office.

'I'd like you to meet him. Will you come for supper with us one evening?' That would save awkward silences, because Helen's chatter could fill the gaps.

'OK,' Helen said, without much enthusiasm. 'Why not?'

Chapter Thirty-Five

In the evening of 12th April, Scott was chatting to Gianni at the curve of the Via Veneto when a shiny black car drew up.

'*Sono loro!*' someone shouted, and all the photographers scrambled into position. Rather than joining the throng, Gianni shimmied up a lamppost and yelled at Scott to hand his camera up to him.

The car door opened and Richard Burton got out on the road side then walked round to open the door for Elizabeth Taylor. No one had been sure if they would come out that evening after the Vatican pronouncement, but here they were, large as life and dressed up to the nines. She was wearing a black dress so tight it looked as though it had been glued to her, and Scott noted there were no creases to indicate any underwear. Round her neck was the famous Bulgari diamond and emerald necklace Burton had bought her recently. He hoped Gianni got a good photo because there was plenty he could write about.

Usually the couple hurried with heads down straight into the bar or restaurant they were visiting, but tonight they lingered, making sure every photographer got the shots they wanted. They didn't respond to reporters who were shouting questions about their reaction to the Vatican outburst, but Scott sensed this was their answer. It was a calculated 'Fuck you, we don't give a damn!' to the cardinals. He warmed to them.

In this day and age, how dare a church single out one individual whose marriage had broken down from the millions of others around the world? Elizabeth Taylor wasn't even Catholic. She'd converted to the Jewish faith for husband number three, Mike Todd. How rude for a country's churchmen to lambast a visitor whose presence had brought much wealth and industry to their country. The latest estimates were that *Cleopatra* would cost twenty-five million dollars. It was the most expensive film ever made by a long shot, and much of that money was being ploughed into the Italian economy and thus into church coffers. Scott decided that was the article he would write: about the ridiculous hypocrisy of the Vatican and the power they still wielded over the Italian government in 1962.

He hung around outside the Grand Hotel until word came from a reliable source that Burton and Taylor were going to the Cha Cha Club after dinner. Scott decided to see if he could get in. Not many of the doormen in Rome knew he was a journalist. They thought he was a smart-looking young American with money so he could still get access to the clubs other journalists were banned from. He was waved straight into the Cha Cha, where he bought a beer and wandered round on the lookout for evidence of drug-taking. To his surprise, he came across Helen, sitting in a corner nursing a drink.

'Hey, I was planning to call you tomorrow,' he exclaimed. 'How are you doing?'

'I'm fine. I came out with a couple of girls from the set but they're off dancing with Italian boys.' She made a face.

'So the vitamin injection is still working, is it?'

'I've had to have a few more but I feel so great afterwards that it's worth it.'

Scott frowned. 'That must be expensive. I thought the doctor said you would need only one more treatment?'

'Trust me to be the one that needs more!' she laughed. 'Pathetic, isn't it?'

'I saw that man – Luigi – in a bar last week openly selling drugs to someone else. He's a sinister kind of guy. How did you hook up with him?'

'One of the other girls recommended him.' The band began to play a popular Italian song '*Quando, quando, quando*' and Helen started to tap her foot to the drumbeat.

'Wanna dance?' he asked. 'I warn you, I'm not very good.'

'I'd love to.' She was already on her feet, grinning broadly. 'I love dancing.'

She gave a little wiggle from her head to her toes and segued into a version of The Twist, her body languid and the movement flowing rather than tight and jerky.

'Wow! You sure can move,' Scott called, and she grinned.

He did his best to keep up but in truth he just wanted to watch her. She had true rhythm in those skinny hips and she kept changing the choreography. Some girls did the same thing from the beginning to the end of a record but she put in her own cute little moves, using her hands, her head, her whole body.

They danced three numbers but when a slow record came on, Scott held his hands up and said, 'I've had enough humiliation. Can we sit down?'

Scott bought some drinks and, once they were sitting down, he asked more about Luigi. 'Does he deal for a living or does he have a day job as well?'

'God no, he only deals. He's busy morning, noon and night. He's got dozens of customers. You wouldn't believe how many people in Rome take drugs.'

'So is he like a boss? Is he Mister Big?'

She considered this. 'He's somewhere in the middle, I think. He controls Via Veneto, which must be an important patch, but I once went with him to a house on the coast where there were some guys who were his bosses. He was really nervous. I saw him put a gun in the glove compartment of the car.'

Scott was aghast. 'Why did he take you with him?'

'I wondered about that. I suppose he was scared of these men and thought they would have to behave well in front of me. Which they did, by the way. There were half a dozen guys there but one of them gave me a smoke of *eroina* that made me all woozy. Then they all started laughing at me.' The words poured out of her and she seemed to have no notion of the danger she'd been in.

'Jesus Christ, Helen! What were you thinking? You could have been killed or raped. Anything could have happened!'

'I know. I only thought of that afterwards. At the time, I wanted a fix and Luigi said he would give me one if I came for a drive with him. So I did.' She shrugged. 'Thank God you got me off that stuff or I don't know what would have happened.'

Scott's brain was ticking. 'Where was this house on the coast? Can you remember?'

'It was somewhere past Anzio. We drove through the town then out the other side where a road goes down the coast. That's where it was. A really big house, right on the edge of the ocean, with palm trees and a swimming pool in the garden. And there was an old tower across the bay.'

'Do you know who owned it? Did anyone mention a name?'

'Not people's names, no.' Her beehive hairdo was slipping and she repositioned it with one hand. 'But I did notice that the house was called Villa Armonioso. There was a sign on the gate. Isn't that odd? The "harmonious villa", and it's actually full of drug dealers. Why did you want to know?'

Scott held out his hands. 'I'm just amazed by the volume of drug trafficking here.'

'Don't mess with Luigi if you see him,' Helen advised. 'He's not nice when he turns on you. He's very cross with me for giving up because he'd been hoping I'd introduce him to lots more people at Cinecittà and maybe even deliver drugs on the set for him. Fortunately, I never got that desperate.'

There was a sudden commotion as the crowds parted and Elizabeth Taylor and Richard Burton arrived and made their way to a table reserved for them and their group. Roddy McDowall and his friend John were among them. Booze was brought by the bottle rather than by the glass, at Richard's noisy request.

'That's the second time I've been with her today.' Helen told Scott about the scene in the dressing room. He tried to memorise the words she said Elizabeth had used, to reproduce them exactly in the piece he intended to send to his editor later that evening: *A source close to Miss Taylor told me that she laughed off being called an erotic vagrant.*

Scott kept an eye on the Burton–Taylor table and noticed that Elizabeth was knocking back her drinks just as fast as Richard, and appeared the worse for wear. Her bra strap was sliding down her arm and her hair was tousled. All at once she got up, knocking over a drink, and bolted for the exit, trotting unsteadily on her high heels.

Scott decided to follow. 'I have to get up early in the morning,' he told Helen. 'It's been great to see you though. Let's get together again soon.'

'My appetite's back. Maybe we could have that dinner?' she suggested.

'I'm busy this week but how 'bout after Easter?' He gave her a hug. 'Look after yourself, sweetheart. And be careful who you talk to about Luigi or you could find yourself in big trouble.'

'I know. I will.' She lifted her face towards his and he gave her a kiss on the cheek. She looked impossibly young, without a hint of a wrinkle, and he felt a twinge of worry for her. Her tongue was too unguarded and she knew some dangerous people.

Outside the club, he found Gianni and asked if he'd managed to take a photo of Elizabeth on the way out.

'Yes,' he said. 'But I don't know whether you will want to use it. Her head was down, her hair was messy, and she was crying.'

'Are you sure?'

'Oh yes. Big crying.' He imitated.

'I'll use it if you've got a clear shot,' Scott told him, then jumped on his Vespa and went back to the office to write his story.

Chapter Thirty-Six

Next morning, an American girl came to the production office looking for Diana.

'Mrs Bailey? Miss Taylor requests a word, if you have a moment.'

For a moment, Diana couldn't think who she meant by 'Miss Taylor' then it dawned on her. 'Do you mean *Elizabeth* Taylor?'

'Yes.'

'What does she want to see *me* for?'

The girl shrugged. 'She didn't say. She's in her trailer over by the back lot.'

Diana stood and picked up her handbag. 'I'll come straight away.'

She walked right down one of the main boulevards that ran through Cinecittà. It was busy because thousands of extras were being arranged in place for the scene of Cleopatra's arrival in Rome. She knocked on the door of Elizabeth's trailer and waited till there was a call of 'Come in!', not wanting to surprise the star in her lingerie.

Elizabeth was sitting in a pink velvet chair, her hair restrained in the netting she wore beneath her Cleopatra wig. Heavy makeup formed a mask over her skin and thick black lines circled her eyes and swooped up to her temples like the wings of a raven. She was wearing the gold chain-mail floor-length gown Diana had seen in Irene Sharaff's studio, the one that weighed more than twenty pounds, and Diana was sure it couldn't be comfortable.

'Thanks for coming. I hope you weren't in the middle of anything important.' She motioned for Diana to sit in a folding chair opposite. 'You must have your work cut out trying to make Joe stick to historical fact. There's an uphill task!'

Diana laughed. 'I gave up long ago.'

'I've been asking about you,' Elizabeth said, fixing Diana with her purply-blue gaze. 'Everyone tells me what a great intellectual you are.'

Diana blushed and shook her head. 'Oh no, not really.'

Elizabeth continued: 'I'm going away for a few days' holiday and I've completely run out of books. We went to the English language bookshop but I couldn't find anything I wanted. Have you been there yet? It's run by two very charming English women who opened late especially for me, so I had to buy a couple of books, but they don't appeal.'

'I didn't realise there was an English bookshop.'

'Anyway, I wondered if you could lend me a book or two on ancient Egypt? I'll bring them back after Easter. I hate not having anything to read and I figured you would be the person to ask.'

'Oh, I see.' Diana tried to picture the books she'd brought with her. 'Most of my books are very academic.' She blushed again. Would Elizabeth think she was insulting her by implying she wouldn't be able to follow them?

She didn't appear to mind. 'Honey, I read everything from potboilers to PhDs so I'd be happy with whatever you reckon is worth reading. I thought I should learn more about Egypt since I'm supposed to be ruling it.' She gave a throaty laugh and took a long sip from a glass at her elbow that looked as though it contained Coke. 'Hey, do you want a drink?'

'I'm fine, thanks. Why don't I bring over a few books and you can choose what you want? I've got some in the office but most are back at my *pensione*. I could bring them tomorrow.' Diana thought she might like Grace Macurdy's *Hellenistic Queens*, a very readable biography.

'I'm planning to leave tonight, but I could send my chauffeur to your *pensione* later. Say seven o'clock?'

'No problem at all,' Diana assured her. It was difficult not to gaze at Elizabeth when you were up close. Diana found herself alternating between staring and looking away, which she worried seemed rude, as though she wasn't paying attention.

An assistant tapped on the door and came in holding the black Cleopatra wig, but Elizabeth waved her away. 'Not yet. I'll put it on at the last moment. I need some time alone with Diana. Would you mind?' The woman left.

'The weather is perfect for your scene,' Diana said. 'It's just as well because there are seven thousand extras being arranged in their places as we speak.'

Elizabeth picked up the glass at her elbow and took another large slurp. 'It's fucking awful timing, coming straight after the Vatican letter. I hope they don't all hate me. You don't think they'll boo, do you?'

Diana was shocked by the swearing but didn't want to appear naïve by showing it, so she stammered, 'God, no. I'm sure they won't. Of course not.'

'I hope you're right, but it's a Catholic country and I'm an "erotic vagrant" after all.' There was a tremor in her voice and Diana realised she was upset. All the criticism had got to her.

'We both know how ridiculous that letter was. I work all over the set and I promise you there's not one person who doesn't think it was ludicrous. Everyone is completely on your side.'

'I fucking hope so.' She gulped her drink thirstily, and it was only then Diana realised it must be alcohol. Elizabeth didn't seem drunk but now she thought of it there was a slight smell of booze in the air.

'Everything's such a mess. I'm sick and tired of worrying about it. I just go round and round in circles.' She sighed heavily. 'How's your complicated love life? Is it as difficult as mine?'

Diana was normally a very private person, but it felt only fair to share her own problems since Elizabeth had been so frank. She found herself wanting to confess, to make their bond more intimate. 'I have a husband back in London but the marriage is not in good shape. Three months ago I started an affair with someone here in Rome and tomorrow my husband is due to arrive for an Easter break. So it's pretty disastrous.'

Elizabeth leaned forward, her eyes gleaming. 'Is your lover Italian or American?'

'Italian and jealous.' Diana raised her eyebrow. 'I should have dealt with the situation much sooner but I've been burying my head in the sand. You're much braver than me.'

Elizabeth threw back her head and snorted. 'Me? Brave? Hell, no. I'd have done the same as you if I could, but the media made that impossible. I love Eddie – I still do – but Richard simply swept me away, like a spring tide. He's too powerful and overwhelming. He calls me "Ocean". Isn't that beautiful?'

'Yes, it is.' Diana remembered a report from the early days of filming that Richard called her 'Miss Tits' but didn't mention it.

'I'm a pushover when he speaks to me in that incredible poet's voice and looks straight through me with those sharp eyes that never miss a thing. I'm lost, vanquished, I surrender completely.' The speech was theatrical but Diana could tell she meant every word. She looked misty-eyed and blinked hard, perhaps remembering that there was no time to redo her lavish eye makeup.

There was a knock on the door and a girl popped her head in to tell Elizabeth that they were ready for her on set. Her assistant held out the wig but Elizabeth waved her away again. 'They'll wait,' she said.

Once they were alone, she said, 'God, Diana, what shall we women do?' She reached out and squeezed her hand. Hers was much warmer than Diana's.

Suddenly Diana felt protective. It seemed mad, when the most famous woman in the world had dozens of servants and hangers-on, but maybe that made it all the more difficult to get good advice. 'I suppose we need to keep our feet on the ground and think sensibly,' she said. 'These are decisions that affect other people besides ourselves so we have to be sure it's not just a feeling that will pass.' She was thinking of Elizabeth's situation and the likelihood that her affair would only last as long as the filming, rather than her own circumstances in which at least there were no children involved.

'Do you believe your feelings about your Italian lover will change?' It was a challenge, a moment for truth.

'No,' Diana whispered. 'I don't think they will.'

'So go with your heart,' Elizabeth breathed. 'People heal in time. I've never known heartbreak to last more than a year.'

Diana had read in the papers that Eddie Fisher was crying on the shoulder of anyone who would listen in New York and wondered if he would have recovered in a year.

There was yet another knock on the door. 'Everyone's waiting, Miss Taylor.'

She sighed and emptied her drink. 'Will you give your address to my assistant? She'll get a chauffeur to pick up the books tonight. And please come see me after Easter to tell me how it goes with your husband.'

Diana promised that she would, and while Elizabeth's wig was being pinned in place she scribbled down her address and said her goodbyes.

She walked straight over to the Forum set, where thousands of extras were standing in their places. The script called for Cleopatra to ride in with her son, Caesarion, atop a thirty-foot-high sphinx. It was taken from a Plutarch version of events, which Diana didn't believe for a moment. In fact, when Caesar returned to Rome in 47 BC, he had entered the city in tribal procession to a certain amount of cheering and some jeering taunts about the Egyptian queen who had bewitched him. It seemed implausible to Diana that Cleopatra would have laid herself open to the taunts (or worse) of Romans in the same way, and much more likely that she sneaked in and installed herself quietly.

The camera started rolling and the giant sphinx, with Cleopatra and her 'son' on top, moved slowly forward, only clearing the Arch of Titus by a few inches on either side. It came to a halt and six gigantic Nubian slaves climbed up to lift the platform on which they sat. Diana gasped inadvertently as they began to descend the steps. If the platform had been rigid, Elizabeth would have tipped forward and fallen to the ground, but in fact it was on a kind of fulcrum that kept it level.

The script called for a take in which the extras chanted her name at this point – 'Cleopatra, Cleopatra'. Diana stood well back and watched the buzz of activity as the camera was positioned and the signal was given for the crowd to start shouting.

'Leez,' they called, 'Viva Leez.' It was a wall of sound that rose and fell then got louder again. She heard other cries of *'Baci, baci'* and saw some of the extras blowing kisses. It was a universal affirmation of their support for her with not a hint of booing and Diana wished she could see Elizabeth's face as it dawned on her that they were emphatically on her side.

Shooting finished but the shouts continued as she was helped down from her perch, the words blurring into one indistinguishable chant.

That's what fame sounds like, Diana thought to herself. *That must be what it's like when you're the most famous woman in the world.*

Chapter Thirty-Seven

Diana decided not to tell Ernesto she'd had a personal conversation with Elizabeth. It might invite too many questions about why the star had chosen to confide in her and, besides, she couldn't risk him repeating it to his journalist contact. It was a shame, because she was girlishly thrilled by the encounter and desperate to discuss it, but she decided there was no one she could tell without betraying a confidence.

Ernesto was subdued over dinner and begged her yet again to tell Trevor on arrival that their marriage was over.

'I can't do that,' Diana told him. 'I can't throw away a six-year relationship in five minutes. But you're the only lover I want. Please give me time to deal with this in my own way.'

He made love to her with great energy that night – almost like an animal scent-marking his territory – and she felt sorry for what she was putting him through. Were their situations reversed, she would be feeling deeply insecure. She had never lied to him about being married and he had always known when he got involved with her that there would be difficult times ahead, but she hated to see him so unhappy.

Diana arranged for a car to collect Trevor from the airport and bring him directly to Cinecittà. She had some work to do for Joe that afternoon, but she also wanted her husband to see the set before the studio closed for Easter. She was sure he would sneer at the oversized mock-up of the Forum and the undersized Temple of Venus but she felt a sense of pride about all that had been achieved there and hoped he would find some merit in it. Ernesto wasn't working so there was no risk of bumping into him, else she would have arranged things differently. She didn't entirely trust him not to make a scene.

As it happened, Walter Wanger was in the production office when Trevor arrived, and he turned on his effusive, old-school charm.

'I'm delighted to meet you at last, sir. Diana's told us all about you. In fact, she keeps promising to lend me a copy of your biography of Plutarch, which I believe is the definitive account. What a great honour that you have come to visit our humble set.'

Diana had seen Walter directing his charm towards everyone from visiting royalty to Italian government officials to recalcitrant journalists, and it seldom failed to win them over. Trevor was no exception, and he positively glowed as Walter insisted on giving him a personal tour of the outdoor sets. She trailed along beside them, saying little, worried about how thin and pale Trevor looked. He stooped as he walked, but kept up an animated conversation with Walter about movies set in ancient Rome, about which both were equally scathing.

'*Spartacus* was a beautifully made picture,' Walter agreed, 'but the plot is a little incredible. Kubrick is a friend of mine, but he should have checked with a few more experts.'

Diana smiled when she remembered his effusiveness at the *Spartacus* party the previous October. He was saying what he thought Trevor wanted to hear.

236

In the car back to Pensione Splendid, she and Trevor chatted about progress on *Cleopatra* and the point they had reached in the story. She rolled her eyes as she told him about Cleopatra's triumphal entry into Rome and the calls of 'Viva Leez'.

He laughed. 'What was it you said Irene Sharaff called it? Hollywood on the Tiber?'

Diana was amazed that he remembered. He must have been listening after all during those awkward, one-sided phone calls.

As she showed him into her room, she felt anxious in case the *padrona* appeared and made some comment about her having yet another male caller. Or what if Ernesto had left some sign that would give the game away? But there was nothing out of the ordinary. Trevor just nodded and walked over to look out the window while Diana unpacked his case and hung up the shirts he had brought.

'So this is your famous view! Very nice.'

They went to the *trattoria* downstairs for dinner and Trevor ate heartily, still in good humour. He had obviously made a decision to be congenial and ask about her life out there. If only he had done that at Christmas, things could have been entirely different.

'I've been keeping up with the Burton–Taylor melodrama,' he told her. 'Did you know that *The Times* now reports on it regularly? What's the world coming to?'

Diana was amazed. *The Times* didn't usually report tittle-tattle, and even if it did, she wouldn't have expected Trevor to bother with it. 'You heard about the Vatican condemnation then?'

'Outrageous! Why doesn't the Pope condemn genuinely evil people like Khrushchev or Ho Chi Minh? It trivialises his church that it should be concerned about an actor and actress doing what actors and actresses have done for time immemorial. There are even reports of thespian affairs in Pliny.'

'Elizabeth is putting a brave face on it but she's distressed.' Diana found herself telling Trevor about the conversation they'd had, and finished by saying, 'She has a lot to lose.'

'Perhaps,' Trevor said, 'but not as much as Richard Burton.'

'What do you mean?'

'For a start, if his wife divorces him he will lose his children. It must be very hard for divorced men only to see their children at times dictated by a court – if they are decent men, that is.'

Diana was startled by the use of the word 'divorce', a subject that was much on her mind of late.

Trevor continued: 'But I also believe he will be taken less seriously as an actor if he hitches his wagon to the lure of global stardom in the form of Miss Taylor. Already *The Times* speculates that this affair was calculated to push up his fees for movie acting, and that if he wants a career starring in the latest Hollywood hit films it was a good move. But his friends in English theatre are openly siding with Sybil and claiming they will have nothing to do with him if he leaves her. Even his family in Wales are saying that. So in making a decision he has to balance his credibility as an actor, his friends, family and children against the undeniable attributes of Miss Taylor.'

'Gosh, I never thought of it like that.' Diana had formed an opinion of Richard Burton as an arrogant womaniser and hadn't stopped to consider his point of view.

'For Elizabeth Taylor to win her prize, she will have to rip him slowly and painfully away from his Welsh roots and everything he believes in. Somehow I can't see her sitting in the

Miners' Arms in Pontrhydyfen drinking ale and singing "Myfanwy" on a Saturday night.'

Diana laughed at the absurdity of the notion. 'They probably don't serve ale in Hollywood.'

'Probably don't even have pubs. And they certainly don't have decent theatre.'

Later, they climbed the stairs to her room companionably arm in arm but Diana made it very clear that sex was not on the cards. She went to the bathroom to change into her nightdress, and when she got into bed she wrapped the covers tightly around her and wriggled as close to the wall as possible, leaving him plenty of space to settle in.

'Goodnight,' he whispered, his voice catching in his throat. He didn't attempt to put his arm round her, as he always did at home.

She whispered, 'Sleep well.' In fact, neither slept for a long while, and both could tell that was the case from the other's breathing, but neither dared to say another word for fear of opening Pandora's box. Once they started discussing their marital problems, who knew where it would end?

Next morning, when Diana awoke, Trevor was lying beside her perusing a Baedeker *Guide to Rome*, tracing a route on a map with his finger. She'd always liked his hands, which were large and strong, but with long, elegant fingers.

'It advises that we should hire a guide to show us round the Colosseum and the Forum. What do you think?'

Diana laughed. 'I think the guide would have to pay *you*. You'd know far more than he did!'

'I can't believe you haven't been yet. How could you spend six months in Rome without having a look?'

She considered this. There were many Sundays when she could have walked around on her own, and she assumed Ernesto would have taken her if she had asked, but in the back of her mind she had always wanted to go with Trevor. He was such a brilliant historian that he would make connections no travel guide would dream of.

Even by the end of her street, he noticed something she had walked past every day without spotting. An old stone waterspout protruded from the edge of a building, and around it, what at first sight appeared to be a series of criss-crosses was revealed on closer examination to be Roman graffiti. Trevor crouched and transcribed it carefully onto the inside cover of his Baedeker, then showed it to Diana.

'Lovers, like bees, lead honeyed lives,' she translated, then blushed to the roots of her hair.

'Very poetic,' Trevor commented. 'Other documented Roman graffiti tells of children who have died, or lists the going rate for prostitutes in the area, but I think there was a romantic fellow in this neighbourhood. Or perhaps it was a woman. Who knows?'

They caught a bus across town to the Colosseum but found it overcrowded with Easter holidaymakers and decided to return just before closing time when the hordes might have thinned out. Instead they wandered up to the Palatine and examined the remains of the houses where the political elite planned their machinations, and visited each other via a series of tunnels and passages. They walked downhill to the magnificent remains of the Republic's temples, statues and official buildings, then finally headed back to the gladiatorial arena, and all day long they never stopped talking. There was so much to think about.

This is why I married him, Diana realised. *This is what we have in common.* She cared deeply about Trevor, she wanted only the best for him, but she wasn't in love with him and wasn't attracted to him. Ernesto had taken that place in her heart. Yet at the same time, she couldn't bear to tell Trevor that their marriage was over. Sometimes she caught him giving her a look of such utter sadness that it almost broke her heart, but neither raised any difficult topics. It was so wonderful to rediscover their closeness that they didn't want to jeopardise it.

The week passed quickly as they toured the Vatican museums, the architecturally famous churches, the art galleries and villas of the city. They ate when they were hungry and stopped for coffee or a beer when their feet were aching. One evening they had dinner with Helen, as arranged, but the conversation was stilted as Helen and Trevor could find little in common. She chattered nervously about the makeup they were using on the film and Diana could see that, although he was doing his best to be polite, Trevor had glazed over.

'She seems troubled,' he said afterwards. 'She hardly ate a bite yet she drank the best part of a bottle of wine. Is she a close friend of yours?'

'I like her,' Diana said. 'She's a true natural. But you're right, she drinks too much. It's probably because it's cheaper here than it is back home. I do worry about her.'

'Some people have less willpower around alcohol than others. Jack Robertson at work always gets sozzled at the Christmas party and has to be hauled into a taxi. He's a bright chap the rest of the time, but put him near the gin and he's soon out of control.'

It was on the tip of Diana's tongue to say that she found herself drinking more in Rome than she would at home, then she bit it back because Trevor might have asked awkward questions about who she went drinking with.

She had arranged to take the whole week off but on Wednesday a studio driver brought a message from Hilary asking if she could drop in for an hour to advise on the dancing in the great procession, which was currently in rehearsal and due to be filmed in just over a week. Trevor said he would sit reading in her room until her return.

As they drove out to Cinecittà, Diana's heart began pounding. Would Ernesto be on set? She was dying to see him. It seemed so long since she had been in his arms, and she missed the smell of him, the way he made her feel so womanly and alive. He had probably taken the week off to be with his family, though. She shouldn't get her hopes up.

When she arrived, she went straight to Joe's office and they walked out together to watch the dancers' rehearsals. The choreography, designed by Fred Astaire's choreographer Hermes Pan, was gymnastic, with back bends, high leaps and rapid pirouettes. It was a celebratory dance, performed for show, and the designers had done their best to create a spectacle.

'You wouldn't have men dancing with women, though,' Diana pointed out. 'If they were in pairs, it would be men with men or women with women.'

'Good point,' Joe said. 'Let's make sure we get that right.'

They watched for about half an hour, fine-tuning details of the display and discussing them with the choreographer, then there was a dress rehearsal. The drumbeat started and girls in multi-coloured costumes that were little more than bikinis danced through the Temple of Venus. Then came the snake-charmers with imitation cobras wrapped around their bodies, writing and twisting to the beat. Red and yellow smoke plumes wafted into the air and arrows were fired with streamers attached. There were pole vaulters, rectangles of gold tinsel raining from above, silver and gold plumed creatures, and hundreds of doves released into the sky. It was an extraordinary sight and would be one of the highlights of the film, a part where you could actually see the phenomenal budget being spent.

As Diana was walking towards the production office afterwards she felt a tap on her back and whirled around.

'You're here!' Ernesto beamed, and pulled her into a close hug. 'Has he gone? Did you tell him?'

She let her body sink into his, not caring who might be watching, filled with the familiar intoxication of lust. 'No, not yet. I had to come in today to check the dancers.'

Ernesto immediately pulled away. 'You haven't told him?'

'I thought I would wait until his last night. It's not long now and I don't want to spoil his trip. He can't change his flight back so we'd be stuck together anyway.' She caught his arm: 'Please don't be cross, Ernesto. I'll see you in a few days because he leaves on Saturday.'

His voice rose in anger. 'You have no idea what it is like for me. I want to burst into your room and kill him just for being near you and you say I should be patient? You ask too much of me, Diana. I don't know any man who would put up with this.'

He was genuinely upset and Diana didn't know what she could say to comfort him. 'I love you. I want to be with you, but I am not the kind of person who can be cruel . . .'

'Yet you are happy to be cruel to me. Well, I'm not sure if I will still be waiting for you in a few days.'

Diana was shocked. 'Are you threatening me?'

'I'm just saying that you are pushing me away and I don't like it.' He was scowling, sulky, like a child who wasn't getting his own way.

She touched his cheek. 'I'm sorry, but you know the situation. Three days is not much to ask. Let's meet for dinner on Saturday evening at that place behind the Pantheon.' It was a favourite of theirs: dark and intimate with good home-cooked food.

'I might,' he said petulantly. 'And I might not.'

He turned and walked off but Diana didn't doubt for a moment that he would meet her. His pride was dented but he would get over that once he had her to himself again. She hurried back to town to meet Trevor and continue their sightseeing for the remaining few days.

On the last night, she knew she had to say something to make her position clear. She had rehearsed many speeches in her head, trying to find the right form of words, but in the end it was Trevor who opened the conversation, and he started with an apology.

'I was wrong to try and stop you coming to Rome. In the brief time I've been here, I've seen how much it means to you, and also how much you are appreciated by your colleagues at Cinecittà. Will you forgive me for being an ass?'

Diana blushed. 'Of course I will.'

'I know it has caused us to become estranged, but I ask one thing of you: please don't make any hasty decisions that you might live to regret. Your thoughts are all focused in Rome just now, but soon these people will go back to their own homes and you will need to think about where you want to be and what you want to do next.'

244

'But I thought . . .' She couldn't find the right words. 'It doesn't seem fair.'

His eyes were sad but he continued calmly. 'Needless to say, I hope you decide to come back to our home and I will welcome you with all my heart . . . but I know we have a lot of problems. Will you at least promise me that you won't make any hard and fast decisions till the end of the filming?'

Diana hesitated. She had promised Ernesto that she would ask for a divorce before Trevor left, but what he said was reasonable. So far her experience of Rome had been like a holiday. She had no idea what it would be like to try to make a life there. She remembered their conversation about how Richard Burton would have to be ripped away from his roots if he were to make a life with Elizabeth Taylor in Hollywood and knew that she had a lot to lose as well. Would she be able to forge a career in Rome? Would their friends take Trevor's side and cut her off? It wasn't a decision she should make in haste.

'I promise,' she said slowly. 'Of course I promise.'

Maybe she was simply being a coward, too scared to let go of her security. Maybe she couldn't bear to hurt Trevor. But she could see no reason to rush headlong towards the divorce courts until she could envisage an alternative future, and so far Ernesto hadn't specified how he saw that working.

She felt immense relief to be given permission to delay the decision, though she dreaded telling Ernesto the next day. He wanted to hear that her marriage was over, not that it was merely on hold. He was going to be very cross.

Chapter Thirty-Eight

Scott was curious to find out who owned the coastal villa Helen had described to him, and his secretary told him that the register of property owners, known as the *Catasto*, would be held in the local council offices of the area – in this case, Anzio. He would be able to request information on the current owners, and perhaps former ones too.

As soon as he had a free morning, Scott rode out to Anzio, taking his camera and the binoculars he'd been given for Christmas. Perhaps he would find a use for them after all. He sat for long hours in a queue at the council offices before being allowed to submit his request for information on the Villa Armonioso. He was told the answer would be ready that afternoon, around five. Immediately afterwards, he headed out of town, past the port and onto the coast road. In fact, the road was some way inland from the sea, separated from it by sand dunes and the occasional building. He stopped to ask directions at an isolated roadside bar and the bartender said there was a turn-off for Villa Armonioso another half a mile further on.

It was exactly as Helen had described. He drove part way down the track past the turn-off but stopped when he saw barbed wire and security guards up ahead. The grounds of the villa were full of palm trees and lush undergrowth, but he could just see the glint of a swimming pool and, beyond the house, the blue of the ocean. When he glanced further along the coast, he could make out an old tower on a headland. This had to be the place where Luigi had brought Helen.

Scott looped back to the main road and hunted for a spot to hide his Vespa. Eventually he found an abandoned shed and slipped it inside, then scrambled over the sand dunes on foot until he reached the shore, about a hundred yards away from the villa. He found a place to sit, just behind a clump of green bushes with tiny yellow flowers on top, and took out his binoculars. Two guards were patrolling the barbed wire fence, and they had a couple of Alsatians on leashes, which was alarming. He'd claim to be a birdwatcher if they spotted the glint of his binoculars and came over, but he would be hard pressed if they asked him which birds he was looking for.

A black car pulled in through the gates and Scott used the binoculars to read the number plate and note it down. That car stayed twenty minutes and, as it left, two more pulled in. They were expensive cars; clearly their owners had money. At one stage there were six cars in the forecourt; the traffic was constant. It was obvious to any bystander that there was something illicit taking place. Why didn't the police keep watch here? If they raided the villa, they would surely find a lucrative haul. He pictured Helen coming there at night with Luigi and the huge risk she had taken amongst those Mafioso types. Her vulnerability was terrifying.

At five o'clock he rode back to the council office and waited in another long queue before being handed a slip of paper stating that the owner of the Villa Armonioso was a company called Costruzioni Torre Astura. He sighed. That was no help at all. He'd been hoping for a name, a person. Now he would have to try to find out who owned this construction company and what it did. Why had he ever thought the trail would be easy to follow? Of course it wouldn't.

Scott spent Easter weekend in his office working on his article about the drugs trade in Rome. He decided to write about Helen but without naming her or giving any details that could identify her: the piece needed an innocent but anonymous victim to demonstrate the evils of the business. He laboured over his description of her drugged to delirium amongst ruthless drug barons: 'like an angel in a school nativity play, but in her veins a poison has taken hold'. He described her in the doctor's surgery: her brittle thinness, the fear in her pretty blue eyes, the way she gripped his hand so tightly it hurt as the doctor administered the injection. He wrote and revised, crossing out unnecessary words and searching for the perfect adjectives in an attempt to convey the pathos of the scene.

On Easter Sunday morning, he got a call from his editor's office in Milwaukee.

'The boss says the *Sunday Times* in London has a front-page story with pictures of Liz and Richard on vacation in Santo Stefano. He wants you to go there.'

'Oh, crap!' Scott swore. 'What time is it for you? Why isn't the boss in bed?'

'It's three in the morning here. He got wind of the piece yesterday and we've been trying to reach you ever since.'

Scott remembered that he had unplugged the phone in his *pensione* a few days earlier after a tearful call from Rosalia. He must have forgotten to plug it back in again.

'Phone's out of order,' he lied. 'I'll see what I can dig up and get back to you later.'

His drugs story would have to wait. Where the heck was Santo Stefano anyway? He called an old college friend in London and asked him to read out the *Sunday Times* article, but it didn't have much information. Liz and Dick had rented a villa under false names and tried to remain incognito, but they'd been spotted sunbathing on some rocks, feeding each other segments of orange, and now every photographer and journalist in Italy and beyond had arrived on the tiny island. There was a large photograph showing her in a bikini and him in bathing trunks. The story read that they were currently under siege, holed up in the villa with press on all sides, calling to try to tempt them out. Scott sighed. He wouldn't get any exclusives by hanging out with a horde of *paparazzi*.

He jumped on his Vespa and sped across town to Gianni's home. Although he was eating Easter Sunday lunch with his family, Gianni immediately agreed to leave for Santo Stefano. Scott went home and plugged in his phone to wait for news but it was the following day before Gianni called to say that Elizabeth Taylor had left the island and was heading back to Rome without Richard. No one knew why. Scott decided to go and wait outside her villa on Via Appia Antica with his own camera, reckoning he might get an exclusive with all the regular *paparazzi* out of town. He parked just along from the entrance gates but saw straight away that he had miscalculated because the place was crawling with photographers. They were perched in the trees, lining the pavements and lounging in cars with their feet up on the steering wheel.

Evening fell and as Scott waited, he chatted to some of the *paparazzi* and was told that Sybil Burton was having dinner with Walter Wanger at the Grand Hotel, where they were having 'crisis talks'. He agreed to buy a picture of them emerging onto the Via Veneto together from another photographer.

At two in the morning, he was about to give up and head home when the gates opened and a car was driven out of the villa. The *paparazzi* began snapping away; Scott peered into the car as it passed and saw a shape on the back seat covered in blankets.

'Is that her? Was she there the whole time? I thought she wasn't back yet.'

'Yes, that's her,' he was assured.

Scott jumped on his Vespa and followed the car through Rome until it pulled up outside a private hospital. He couldn't get through the security gates but saw the figure covered in a blanket being led inside. Was she ill? No one was prepared to issue a statement.

Gianni arrived back in Rome the following day, but none of his contacts could find out why Elizabeth Taylor was in hospital, so Scott decided to call on Helen, to see if he could winkle any information from her.

She opened the door looking bright as a button, nothing like the frail creature he'd been writing about in his drugs story.

'Wow! You look incredible!' he said and she beamed. 'How 'bout that dinner we talked about?'

'Lovely!' She seemed delighted. 'Give me half an hour to get changed.'

Scott waited in a bar across the road until she reappeared in a knee-length polka-dot dress with a large bow at the waist. She had to sit side-saddle on the back of his Vespa as they drove to a nearby *trattoria* because her dress was too tight for her to straddle the bike.

250

'How's it going at Cinecittà?' Scott asked as they drank cocktails and perused the menu. 'Were you shooting today?'

'No. We were supposed to be, but Elizabeth Taylor couldn't make it so I've been sitting around doing nothing. It was deadly dull.'

'Oh dear. Why wasn't she there?' Scott asked. 'Did they tell you?'

'I shouldn't really say . . .'

'Say what?'

'Well . . .' she hesitated, and he knew she was going to tell him. She didn't have the ability to keep a secret. 'So long as you don't tell anyone else . . . Elizabeth and Richard were on holiday at the weekend and they had a big fight and he hit her.'

Scott was surprised. 'Are you sure?'

'Yeah, she's got a black eye. Joe – that's the director – came to talk to her makeup artist about how they're going to cover it. They'll have to wait for the swelling to go down first. Sometimes I think we're going to be stuck making this film forever because it's one delay after another. I was originally hired for ten and a half weeks and it looks as though it could be ten months by the time we finish.'

The waiter came to take their order and Scott asked for a bottle of Chianti. 'Do you get to talk to Elizabeth Taylor much or is her makeup done in a separate place from everyone else's?'

Helen slurped the last of her cocktail. 'It's usually done in her dressing suite, but I've met her loads of times. You wouldn't believe how nice she is. Everyone likes her.'

Scott asked for her opinion of Richard Burton and Helen screwed up her nose. 'I don't think he's a very nice person. First of all, he used to make fun of Elizabeth behind her back. And then when they broke up for a while in February he

251

brought over that other girlfriend, Pat. That wasn't very nice of him, was it?'

'It's not very nice to give her a black eye either,' Scott commented.

Helen shrugged. 'Men are like that sometimes. They like to show who's boss.'

'Hey!' Scott laughed. 'Don't put me in that category. I never hit a girl in my life.'

Helen smiled at him. 'You're an angel. You saved my life. I don't think you have a bad bone in your body.'

Scott felt embarrassed. She might be disillusioned if she found out he was writing about her. He hoped she would never see the story. 'So the vitamin injections have worked, have they?'

Helen beamed. 'That doctor is a miracle worker. I've got my energy back and I feel like myself again, you know? It's strange to remember how different I was on drugs. Instead I'm a vitamin addict now!'

Scott made a mental note to ask the doctor for more information about his miracle cure. If it were that simple, why wasn't every heroin addict prescribed it as a matter of course?

Scott was sitting on a long couchette with his back to the wall while Helen was in a chair opposite, but after they finished eating, she came round to sit beside him.

'You are absolutely the nicest person I've met in Rome, apart from Diana,' she said. 'She's the nicest woman and you're the nicest man.'

She leaned up to kiss him but he turned his head so that she kissed his cheek alongside his mouth.

'Sorry, Helen, but I'm not the right guy for you. I'm not nice enough to girls. Best if you and I are just friends.'

Helen smiled. 'Yeah, I guessed that was the case after you told me about Rosalia. I'm not having much luck with men here. I thought there was someone last week but he hasn't called since. I don't suppose you could fix me up with a friend of yours, could you?' She was staring at him, her pupils huge and black, and she'd never looked lovelier.

'I'll think about it,' Scott promised. 'It would have to be someone pretty special. Leave it with me.'

Chapter Thirty-Nine

Trevor left Rome on the Saturday after Easter and Diana waved him off with genuinely mixed feelings. She would miss his company but she wouldn't miss the discomfort she felt when he put an arm around her shoulders or took her hand, or if their legs accidentally touched in bed. It felt wrong to be touched by any man but Ernesto.

She missed her lover but part of her wished that she had an evening on her own, in order to clear her head, instead of meeting him for dinner later. At the same time the thought of lying in bed with him, skin to skin, and feeling his lips on hers was thrilling. She missed him with a physical ache in her belly and when he arrived at the restaurant, ten minutes late, she leapt from her seat and ran across to throw her arms around him.

Ernesto returned her hug, but when they sat down he seemed cool and distant. Diana chatted about the sightseeing she had done, sharing anecdotes about the city, but when she asked about Ernesto's Easter with his family he was monosyllabic.

'What's the matter?' she asked at last. 'Have I done something to upset you?'

He shrugged. 'You've spent the last ten days sleeping with another man. Why should that matter?'

Diana sighed. 'I swear to you there was no physical contact. He's like an old friend now. He didn't even *try* to make love to me.'

'So when are you getting a divorce? You haven't mentioned this.'

Diana took a deep breath before explaining their agreement that they wouldn't do anything irrevocable until filming had finished. 'You must see that it's not straightforward. For a start, where will I live when I leave Trevor? Where will I work? I can't risk being homeless.'

'So you stay with him for a roof over your head? That makes you a *puttana*.'

She gasped at the cruelty. 'I know your feelings are hurt, but there's no need for insults. You're being unreasonable.'

Their food arrived and she could tell he was trying to snap out of his black mood. 'I can't help it.' He looked at her sadly. 'I love you too much. Forgive me.'

Over the meal, they talked about the film and Ernesto told her about Elizabeth Taylor having a black eye and a badly bruised nose. 'The story is that she hit her face when her car braked suddenly on the way back from Santo Stefano.' He raised his eyebrows. 'But no one believes it for a moment. They say it will be at least three weeks before the bruising goes down enough for filming to resume.'

'Oh God, poor Elizabeth. What's the next disaster going to be? This film is jinxed.'

'The next disaster is that Joe wanted to film the outdoor scenes at Torre Astura this week but the army have a training exercise in the land next to the set and there will be guns firing. We are paying rent and they have built the set but still nothing has been shot there. Walter blames me, of course.'

'That's not your fault. I'm just astonished at the way this film is being created in such a haphazard manner, lurching from crisis to crisis. If they end up with any kind of coherent narrative, it will be a miracle.'

They rode back to her *pensione* after eating, and as they climbed the stairs Ernesto's mood flipped again. 'Have you changed the sheets since he was here?' he demanded.

'Of course I have. I gave them all to the *padrona* this morning. Everything is fresh.'

Ernesto picked up a pillow and sniffed it. 'Did you turn the mattress over?'

She sighed. 'I didn't think that was necessary.'

Instantly, he ripped off the covers and insisted on turning the mattress and remaking the bed. When it was done, he pulled her down onto it and made love to her in a rough, unaffectionate manner. There was no kissing, no stroking, no attempt to make her happy. It was about possession, pure and simple, and she lay there feeling lonely and miserable.

Afterwards, Diana turned to the wall and tears started rolling down her cheeks. She tried to stop them but attempting to suppress the emotion made it worse.

Ernesto tried to placate her. '*Cara mia*, don't cry. I don't mean to be horrible. I'm just a jealous, possessive Italian man and I can't bear the thought of you with anyone else. It eats me up inside.' She was crying harder now and he began stroking her hair. 'I love you, please stop crying.' He rolled her over to kiss her tears. 'I will keep kissing you until you stop crying. I'll kiss every part of you, in places you've never been kissed before, until you beg me for mercy.'

She calmed down at last and when they made love again it was tender and beautiful and she felt better. She lay awake in his arms afterwards thinking about the bewildering twenty-four hours since her promise to Trevor through to her reconciliation with Ernesto. She noted that the latter hadn't made any promises at dinner when she mentioned that she had to consider where she would live if she and Trevor divorced. He hadn't offered to get an apartment with her in Rome, hadn't asked her to marry him when the divorce came through. Even if he did, could she relocate to Italy? She realised she didn't even know if Ernesto wanted children. She assumed he did. All men did. Would he want her to have his children and become an Italian housewife? She couldn't imagine herself in that role. There were a lot of conversations to be had.

The next day, she got back to a pile of work on her desk: requisition notes for extras' costumes for the grand procession scene, and plans for the Alexandria scenes that would be shot at Torre Astura as soon as the army exercises were over. At lunchtime, she went to find Helen but she was nowhere to be seen in the makeup department and no one seemed to know where she was. Diana scribbled a note asking her to get in touch. Perhaps she had been told not to come in since they weren't shooting. The lot was very empty.

On her way back to the production office, Diana saw a car pull up and Elizabeth Taylor stepped out just beside Joe's office. She was wearing huge dark glasses and a leopardskin-patterned coat and looked very small and fragile.

When she spotted Diana, she waved and called 'Hi there!' but didn't come over to chat.

'Hello,' Diana called back, before Elizabeth turned and walked into Joe's office. She had said Diana should stop in after Easter but obviously this wasn't a good time.

'Richard's wife and children are here,' Hilary told her. 'He's spending time with them at their villa. Meanwhile, Elizabeth's parents have flown from LA to stay with her. I think everyone is trying to make the pair of them see sense and put an end to this crazy affair. There are too many people getting hurt.' She looked sternly at Diana, and Diana blushed, wondering if this was also a comment on her own affair.

How was the outwardly stoic Sybil coping? Had she decided to put her foot down and make Richard behave responsibly? How was their handicapped daughter? And what about Elizabeth's children and the newly adopted baby Maria? At least in Diana's own situation there were only three people being hurt: Trevor, Ernesto and herself. The Burton–Taylor romance was much more complex.

Diana wondered if Elizabeth felt guilty about the harm she had caused. To everyone on set, she seemed to be the one doing the chasing. She was forever running to Richard's dressing room and hovering on the sidelines while his scenes were shot. She had decided she wanted him and wouldn't take no for an answer – at least, that was the perception in Cinecittà.

When Diana went to the bar to pick up a sandwich and a coffee, she eavesdropped on an animated conversation between a group of American camera crew and realised they were running a sweepstake. Would Richard leave Sybil for Elizabeth? The odds they were taking were three to one against.

Chapter Forty

Scott had been keeping the packet of cocaine he'd bought from Luigi on the dressing table in the room where he lodged, hoping to try it next time he got lucky and had a girl back to stay. However, he was startled one day when he returned home to find that the *padrona* had come in and tidied up and his paperfold was stacked neatly in a pile with some matchbooks. Had she been at all streetwise she would have recognised what it was and called the *carabinieri*. Perhaps he should throw it away rather than risk a criminal conviction in a foreign country? But it seemed like evidence of a sort, so he decided to take it to his office and hide it somewhere. That way, if anyone found it, he could blame it on his predecessor.

When his secretary went out for lunch, he searched the office for a secure hiding place. First he checked for loose floorboards that he could slide the packet underneath. That was what they did in the movies, wasn't it? He couldn't find any, though. He checked behind the filing cabinets for an odd surface that might form a little shelf but there was nothing. The walls were covered in wood panelling and he ran his fingers along it. He noticed that there was an odd piece of panelling by the window shutters that protruded a few inches, as if some part of the shutter mechanism folded into it. He closed then opened them but could see no reason for the panelling to be deeper there. He slipped his fingers underneath and pulled outwards, but it wouldn't move. Then he tried pulling sideways, towards the window, and still it didn't move. It was only when he pushed upwards that the panel slid, stiffly, and behind it he saw a cubbyhole about a foot tall and six inches wide. Inside there were several sheaves of paper, stacked neatly and separated by paper clips.

Scott pulled out the papers and glanced at the scrawled writing that covered them. Straight away he recognised Gregg's shorthand, the system he had learned, which wasn't used in Europe. That implied the writer of these papers was American. He sat on the edge of his desk and slowly read the top page, making out the name of a prominent government minister. The author said that on the 12th of January 1960 he had accepted a bribe of four million *lire* to draft a bill concerning some technicality to do with ships that collect cargo from Italian ports without coming into port themselves. Scott scanned the page but couldn't make out who was alleged to have made the bribe in question. Behind it there was a customs document covered in tiny print. He flicked through more pages and on top of one sheaf of papers he made out the name Ghianciamina. It was something to do with a meeting with a government official.

Suddenly he became concerned that his secretary could return at any time. He thrust the sheaf of paper with the name Ghianciamina into his inside jacket pocket and stacked the rest back in the cubbyhole, along with the cocaine, before sliding the wood panel into place. It moved smoothly and Scott wondered who was responsible for the clever piece of carpentry. There was only one explanation he could think of: the dates on the papers were around 1960, so they must have been left by the previous Rome correspondent, Bradley Wyndham.

All afternoon, Scott sat at his desk, listening to the *click-click-ping* of his secretary's typing across the room, and worrying about the documents in his pocket. He didn't dare take them out to read them but imagined they must be incriminating; otherwise, why the special hiding place? What if he fell off his Vespa or got mugged and they were found in his pocket? He could be in serious trouble.

Suddenly it seemed imperative that he track down Bradley Wyndham and ask about his research. As soon as it was morning in the Midwest, he called his editor and asked if he could have a forwarding address for Bradley, saying he had found something of his in the office and would like to return it.

'He never gave a forwarding address,' the editor told him. 'I was furious. He called on a Friday to say he was leaving, asked me to pay his last month's salary into a Swiss bank account, and when I rang on the Monday he'd gone. We've never heard from him since. It was pretty unprofessional and if he'd asked for a reference I'd have given him his head on a platter.'

Scott's stomach clenched. It sounded as though Bradley had upset someone in Rome and been forced to leave in a hurry. What other explanation could there be?

He looked at his secretary, a grey-haired spinster in her fifties who had also worked for Bradley. Might she know anything, he wondered.

She shook her head. 'He didn't even say goodbye. I came in to work on the Monday as usual and he didn't appear. I never saw him again.'

Scott tapped his finger on the desk. 'Can you think of any way I could get in touch with him?'

She thought for a moment, then flicked through a Rolodex card file on her desk until she came to 'W'. 'I'm sure I used to have his brother's address. Bradley asked me to ship some Christmas presents to him and he wrote the address on a piece of paper so I filed it afterwards. Here it is. He's in Ohio.'

Scott walked over to have a look. 'You've got the phone number as well,' he said, pleased.

'Yes, they needed it for customs.'

'I think I'll give him a call later.'

He waited until his secretary had left for the evening, then he rang the operator and asked to be connected. When a man answered, Scott said, 'I'm calling from Rome, trying to get in touch with Bradley Wyndham. I took over his job here.'

'I don't know anyone called Bradley Wyndham,' the voice said. 'You must have the wrong number.' The line went dead abruptly.

Scott thought about this for a moment. Why the abrupt hang-up? If the person on the end of the line genuinely didn't know anything, wouldn't they have asked more questions to make sure it wasn't a case of a misheard name? He rang back and as soon as the call connected, he said quickly: 'Tell Bradley I've found his papers and I want to meet.'

The line went dead.

Chapter Forty-One

On the 8th of May, the procession scene was being filmed at Cinecittà. Seven thousand extras had to pretend they were watching dancing girls and snake-charmers coming through the Temple of Venus, for a scene that would precede the arrival of Cleopatra and her son on a sphinx. When Diana arrived at the studio, she could hear a sound like the buzzing of a gigantic beehive as the extras flocked into the back lot through a separate entrance and made their way to massive warehouses to be kitted out with costumes, hair and makeup. Some interlopers clustered in a timid group outside Elizabeth Taylor's dressing-room suite, unaware that she wouldn't be in that day. Her black eye still hadn't faded.

Ernesto was sitting on Diana's desk chatting to her when Hilary came into the production office, looking harassed.

'The gate man hasn't been doing a proper check on passes so loads of unauthorised people are getting in and it's driving me crazy. The place is full of strangers gawping and getting in the way!' She flopped down at her desk and pulled out a cigarette. Ernesto leapt across to light it for her.

'Can we help?' Diana asked.

'Actually . . .' Hilary inhaled hard and screwed her eyes against the smoke. 'I don't suppose you two could get into costume and mingle in the crowd, to watch out for anachronisms, like newspapers or wrist watches?'

Diana looked at Ernesto and he shrugged. 'Why not? When the film comes out, maybe we will spot ourselves on the big screen.'

'We haven't been fitted for costumes, though,' Diana said.

'They're bound to have some spares your size.' Hilary glanced at them both. 'Better hurry though. We start shooting at one.'

Diana giggled as they ran to the costume department. How funny that she was actually going to appear in the film she'd been working on for the last seven months and Ernesto had been involved in for over a year. Of course, she knew it was unlikely she would ever be able to pick herself out of the crowd in the finished picture, but she was tickled to think of the possibility.

There were loads of unclaimed costumes so she picked an authentic-looking tunic and an imitation pearl necklace, pulled them on, then went to the makeup area to join a queue. There was a strong scent of singed hair as tongs were used to create curls, which were considered more 'Roman' than straight hair. When it was Diana's turn, one of the girls wiped her face with an orange cream, giving her a hasty tan. 'The hair's fine. You'll do,' she said, glancing in consternation at the queue stretching behind her.

She had arranged to meet Ernesto in the bar by the sound stages, and he was already standing there in a centurion's short tunic and helmet. Strangely, it suited him. He had classic Roman bone structure with a sharp nose, and well-muscled legs, just as a centurion would have done.

He laughed when he saw her: 'Your arms don't match your face. It's as if you've been bleached from the neck down.'

'I'd better keep my arms out of shot in that case. Let's go and see what we can do.'

Ernesto offered her a gulp of his beer but when she refused, he drained it and followed her to the back lot. Diana had heard stories of bottom pinching and men pressing themselves against scantily clad girls in the crowd at the rehearsals, but there was none of that in evidence. People stood with serious expressions, watching Joe Mankiewicz where he crouched on a platform in deep discussion with one of the cameramen.

Diana and Ernesto set to work, making their way through the crowd asking people to remove watches and jewellery. One girl was sporting a modern beehive hairstyle and Diana sent her back to get a wig. One o'clock came and went and no instructions were issued. The heat was sweltering and Diana could feel the heavy makeup starting to melt on her face. She wondered how Elizabeth could bear to wear her makeup and wigs for hours on end. What with the elaborate costumes and the stifling atmosphere of the sound stages, she must be very uncomfortable.

At last Joe spoke through a loudspeaker, announcing that filming was about to start. He wanted the extras to look amazed by the sights they were witnessing and remember that these were things they would never have seen before. Cues would be given on signs. That was the only acting required of them. Diana heard the familiar commands of 'Quiet on set, going for a take, roll sound, roll camera . . . And action!'

'Cut!' came the order over the loudspeaker, almost straight away. Joe spoke to someone beside him who leapt down from the raised platform and came running over towards the crowd.

Diana followed him with her eyes. What had gone wrong? Standing on tiptoe, she saw the problem: a stout man with a cool-box strapped to his chest. In the vicinity, several extras were hastily gobbling ice creams. They were allowed to have refreshments between takes but shouldn't be seen on film, of course.

'That's the spirit,' Ernesto chuckled. 'We Romans never miss a business opportunity!'

'Incredible!' She shook her head as she watched the offender being led off to the side. It didn't matter so long as he didn't try to sell ice cream while the cameras were rolling.

'Italians invented ice cream, you know,' Ernesto claimed.

'No, they didn't. There are records of something similar in China in 3000 BC, and it's likely the idea was brought to Italy by Marco Polo.' She stopped, realising how pedantic she sounded, but Ernesto just laughed and rubbed her shoulders.

'My little brainbox,' he whispered adoringly.

Finally, filming started again, and the crowd roared and cooed and aahed, as they were instructed, craning their necks to watch the imaginary procession that had already been filmed. It felt like a real celebration, a proud moment for all involved, something they could tell their children in future. Diana and Ernesto cheered along with the rest of the crowd, and hugged and kissed each other openly. She felt so happy. Life at Cinecittà was exciting, she had a wonderful lover and the sun was shining.

There were several retakes but no one complained, despite the intense heat. They wanted the moment to last as long as possible. There was even a disappointed groan when Joe called out in Italian to thank them for their involvement and ask them to take their costumes back to wardrobe.

The women's changing area was heaving with people so Diana grabbed her summer dress from the corner where she'd left it and made her way towards the production office to change and wash off her makeup. She waved at several people along the way and stopped in the bar to pick up an iced lemonade. Just as she passed the main gates of the studio, a young Italian woman stepped into her path, screeching in anger and gesticulating wildly. At first Diana got the impression she had lost her child, but the woman was pointing and screaming '*Sei tu!*' which didn't make sense. How could it be Diana's fault?

'*Hai rubato mio marito. Hai rubato il padre dei miei quattro figli.*'

Her words were hysterical and hard to distinguish. Diana looked around for someone to help her make sense of what the woman was saying, but there were no Italian speakers in sight. Frustrated, the woman opened her bag, fumbled around and pulled out a photograph, which she handed to Diana. It showed Ernesto with a baby in his arms and three small children grouped round him. A little girl was sitting on his knee. Could this be his sister's kids? Diana tried to remember which one he'd said had children.

'Are you his sister?' she asked in Italian.

'No, I'm his wife. These are his children. And you are a whore.'

Diana felt as though she was going to faint. '*Ma lui non è sposato*' – 'But he's not married.'

The woman held out her hand to show a wedding ring. 'Ten years we are married,' she insisted. 'Ten years. But since January this year my children have hardly seen their papa because he is staying with his English whore.' She spat on the ground in disgust.

267

Diana looked at the photo again, trying to think of some reason why the woman would say all this if it weren't true. She couldn't come up with one. But Ernesto had been planning to introduce her to his mother. How could he have done that if he were married? The answer came to her: he would never have gone through with it. He was all talk. What about the girlfriend who broke his heart? Had she even existed? Was anything he'd ever told her true?

His wife was sobbing now.

'I'm so sorry,' Diana told her. 'I had no idea he was married.'

Still the woman was crying and Diana didn't know what to do. It wasn't her place to offer comfort to this stranger. 'I will stop seeing him straight away. I'm sorry.' She handed back the photograph.

'*Puttana inglese!*' the woman cried. '*Sgualdrina!*'

She placed the photograph back in her bag and walked slowly out the gates of the studio, still crying. Diana watched as she made her way across the road to the bus stop, feeling so shocked that for several minutes she couldn't move.

Once at the stop, the woman turned to glare back through the gates, and it was only then that Diana found the strength to continue towards the production office.

Chapter Forty-Two

Diana changed quickly, removed her wig and called for a studio driver to take her back to her *pensione*. She was still wearing her heavy pancake makeup and eyeliner and the driver tried to joke with her about it but she was lost in her own thoughts.

I'm such a fool. Why didn't I guess? How could he?

It didn't occur to her to question the woman's story. Her distress had been genuine and that photograph was proof. She must have grabbed the opportunity to sneak onto the set when so many strangers were there for the procession scene. It was the only way she could catch her husband red-handed with his mistress – *her!* How could she have been so wrong about Ernesto? Was she such a bad judge of character? More to the point, what was she going to say when he arrived at her *pensione* later?

She had a bath to wash off the grime of the day and lay on her bed, staring at the ceiling as the fierce heat of the sun subsided. Her cheeks and arms were tight with sunburn. A faint breeze blew her curtain inwards. She decided she couldn't face a long, drawn-out argument with Ernesto. She would simply tell him it was over and ask him to pack his things and leave. She didn't want to hear dozens of excuses. What was it errant men always said in the movies? 'My wife doesn't understand me.' Well, maybe she didn't, but he'd had children with her and that changed everything as far as Diana was concerned.

Ernesto didn't attempt to deny that he was married and a father, but he had a million excuses for his behaviour. 'I couldn't help falling in love with you, Diana. During that trip to Ischia, I knew you were the person I should spend my life with. I got married too young and we have nothing in common. My wife is uneducated, simple, but you – you are a genius.'

'You lied to me, and you've gone on lying and lying.'

Ernesto looked pained. 'I had no choice. I hated lying to you but if I'd told you I was married you wouldn't have been with me. I wanted you to love me. I need you, *cara mia.*'

Diana clutched her head in her hands, wanting to scream. 'You could never have married me. Divorce isn't legal in Italy, yet you tried to make me divorce my husband. Why would you do that?'

'I didn't want to share you. The thought that this man slept in our bed makes me crazy. Diana, we can still be together. I will leave my wife and we will get an apartment. I want to wake up beside you every morning for the rest of my life.' He reached out to touch her cheek and she flinched.

'Absolutely not. I can't believe you've turned out to be such a louse. I want you to collect your things and get out, and I don't want you anywhere near me from now on.'

'Don't decide so quickly. Take a few days to think it over. Please don't break my heart.'

He sounded very upset, but she noticed there was no remorse for what he had done. For Diana it was a black and white decision. 'There's nothing to think about, Ernesto. Go back to your wife and children. Tell her I'm sorry. And stay away from me.'

He began to fold his shirts and trousers and Diana watched, willing him to hurry. It was unbelievable that just a few hours earlier they had been kissing on the film set, delighted in each other's company, perfectly happy in the moment. How naïve she had been.

'Can I have one last kiss?' Ernesto asked, his brown eyes sad, and her traitorous body yearned to press against his and feel his lips one last time, but she was too angry.

'Just get out!' she ordered, and with a reproachful backwards glance, he did.

Diana poured herself a glass of water then sat on her balcony watching as the light faded and the evening traffic hit the streets. She felt old, cynical and exhausted.

What's the big deal? I've simply had an affair. All over Cinecittà, men and women were having affairs. That's what happened on film sets. Most of them went back to the lives they'd had before and forgot all about it. That's probably what would happen with Elizabeth and Richard, if word on the set was to be believed. But to her, it *was* a big deal – a huge deal. She felt dirty and used. She was horrified at the suffering she had inadvertently caused to Ernesto's wife. And she felt sheer rage with him for the damage he had done, both to her and to Trevor. She didn't cry – couldn't cry – but she sat on her balcony long after darkness fell, watching the lights of the city and listening to the drone of Vespas speeding their drivers to bars and nightspots. Her love affair was over and life went on.

Next morning, when she reached the production office, she asked Hilary if she might have a private word and explained

271

to her what had transpired the previous evening. Hilary immediately threw her arms round her.

'Hell's teeth, you poor old stick! I worried that he might be married but you seemed so sure . . . I'm so sorry. The truth is that you can't trust any Italian men and that's been the case since Cleopatra's day.' She pulled back, patting Diana on the shoulder.

'I'm OK. I just feel such a fool. Do you think anyone knew, apart from you?'

'Goodness, don't concern yourself about that. If anyone knows, they'll blame him, not you.' She frowned. 'However, it does present one problem because I suppose you won't want him to accompany you to Torre Astura. I've just had word we're allowed on the set tomorrow and I was going to ask you two to check it out.'

Diana was alarmed. 'Can't I go on my own? Ernesto didn't do anything in Ischia except drive me around. My Italian is fluent enough. If you send me with a driver and tell me who to talk to, I'll be fine by myself.'

'Yes, that's the best plan. I'll tell Walter what we're doing.'

'You won't tell him why, will you?'

Hilary patted her hand. 'No one will hear about it from me. Not one word.'

'I'll go down first thing tomorrow morning. It will do me good to get away.'

'Take an overnight bag and stay a couple of days. The sea air might help to clear your head.'

'I think I will. Thanks.'

They walked together to the script meeting, then back to the office. All the time Diana felt nervous that Ernesto would appear; she didn't feel strong enough for a confrontation. But fortunately there was no sign of him. At lunchtime she made her way to the makeup department to look for Helen and found her organising lipsticks in a gold-coloured box.

'You hungry?' she asked.

'No, but I'll keep you company.' She looked tired and pale.

'You must be worn out after yesterday. How many people did you make up?'

'We weren't allowed to make up the extras. Union rules or something. But I hear it was crazy over there. We've run out of Max Factor pancake foundation, and they've sent off for more. There's not much I can do till that arrives.'

Diana bought a sandwich of mortadella sausage and got them two Cokes, then sat down with Helen at their usual table. 'So what's been happening to you?' she asked. 'Seems like ages since we caught up.'

'Well . . .' Helen gave a sly smile. 'I know I'm always saying this and it never comes to anything, but there's someone I'm keen on. A man.'

'Oh yes? Anyone I know?'

'Actually . . .' There was a pause before she announced with a wide smile, 'It's Ernesto, that guy who works as a fixer. Don't you think he's lovely?'

Diana stared at her, utterly aghast. Had Helen really never got wind of their affair? How peculiar that she should pick this very day to announce him as her new crush. 'I've got bad news for you,' she said. 'He's married with four children.'

Helen gave a dismissive gesture. 'Everyone's married here. It doesn't make any difference, does it? I could still have a fling with him. We're only here once. You keep saying it's a once-in-a-lifetime experience and we should make the most of it . . .'

Her words tailed off as she noticed the expression of horror on Diana's face.

'I can't believe you would do that to his wife! It's immoral.' She felt sick to her stomach and pushed the sandwich across the table. 'You're the one who was so disapproving about Elizabeth and Richard.'

Helen tried to justify herself. 'He came on to me, you know. It's not as if I chased him or anything. You know how hard it's been for me to find a boyfriend even though everyone else has one and I just thought it was my turn to have a bit of fun.'

Diana spoke slowly. '*When* did he come on to you, Helen?'

She thought back. 'The first time was over Easter. You were off with Trevor so I didn't have a chance to tell you about it. Then he arrived at the club where we went dancing last night and was lovely to me.' Suddenly she burst into tears. 'I'm sorry you don't approve, but it's alright for you with your cosy marriage and your PhD and everything in your life being perfect. I'd like to get married too one day.'

Diana felt herself losing her temper, as if she was standing on the edge of a cliff as the grass gave way beneath her feet. 'If you want to get married, you should try going out with single men. Stay away from Ernesto!'

'But I like him,' she whined through her tears.

'You stupid, thoughtless girl!' Diana was shouting now, vaguely aware that other customers in the bar had stopped to listen. 'Does it mean nothing to you that people will get hurt because of your actions? Is it all a game? Is it just sex you're after? I'm sure there are plenty of men here who would give you just sex, if that's the kind of girl you are.' She was being cruel now, and reined herself in. 'Look, I'm sorry but please don't go out with Ernesto. I've met his wife and she's a decent woman. She doesn't deserve this.'

Helen laid her head on her arms and sobbed. Diana stood up and scraped her chair back. She should comfort her. It wasn't Helen she was angry with, but Ernesto. He must have gone straight out on the prowl after leaving her room the previous evening. And he knew Helen was a friend of hers, so why did he target her? The suspicion entered her head that he was trying to hurt her as revenge for ending the affair.

She considered again whether she should comfort Helen but she didn't have the patience. She was too cross. Besides, she wanted Helen to take her seriously and stay away from Ernesto, so she picked up her bag and walked out of the bar without another word. The other customers watched her go.

All afternoon, Diana felt bad about their falling out. Helen was an innocent and would have been childishly delighted when Ernesto made a play for her. He was the villain. Diana hoped he hadn't taken advantage of her already. Surely he didn't work quite so fast? She frowned. Of course, Helen had mentioned something about Easter as well. If he had targeted her back then, he really was a louse.

The argument preyed on her mind so at five o'clock she went to the makeup department to apologise but the Italian women there told her that Helen had left earlier. Diana hurried towards the main gate to ask the guard on the gate if a car had picked her up yet. If not, she'd invite Helen for dinner that evening so they could talk it through. She should confess about her own affair with Ernesto so that Helen understood why she had snapped.

'*Sta in quel bar di là,*' the guard told her, pointing to a seedy-looking place down the street.

Diana walked down the dusty main road, past a lone *paparazzo* and some waste ground where a few goats were grazing, and when she reached the bar she saw Helen sitting inside with the Italian man called Luigi. Diana hesitated. She had never liked the look of him and decided not to interrupt them. She'd explain everything to Helen on her return from Torre Astura. They could make things up then.

Chapter Forty-Three

Every evening, Scott replaced one batch of papers in the office cubbyhole and took out another. The author had done his homework and the picture that was emerging was disturbing. The papers explained that in 1955 two Sicilian Mafia bosses, Gaetano Galatolo and Nicola D'Alessandro, were killed in a dispute over protection rackets, and since then the balance of power in what was known as 'Cosa Nostra' had been shifting towards Michele Cavataio, a much-feared gangster nicknamed the Cobra. They said that Rome was the centre of European heroin trafficking, with opium arriving from North Africa or the Middle East and being processed in labs around Italy then smuggled out to the US or the rest of Europe. Cavataio had multiple contacts in Rome where he bought the allegiance of government ministers, judges and anyone else he needed. There were different levels of people working for him, and Don Ghianciamina was near the top. There was a photograph of him, corpulent and silver-haired, with half-moon glasses on his nose.

Scott got excited. This was the first document that would help him to tie the Ghianciaminas into his drugs exposé. So far all he had was a young girl who had dabbled in heroin, a man who drove drugs up from the south of Italy and left them in a garage, and a dealer who worked in the bars and clubs round the Via Veneto. If he could implicate someone higher up the chain and round out his piece with this extra information that had dropped into his lap, then it could be genuinely good journalism. This could be the Pulitzer Prize-winning piece his father wanted him to write – and it could cause trouble for the Ghianciaminas as well, so Scott would have his revenge.

Suddenly he wondered whether Don Ghianciamina or his son Alessandro had been amongst the men Helen had met at the villa on the coast. From the fancy cars he spotted there, it appeared to be the top people who came and went. It would be wonderful if she could identify them.

At seven o'clock, the hour when many Romans went home after work before heading out for the evening, Scott decided to drive to Helen's place. The *padrona* wasn't sitting in the courtyard and he wasn't sure which room was Helen's, so Scott knocked on the first door. It was opened by an Italian woman with a baby on her hip.

'*Sí?*'

'*Una ragazza inglese. Con i capelli biondi. Dove abita?*' Scott asked.

The woman stepped outside and pointed to an apartment on the next floor and two doors along.

'*Grazie.*'

'*Prego.*' She remained outside and watched as he ascended.

He knocked on the door and waited. He could hear movement inside but there was no reply so he knocked again and at last Helen opened the door a crack. She held up a hand to shield her face from the light but he could see she had been crying.

'Are you alright? What's happened?'

'Nothing. I'm OK.' She was breathing in huge gasps and seemed extremely distressed.

'You don't look OK. Why don't I buy you a drink and you can tell me about it?'

She blew her nose noisily into a crumpled handkerchief. 'You can't help. Forget about it.'

Scott held out his arm, wanting to give her a hug, but she pulled away. 'Why not dinner? Maybe I could cheer you up. I'll tell you my best jokes.'

'I can't. Why are you even asking me? You don't fancy me and I don't want your pity.' Tears were rolling steadily down her cheeks.

'I've never pitied you!' he protested. 'I like you. We're friends. I'd like to spend the evening with you.'

'I'm sorry, I have to go now.' She tried to shut the door but he stuck out his hand to stop her.

'Helen, this isn't anything to do with drugs, is it? You haven't started taking them again, have you?'

She began to cry even harder. 'I had no choice. I couldn't afford any more of those vitamin shots and I feel awful when I don't have them. There's nothing else I can do if I want to keep my job.' Her words were almost incoherent.

'But I thought you were only going to need one or two vitamin shots. Why did you keep going back? They cost a fortune!'

'I needed them. I suppose I'm weak, but I couldn't manage without them – and now I can't afford them any more.'

'That's crazy! We'll go back to the doctor and make him help you. Or we'll find another doctor. Don't give up, Helen. I'm on your side. I promise we'll solve this. Why don't you let me come in?'

She grabbed the door in panic. 'No, you can't. It's not a good time. Please go, Scott. I can't come out with you and that's all there is to it.'

She tried to close the door again but still Scott held on. He couldn't leave her like this. Besides, she might be his only way of linking the Ghianciaminas to his drugs story and he had to persuade her to cooperate. He improvised as he went along.

'Listen, I'm going to tell you the truth, Helen, but you'll have to keep this to yourself. I actually work for the CIA. We're trying to crack down on the drug shipments coming back to the US by catching the big dealers and I really need you to look at a couple of pictures and tell me if you saw any of these people at the Villa Armonioso.'

She stopped crying and stared at him wide-eyed. 'Are you really in the CIA? Do you have a badge?'

'I didn't bring it with me because I'm working undercover. This is very important. You could be saving a lot of other young people from going through what you have. You could even save their lives.'

Would she really be gullible enough to buy it? She stared at him, making up her mind. 'You told me you were a writer.'

'Yeah, that's my cover story. It's a mark of how much I trust you that I'm telling you now. Please will you look at the pictures for me?'

'I was pretty stoned so I'm not sure how much I remember. They were old, you know. Like, forty or something.'

'Does this face seem familiar?' He handed over the newspaper photo of Don Ghianciamina.

She stared at it, then shook her head. 'No, I don't think there was anyone *that* old.'

Scott took it back and handed her his snap of Alessandro.

280

She peered at it for a while. 'Yes, he might have been there. I'm not positive, but I remember thinking he had lizard eyes.'

'He does. You're right. That really helps.'

She sniffed hard, as if she might start crying again.

'Do you want me to take you back to the vitamin doctor for another shot? I'll pay.'

'No, I'd rather go on my own.'

Scott took out his wallet and peeled off some notes. 'You sure? This is enough for one more, just to keep you going, but I'm going to talk to that doctor and find out why you aren't better yet. I'm sure there's something else we can try. Don't give up hope, will you?'

She hung her head.

He put his fingers under her chin and lifted it gently. 'I'm not going to leave until you convince me you're OK.'

She nodded very slightly. 'Yes, I'm fine.'

Scott kissed her cheek and let her close the door but he stood there a few moments longer. It felt wrong to leave her in that state but he didn't know what else to do. He wished he had met her friend Diana. Maybe she would talk more readily to another girl.

At last he turned and walked slowly down the stairs again. The woman with the baby gave him an indignant look, as if it were he who had made Helen cry.

Chapter Forty-Four

During the drive to Torre Astura, Diana opened the car window and let the hot, dusty breeze blow over her, not caring about the mess it made of her hair. It didn't matter what she looked like any more. There was no one to care. In her head, she kept rerunning all the lies Ernesto had told her: his mother's shingles, the stories about his sister's children (she now assumed he had been talking about his own) . . . and the biggest lie of all – that he loved her. She realised she hadn't known him. She'd seen him as one person whereas he was someone else entirely, someone she couldn't fathom. Why would you try to break up a person's marriage when you had no intention of marrying them yourself? To her, it made no sense. She supposed that it meant she hadn't truly loved him. She had been in love with a fantasy, an invention that didn't exist.

The journey took an hour and a half, through fields and across rivers, until eventually they pulled up at some gates set in a fenced-off area. She showed her studio pass to a security guard and was driven into the lot.

Straight away, Diana saw the Alexandria set along the waterfront and she caught her breath. It was so much better than the one she'd seen at Pinewood the previous year, with the turquoise Mediterranean forming a backdrop and white sun bleaching the imitation buildings. The Serapeum was magnificent, with several flights of wide steps leading up to the colonnaded frontage. Hawk-headed sphinxes sat on pedestals and giant sculptures of Cleopatra II and Cleopatra III greeted boats that moored at the C-shaped jetty. To the side was the black pyramid of Cleopatra's mausoleum, still under construction. It wasn't bad at all. In fact, it was rather good.

Leaving her overnight bag in the car, she walked down to the jetty, where carpenters were at work on a Roman battleship. The rigging of the sails, the eyelets through which oars protruded, the curved helm – all seemed to follow the advice she had given. There were a few issues to correct: the moorings to which it was tied were wrong, and some of the little craft anchored in the water, which would have transported goods to shore, were too modern-looking. Some fishing pots sitting on the jetty were Greek in style rather than Egyptian but that was plausible. She sat on the edge of the jetty, dangling her feet over the water, and took out her notebook.

Soon after she arrived, at one o'clock, the carpenters abandoned their tools and headed for lunch but Diana stayed where she was, glad for the opportunity to lose herself in work. When she had finished making notes on the jetty, she walked up to the Serapeum. Of course, it was only a frontage with scaffolding behind, but it was majestic – as it should be. Contemporaries had described it as the most magnificent building in the world. The real one had been destroyed in AD 391 by a Christian mob but enough records remained to make historians fairly sure about the scale, the design and the decoration of the temple to the god Serapis, which had been built in 300 BC.

Next she examined the black marble-effect pyramid representing Cleopatra's mausoleum, in which she would take her own life. According to Plutarch, Mark Antony was hoisted up to it in chains as he lay dying because the great front door could not be opened once it had been sealed. The pyramid was at least two storeys tall and the roof was unfinished because Cleopatra had ordered it to be built in a hurry, but it would have been a huge, impregnable structure that Octavian's armies could not easily breach so the flimsy film version was unconvincing – but she hoped it would look fine on screen.

Her head began to ache from the heat and she felt mildly sick. She hadn't eaten breakfast; perhaps she should find out where the men were having their lunch. She would no doubt feel better after some food and a bit of shade from the ferocity of the sun.

The studio car had gone but the driver had left her bag in the security guard's hut at the entrance. He directed her to a *pensione* just up the road where a room had been reserved for her – room number eleven, he told her, consulting a list. A *trattoria* situated round the bend in the other direction would be serving lunch until three. She checked her watch and decided to go for lunch first. The menu offered a full range of pasta, fish and meat dishes but a bowl of minestrone soup and a bread roll were all she could manage. Her stomach was taut with nerves and she felt like an invalid, as if she had been beaten up or run over by a lorry. She decided to treat herself gently for the time being, until her emotions settled down and she could come to terms with Ernesto's huge betrayal.

Throughout the summer months, when midday temperatures soared into the 80s, Italian workmen took a break from one till four o'clock. Diana wanted to discuss her notes with the chief carpenter but she knew no one would be back on the set till later. She was hot and sticky from the journey and considered going to the *pensione* to bathe, but then changed her mind: she was by the seaside, so she might as well go for a swim. There was a swimsuit and towel in her bag so she went back to fetch them from the gatehouse then walked down to the seafront to search for a quiet spot.

She could see the army camp in one direction, so she walked the other way, past the back of the set, and stepped over a waist-high fence into no-man's land. Waves were lapping onto a shingly beach of yellow-gold stones. She walked for some time until she couldn't see anyone in either direction, and a large rock offered some shade from the sun. Under cover of her sundress, she slipped off her underpants and pulled on the striped swimsuit, a recent purchase from Rinascente. She'd considered getting a bikini but hadn't felt brave enough to expose her midriff. With a struggle she managed to unclasp her brassiere and pull up the top half of the suit, keeping her dress loosely fastened over her shoulders. She was pretty sure no one was watching, but didn't want to take any risks.

The water was shallow and warm by the shore, but ten feet out there was a deep trench beyond which it became cooler. She swam for a while, watching a shoal of tiny silver fish gliding below her, then she turned on her back to float. Out there in the water, her emotions felt more manageable. She'd made a mistake in falling for Ernesto – what a fool she had been to trust him – but it wasn't the end of the world. It would have been better if it hadn't happened, but it had, and now she would have to readjust to the sudden change in circumstances. It was hard to see how her marriage could survive but fortunately she had time to consider it rationally, with her mind unclouded by thoughts of Ernesto. Poor Trevor. It was difficult to imagine them ever making love again. If she went back to him, should she confess her infidelity? He would be so hurt. But it seemed unfair to keep it from him.

Her thoughts turned to Helen and the argument they'd had: poor, childish Helen, who believed at last a man was interested in her. How rotten that it should turn out to be a married man. She desperately needed to find someone who could see the beauty and innocence of her soul, who would fall in love with her and give her confidence in herself. Diana resolved that she would spend a lot more time with Helen now she was on her own. If they went out together in the evenings, she could make sure Helen didn't drink too much and vet any potential suitors. Perhaps she would help her to find a nice boyfriend before filming was over.

She swam back to the shore and lay on her towel to dry off, feeling the salt itchy on her skin. She was going to be very sunburned later but she was pretty sure she'd brought some calamine lotion in her toilet bag. The shingle was hard beneath her spine but she nodded off and woke some time later, disorientated from a muddled dream. The sun had moved across the sky and when she checked her watch she was shocked to see that it was six o'clock. The carpenters would be going home soon if they hadn't left already. She'd have to speak to them in the morning. Meanwhile, she'd go to the *pensione* and freshen up.

The coast bulged outwards at that point and she sensed it would be quicker to walk across a field towards the main road behind her rather than go back the way she had come through the film set. She pulled her dress over her swimsuit and set off in that direction. Halfway across the field, she saw a rapid movement out of the corner of her eye and suddenly panicked that there might be snakes. She wasn't sure if there were poisonous snakes in Italy but, if there were, this kind of waste ground covered in scrub would be exactly where they were likely to be found. She walked faster, stamping hard on the earth to scare them away.

The field was divided from the road by a thicket of wispy bushes. She sought a place where there was a natural gap and pushed through, but a sharp branch sprang back across her cheek, scratching it.

'Drat!' she exclaimed, and touched the wound. The salt made it sting, and when she pulled her fingers away there were traces of blood. That wasn't going to look very attractive.

She collected her bag from the security guard then walked up to the *pensione*.

'Room number eleven?' she asked the *padrona*, but was told that number eleven hadn't been cleaned or prepared.

'You can have number two instead. It's a better room,' the woman said. 'Round the back, with its own patio and a view to the seafront.'

It may have been better than the rest but to Diana's eyes it seemed very basic. The actors and actresses, production, hair and makeup staff wouldn't stay here when they were shooting the Alexandria scenes but would be bussed down from Rome every morning and taken back each evening. These rooms were just for the men building the set and the place was very run-down, with mould growing on the bathroom ceiling and mattresses that had barely any spring to them. Still, it would do for one night.

Diana bathed to wash the salt from her skin, trying not to think about what might have caused the brown stains on the bath enamel, then she went to sit on the patio to dry her hair. The sun had almost set but she could still make out the hazy shape of the Serapeum and the sea behind. Her stomach growled but she decided she couldn't be bothered to walk back down the road to the *trattoria* for dinner. She would feel self-conscious sitting on her own among the evening diners. She'd rather wait and pick up a *cornetto* with a coffee on her way to the set at breakfast time.

As soon as her hair was dry enough, she climbed onto the bed, pulled a sheet over her and fell sound asleep.

Chapter Forty-Five

A telegram arrived at the office for Scott: '*Re. recent find, if you want to talk come to Geneva, Best Western Hotel, tomorrow.*' That's all it said. The name of the sender wasn't recorded on the slip of paper, but it had been sent from a Geneva post office. It had to be from Bradley Wyndham. No one else could possibly know that he had a 'recent find'. Scott didn't hesitate. He called the airport to check the departure times to Geneva then drove to a travel agent in Via del Corso to book and pay for a flight the following morning. It was expensive but he hoped he would be able to reclaim the cost on expenses.

It was an Alitalia flight on a jet airliner, and the air stewardesses were particularly attractive, in short skirts and livery-green jackets. Scott sat back as a girl brought him a cup of coffee and a cream-filled *cannolo*. As she leaned across to open his tray table, the man in the opposite row pinched her bottom and she shrieked and scolded that he was a naughty boy. Scott could tell she wanted to say more but was suppressing her annoyance.

On arrival he caught a taxi to the hotel and, when he checked in, the receptionist handed him a note that had been left for him. '*Come to the outdoor café in Place du Bourg-de-Four at four o'clock.*' Scott almost laughed. He felt like some third-grade secret agent in a dubious Cold War movie, but all the same he caught a taxi to the square at the appointed time. There was a fountain in the middle and just one café with outdoor tables. He examined the clientele but no one appeared to be looking for him so he sat down in a vacant place, wondering how his correspondent expected to recognise him.

'Scott Morgan?' a voice behind him asked, and he turned to see a wiry man wearing a business suit and dark sunglasses. 'Bradley Wyndham.' They shook hands and he sat down.

'Good to meet you, Bradley. This all feels a bit hush-hush. Was it really necessary?'

Bradley removed his glasses to reveal intense blue eyes. 'Yes, it was. You could have been a Cosa Nostra member who'd found my papers in the office and was trying to trick me into meeting. I'm extremely relieved it's you.'

'How do you know *I'm* not from Cosa Nostra?' Scott grinned.

Bradley wasn't smiling. 'I've checked you out: Harvard degree in international relations, minor success in the athletics team, and a media mogul father. I've seen your photograph in the *Harvard Crimson*. I wouldn't have approached you otherwise.'

'Jeez! You're that scared of them?'

'Sure I am. So should you be. These people don't mess around. I was told I had two days to get out of Rome and disappear for good and I took the hint. It's not just me on my own – I have a wife and two kids to protect.'

He had a trustworthy face, Scott decided. Probably in his forties, receding hairline with grey hairs beginning to outnumber brown, and a lithe frame. He looked fit. But it was the way those eyes fixed on you directly that made you believe him.

'Who warned you to leave?'

Bradley glanced around, checking there was no one close enough to overhear. 'A man named Alessandro Ghianciamina.'

Scott's chest tightened. 'My old friend Alessandro,' he remarked drily. 'That's who was responsible for the shape my nose is in.' The constant dripping had eased off but it was still skewed to one side.

'Oh Christ! If he already knows you, you can't write about this stuff. He'll be after you before the ink's dry on the paper.'

'He doesn't know I'm a journalist.' Scott explained what had happened and Bradley gave a long, low whistle.

'You made a play for Alessandro Ghianciamina's sister! Of all the bad luck . . . Look, I can see you are young and ambitious, but there are easier ways to earn prestige as a journalist than going after these guys. They won't hesitate to kill you. In fact, killing would be merciful.'

A waiter came over and they ordered black coffees.

'But you must want the story to come out,' Scott protested. 'Otherwise, why go to all the trouble of hiding the papers in a place where sooner or later someone would find them?'

'You liked my little carpentry project?' He smiled. 'I created that to keep the documents out of harm's way. When I was ordered to get out of town, I just left them.'

'Funnily enough, I was working on the same kind of stories. I found someone – a drug addict – whose dealer took her to a villa on the Anzio coast where heroin was being distributed and she identified Alessandro Ghianciamina as one of the guys there. The villa is owned by a company called Costruzioni Torre Astura . . .'

'Which is one of the Ghianciaminas' companies,' Bradley intervened.

'Is it really?' Scott was excited.

'Yes, construction is a popular way of laundering drugs money. The Ghianciaminas have built luxury villas right along that coast. It's interesting your witness saw drugs being dealt there, but you can't print it, can you? Not based on the word of a single addict. You'll have to find more than that. It's just a hunch, but I bet there's a motorboat moored at the villa that takes packages out to container ships in the bay by night. The coastguards will all have been paid to turn a blind eye. If you could get evidence of that, you'd be onto something – but still you'll only get the little guys who drive the boat. No prosecuting attorney will ever make anything stick to Gaetano or Alessandro, the indomitable father and son team.'

The coffee arrived and Bradley tipped a single spoonful of sugar into his then stirred it thoughtfully. 'My prediction is they'll be wiped out by a rival family within the next five to ten years. American crime bosses are being deported from the US and coming back to the home country looking for a piece of the action. There's a lot of rivalry in the construction industry, and I wouldn't be surprised if there's full-scale war over the next few years, with bodies turning up in the streets of Rome. I just hope yours isn't one of them.'

Scott felt the hairs on the backs of his arms prickle as he remembered lying on the ground while Alessandro and his friends laid into him. They had been prepared to kill him that day. He could easily have died if one of their vicious kicks had connected with his head. Maybe Bradley was right. Perhaps he shouldn't pursue this. 'Are you still working as a journalist?' he asked.

'Well . . .' Bradley screwed up his nose. 'Journalism of sorts. I'm employed by a Swiss bank to write a magazine for their investors. We have a great lifestyle, with sailing on the lake in summer and skiing in winter. As jobs go, it's lucrative, safe and dull. It's certainly not what I imagined I'd be doing when I graduated college.'

'Couldn't you go back to the States and work for a paper out there? Or London? Surely the Ghianciaminas wouldn't come after you so long as you weren't writing about them?'

Bradley's face took on a haunted look. 'At first, I thought I might tough it out in Rome. I was ambitious, hungry to get the story in print – like you. And then the day after delivering his warning, Alessandro picked up my six-year-old daughter from school. The teachers just let him, then telephoned us. He took her for a ride in his flashy Alfa Romeo and bought her candy before dropping her off at our front door.' He blinked hard. 'They were only gone half an hour but my wife and I were frantic. I ran outside when I saw them and Alessandro beeped his horn and waved at me before driving off.'

'Holy shit!'

'So you see, I might write for a newspaper again one day, but not while my children are young and the Ghianciaminas are walking free. Even if I wanted to, my wife wouldn't let me. She didn't even want me to meet you today . . . And that reminds me: I don't know where you got my brother's number, but will you destroy it? Nothing in that office can give any clue to my whereabouts. I'm placing my trust in you, Scott. Do whatever your conscience dictates about your own research but promise me that nothing you dig up will ever lead to my door. After today's meeting, you're on your own.'

He nodded. 'Message understood.'

Scott asked some questions about the government ministers on the Cosa Nostra payroll and the legislation that had been passed by them in return for bribes, then they went on to talk about the editor of *Midwest Daily* and his taste for stories about the rich and famous. Scott made Bradley laugh with some of the more ludicrous articles about Elizabeth Taylor and Richard Burton.

'The latest news is that Sybil Burton finally broke her silence and gave an interview to the *Express* in London saying that Elizabeth is a close friend of both her and her husband and that Richard is only taking her out for dinner to comfort her since her latest marriage breakdown. Isn't that exactly what Debbie Reynolds used to say when Eddie started dating Elizabeth? That he was comforting her after Mike Todd died? History repeats itself.'

'Poor Sybil. I don't think she believes it for one moment. She's desperately trying to maintain her dignity but she's fighting a rearguard action.'

'It's as if the circus has come to Rome. No one will emerge from this with any dignity.'

They talked about the foreign press hacks who frequented the bar of the Eden Hotel. According to Bradley, Joe was a once-great writer who had gradually pissed away his talent in the bars of each city he was posted to.

'Do you think he really knows Truman Capote?' Scott asked.

Bradley was scathing. 'Is that what he says? Maybe they were introduced at a party once but I wouldn't count on Mr Capote remembering his name.'

Suddenly he checked his watch and rose abruptly to his feet. 'I have to go. My wife is waiting and she'll be nervous if I'm late.'

Scott stood to shake his hand. 'Thanks for meeting me. I appreciate it.'

'Take care of yourself, Scott. Think about what I've said.' Bradley put on his sunglasses then, with a final nod, he hurried across the square and disappeared down an alley between buildings.

It was too late to catch a flight back to Rome, so Scott had dinner in the hotel then went for a drink in the bar, where he met an English air stewardess called Cheryl. He bought her a few cocktails and managed to lure her upstairs to his room where they had satisfactory if somewhat drunken sex. Next morning she gave him her phone number in London but he lost it on the way to the airport.

Chapter Forty-Six

───────✦───────

Diana was wakened just after dawn by a man's voice shouting from far off. She lifted her head to try and make out the words. It sounded like '*Aiuto!*' – 'Help!' She opened her patio door and looked out. A pinky-yellow sun had just begun to rise above the horizon and the Mediterranean was steel-grey in the distance.

Then it came again: '*Aiuto. C'è qualcuno?*' It sounded urgent.

Diana pulled her nightdress over her head and scrambled into her clothes. She took her room key, shut the patio door behind her and walked out across the scrubland separating the lodging house from the waterfront. As she had done the previous day, she stamped heavily and scanned the ground in front of her for snakes.

The Alexandria set loomed on the horizon. Beyond that, she thought she could see a figure in the water, moving towards the jetty. She walked faster. It was a man and he was carrying a bright red object. Something must have fallen in the water and he was retrieving it. He climbed the steps onto the quayside, and it was only as he laid the object on the ground that Diana realised it was a person. Another man appeared and they both leant over it. She broke into a run.

'*Cosa è successo? Sta bene?*' she shouted as she reached the edge of the set.

'*E' annegata una ragazza*,' one of them men called. A girl had drowned.

'Are you sure?' She saw that it was a blonde girl, wearing a red dress, and that she was very thin. The legs were splayed out like those of a fawn. Suddenly it struck her that there was something familiar about those legs.

When Diana reached the spot, her knees gave way. Beneath the mass of matted blonde hair was Helen's face, streaked with black makeup. Diana screamed, an animal sound forced from deep within her, then pushed the man out of the way and began to administer mouth-to-mouth and compress Helen's chest. She had learned how to do it on a first-aid course in the Girl Guides – two breaths, four chest compressions – but the last time she tried it had been after her father had a heart attack right in front of her and it hadn't worked then.

'You know her?' one of the men asked.

Diana gasped between chest compressions: 'It's Helen. My friend. Get help!' She noticed that the first man was dressed in a soldier's camouflage trousers and jacket, and the other looked like a security guard. '*Quick!*' she yelled, wondering at his lack of urgency.

'It's too late,' the guard said in English. 'She is dead.'

'No!' Diana screamed. 'She can't be. Please call an ambulance. *Chiami un'ambulanza.*' She pointed to the gatehouse. What was their problem?

The guard got up and sprinted in that direction. Diana continued, and in her head raced the words: *I have to save her, I have to. She's too young to die.*

'Come on, Helen,' she urged during the chest compressions. 'Come on, *try* at least.' She gulped air and breathed it into Helen's mouth, holding her nose. The chest rose and fell with

297

her breaths but there was no sign of a pulse, no sign of the heart restarting.

Tears began to roll down Diana's cheeks but still she kept going. *Helen, come back. You can do it. Please. For me.*

She remembered stories from the newspapers of doctors restarting someone's heart after they'd been dead for twenty minutes. She had heard that being in cold water made the metabolism slow down. All sorts of miraculous recoveries came to her as she kept up the rhythm of two breaths, four compressions, two breaths, four compressions. But Helen's skin felt cold as stone. Diana tried to feel a pulse in her neck, but there was nothing. She lifted her arm, expecting it to be floppy but there was a stiffness. The elbow wouldn't bend. The guard's words – '*She's dead*' – came back to her. How long had Helen been in the water?

'I was just over there,' she whispered. 'Why didn't you come and find me? Why?'

She lifted Helen's head and cradled her, rocking her back and forwards and speaking to her softly. 'I'm sorry, I'm so sorry. You're safe. I've got you now.' She felt like a mother holding her daughter. Nothing more must harm her. She'd failed to save her life so all she could do now was protect her body from further damage.

The security guard returned and told her the police were on their way. He was looking at her oddly so she explained: 'She's my friend. She was my best friend here in Italy.'

The soldier took out a cigarette, offering one to the security guard but he shook his head. Diana felt it was wrong to smoke with Helen lying there and opened her mouth to say so but the words wouldn't come out. *They're so casual about it. How can they be so indifferent to a young girl's death?* She bent to kiss the white marble forehead and again she begged her, 'Please forgive me. I'm sorry, I'm so sorry.'

When the ambulance got there, Diana didn't want to let Helen go. She asked if she could accompany her – it seemed wrong to leave her on her own – but the policeman said they wanted to take statements from all of them. There were procedures to be followed. She argued, but they wouldn't budge.

The ambulanceman who lifted Helen onto a stretcher seemed surprised at how little she weighed. There was hardly anything of her. Diana walked alongside as she was carried back towards the ambulance, which was parked just inside the gates. She tried to read the expression on Helen's face. Had she been scared when she died? Upset about something? The look was blank and unseeing, offering no clues. Helen simply wasn't there any more.

Diana gave her friend's hand one final squeeze before she was lifted into the ambulance and the doors closed. As it drove away she began to shiver. There was a rushing sound in her ears and in a separate part of her mind she realised she must be in shock. What happened now? What should she do? She should telephone someone to tell them – but who?

A man she'd never met handed her a cup of sweet scalding coffee and she sipped a little, burning the roof of her mouth. Someone else brought a towel and she realised she was soaking wet from cradling Helen. The soldier was also wrapped in a towel. She sat down on the steps of the Serapeum, the most magnificent building of the third century BC, and a police officer came over to talk to her.

First they asked who Helen was and how they knew each other, and she explained. Then they asked why she was at Torre Astura and she told them it was her job to check the set but that she had no idea why Helen had been there or when she had arrived. She hadn't seen her there – not until that morning, when it was too late. She gave the telephone number of the production office at Cinecittà, because someone would have to phone England and tell Helen's parents. Fresh tears welled at that thought. Who would be responsible for delivering the worst news any parent could ever receive?

Then the policeman asked if Helen had any enemies. It was such an absurd question that Diana laughed in disbelief, a strange kind of laugh that came out as more of a snort. 'God, no. She was an angel.'

Why were they asking that? Did they think someone had been involved in her death? Ernesto's name popped into her mind but she dismissed it instantly. He could have no possible reason to kill Helen. That was silly. 'She had no enemies,' she said out loud, then repeated it in Italian for emphasis.

'The soldier tells me that you kept saying you were sorry. What were you sorry for, Mrs Bailey?'

Diana explained about their argument two days earlier. She said that Helen had wanted to go out with a man she had had an affair with and she hadn't liked the idea because he had a wife and children. The policeman peered closely at her before writing that down, and she felt ashamed. It sounded immoral and not like her at all. He asked the name of the man and she gave it. Ernesto would be annoyed.

Diana was shivering hard now, although she could feel the sun was already hot. It was a curious sensation, as though she was separate from the physical world.

'Perhaps you should go and lie down for a while,' the policeman suggested. 'But stay here. Don't go back to Rome until we give you permission. We will need to speak to you later.'

Diana got up and started to walk back towards the *pensione*, her legs feeling as though they didn't belong to her. There was a buzzing noise in her head and she felt as though everything was very far away. Nothing was real. Had it definitely been Helen? Could she have made a mistake?

But she knew she hadn't. Helen was dead. The policeman was right; she should lie down somewhere until the world stopped feeling so very far away.

Chapter Forty-Seven

Diana lay on her bed staring up at the cracks in the ceiling. Out in the corridor she could hear other lodgers using the bathroom, one after another. The sound of water gushing through the antiquated plumbing was like a waterfall pounding onto a tin roof. How could Helen be dead? How was it possible? She was too young for death. She couldn't even begin to guess what had happened.

The house fell silent as the workmen headed off to their jobs on the set. She remembered she had meant to talk to the chief carpenter but couldn't for the life of her think what she had meant to say.

Her left eye started twitching and wouldn't stop and that made her realise that she hadn't cried properly yet. Tears trickled out unbidden but that was all. When would the crying start? There would be crying, that was certain, but she couldn't cry yet because she had to decide what to do. She should telephone people to tell them – but who?

Hilary. Suddenly she yearned to speak to sensible, practical Hilary. The security guard must have a telephone. Maybe he would let her use it if she went over there.

She sat up. The shivering had stopped but she was still in her damp clothing and it was making the bed damp beneath her. She'd brought another dress with her but it had a bright summery pattern of tiny sprigs of orange blossom on a pale green background and didn't seem appropriate. She hesitated for a long time, wondering if there was anywhere to buy a black outfit nearby, before realising that it didn't matter in the slightest what she wore. Helen was gone and nothing could bring her back.

It was a different security guard and he gave her an odd look, but immediately agreed that she could come in and use the telephone. Her hands were shaking hard so he dialled the number for her then passed over the receiver.

Candy answered the phone.

'Can I speak to Hilary?' Diana asked, her voice cracking.

There was a pause and a murmur of voices, then Hilary's voice came on the line. 'Is that you, Diana?'

Diana opened her mouth to speak but no words came out. Instead the tears came and she couldn't stop them. 'It's Helen . . .' she gasped between sobs.

'I know. The police rang us. God, it's simply awful. Walter wants me to ring her parents because he thinks it's a woman's job but I haven't a clue what to say. Oh Diana, you poor thing, do try to stop crying.'

Diana's chest hurt with the force of her sobs and she struggled to speak. The security guard passed her a handkerchief and she blew her nose hard. 'I t-tried for ages to save her but it was t-too late. She was g-gone.'

There was a tutting sound down the line. 'You shouldn't be there on your own. I'm sending a taxi to bring you back to Rome. If I hire a local firm they should be with you in the next half hour.' Hilary sounded calm and in control. 'Come straight to Cinecittà,' she said. 'You need to be among friends.'

'B-but the police told me to stay here.'

'That's ridiculous. I'll get our lawyers to speak to them. Go back to the *pensione*, pack your things and wait for the taxi. You'll be here in a couple of hours and we'll talk properly then.'

'OK,' Diana agreed. It was good to have a plan. She handed the phone back to the guard and offered to return his handkerchief as well, but he motioned that she should keep it.

The taxi arrived promptly and Diana calmed down a little on the drive back to Rome. She wondered what everyone on the set would make of it. Hilary hadn't known Helen personally; neither had Candy. They didn't know how deflated she had been recently and they certainly didn't know about her flirtation with Ernesto, so they were unlikely to be able to shed any light on what had happened. But perhaps they would be able to explain why Helen had been there at all. Had she been sent on some errand – perhaps to check the makeup stocks at Torre Astura? It seemed unlikely. Anyone could have done that.

Hilary was waiting in the office when Diana arrived. She sent Candy out to pay the taxi driver before pulling Diana towards her for a warm hug.

'What a hideous experience! She was a good friend of yours, wasn't she?' She patted Diana's shoulder. 'Sit down and tell me all about it while I make some tea.'

'There's hardly anything to tell,' Diana shook her head, holding back the tears. 'I woke this morning to hear a soldier shouting for help and when I ran down to the set, he'd pulled Helen out of the water and she was dead. I tried to revive her but . . . but it was useless.' She sat at her desk and gazed blankly at the familiar filing tray and telephone.

Hilary plugged in the kettle. 'Didn't she find you last night? She told the girls in the makeup department she was going to look for you. Said she had to speak to you urgently.'

'Really?' Diana felt a plummeting sensation in her stomach. She buried her face in her hands and groaned. 'We'd argued. She must have wanted to make things up.' Hilary looked at her quizzically. 'We fell out the night before last, about Ernesto. Immediately after our affair ended, he seduced Helen and she was keen on him, even when I told her about his wife. I yelled at her, and I shouldn't have. I feel simply awful about it now.'

Hilary sat down to wait for the kettle. 'So you didn't see her? That's odd. The policeman who rang gave us the impression you were with her when she died. They must have got it wrong.'

'No, they're confused. I didn't know anything about it till this morning. I suppose she was alone.'

Hilary pursed her lips. 'Do you think she committed suicide?'

The thought hadn't occurred to Diana, and she was shocked that Hilary could consider it. A young woman would have to be utterly hopeless to take such a drastic step. She ran through possible reasons for suicide but couldn't come up with any. Even if Helen had been pregnant, there were things that could be done. She'd heard that it was relatively simple in London to find a midwife who would terminate an unwanted pregnancy, though, admittedly, in the Pope's hometown it was likely to be much harder. But if Helen were pregnant, whose could it be? Surely not Ernesto's?

Diana realised she hadn't yet answered Hilary's question. 'No, it doesn't add up. Why would she come all that way to see me then kill herself before finding me? . . . Unless she was very drunk. Sometimes she drank more than was good for her.' Diana felt disloyal saying that when Helen wasn't around to defend herself, and wished she could take back the words.

'Did you mention that to the police?'

Diana shook her head. 'To be honest, I can't remember what I said to the police. I was so distraught this morning I could barely speak. I'm going to have to talk to them again, no doubt.'

Candy came back into the office. 'Did you tell Diana about Helen's mom?' she asked. Hilary gave her a warning frown.

'Have you talked to her? Oh God, how did she take it?'

Candy answered. 'She didn't believe it at first, and then she screamed so loud I could hear her on the other side of the office. I suppose her folks'll come out here, don't you think? I wonder where they'll have the funeral? The whole cast and crew should go. That's what I'd want if it was me: lots of flowers and some great music.'

Diana was uncomfortable with the way Candy was treating it, almost as another piece of gossip on the set. She didn't feel like discussing it with her. Hilary brought over her cup of tea.

'I think I'll type up my notes from the trip,' Diana told them. 'I need to keep myself busy and I don't know what else to do.'

'Are you sure?' Hilary frowned again. 'You look very pale and shaky. Have you eaten anything today?'

Diana remembered that she hadn't eaten since lunchtime the day before.

'Let me take you to the bar,' Hilary said firmly in her head-girl voice. 'We'll get some food inside you then send you home to bed. Drink your tea first.'

Diana looked at the phone. It would be good to call Trevor. He'd met Helen and would sympathise with the shock she was feeling. But he would ask questions about why Helen had come to Torre Astura, and Diana couldn't tell him about their argument because then she would have to confess about Ernesto. It was a tangled mess.

She couldn't think straight for herself, so she obeyed Hilary's orders, drinking her tea then following her to the bar. It was after three and they were no longer serving sandwiches but they made one up for her with fresh tomatoes. She chewed mechanically without tasting it.

'Take the weekend off,' Hilary suggested. 'Get lots of rest and eat regular meals. Don't come back to work till Monday morning. We're only shooting a few fill-in scenes, nothing vital.'

I don't want to be on my own for two days. What will I do with myself? Diana was about to protest, then realised that she was really very tired. Perhaps she could just sleep.

After the food, Hilary ushered her into a studio car and sent her back to Pensione Splendid. Diana unlocked the door and went to sit at the window and gaze out across the rooftops, trying to think clearly.

If only she had gone back to resolve the argument with Helen the same afternoon. If only she had gone into the café where she saw her with Luigi. She still couldn't imagine what had happened but it was becoming clear that if she had made peace with her Helen would be alive today – and that was a hefty burden to bear.

Chapter Forty-Eight

Next morning, Diana was wakened by loud knocking. She pulled on a robe and opened the door to see two policemen standing there, with her *padrona* behind them.

'Mrs Bailey, you were supposed to stay in Torre Astura. We need to ask you some questions,' one said in English.

Diana folded her arms protectively across her chest. 'Yes, of course. If you'll just let me get dressed.' She nodded to the *padrona*, who didn't seem best pleased at this visitation.

'Meet us downstairs and we'll drive you to the station. Bring your papers.'

As she dressed, Diana shook herself mentally. She had to give the police all the information she could to help them find out what happened to Helen. It was imperative that they solved the mystery or her family and friends would be left hanging on, wondering. She still didn't know what she thought herself but the police were better at this kind of thing. If she gave them the information, they'd work it out. She felt a frisson of nerves, but quelled them. She was an intelligent woman with a PhD from Oxford. She could handle this.

She sat in the back of a police car and was driven out in the direction of Cinecittà for about twenty minutes, until they pulled up outside a large building with a sign saying *Questura Polizia di Stato* over the door. They led her straight into a small room with a table and three chairs. The only window was high up in one wall. Her stomach rumbled and she wished she had grabbed some breakfast before she left.

'Could I have a glass of water, please?' she asked in Italian.

'Sit down, Mrs Bailey,' an officer told her. 'We are going to go through the entire story from the beginning. Someone will bring your water in due course. Can you answer in Italian or would you like us to find a translator?'

She could tell he didn't want the bother of finding a translator, so agreed to speak Italian.

They wanted to see her passport, her residence permit and the permit to work that had been obtained for her by Twentieth Century Fox. They asked about her job in England and that of her husband, how she had got the post at Cinecittà and when she first met Helen. Many of the questions seemed inconsequential but Diana answered them with painstaking honesty. A young officer was writing everything down and sometimes she paused to give him time to catch up.

They were stony-faced when she talked about her affair with Ernesto. They had already reacted with disbelief that she would leave her husband to take a job in another country so she couldn't expect them to understand the terrible mistake she had made getting involved with a married man. They'd written her off as a scarlet woman. At last the glass of water arrived. It was warm and tasted stale but she gulped it down gratefully.

Next she had the difficult task of explaining her argument with Helen. She lowered her head and chose her words with great care, trying to make them understand exactly what had happened. She mentioned going back to try to find her at five o'clock then seeing her in a café with a friend of hers called Luigi.

'Who is this Luigi?' the officer asked instantly.

'I don't know,' Diana told them honestly. 'Helen never talked about him. We often saw him in clubs or bars but she didn't seem close to him. I'm not sure why she was with him last Wednesday.'

'What does he look like?'

Diana described him as best she could. Dark, curlyish hair. Swarthy.

'Do you know where we could find him?'

'He usually hangs around the Via Veneto in the evening, but I don't know where he lives or works. Sorry.'

'Do you know a young American man with short fair hair? According to a neighbour he visited Helen at her apartment on Wednesday evening.'

Diana ran through a mental list of the American men Helen might have known at Cinecittà but couldn't imagine who the visitor might have been.

'She was very distressed during his visit. The neighbour heard her crying. Next morning she went to the film studios but didn't do any work. She said she felt ill and lay down in a spare dressing room, and then in the afternoon she decided to come and find you. Do you have any idea why?'

Diana repeated that she could only presume Helen wanted to make up their argument, but when she reached Torre Astura she couldn't find her.

It was stuffy in the interview room and she felt weak with hunger. Suddenly the officer stood and left the room without explanation. She addressed the younger man, the one taking notes. 'Do you think I could have some more water, please?' She had to repeat it twice before he understood what she was asking, and she worried that if he had trouble understanding her Italian it didn't bode well for the accuracy of the notes he was taking.

'Soon,' he said, without indicating when that would be.

The first officer reappeared. 'We want to find both of the men she met the night before she died. Perhaps you will be so good as to come out with us tonight and help us to identify this Luigi?'

Diana agreed. 'Yes, we can certainly have a look.'

The police dropped her off at home around lunchtime and she hurried straight into the *trattoria* for some food. She was starving, and ordered more than she could eat. 'Eyes bigger than your stomach,' she remembered her dad teasing her and that made the tears come.

At ten that evening the same police officer picked her up and drove her to Via Veneto, accompanied by another officer she hadn't met. She felt self-conscious walking into bars and nightclubs with two uniformed policemen by her side. People turned and stared. In one bar, there was a group she recognised from Cinecittà and they whispered behind their hands as they watched her gazing around the room.

She took the police to four different places without success but as they came out of the last one, suddenly she saw Luigi walking up the hill towards them.

'That's him,' she pointed. 'That's Luigi.'

He saw her pointing and his eyes darted quickly from her to the policemen as if trying to decide whether to flee. They drew alongside him and the first officer asked if he would mind answering some questions about Helen.

'No, of course I wouldn't mind,' he said straight away. 'I was very sad to hear about what happened to her. A mutual friend told me earlier.'

'Can you come with us?' they asked, and he agreed.

'Thank you. That's all we need from you for now, Mrs Bailey,' she was told. 'Call us if you have any inspiration about who the American man might be.'

She agreed that she would, and watched as the officers walked towards the police car with Luigi between them. Suddenly he turned and gave Diana a look of such venom that she froze. His lip was raised in a sneer and hatred blazed in his eyes. He looked as though he wanted to kill her, and might well have tried had the officers not been present.

Diana leant against a wall feeling deeply shaken. At that moment she became convinced that Luigi had been involved in Helen's death. Maybe Helen had been running away from him when she came to Torre Astura but he caught up with her and killed her before she could reach Diana. How on earth had Helen known someone like that? At that moment he certainly looked capable of murder.

The police car drew off with Luigi in the back. With a wave of panic, Diana remembered that he knew where she lived. The very first evening she went out with Helen, Luigi had been in the taxi when it picked her up. Would he remember? She was on the second floor and usually left her shutters open at night but she decided to close them before going to sleep that evening. She would bolt her door from the inside as well. Suddenly she didn't feel safe any more.

Chapter Forty-Nine

As soon as he got back to Rome, Scott called and arranged to have a beer with Gianni to catch up on any news he had missed.

'What's the story with Liz and Dick?' he asked. 'Is it on or off?'

'Sybil is in town,' Gianni told him. 'So it's off. I have some pictures of her dining with Richard last night. Elizabeth stayed at home with her parents, who are visiting from America. I expect she is not pleased about this.'

'No, I'm sure she's not.'

'The big news is that Twentieth Century Fox may be about to fire their president, Spyros Skouras, because the *Cleopatra* budget has overrun so badly. It looks as though it's going to end up costing thirty million dollars instead of the original budget of two million. If he survives the vote at the board meeting next week it will be a miracle. He's been in town for talks with Walter Wanger but flew out again today.'

Scott grinned. 'I think I'll give my friends in the press department a call about that.'

'And a crew member drowned at one of their locations near Anzio but they haven't been identified yet.'

'Do you think there's a story in it?'

'Who can tell?'

It was a Saturday night, but Scott popped in to the office to make a couple of phone calls. First he rang his editor and, as they chatted, he wondered what he would say if he knew Scott had just been in Geneva with Bradley Wyndham. He didn't mention it, of course. He'd have to invent some fictitious reason for the trip if he wanted to get the cost reimbursed as expenses.

'I've sent over some pictures from the wedding of King Juan Carlos of Spain and Princess Sophia of Greece,' the editor told him. 'They should be on your desk by now. I'm told it's a who's who of European royalty and our women's page wants to run a feature on the fashions but no one can identify the damn people. Could you find out and ring back in a couple of hours?'

So much for his Saturday night, Scott mused. He wouldn't have minded if it had been a decent story instead of a women's piece.

'Next week, I want you to profile the new Italian president, Antonio Segni. You can have fifteen hundred words and a byline. What does it mean to be Christian Socialist? How is he different from his predecessor? Where does he stand on the Soviet Union? Is he kind to children and animals? You know the kind of thing, Scott. Give it your best.'

Scott exhaled loudly. That was the kind of story that took a lot of time and research. His editor would expect more than a rehash of items from the cuttings file but he knew he didn't have a cat in hell's chance of getting an interview with Segni. Why had he ever written that hatchet job about the Communist Party? The repercussions followed him around like a bad smell.

'Oh, and if you can get your piece on the *Cleopatra* budget to us tomorrow, we'll print it in the paper the day before their board meeting. Try to tie in something about the profligacy of the movie's stars, won't you?'

Scott agreed that he would.

When he came off the phone, he opened the envelope full of wedding photographs and glanced through them. He didn't recognise a soul but he'd take them up to the Eden bar and get the press hacks there to help him.

Before he left the office, he dialled the *Cleopatra* press office.

'Hey, it's Scott Morgan here. I heard Spyros Skouras is up for the chop and wondered if he's going to take Walter Wanger down with him. Any comments I can use in my piece?'

'We only discuss events here in Rome,' came the response. 'I can't tell you anything about the business in Hollywood.'

'OK, can you tell me whether Elizabeth Taylor and Richard Burton are going to get together again any time soon?'

'I've left my crystal ball at home. Can't help you with that one.'

'Any chance of an interview with Miss Taylor?'

'Not gonna happen.'

Amidst their banter, Scott clean forgot to ask about the person who drowned at the Anzio set.

Chapter Fifty

When Diana reached the production office at Cinecittà on Monday morning, a middle-aged couple were sitting talking to Hilary. And then she looked at the woman and realised who they were, because her face was an older, more tired version of Helen's. She had carefully set bleached blonde hair and huge bags under her eyes.

'These are Helen's parents, Mr and Mrs Sharpe,' Hilary introduced them, and Diana felt humbled as she shook hands and muttered words of condolence.

'Helen told us what great friends you were,' the mother said. 'I know it must be hard for you, but I wondered if we could ask you a few questions? We're trying to piece it together and we don't have a clue . . .' She broke off, close to tears.

'The police don't seem to have much idea what happened,' Helen's father said. 'And that makes it harder.'

Diana took them to a waiting room outside the admin office, fortunately quiet at that time of the morning, and answered all their questions about the morning at Torre Astura when she'd tried frantically to revive Helen. They listened intently, not wanting to miss a single word.

Helen's father asked what Diana knew about the police investigation, and was surprised when she told them that an Italian man called Luigi had been taken in for questioning.

'The police didn't mention him. They said they are looking for a fair-haired American man who visited her the evening before . . . They're bringing the neighbour who saw him to Cinecittà today to see if she can identify the man in question. They seem to be convinced that foul play was involved.'

Diana wondered why the police hadn't mentioned Luigi. Perhaps they were still trying to gather evidence. Helen's father asked if Diana had known him and she said no, not really. They had never been introduced.

When they had finished asking questions about Helen's death, Diana took them for a tour of the studio, stopping first at the makeup rooms. She showed them Helen's set of brushes, all neat and clean in a plastic wallet, and the autograph book with Elizabeth Taylor's signature. Helen's mother picked it up and staggered slightly, overcome by emotion. Her husband put an arm round her to support her.

Diana told them that Helen had been a walking encyclopedia of information on the stars. She told them she had helped to restyle her wardrobe, dragging her into the 1960s, and that she used to do her hair and makeup for special occasions. 'She was very happy here,' Diana said, not entirely truthfully. 'She was doing a job she loved, surrounded by glamorous film stars, in a wonderful city.'

'I suppose that's some consolation,' her father said, in a tone that implied it was no consolation at all.

'She was always the sensitive one of my two,' her mother remarked. 'Julia – that's my elder daughter – got all the confidence, while Helen worried too much what people thought of her. She could never see how special she was. Even as a toddler, she was a lovely singer and dancer, but she'd be too

317

shy to perform in front of anyone except family no matter how much we encouraged her.'

'Yes, I saw her dancing. She was tremendous,' Diana told them. She remembered Helen singing snatches of pop songs as well.

Suddenly she could hear the sweet pure voice in her head and a wave of grief swept over her. This was so hard. She knew she had to be strong for Helen's parents, but their presence made her feel even more guilty that she hadn't been a good enough friend to their daughter.

'We did everything we could to boost her confidence but she got it into her head that her sister was the one we were proud of. It wasn't true, you know.' Her mother sniffed hard. 'Do you have children yet, Diana?'

Diana shook her head.

'Let me tell you, if anything you love the sensitive ones just a little bit more, because they need you more. You can't help it.' She took out a handkerchief and blew her nose, then apologised: 'Excuse me.'

Afterwards, Diana was haunted by the way they seemed dazed by what had happened. They were still in the early stages of grief and shock; they were only starting to come to terms with the fact that this tragedy would overshadow the rest of their lives.

As she walked back towards the production office, she didn't notice Ernesto sitting outside the bar until she was right along-side and couldn't ignore him.

'I heard about Helen,' he said. 'How are you?'

'A bit shaky,' she replied, stopping by his table. 'It's all so strange. I can't begin to make head or tail of it. I suppose you heard I'd had an argument with her?'

He nodded, and had the good grace to look embarrassed. 'Did you tell the police about that?'

'Yes, I expect they will want to talk to you.'

He shrugged. 'There's nothing I can tell them. I hardly knew her.'

Is that so? Diana thought cynically. *You tried to seduce her without any attempt to get to know her?* She let it pass, though. 'They're looking for a man she saw the night before she died: a fair-haired American. Can you think who that might be?'

Ernesto considered this, then shook his head.

'And they are questioning an Italian man called Luigi. I saw her with him in a café near the studio and the police wanted to talk to him, so we went out and found him on the Via Veneto on Saturday night. I identified him . . .' Her voice trailed off, as she noticed Ernesto was staring at her in alarm. 'What is it?'

'You're so naïve, Diana. Do you really not know who Luigi is?'

'No. Helen never introduced us.'

Ernesto blew air through his teeth. 'He's a drug dealer. He used to supply Helen. He's not going to be pleased with you for tying him into this.'

Diana jerked backwards. 'Drugs! Helen didn't take drugs. She sometimes drank too much but . . .'

'She took drugs, believe me. She was a very good customer of Luigi's. Did you never notice her mood swings? Sometimes she was the life and soul of the party and other times she could barely move.' Ernesto looked directly into her eyes. 'She was very troubled.'

'But why didn't she tell me?'

'I expect she was ashamed. She looked up to you.'

Diana was reeling. She tried to think of reasons to refute Ernesto's story, but she didn't know enough about drugs. 'Why didn't *you* tell me?'

He looked away. 'I don't get involved in things that are none of my business.'

What rot! she thought. *He sells news about the stars of the film to journalists. Who does he think he's fooling?*

Ernesto stood up and spoke quietly but insistently. 'I am going to give you some good advice, Diana. Tell the police it was dark in the café and you might have been mistaken in thinking you saw Luigi with Helen. You don't want to have him as your enemy.'

'But he might have killed Helen. I can't tell a lie.'

Ernesto patted her shoulder and she drew back from his touch. 'You should think about it very carefully. Even if Luigi was responsible, he will never be convicted. His kind of people never are. You'd be putting yourself in danger for no good reason.'

He leaned in to kiss her on the cheek but she twisted away so he shrugged and said, 'Goodbye, Diana. Take care of yourself.' He walked off towards the front gate.

Diana was very disturbed by their talk. What a bad friend she had been if Helen couldn't even confide in her about a drugs problem. She'd been so caught up in her own affair that she had paid no attention to all the warning signs that were staring her in the face. She felt ashamed for letting Helen down, ashamed of her own self-absorption – and a deep contempt for Ernesto, who had seduced a vulnerable young girl. What a complete and utter bastard he had turned out to be!

She knew she wouldn't take his advice and retract her statement about Luigi. She planned to do everything in her power to help the police find Helen's killer and have him put behind bars. It was the very least she could do.

Chapter Fifty-One

On Monday morning, the Italian press printed a grainy photograph of Helen sitting in an outdoor café with some other girls from the *Cleopatra* set, and it was only then Scott realised that she was the person who had been killed at Torre Astura.

'Jesus Christ!' he yelled, startling his secretary. 'I know her.'

She was beaming at the camera, holding up her drink as if toasting someone, and she looked heartbreakingly young and pretty. Tears came to Scott's eyes. What the hell had happened?

The story alongside the photograph said that the police were treating her death as suspicious and straight away Scott guessed she had been killed because she'd blurted out something about drugs to the wrong person. Maybe Luigi had got wind of it. It had been foolish of him to take her to the Ghianciaminas' villa. She was young and garrulous and seemed to have no sense of caution. If word got back to Luigi that she was talking about it, he would have had no option but to shut her up.

Scott checked the date on which she had drowned and realised it was the day after he last saw her. She'd been distraught that evening. Maybe she already knew that Luigi was after her. He tried to remember exactly what she had said: she'd complained that she couldn't afford the vitamin treatments any more, and implied that she was taking drugs again. Scott had assumed that she was upset because she hadn't managed to get off the heroin as easily as she'd hoped – but perhaps there had been something else going on. Had Luigi been threatening her? Was he even inside her room at the time? Is that why Helen wouldn't let him come in?

Scott was determined to get to the truth. First, he decided to ring the vitamin doctor to find out whether she had gone for the vitamin shot that night, the one he gave her the money for.

'Helen Sharpe? I haven't seen her in almost a week.'

'Did you realise that she is dead?' Scott asked. 'She drowned last Thursday night. It's all over the morning newspapers.'

There was a sharp intake of breath. 'I had no idea. I'm sorry to hear that.'

'I saw her the night before she died and she told me she'd had to start taking drugs again because she couldn't afford any more of your treatments. But that made me curious, because I thought you said she would only need one or two injections before she would be cured.'

'Yes, that's how it should have been,' the doctor told him. 'But Miss Sharpe was a very anxious young lady who didn't believe herself capable of beating the addiction on her own. If I'd known she was struggling I would have offered her free treatments.'

As they spoke, Scott was scribbling down the doctor's responses in shorthand. 'What else is in those shots? Why did she need to keep coming back for more?'

'I don't need to tell you . . .'

'Shall I suggest to the police that they come and test your formula to see if it could have contributed to Helen's death?'

There was a long pause. 'I always include some ampheta-mines to give patients a boost. You'll find that's normal practice. Otherwise it's mostly vitamins B and C.'

'Oh Christ!' Scott was furious with himself. Looking back, all the signs were there but it had never occurred to him. Lots of doctors gave amphetamine shots – it was said that the *Cleopatra* director Joe Mankiewicz had one every morning – but it was the last thing Helen needed in her fragile condition. She'd gone from one highly addictive drug to another. 'You'd better tell the police about that.'

The doctor cleared his throat. 'I don't see why I should. It's not as if she died of an overdose, is it? I thought you said she drowned?' He sounded defensive.

'The police are treating her death as suspicious.'

'That has nothing to do with me. I'm bound by the Hippocratic Oath not to discuss my patients, so I'm afraid I'm going to have to terminate this call.'

'Surely the Hippocratic Oath—' Scott had been going to say that he thought it no longer applied when a patient died, but the doctor had hung up.

Scott was furious with himself. Why had he taken her to someone he couldn't personally vouch for? He should have made more enquiries first. That evening, as he nursed a Peroni in the piano bar where he'd often seen Helen and her friends, Scott felt very emotional. He gazed at their usual table and tried to imagine her sitting there. She'd been troubled, for sure, but she was a lovely girl, entirely without guile. If only he hadn't left her that last evening. He should have insisted she told him what she was upset about.

He knew he should go to the police and tell them about Helen's drug habit, in case they hadn't figured it out already.

He'd say he was a friend who met her in a nightclub and was trying to help her to break her addiction. He should also tell them about seeing her the night before she died.

Scott wondered what theories they were pursuing. Maybe they already had someone in custody. *Oh crap!* Suddenly it occurred to him that he could find himself being called to testify in court against Luigi or one of his cronies. That wasn't a position he wanted to find himself in. Apart from anything else, it would make it very difficult to continue writing his story. Perhaps Alessandro Ghianciamina would remember him as the guy who chatted up his sister. It was far too dangerous.

All in all, he decided he would wait a few days and see if the papers reported any more before he raised his head above the parapet. One way or another, there was a lot at stake.

Chapter Fifty-Two

On Tuesday morning, the 15th of May, two policemen appeared at Diana's *pensione* just before nine as she sat with a cup of coffee waiting for the studio car to arrive. She'd grown to like Italian espresso, with its rich aroma, quite unlike the insipid Lyons coffee grounds that Trevor preferred back home. It certainly jolted you into the day, making you feel wide awake.

'Signora Bailey? We need to ask you more questions. Please would you accompany us to the station?'

Diana was surprised. 'I was there for hours on Saturday. Do I really have to come again today? Can't you ask me your questions here?'

'I'm afraid not. You must come with us.'

She sighed loudly. 'Will someone give me a lift to Cinecittà when you finish? I have a meeting to attend.'

'We'll arrange something.'

Diana asked them to wait until the studio car arrived and she told the driver to get word to Hilary that she would be late, then she climbed into the police car and was driven back out to the Questura Polizia di Stato. At least she'd had breakfast this time.

She was led into the same airless room with one window set high in the wall, and the senior officer, the one who had questioned her on Saturday, walked in.

'Thank you for coming,' he began. 'I have a number of matters to clear up so if you don't mind we will go through them one by one.' Diana nodded her agreement. 'First of all, I am puzzled about the fight you had with Helen on the 9th of May. Several witnesses have described it to me and they say that Helen was crying and you were shouting at her. Is that a fair description?'

Who had he spoken to? Diana tried to remember who had been in the bar that day but could recall only blurred faces: one of the camera crew, and an assistant director whose name she didn't know. 'I only raised my voice once, towards the end. At the beginning we were chatting normally, then I got angry with her so I raised my voice and she began to cry. Rather than continue the argument, I went off to calm down. That's all that happened.'

'You were angry with her because she wanted to have an affair with a man you had just finished an affair with. Why would you object if you were no longer with him?'

God, this was complicated. 'Because he was married. It wasn't fair on his wife and children.'

'But you were happy to go out with him yourself.'

'I didn't know he was married at the time. He lied to me. I broke up with him as soon as I found out.' As she spoke, she realised they hadn't picked that up before. No wonder the officer appeared to think badly of her.

'It seems to me that you fell out because you both wanted the same man and you were fighting over him. Is that not the truth?'

It would have been laughable, if it hadn't been so sad. She spoke slowly, trying to clear the matter up once and for all. 'Helen didn't know I'd been seeing Ernesto. We kept it secret

327

at work. I finished the relationship when I found out he was married. He then tried to seduce Helen. Our row occurred because she wanted to go out with him and I told her not to, because he had a wife. Does that answer your questions?'

'No, I have many more,' he said, looking down at his notes. A younger policeman was jotting everything down studiously.

'Tell me, Signora Bailey, how did you get that scratch on your cheek?'

Diana's hand flew to the place where there was still a jagged pink line, about two inches long. She told him about the branch that scratched her face as she walked up from the beach. Why would he ask about that?

'Tell me again why you think Helen might have announced to her friends at Cinecittà that she was coming to Torre Astura to find you. Is it not possible that she came to continue the fight with you over this man?'

'No.' Diana shook her head emphatically. 'She wasn't that kind of person. I don't know why she came but I think she might have been scared of someone, or that she was very upset and wanted a friend to comfort her.'

'But you say she didn't find you. You didn't see each other at all once she got there. Is that true?'

'Yes, it's true. I didn't see her until the following morning when the soldier pulled her out of the water. I've got no idea what happened, but if she was scared of someone, maybe he followed her down there and they got into a fight, which ended with her being drowned. That's all I can think of.' In her mind, she saw an image of Helen thrashing around in the water while Luigi held her head under. She would have fought with all her strength to get free, but she was tiny and he was a strong man. She wouldn't have stood a chance.

'This is what you want me to type up and put in your statement. Are you sure?' the officer asked, peering closely at her.

She racked her brains, trying to think of any detail that she'd missed. 'The last time I saw her alive was when she was in the café with Luigi the night before. Has he told you anything about her state of mind at that meeting?'

He looked at her coldly. 'The man you identified was nowhere near Cinecittà at that time. He has an alibi. We've checked and it's true, so you were mistaken.'

She gasped. 'He can't have an alibi! I saw him with my own eyes. Did you know that he's a drug dealer? He's a bad person. I'm scared of him. I hoped you would still have him in custody.'

'What makes you think that he's a drug dealer? Do *you* take drugs, Signora Bailey?' His tone was very stern now.

'No, never! Ernesto told me. He said Helen was taking drugs and she bought them from Luigi. You should investigate that. I'm sure he was involved in Helen's death. It was the way he looked at me on Saturday that convinced me . . .'

The officer stood up. 'We'll type your statement and I'll bring it back and ask you to sign it in due course.'

Diana looked at her watch. It was almost half past ten so it looked as if she was going to miss the script meeting entirely. Why were the police being so slow to pick up the most obvious suspect? If Luigi were innocent, he wouldn't have given them a false alibi. That was the action of a guilty man. *Oh Christ, poor Helen.* It was unbearable to imagine her trying to run away from him, thinking she'd be safe with Diana, and then being caught before finding her. She must have been petrified. She wondered what Luigi was chasing her for and assumed Helen owed him money.

329

It took over an hour for the statement to be typed, during which time she was left on her own in the room without so much as a glass of water. Surely in Britain the police were supposed to give you a cup of tea or something? At last the door opened and her statement was brought in and put in front of her. It was in Italian so she read it carefully, unsure about the nuances of some of the vocabulary choices, but it set out the bare facts as she had told them and she wanted to be allowed to leave, so she signed it.

She stood and picked up her handbag, ready to go, but the officer came back into the room, checked the signature on her statement, then said something that was so bewildering she had to ask him to repeat it.

'Signora Diana Bailey, we are arresting you on suspicion of killing Helen Sharpe some time during the night of 10th to 11th May. You will be held in custody until the evidence can be presented to a judge, at which point you may be represented by a lawyer if you wish.'

She sat down hard and gripped the edge of the table. '*No!*' she cried. 'You've got it all wrong. I couldn't have killed Helen. She was my *friend*. I couldn't kill anyone. It's ridiculous.' She reached out to grab the statement, wondering if she had accidentally signed something incriminating, but the officer whisked it away.

'These officers will take you into custody.' Two men approached and one caught hold of her wrist.

'Please listen to me. This is all a huge mistake. Perhaps we should have had a translator present. I don't know how you could misunderstand me so badly.' Surely there must be something she could say to make him see? But he turned and walked out of the door without another word. The man holding her wrist pulled her to her feet, at which point the other man produced a set of handcuffs.

'No,' she shouted. 'Call the British Consul, please. This is all wrong.'

Her hands were yanked behind her back and the cuffs clicked shut. As they led her out of the back of the police station to a waiting car, she kept pleading with them. 'Please call the British Embassy. Call Hilary Armitage at Cinecittà. Please tell *someone* I'm here.'

But they gave no sign that they would do anything of the sort. As far as she could tell, she was entirely on her own.

Chapter Fifty-Three

Diana was ushered into the back of a police car and a policeman got in the front to drive. He looked young, and she sensed he was of junior rank and unlikely to be able to help her but still she bombarded him with questions.

'Where are you taking me?'

'To Mantellate, the women's section of Regina Coeli prison.'

'But I'm not guilty. What should I do?'

'A judge will decide if you are not guilty.'

'When will I see a judge?'

'Soon,' he said. 'Within forty-eight hours.'

That was two whole days – and two nights as well. She couldn't possibly spend two days in jail. This was ridiculous. She had to speak to Hilary and get a lawyer.

'I need to make a telephone call. Where can I use a telephone?'

'At Regina Coeli.' He was a man of few words and after a while she gave up.

Regina Coeli was by the riverside in Trastevere, overlooked by the Janiculum hill, and the yellow-painted Mantellate was a former monastery down a side street. Her driver helped her out of the car and into a reception area.

'Can I make a phone call please?' she asked a prison guard, but was told 'Later, later.'

The contents of her handbag were searched and she was patted down to check she didn't have anything in her pockets, then the handcuffs were removed and she was led by a guard down a narrow corridor and up a flight of steps. Their footsteps echoed, and she could hear far-off clangings of metal. It was a place of stone and metal.

'Here you are,' the guard said, opening the door of a tiny cell and gesturing for her to enter.

'No, I must make a phone call,' Diana said in her firmest voice. 'I am expected at work.'

'You can call later,' the guard told her.

There was no negotiation, no sympathy. He wanted to get on with his job. She stepped into the cell and immediately the door was slammed shut and locked behind her. Panic gripped her. *Oh God, what would become of her?*

The cell was cool, with thick walls, and one high window through which she could see blue cloudless sky. For the first hour, Diana sat trembling on the edge of the narrow bed. She wanted to clear her head so that she could think, and decide what to do – but in fact there was nothing she *could* do, not for the moment. She felt sick with anxiety and at one point crouched over the covered bucket in the corner thinking she was going to bring up her stomach contents. She retched but with no result apart from hurting her throat. Once she stopped feeling so nauseous, perhaps she could run through events from start to finish and find the missing piece of evidence, the one thing that would persuade them they had made a terrible mistake.

Her mood swung between wild optimism – as soon as Hilary heard what had happened she would call a Twentieth Century Fox lawyer who would have her out in no time – and abject pessimism. What if everyone believed she was guilty? What if Helen's parents thought she had done it? She might be found guilty and she wasn't sure whether they still had capital punishment in Italy. Were criminals executed by hanging or by firing squad?

Ruth Ellis had been hanged in Britain just seven years previously after shooting her lover, David Blakely. It had caused a huge scandal, with all kinds of public figures speaking out against it, but she had a feeling that Italians might be keen on 'an eye for an eye' justice. They'd only just emerged from the dark ages of Fascism, and had been on the other side from Britain in the war. Maybe they still harboured anti-British sentiment.

Stop! I can't go on thinking like this or I'll go mad! Focus, Diana, focus.

Nothing in her life experience to date had prepared her for this ten-foot by ten-foot cell, with its narrow bed and covered bucket. She walked to the door and held her ear against it, trying to listen to the sounds outside. There were clanking noises and she thought she could occasionally hear human voices but there was no reply when she shouted, 'Hello! Is anybody there?'

She thought of newspaper stories she had read about people imprisoned abroad, and felt sure they were allowed a visit from the British Consul. Presumably they should inform the next of kin as well – in her case Trevor. But she had no idea what rights she had in Italy. Oh, if only she could talk to Trevor. He could call the Foreign Office and get them involved. He was such a clever man, he'd be sure to think of something to get her out of there.

As the afternoon wore on, she became very thirsty. There was no water in the cell, no refreshment of any kind, not even a tap at which she could wash her hands. Her mind leapt from subject to subject. Couldn't the *padrona* at the lodging house in Torre Astura confirm that she had been tucked up in bed all night? No, because her patio led straight out towards the seashore. Anyone who knew Helen would testify that she was a gentle soul who would never have engaged in a physical fight, and surely they would say the same about her? And then she couldn't think any more because her throat was parched and all she could picture was a long, cool drink of lemonade.

She watched the hands moving round on her watch and calculated how long it would take the Embassy to send someone. If they heard the news at, say, noon, it should have been possible to get someone there by two – but according to her watch it was already after four. Then she remembered that Italians don't work during the heat of the afternoon in summer, so maybe someone would come around five.

Just after five, there was a rattle of keys and she stood up expectantly, but it was a female guard holding a tray of food. She glanced at it: a plate of stew, a small salad and an unidentifiable pink dessert.

'*Acqua, per favore.*' She held her throat to indicate her thirst and the guard nodded. She put the tray of food on her bed and left the cell door unlocked while she went to fetch a jug of water and a glass. For a split second, Diana considered making a run for it but she knew that was crazy thinking. The guard returned, gave her the water and began to shut the door again.

'*Chiami l'Ambasciata Americana, per favore,*' Diana begged – 'Call the British Embassy.'

'*Domani, domani,*' the guard replied, and Diana's spirits plummeted. That meant 'tomorrow'. How could she be expected to stay overnight in this place?

Helen, where are you? If only you could come back and tell them the truth . . .

The door closed and she sat down and poured a glass of water. Bile rose in her throat at the smell of the food and she knew she wouldn't be able to touch a morsel. Even the water made her retch, although it was fresh and cool.

At five-thirty, the guard returned and Diana assumed she'd come to collect the tray so she lifted it to hand over but she said, '*No, hai un visitatore.*'

Oh thank God! Someone had come to get her out.

She dropped the tray on the bed with a clatter and followed her out and along the corridor then up some stairs to a room with a table and several chairs. The door was open and inside sat a very suave-looking man with silver-grey slicked-back hair, wearing a pale grey suit.

'Hello, Miss Bailey,' he said, standing up and holding out his hand. 'Bartolomeo Esposito. I am your lawyer.'

As she reached out her hand to shake his, a whiff of sweat reached her nostrils and she realised she had sweaty armpits. She was sure she had used her Arrid deodorant that morning. The words from the advertisement – 'Dry as the desert' – came into her head. It hadn't worked, though. Perhaps her fear had caused an unusual amount of perspiration. She worried that Signor Esposito might be able to smell it and clasped her elbows firmly to her sides.

What a ridiculous thing to be worrying about! This was the man who could establish her innocence. That's what mattered. She needed to convince him that she was honest, rational and reliable, and that she was being treated with great injustice.

'Please take a seat,' he said, in a business-like tone, sitting down and opening a folder of papers.

Diana sat.

Chapter Fifty-Four

———◆———

Signor Esposito was probably in his early fifties, she thought, and he looked expensive. She watched his hands as he flicked through papers. They appeared to be manicured, with short nails and neat cuticles. Did Italian men have manicures?

'Hilary Armitage hired me on behalf of Twentieth Century Fox.'

A lump formed in Diana's throat. It was wonderful to know that Hilary was aware she was there and trying to help.

'I've read through your statement and the police case against you and it seems we have two problems: the fact that you were both rivals in love for the same man, and the witness who says she saw you together at Torre Astura.'

'What?' Diana exclaimed. 'That's impossible! I didn't see Helen at Torre Astura. And we weren't love rivals – that's all wrong.'

He nodded. 'Good. They're bringing the woman up for an identification parade so if she is not able to identify you that will be helpful.'

Diana was aghast. 'Who on earth is she? When will they hold this parade? I hope it's going to be soon, so I can get out of here.'

He frowned, creating a furrow above the bridge of his nose, and leaned forward on his elbows. 'I hope it will be

338

tomorrow. On Thursday there will be a hearing at which the public prosecutor will request validation from a judge for the preliminary investigation.'

Diana gasped and her stomach clenched into a knot. 'I *can't* stay here till Thursday. I simply can't. I have a job to do.'

He continued in the same matter-of-fact tone. 'There's no possibility you will be released before Thursday. Murder is a very serious charge. But we'll make it as comfortable as possible for you here while we build up your defence.'

'And I'll definitely get out on Thursday?'

'No, not definitely. Only if we can convince the judge there are no grounds on which to hold you. We have to overturn all the circumstantial evidence against you and that could take time.'

The enormity of events began to sink in and Diana started to cry, quietly.

'Compose yourself, Miss Bailey,' he said, but not unkindly. 'I'd like you to describe to me your relationship with Helen. What kind of friendship was it? How much time did you spend together? And then tell me in your own words about your relationship with this man' – he glanced at his notes – 'Ernesto Balboni, and about Helen's interest in him.'

She sniffed back her tears to answer his questions. As she spoke, he made notes, and that calmed her. His English was completely fluent and she could tell he understood everything she was saying. She felt as if she was doing something productive. If she could be clear, precise and accurate in her statements, they would realise, surely, that she was a good person and would never have been capable of murder. She hadn't even bought a mousetrap to kill the little mouse that sometimes darted across the room in her *pensione* at night.

'Look at me!' she said, holding up an arm. 'I'm not strong. How am I supposed to have wrestled Helen over to the water and held her head under until she drowned?'

He looked at her closely, then made a note in his papers. 'Interesting. So you didn't realise she had a head injury?' Diana shook her head, wide-eyed. He continued. 'Yes, she appears to have been hit over the head and was unconscious when she entered the water. It's why they have discounted suicide.'

'You believe me, don't you?' Suddenly it was very important to her that he did.

He nodded. 'Having listened to what you say, I do.' He patted her hand. 'But we need to find hard evidence. I don't suppose you have any idea who might have killed her?'

'Yes, I think it was a drug dealer called Luigi – I don't know his surname. But the police have already questioned and released him. He's lying to them because I *definitely* saw him with Helen the day before she died even though he claims to have an alibi.'

Signor Esposito made some notes about that, and said he would see what he could find out. Perhaps the staff at the bar where he met Helen would remember him – but if he was a known drug dealer, it's likely they wouldn't want to get involved.

'Now, let me explain your rights while you are in custody. You can have one visitor a day and you can ask them to bring clothes and toiletries for you. You are allowed to make one phone call a day and you should be given access to a bathroom to wash at least once a day. I understand they have put you in a cell on your own for now. Normally you have to pay extra for that but I expect they are waiting for the outcome of the hearing before putting you in a shared cell. We'll deal with that on Thursday, if necessary.'

It was Tuesday. Thursday seemed a lifetime away. He noticed her terrified expression. 'I assume you've never been in jail before.'

'Of *course* not!'

'The time will pass. Perhaps you could have some books brought in. Please try to stay calm and keep racking your brains for any tiny fact you might have overlooked that could help your case.'

She was still very tearful but his tone calmed her a little. Two days wasn't so much out of an entire lifetime. She just had to get through it. 'Would it be possible to have some belongings brought from my *pensione* today?'

'Write a list of what you want and I'll ask Hilary Armitage to arrange it.'

He passed her a pen and paper and she wrote her list: toothbrush and toothpaste, washcloth and soap, shampoo, day clothes and night clothes, books, pens and paper and lots of bottles of water.

'Can I make a phone call? Do you think they will let me call my husband in London?'

The lawyer looked surprised. 'You're married?'

She supposed it hadn't occurred to him because they'd been talking about her having a lover. She held out her ring finger to show him the plain gold wedding band she wore. 'Yes.'

'Of course they will let you call him. Do you want to do it now?'

She checked her watch. Taking into account the hour's time difference, Trevor would just have left work and should be heading home. Did he have any society meetings on Tuesdays? She thought not. 'Perhaps in about an hour.'

'OK. I'll tell the guard to fetch you in an hour and I'll explain that you will be calling England.'

'Thank you,' she whispered.

He gathered his papers into a pile, tapping the edges on the desktop to align them, then slipped them inside a folder and scraped his chair back. Helen felt panicky that he was about to leave her and she'd be led back to that cell and left alone again.

'Signor Esposito, one final question,' she asked in a small voice. 'Do you . . . do they have the death penalty here?'

'Absolutely not! We think it's barbaric that your country still executes people. The death penalty was banned in Italy in 1889. It was brought back briefly under Mussolini, but the last time people were executed here was in 1945. You will find our legal code very humanitarian, Mrs Bailey.'

That was something. And yet they had made such a huge mistake in her case that she found it hard to take comfort. 'When will I see you again?' she asked.

'I will see you on Thursday morning before the hearing. In the meantime, you can call me if you think of anything else.' He handed her a gold-embossed business card. 'You'll be fine, Diana. You'll get through this.'

She pursed her lips and nodded.

He summoned a guard and spoke to her in rapid Italian, explaining about the phone call, then with one last wave he was gone. The only thing that kept her calm was thinking that in an hour she would be able to speak to Trevor. She would tell him everything and he would think of a plan. He'd know what to do.

342

But when the guard led her back upstairs and the call was put through, it rang and rang unanswered. After twenty rings, the Italian operator told her that there was no reply and she should call again later.

'Please try for longer,' she begged, but after a further twenty rings the operator terminated the call, and it was then that Diana fell apart. As the guard led her back down to her cell, she sobbed uncontrollably, and she continued to sob well into the night.

Chapter Fifty-Five

On Wednesday morning, some Italian newspapers ran stories saying that Diana Bailey, a twenty-six-year-old researcher on the *Cleopatra* movie, had been arrested in connection with the death of the makeup artist who'd been found in the water at Torre Astura. Under the lurid headline '*Gelosia!*' one said that Diana was a married woman who had left her husband at home in England to embark on a torrid affair with an Italian man. When her younger, prettier colleague lured him away, she couldn't contain her rage and attacked her rival, leaving her covered in cuts and bruises, before drowning her. The article went on to lambast the immoral atmosphere on the Cinecittà set, where everyone was sleeping with someone else's husband or wife. It reported that Sybil Burton had left for England and already Elizabeth Taylor and Richard Burton had been seen together again, pawing each other like animals. No wonder other people on the film followed their example.

Scott read each of the stories in turn, trying to square the facts with what he knew of Helen's life, but they didn't add up. Drugs or no drugs, she was too gentle. She wouldn't steal another woman's boyfriend and engage in a cat-fight over him. Scott had never seen her with a boyfriend. The coverage had a hysterical tone that he instinctively distrusted. Helen had always described Diana in glowing terms. When he spoke to Gianni later, his photographer agreed.

'I think I have a picture of Diana at home,' he said. 'I'll bring it for you and you'll see she doesn't look the type. Still, sometimes the quiet ones have the most secrets.'

He zipped home and met Scott later at a café on the Via Veneto where they pored over his shots of a mousy-haired woman going into the Grand Hotel on the occasion of the *Spartacus* party the previous October. She looked startled by the flashbulbs and uncomfortable in a tight-fitting, above-the-knee frock and backcombed hair. Somehow they didn't suit her. She appeared trussed up and unnatural.

'I hadn't seen her before and I took the photos in case she was important,' Gianni explained, 'but when I showed them to my contact on the set he said she was just the new researcher.'

'It's handy you kept them. I'll send one to my editor tonight. Why don't you sell the others? You might as well make some money from them.'

Gianni beamed. 'I wasn't sure if you would let me sell them to other papers.'

'Sure you can. Take them to Jacopozzi at Associated Press and get the best price you can. They should be worth a bit if you release them before anyone else has one.'

'Will do, boss.' Gianni stood up eagerly.

'Hang on! Are you expecting Liz and Dick to come out tonight? What's the word on the street?'

'She won't come today, I don't think. She got a letter threatening to kill her and her children, so they've trebled the security around her villa. I went past earlier and there are armed police patrolling and a police car parked outside.' He sniffed in annoyance. 'It's going to be hard to get shots of her because they

345

have thrown out all the photographers who used to sit in the trees overlooking her garden.'

'Have you ever done that?'

'Sure,' Gianni grinned. 'Why not?' He slung his camera diagonally across his shoulders, then straddled his scooter and waved as he drove off.

Scott sat deep in thought as he stirred his espresso. He was convinced that Helen's death must have had something to do with her drug habit. Maybe it had caused her to behave out of character and get into a fight. Perhaps she was distressed the night before she died because Diana had confronted her. But what was she doing in Torre Astura, presumably not far from the Anzio villa she had told him about? Poor Helen. He just hoped that if the Ghianciaminas had killed her, it had been quick and she hadn't suffered.

He decided the time had come to go to the police and tell them what he knew. He jumped onto his Vespa and drove out to the police station to the east of the city. At reception, he said he had information about the death of the makeup girl from *Cleopatra*, and asked if he might speak to someone involved in the case. He was led into an interview room, where he had to wait about half an hour before an officer came in.

Scott explained that Helen had been a drug addict and that he had been trying to help her quit the habit.

'You were a boyfriend of hers?' the officer asked.

'No, just a friend.'

Scott told him about the vitamin doctor and wrote down his name and address on a piece of paper torn from his journalist's notepad. The officer took it without looking at it.

'I saw her the night before she died and she was very upset

because the treatment wasn't working. I think she might have started using heroin again.'

'Where did you see her?' He had the officer's interest now.

'I went to her apartment at about seven in the evening.'

'Ah,' the officer exclaimed, pleased with this information. 'So you were the American man seen there. Our witness said she was crying, yes?'

'She was very upset,' Scott agreed.

'And you talked to her. Did you go in?'

'No. We talked for a while on the doorstep and I asked her to come out for dinner with me but she didn't want company so I ended up leaving her. I wish I hadn't now.'

'Did she tell you about her new boyfriend?'

'No. I never saw her with a boyfriend and she never mentioned one.' *Only guys she liked who didn't call her*, he remembered.

'Uh-huh. Well, thank you for your help, Mr . . .' He rose to his feet.

'Morgan.' Scott was surprised. 'Don't you want me to make a statement? You haven't written down anything I've said.'

'We're confident we have the culprit in prison. There is evidence against her the public haven't been told about. If Helen occasionally took *eroina*, it is not relevant to our case.'

'I'm sure it's relevant,' Scott insisted. 'The night I saw her she was upset because of drugs, not because of a boyfriend. Helen spoke about Diana a lot and always said she was her best friend.'

'That's why the argument became so bitter when they fell out.' The officer was still on his feet and he seemed impatient. 'Now if that's all, Mr Morgan, I have a lot to do.'

Scott stood up reluctantly. 'One last thing: can you tell me anything about the threatening letter sent to Elizabeth Taylor? Was it in English or Italian?'

'Italian. Goodbye, Mr Morgan.'

Scott walked out of the station, pondering that. The letter could have been from a religious maniac, adopting the Vatican's view that Elizabeth Taylor was a promiscuous tart. That was one theory. But he wondered whether she could have done anything to antagonise the Cosa Nostra in the city. It was a possibility.

Back at the office, he rang the *Cleopatra* press team to ask for a statement, but they played it down, saying that Elizabeth wasn't remotely worried. She had been receiving crank letters since she first put her arms round Lassie at the age of twelve and in her view this was just another of the same. The heightened police presence would be maintained for the rest of her stay in Rome, though. The Italian police couldn't ignore the world's biggest star being threatened on their watch.

Chapter Fifty-Six

During her first night in prison, Diana lay gripped by anxiety. At ten o'clock a church bell rang then the lights were switched off, leaving her in fuzzy blackness with just a pale rectangle of moonlight by which to get her bearings. She dozed off briefly then woke feeling disorientated and had to feel her way along the wall to reach the covered bucket to urinate. There were distant clangings, a vague murmuring and at one stage she heard movements in the air overhead, as if she was sharing her cell with bats or some very large moths. Every noise caused a fresh wave of panic.

At seven a.m., the church bell rang again and the lights were abruptly switched on. Diana calmed herself by picking up one of the books from the package that Hilary had arranged to be delivered the previous evening. Tarn and Griffith's *Hellenistic Civilisation* was a classic that she always used to enjoy rereading. The words were jumping around and she had no concentration, but the simple act of holding a book and turning the pages were familiar sensations that comforted her.

The door opened and a new guard appeared, holding a tray with a cup of milky coffee and some bread, as well as a letter. She discovered she was ravenous, and took a big gulp of coffee and a mouthful of bread before tearing open the envelope.

The handwriting looked like Hilary's, and a quick glance at the signature confirmed it.

My dear Diana, I simply can't believe what has happened! We are all in a state of shock. No one believes a word of the case the police have concocted against you. It's utterly ludicrous and we've told them so, as have Helen's parents, who said to send you their warmest regards. Keep strong and know that we are doing all we can. Signor Esposito is one of the top lawyers in Rome and I'm sure he'll get you out before long.

Today we start shooting the mausoleum scenes and Joe is not happy with the baskets the asps will be kept in. He was cursing the fact that you are not here to advise, so if you have any thoughts on baskets (or asps) and it will distract you from your plight, do send word.

Keep a stiff upper lip. We are all behind you and can't wait until this hideous experience is over and you are back with us at Cinecittà again.

All my love, Hilary

Hilary didn't mention how Diana should send word, but she decided to make some notes for them about the basket of asps, simply to occupy her thoughts. Few historians believed that Cleopatra had been killed by a snakebite, a story first recorded well after her death and not mentioned by contemporaries like Plutarch and Strabo. For a queen who liked to be in control of every detail, it seemed unlikely that she would rely on a wild animal smuggled in to her in a basket of figs. Asps were notoriously sluggish and it could have refused to bite her. Even if it did, she faced a slow, painful death. Much more likely she would have taken one of the many poisons known to the Egyptians, poisons with which she was well familiar, having used them many times on her enemies.

Alternatively, Diana had a theory that she could have been killed by Octavian himself, who then arranged it to look like suicide. A captive Cleopatra was a political problem he could do without, yet to have ordered her execution openly would have alienated her people. She was the mother of Caesar's son, and Egyptians believed her to be the incarnation of the goddess Isis. He wouldn't have wanted to risk being accused of killing a goddess, so to poison her and frame it as suicide made perfect sense.

She wrote all this, knowing she was wasting her time. Joe and Walter were undoubtedly set on the dramatic ending popularised by Shakespeare, whereby Cleopatra hoists the body of her dying lover into her mausoleum, then dispatches herself by holding an asp to her breast. She sketched a picture of the type of lidded basket in which the asp might have been smuggled, a basket normally used for carrying fruit. There were many images of such baskets in wall paintings.

She finished her note and glanced at her watch to find, to her horror, that it was still only nine-twenty in the morning. How on earth would she manage to fill the day?

A female guard came to escort her to the bathroom and Diana asked if she could arrange for her letter to be delivered. The guard suggested that if Diana had a visitor later, perhaps they could help. She seemed nice, this morning guard, and Diana kept her chatting for a while after she had finished her ablutions. She asked how long she had been in the prison service (two years) then told her about her job on the film, and her efforts to make everything historically accurate while they wanted drama and ostentation.

'Have you met *La Taylor*?' the guard asked, using the name given to her in the Italian press.

'Yes, she's a nice woman,' Diana replied. 'When I first met her, it was hard to stop staring because she is far more beautiful than anyone I've ever seen. But when I got to know her better I realised she's only human: she drinks, she smokes, she swears a lot and she is actually very witty. She's spoiled because of the lifestyle she leads but still friendly and considerate of those around her.'

'She's OK. I think my daughter is more beautiful,' the guard told her, and when she pulled out a photograph to show a sweet-faced Italian girl, Diana agreed that she was gorgeous.

The guard had to get on with her duties, but every time she came back to Diana's cell with food or a cup of coffee, she had more questions about the stars on the set and would linger for ten minutes or so. It passed the time.

Diana wondered if Elizabeth Taylor had heard of her arrest. Would she believe in Diana's innocence and, if so, were there any strings she could pull? She must have many friends in high places.

And then her thoughts returned to the case against her, puzzling through every minor detail to try and make sense of it all. Who on earth was this witness who claimed to have seen Helen fighting with another woman? Why would Helen be fighting, unless she had been attacked and was fighting for her life? And why hadn't the witness intervened to help her? Perhaps it had been Luigi she was struggling with and not another woman at all. Diana hoped that after the identification parade when the woman failed to identify her, someone would question her story more closely. Perhaps Signor Esposito would have a chance to do so.

She also hoped someone would interview Ernesto, who would confirm that she and Helen were hardly 'love rivals'. Why would she be fighting Helen for him when it was she who had ended the relationship? She guessed he would be reluctant to testify because it didn't show him in a very flattering light, but this was an emergency. Every time she thought of a new point, she wrote it down and soon the list was running to many pages.

And all the while she thought constantly about Helen, wondering what had really happened that night. She hoped the blow to the head had been quick and that her friend hadn't known any fear or pain. It was unbearable to imagine her being so near yet not able to reach the boarding house. Diana could only think that Luigi must have intercepted her.

A bell rang and a guard brought lunch. It seemed that every stage of the day was punctuated by the ringing of the old monastery bell. Diana asked if she might make a phone call. Trevor was always in his office at that time, usually munching a fish-paste sandwich. She was led upstairs to a little office, where she told the operator the telephone number and sat waiting to be connected. There were interminable clicks, buzzes and screeches down the line before the phone began to ring in City University, London, almost a thousand miles away.

'Dr Bailey's office,' came the voice of his secretary.

'It's Diana, calling from Rome. Could you put me through to Trevor, please?'

There was a hesitation or a delay on the line, she wasn't sure which. 'He's not here, Diana. I don't know where he is. He's got a tutorial at three so I expect he'll turn up later. Shall I give him a message?'

Her spirits sank. She was only allowed one phone call a day

and this was it. How awful to miss him. 'Could you please ask him to call Cinecittà and speak to Hilary Armitage? Tell him it's urgent.'

She had to spell Cinecittà and give a note of the phone number, which Trevor would no doubt have left at home on the pad by the telephone in the hall.

'Are you having fun out there?' the secretary asked. 'It's horrid weather here.'

Diana ignored the question. 'Please don't forget to tell him. Thank you so much.'

At least he would know soon. He would think of something to do.

Back in her cell, she reread the letter from Hilary and wished she had used her phone call for the day to ring her instead. Would Signor Esposito tell her that Diana was allowed a visitor? Might she come by later? If she did, Diana could give her the notes about the basket and the asps. She felt a strong desire not to be sidelined from the film and decided to pass her time making notes on all the scenes still to be shot: Antony's suicide and Cleopatra's death in the mausoleum, the sea battle of Actium and the arrival of Cleopatra's boat at Tarsus. It was one way of keeping busy – that, and talking to her friendly guard.

Around five o'clock the door of her cell opened and another guard appeared, a man. '*Un visitatore,*' he told her. '*Venga con me.*'

Excellent, she thought. *I hope it's Hilary. Or perhaps the British Consul.*

She followed him down the stairs to the meeting room, clutching her notes, but when she looked through the doorway her knees almost gave way beneath her. There, standing by the table with a battered brown suitcase by his feet, was an exhausted-looking Trevor. The relief was overwhelming. She ran straight into his arms and hugged him tightly, tears leaking out of her eyes. When she looked up, his eyes were shining.

'Walter Wanger called me yesterday afternoon,' he told her. 'He was very apologetic. Didn't say much; just that you had been arrested for murder and it appeared to be a case of mistaken identity. It sounded like a ridiculous made-up story but I got the first flight I could this morning just in case.'

'I rang your secretary earlier. She doesn't even know you've left the country.'

'I'll telephone later and tell them to find someone to stand in for me because I'm not leaving Italy again until I'm able to take you with me. What kind of a country is this? It's outrageous that you should be treated this way.' His expression was a mixture of anger and bewilderment. He wasn't the kind of person things like this happened to. Neither was she.

They sat and linked hands across the table. 'Wasn't the dead girl that friend of yours, the one I met?'

Diana took a deep breath. She had hoped this moment would never come, but now she had no choice but to tell him everything, including the fact that she'd had an affair.

'Yes, it was Helen,' she began. 'I'm so sorry, Trevor. I've let you down.'

Both of them cried as she described the way she had been taken in by Ernesto and the consequences of her affair. Trevor didn't let go of her hand throughout, but the tears slid unchecked down his cheeks. The news didn't seem to come as a surprise and she wondered if he had suspected something of the sort at Easter when he asked her not to decide about the future of their marriage until filming was over. Perhaps he had been able to sense a change in her that went deeper than a few new outfits.

Next she described to him what had happened to Helen, and the desperate attempt to save her life on the jetty.

'Why didn't you telephone me?' he asked.

'I wish I had, but it would have meant telling you about Ernesto.' She finished her story, describing Luigi, the witness who claimed to have seen her fighting with Helen and the suave lawyer who was representing her.

The guard was standing outside the door to give them privacy, but now she popped her head in to say '*Solo dieci più minuti*' – ten minutes more.

They turned to practicalities. Diana wrote down Hilary's number and gave Trevor the notes to pass on, then she opened her handbag to give him the lawyer's phone number and the keys to her room in the Pensione Splendid, where he could stay the night. With any luck, she would be joining him the following day.

'I'll find out from Signor Esposito where the hearing is, and what time, and I'll make sure I'm there,' Trevor told her. 'I'll keep a taxi waiting outside for us to leave together.'

'Oh, that would be bliss. We can go for lunch somewhere lovely to celebrate.'

The guard stood in the doorway clearing her throat. '*Signora, è ora.*'

She stood up and Trevor's voice cracked as he spoke: 'I can't bear to leave you here, Diana. I wish I could take your place.'

'It's OK,' she told him firmly. 'It's not too bad. I'll manage.'

After he'd left, back in her cell, she felt more worried for him than she did for herself. He belonged in academia and had no resources for dealing with a world peopled by movie stars and drug-dealing criminals. He didn't even speak Italian. But it was wonderful to know that he was there in Rome and still on her side after all she had told him. It was extraordinary, in fact.

Chapter Fifty-Seven

On Thursday morning, Diana was driven across town in a prison van, which drew up outside a limestone baroque building with a sculpture of a chariot and four horses on top, and a statue of Justice over the door. It was an austere building that seemed to have the weight of history in its stones. She was led through the entrance hall into a high-ceilinged chamber. Her heart was pounding hard and she focused on simply putting one foot in front of the other. Signor Esposito was already there, and he waved her over to sit beside him. A judge came into the room, an elderly man who wore thick, heavy spectacles. He nodded at both lawyers and proceedings began.

First the prosecuting lawyer presented his evidence, and Diana listened hard. She reeled when he said that Ernesto Balboni would be testifying that he'd had a sexual relationship with both her and Helen. It was a horrifying thought, but she simply didn't believe it. Helen would have told her; she could never keep a secret. She wrote a note to Signor Esposito: 'I don't believe it. He's lying.'

After that, the prosecutor read the evidence about their argument in the bar, Helen being distressed the next day and telling everyone she had to find Diana, and then there was a statement from the security guard at the Torre Astura film set who said he had directed Helen to Diana's room and that she was alone. That was odd. What had happened to her between the gatehouse and the *pensione*, where the *padrona* said she hadn't seen her? The prosecutor said a local resident claimed to have seen the two girls fighting by the roadside, pulling hair and screaming, at around midnight. Unfortunately, she couldn't be asked to pick Diana out of a line-up because her photograph had appeared in the Italian press that morning.

Diana was aghast. 'Where did they get my photo?' she scribbled in a note and Signor Esposito raised his hands in a shrug.

Then the lawyer spoke of the soldier's testimony that, after he pulled Helen from the water, Diana had come running down straight away, almost as if she had been waiting for someone to find the body and wanted to try to establish her innocence with ostentatious attempts to save someone who was clearly already dead. He said that Diana kept repeating 'I'm sorry, I'm sorry.'

Diana shook her head. She'd been in shock. How could they misinterpret that?

Finally, the policeman who had interviewed her at Torre Astura testified that she had a nasty scratch on her cheek, and that she had left the area despite his specific instructions to the contrary.

It all sounded very damning when put that way, and she watched the judge making notes on a sheet of paper in front of him. From time to time he glanced at her with a stern expression.

Now it was Signor Esposito's turn and he stood up and began to explain first of all that Diana's marriage had been troubled and that she had made the grave error of turning for comfort to a man who transpired to be married and a seasoned seducer. Diana was grateful that Trevor was waiting outside and couldn't hear what was being said. It made her sound desperately naïve, which she supposed she was. Signor Esposito mentioned that she had no family and was lonely in Rome, where she was fulfilling a very responsible role on the Cleopatra film. Perhaps it was unsurprising that she sought comfort elsewhere.

He dwelled at length on Diana's professional achievements, trying to correct the erroneous picture of her that had been promoted in the Italian media and establish her as a well-brought-up woman of good repute, before setting out her version of the events of the night Helen died. He mentioned that Helen had been struggling with a drugs problem and had become mixed up with some unsavoury characters as a result, although he didn't mention Luigi by name. The picture he painted was of a fragile, troubled girl who didn't fit in well amongst the older, more sophisticated crowd on the film set. He said Diana had tried to help her, but they had unfortunately fallen out the day before Helen died. And he made the point that Diana had already finished the relationship with Ernesto Balboni when he seduced Helen; she broke up with him as soon as she found out he was married.

'We don't know what happened to the poor girl at Torre Astura that night but my client did not see her. The police must continue their investigations until they find the true culprit and we will do all we can to assist them.'

Diana bit her lip. It sounded convincing if you understood that both she and Helen were gentle types. The idea of them getting into a physical fight was ludicrous. She gazed at the judge, trying to guess what he was thinking but he gave nothing away.

After hearing all the evidence he stood up and left the courtroom to consider his decision.

'How did it go?' she asked.

'We'll have to wait and see,' Signor Esposito told her. 'There were a couple of surprises in their evidence.'

For Diana, the biggest surprise of all was that Ernesto would testify for the prosecution. She was sure he was lying that he had a 'relationship' with Helen but why would he do that? He must truly hate her.

Just ten minutes later, the judge came back into the room. His judgement was short and to the point. Given the mass of circumstantial evidence against Signora Bailey, he ruled that her arrest for the murder of Helen Sharpe was validated. And given the seriousness of the crime, the fact that she had already left the area despite the police requesting her not to, and because she was a foreign national who might decide to flee, he was remanding her in custody while the investigation continued.

Diana clasped her face in her hands to stifle a scream. 'How long will that be?' she asked as soon as she could compose herself.

'Murder trials can take over a year in preparation.' Signor Esposito patted her shoulder. 'But don't worry – we'll get you out long before then.'

A guard came to collect her and she stood up, feeling utterly dazed.

'Will you explain to Trevor?' she asked. 'Tell him not to worry.'

'Of course.'

As she was led through the hall back out to the police car, she saw Trevor in a waiting area. She called his name and when he looked up, she managed to blow a kiss before she was led through a doorway and down to the car for the short journey back to Regina Coeli.

Chapter Fifty-Eight

Scott Morgan went to the Palazzo di Giustizia for the judicial hearing regarding the arrest of Diana Bailey, hoping that he might be permitted to listen to the evidence, but he was told by an official that it was just the judge, the lawyers and the defendant. Still, he decided to hang around and get the news as soon as judgement was declared. He asked a clerk which courtroom it was in and sat near the entrance. A dozen other journalists were hanging around, some of whom he recognised. On the next bench along there was a bookish sort of man who looked anxious and out of place, and Scott guessed he might be a friend of Diana's. He was dressed like an Englishman, in a shirt and tie, trousers and socks with gladiator sandals.

Sooner than he expected, the courtroom door opened and Diana was led out in handcuffs.

'Trevor,' she shouted, and blew a kiss at the waiting man. He half stood and spread his arms wide, obviously expecting her to run to him. When she was led off through a doorway instead, he hurried after her calling, 'Diana! Wait! Where are you taking her?'

A lawyer emerged and summoned the man, Trevor, and they sat in a huddle, head to head. They weren't far from Scott but their voices were lowered so he couldn't hear anything.

He seemed distraught and that's when Scott guessed he must be Diana's husband.

The lawyer spoke to him quietly for about ten minutes, then got up to leave, whereupon some members of the Italian press surrounded him, clamouring for information. Looking dazed, Trevor wandered towards the main doors of the building.

'Mr Bailey,' Scott approached him. 'Scott Morgan. I was a friend of Helen's and it's possible I can help with Diana's case. Can we talk?'

'Who are you?' he frowned.

'I'm a journalist, but I knew Helen. I'm convinced your wife is innocent, and I might have some information that can help her.'

'What paper do you work for? You're not planning to write about this by any chance?'

'I understand why you are suspicious, but I guarantee I won't write about anything you tell me. I promise.' He held out his hand. 'Can I buy you a coffee?'

'Alright,' Trevor agreed, and they shook.

They went to a nearby bar, which was empty apart from the owner and a scruffy dog snuffling on the floor. Scott began by telling Trevor about his article on the drugs trade in Rome, and how he had come to know Helen.

Trevor listened carefully. When the coffee came, his hand trembled as he raised the cup, sloshing some into the saucer.

'Want a brandy to go in that?' Scott asked. 'I'll join you.'

'Perhaps I will,' Trevor said. He was on the verge of tears and needed something to stiffen him up.

Scott told Trevor about his encounters with Luigi, then he described his visit to Helen the night before she died when he had found her in such a distressed state.

'She was very indiscreet about Luigi and I wonder if he had threatened her. It was pretty obvious that she was close to rock bottom but she wouldn't tell me why. Diana was her closest friend in Rome, so I'm sure that's why she decided to try and find her the next day. Except she didn't quite get there.'

Trevor nodded, thinking it over. 'But what can I do, Mr Morgan? They don't let you out on bail in this country and I can't have my wife spending a year in prison. It's extraordinary! We are not this kind of people.'

'I know you're not,' he soothed. 'I can see that a mile off. I don't know what the judge was thinking of.'

Trevor shook his head. 'I can't understand why a witness would claim to have seen them. She must be mistaken. And Ernesto Balboni, the man with whom Diana had an "affair"' – he grimaced – 'appears to be testifying that he was seeing Helen at the same time. Diana doesn't believe it, but why is he lying? That's another thing we need to find out.'

'It would be difficult for you to make contact with Balboni. You'd probably feel like slugging him, but I could try if you like. I bet I can find a way to catch him off guard.'

'Are you sure it's not against the law to contact witnesses?' He had finished his brandy and seemed more composed.

'Only if we intimidate them.' Scott pursed his lips in a half-smile. 'Let's trade addresses and phone numbers and keep in touch.' He scribbled his on a sheet of paper torn from his reporter's notebook. Trevor wrote the address of Diana's *pensione* on the bottom of the page and ripped it off to hand back.

'The telephone is out of order, I'm afraid, but you will catch me in the room after dinner every evening. I have nothing to do but go back there and read.'

Scott didn't know what to say. 'We're going to solve this, Trevor. Try not to worry too much.'

Trevor tilted his head to one side. '"Don't worry?" You're not married, are you, Mr Morgan?' Scott shook his head. 'No, I thought not.'

When they left the bar, Scott asked if he could give him a lift anywhere but Trevor said he would rather take the bus. The Rome bus service seemed to work rather well. He shuffled off, his shoulders hunched.

Back at his office, Scott rang the *Cleopatra* press office. 'One of your crew is dead and another is being investigated for murder. Do you have a comment?'

'It's a private matter, in police hands. We have nothing more to say.'

'I wonder if it would be possible to talk to Ernesto Balboni?'

'No.'

'Do you think the threat to kill Elizabeth Taylor might have anything to do with the death of Helen Sharpe?' He was fishing, but it didn't get him anywhere.

'Now you're being ridiculous,' he was told, and the line went dead.

Chapter Fifty-Nine

———•◆•———

Diana felt numb as she was driven back to Regina Coeli prison after the hearing. A year of her life might be spent there – more if she was found guilty at trial. Perhaps she would never leave the Mantellate wing's yellow walls again.

The guard met her at the entrance and told her he was taking her to a different cell.

'Why am I moving?'

'You'll share a cell now.'

'With another prisoner?' *Stupid question: of course it would be. Oh God, what kind of person would it be? They wouldn't put her in with anyone violent, would they?*

She was led to her original cell first, where she gathered her books, clothes and toiletries, then they continued up two flights of stairs. Noises echoed through the stairwells: footsteps on ancient stone, voices calling and strange unidentifiable clankings. The high ceilings amplified every footfall.

The warden took her along a corridor and unlocked the door of a cell. Inside Diana saw a woman of roughly her own age sitting on a narrow bed. There was an empty bed along the other wall. The woman looked up at her with suspicion, taking in her pale skin and mousy-brown hair.

'*Parli italiano?*' she asked.

'*Sì.*'

'*Quello è il tuo letto là.*' She pointed to the other bed.

Diana sat down on it, and the warden locked the door behind her. 'My name's Diana. I'm English,' she said in Italian.

'Donatella.' She had thick dark hair that hung below her breasts, and manly features. 'What are you in for?'

Diana explained that she had been accused of murdering a friend but that it wasn't true. 'And you?' she asked.

'*Pah!*' The woman spat in disgust. 'Theft. From my own brother-in-law, the son of a whore.'

She launched into a long explanation, gesticulating wildly to stress the crucial points, almost as if she were signing for a deaf person. Her husband died two years ago, she said, leaving her with no income and three children to feed. Her brother-in-law was rich, with a string of shops, and she asked if he could help. He gave her a job in one of his stores but paid her only a pittance and she got behind on the rent. There was nothing else she could do but slip a few hundred *lire* from the till every now and then. She had no choice. But her brother-in-law had set a trap for her by marking some notes. 'I took one – that's all. One hundred thousand *lire*! He called the police and they searched my bag and then I was arrested.'

'How could he?' Diana gasped. It was roughly fifty-seven pounds' worth, not a huge sum for a family member to take. 'Your children's uncle did that to you?'

Donatella shrugged dramatically. 'He's a bastard. When I see him I will scratch his eyes out, so help me.' Her face hardened and Diana thought she looked easily capable of it.

'So tell me your story,' Donatella challenged. 'If you are innocent, why are you here?'

Diana explained about the circumstances surrounding her arrest, and her suspicion that a drug dealer was the real culprit.

Donatella made a face. 'That's a problem. The big dealers don't tend to get convicted. But if you work for the film studios, get them to buy you a fancy lawyer and you should get off. Hey, did you know that if you have money, you can pay for a cell of your own and extra food here?'

'Can you?' She vaguely remembered Signor Esposito mentioning it but she had been so sure she'd get out today that she hadn't paid much attention. 'I've been in a cell on my own for two days and I think I'd rather have company – if you don't mind, that is. But I'll ask about getting extra food. Maybe we could share it.'

'Good idea.' Donatella grinned, and Diana saw that one of her front teeth was missing. 'So have you met *La Taylor*?'

'Yes, of course!' Diana told her about working on the film, and the obsessive character of its star. She saw no need for discretion in the present circumstances, so she described the way Elizabeth pursued Richard relentlessly yet still he kept returning to his wife. 'You'd think she could get any man she wanted but she may have set her sights on the one man who will reject her in the end. Isn't it strange how some women do that?'

'I'm the same. Why do we fall for the bad guys every time?' Donatella rolled her eyes. She had a million questions about the stars of the film and the time passed. A meal was brought and then they were allowed out of their cells for an hour's recreation. Donatella introduced Diana to a crowd of other women and she found herself the centre of attention as she described life on the film set and the peccadilloes of its international stars.

'What time is visiting hour?' she asked Donatella. 'I hope my husband will come to see me.'

'It's just after lunch. You've missed it for today,' came the reply, and Diana's face fell. 'But you can phone him if you have *gettoni* for the telephone.'

Diana nearly burst into tears. 'I have *gettoni* but the phone's out of order at the *pensione* so there's no way of contacting him.' She was miserable when she thought of Trevor hearing that he wasn't allowed to visit her that day. Maybe he would come to the jail only to be told at the gates. She wished she could get word to him that she was fine. She couldn't bear to think of what this must be doing to him. He had looked thin and tired before and now he must be beside himself with worry.

Back in the cell, while Donatella washed herself, Diana lay on her bed feeling crushed by misery. She'd been so happy. She loved the job. She loved living in Rome. She loved her friendship with Helen. For a while she had thought she loved Ernesto. Now they had all been taken away from her. Even if she were released from prison, life could never be the same again.

Chapter Sixty

The morning after the hearing, Trevor got up at the crack of dawn, determined to do something useful before visiting Diana so that he could report some progress. He consulted his elderly Baedeker, which told him that the British Consulate was on Via Septembre XX. He walked there using the maps in the guidebook only to find the building in ruins, with rubble strewn around. A solitary guard in a gatehouse wrote down another address for him – the Villa Wolkonsky – but when he consulted his Baedeker he found that it was a long way off, just inside the Aurelian walls which surrounded one of the city's seven hills, and he was forced to hail a taxi.

'Yes, we were bombed out of the old building in 1946,' a consular official told him when he finally found it. 'Zionist terrorists were responsible. There are plans being drawn up for a new one but meanwhile we are stuck out here in the back of beyond. Now what can I do for you?'

Trevor explained who he was and the official nodded in sympathy. 'We are familiar with the case and were planning to send someone to visit your wife. How is she coping?'

'She's a strong woman, but being wrongfully imprisoned would test anyone.'

'Yes, of course. The Italian press have been having a field day, trying to paint her as immoral. My advice would be that you ask any prominent friends to write testimonies in her support. It could be colleagues of hers back in England or here in Rome. Get your lawyer to release them to the media and you might start to swing public opinion in her favour. Is she religious?'

'No.'

The official tutted. 'That's a shame. You can't say that she is spending her time praying?'

'It would be a lie.'

'Not to worry. See how you get on with collecting testimonials, and do get back in touch if you need any further help.'

They agreed to let Trevor use a telephone, so he called his university department head to ask for compassionate leave, which was immediately granted. The story had broken in the British press that morning and they guessed that's why Trevor had failed to turn up for his lectures.

He telephoned Diana's old boss at the British Museum then her Head of House at Oxford and asked if they would write testimonials. Everyone was immensely sympathetic, and quite baffled at the predicament in which Diana found herself.

Next he phoned the production office at Cinecittà and made an appointment to see Hilary. He felt fine as long as he had tasks to fill the time, but as he sat having coffee on his own in a little café near the Colosseum, he felt his spirits plummet. The Consul had really been very little use. He'd been expecting a lot more support, but it seemed it was going to be up to him and Signor Esposito if anything were to be done.

It had been his worst fear all along that Diana would fall for another man in Rome. He was too old for her, and too set in his ways. He'd long suspected that the only reason he'd won the hand of such an extraordinary woman was because she was feeling adrift after the death of her father and had clung to the nearest life-raft. Well, perhaps she would still leave him, but for now she needed her life-raft and that's what he would be. He would apply his intelligence to this problem, do every-thing he possibly could, and not rest until he had solved it. He hoped he wouldn't have to meet Diana's lover, though. That would be a step too far.

He set his mind to considering who else he might approach to provide testimonials for Diana. He compiled a list then wrote little notes to each of them, which he would ask Hilary to distribute on set or send to London via the Cinecittà courier service. He didn't know where to buy envelopes but perhaps she would be able to lend him some.

He took the bus across town to Regina Coeli, arriving over an hour early for visiting because he wanted to make sure they had as much time as possible together. On this occasion they weren't alone but in a room full of other women receiving visitors, and Diana was waiting for him. As soon as he saw her he could tell she was depressed – who wouldn't be? – but she made an effort to appear cheerful and he did the same. He reported all the friends he was asking for testimonials and she seemed embarrassed.

'How awful it should come to this, that I need people to vouch for my good character.'

She gave him a thick pile of notes that she had written about forthcoming scenes on the film and asked him to pass them to Hilary. 'And will you pick up a copy of the latest shooting schedule from Candy?'

He agreed that he would. 'I met an American journalist called Scott Morgan – did Helen ever mention him?' Diana shook her head. 'Well, he's agreed to help. He's going to contact Ernesto Balboni and try to get the truth out of him.'

Diana hung her head, ashamed that Trevor should have to say that name. 'That's good.'

'How is the food, darling?' he asked.

She wrinkled her nose. 'Stews, stodgy pasta, soup, that kind of thing. It's quite edible, although the crockery has seen better days. I won't starve. But if we can afford to pay for extra rations, I will share them with my colourful room-mate.' She described Donatella and imitated her expressive way of talking with arms, head and whole body sometimes involved.

'Can I bring you anything else? Any treats?'

'Not really. Maybe some teabags. I think I may be able to get hot water for tea.'

With business complete, they sat holding hands for the comfort of it. Trevor's heart ached. He couldn't look her in the eye because he could read in her expression how miserable she was, and he didn't want to add to her misery by letting her know his own anxieties. It was awkward yet companionable at the same time. When the guard called '*È ora!*' he squeezed her fingers tightly.

'Every minute I am not here, apart from when I am sleeping, I will be working for your release. Trust me, Diana. I'm going to get you out.'

'Thank you,' she whispered. She thought, but didn't say out loud, *I don't deserve you.*

When he left the prison, he checked all the bus stops he could find but none seemed to go all the way to Cinecittà so he had to take one bus to Termini station and find another from there. Hilary met him at the studio gates and waved him in past the guard. She took him to the bar, where they ordered iced lemonades because the heat was fierce.

'How is she doing?'

'Remarkably well. Perhaps she is trying to be strong for my sake, but she does a good job of it.'

'I don't know how she copes. I'd be a nervous wreck.'

'She's keeping busy. I think that helps.'

Trevor handed over the reams of notes Diana had made, and Hilary said she would deliver them to Joe Mankiewicz. He also handed over his testimonial requests. Some were to go back to London by courier but needed envelopes, while the rest were for people working on the film.

'I've written a note for Elizabeth Taylor. Diana doesn't know about it, but I wondered if she might be able to bring any influence to bear.'

Hilary reluctantly took the note from him. 'She's very busy. I wouldn't hold out any hope but I'll give it to one of her secretaries.'

'Thank you. Now, is there any sign of Ernesto Balboni?' He hated the sound of the name, its syllables, everything about it. 'Diana's lawyer needs to talk to him urgently.'

'He's off sick. No one has heard from him. We're very cross with him.'

'Do you have his address?'

'You'd think I would, but I checked our records and he listed Diana's *pensione* as his address. There was another one before that but it's been crossed out and I can't read it. I'm so sorry.'

Trevor was quiet for a moment. It really was too bad. How would Scott Morgan track him down without an address? You'd think if the chap had any decency at all he would have volunteered to come forward. It was hard to fathom how Diana could have chosen such a rogue, but those were always the pushy ones, he supposed. There was a chap in the Latin department at university who was a real womaniser and Trevor had watched at a party once as he seduced a colleague with unctuous flattery, but he had never thought Diana would be susceptible to that kind of thing. It made him shudder.

After they finished their drinks, Hilary took him back to the office, where he addressed all his envelopes and picked up a copy of the shooting schedule.

'Do give Diana our love,' Hilary said. 'Tell her we're all rooting for her.'

After leaving, Trevor consulted the sign on the bus stop opposite Cinecittà and took a bus back into town. He stopped at a *trattoria* near Diana's *pensione* and ate some chewy type of pasta, drank a whole bottle of a dark, heavy wine, then threw it all up in the gutter outside.

Chapter Sixty-One

On Friday evening, Scott noticed Luigi in the piano bar Helen and her friends used to frequent and sidled up to chat.

'How's business?' he asked.

Luigi shrugged. 'The usual. Did you want something?'

'Maybe,' Scott replied. 'What's on offer this fine evening?'

'Everything. I can get anything you want.'

'Can I buy you a drink?'

Luigi accepted a shot of whisky, requesting Johnny Walker, the most expensive brand they stocked. Scott had a beer. He wanted to work round to asking about Helen but without being too obvious.

'Your job must make you very popular,' he said. 'Does it help when you are sweet-talking the ladies?'

Luigi was heavy-set, and the open buttons at the neck of his shirt displayed a carpet of curly dark chest hair. There was dark stubble on the backs of his hands where he obviously shaved them. The man resembled a gorilla and Scott couldn't believe he would have much success with women based on his physical merits.

'Who needs it?' Luigi bragged. 'The ladies come to me. They all want something so I get what I want in return.' There was an ugly glint in his eye and Scott noticed a cloying aftershave scent hung in the air around him.

'I could do with some of that. I'm not having much luck with the chicks here in Rome.' Scott found self-deprecation worked to his advantage, especially when dealing with arrogant types. It underpinned their sense of superiority.

'You want me to introduce you to some?'

Scott couldn't think of anything he wanted less. 'I'm pretty picky. Some of the girls in the *Cleopatra* crowd are cute but they can be full of themselves.'

'I know some of them, for sure. There are none in tonight though.' They both gazed round the bar, which was quiet for a Friday evening.

'Say, didn't you know that makeup artist girl who drowned? I was reading about it in the paper.'

'Not really.' Luigi wouldn't meet his eye. 'I saw her around.'

'I gave her a ride home once and I got the impression she was an addict. She always looked like she was blitzed.'

'Did she put out for you?' Luigi asked, with interest.

'Nah. We kissed a little but she seemed uptight.' It felt awful to be talking about Helen in this way but he wanted to lure Luigi into confessing. There was a knowing smirk on his face and Scott could tell he was dying to boast. 'Did you ever get anywhere with her?'

'Sure I did. She would do anything when she wanted a fix. Well, not quite anything – she was a virgin – but a few times she gave me a hand job or a *bocchino*.' He made an obscene gesture, thrusting his thumb in and out between his lips.

Scott felt like smacking him on the nose. His fists clenched, but he managed to control his temper. 'Gee, I wish I'd known about that. When did you see her last?'

There was a flicker of suspicion, then Luigi relaxed again. 'Last week. Usual thing: no money, desperate for a fix, so I took her out the back of the café for a quick one. Probably the last sex she ever had.' He grinned, hideously.

'What do you reckon happened to her? That story about the researcher doesn't add up somehow.'

Luigi's face took on a guarded look. 'I don't know, and I don't care. One less slut in the world doesn't bother me.' A muscle twitched in his cheek and Scott felt sure he was hiding something.

'Don't you think it's a bit weird that she travelled all the way down to the coast? I wondered if she knew another dealer down there and went to buy drugs from him, perhaps if she couldn't find you.'

Luigi was definitely rattled. 'How the hell should I know? Listen, do you want something or not? I'm not going to do any business with you standing here yakking.'

'I'll have some coke. Meet you in the gents'?'

As Scott handed over the money by the urinals, Luigi revived their little joke: 'So is this for Elizabeth Taylor?' He grinned broadly, and Scott saw he had a gold filling in one of his molars.

Scott tapped the side of his nose. 'That would be telling.' He accepted the paperfold that was slid into his palm, then said, 'Thanks, buddy. See you around.'

When he got outside, he turned the corner into a service alleyway and leaned against a wall, utterly sickened by what he had heard. Was Luigi just boasting or had Helen really been forced to offer sexual favours to feed her drug dependence? That pretty, innocent girl touching such revolting flesh . . . If it were true, that might explain why she was so distraught the last time he saw her: she couldn't afford any more vitamin injections but felt so bad when she stopped them that the only thing she could think of was going back to that vile man.

She was caught between a rock and a hard place. If only he had been able to rescue her. He should have done more. Now his drugs exposé had another purpose apart from revenge on the Ghianciaminas: he owed it to Helen to get Luigi put behind bars.

Chapter Sixty-Two

Trevor woke on Saturday morning to the sound of an envelope being slipped under the bedroom door. He blinked and called 'Hello?' but whoever it was had started back down the stairs again.

He got up and examined it but all it said on the outside was 'Professor Trevor Bailey', and the address of the *pensione*. He sat on the bed to open it, and his eyes widened as he read the ornate signature at the bottom: Elizabeth Taylor. The handwriting was neat, with florid loops and swirls.

Dear Professor Bailey,

I'm very sorry to hear of Diana's troubles. I'm not sure how I can help but please come to my villa for cocktails at 7 this evening and we'll talk. My driver will pick you up at 6.45.

Sincerely,

Elizabeth Taylor

'Oh my gosh!' he exclaimed out loud. How very kind of her. How extraordinary, in fact. He would have to wear a suit and tie, and he decided to pop in to a local barber's shop and have a proper shave and hair trim. It felt as though one should be well turned-out when meeting Hollywood royalty.

At the daily visit, Diana was touched when she heard of

Elizabeth's invitation, although embarrassed that Trevor had contacted her in the first place.

'I hope she doesn't think badly of me. Please make sure she understands the truth.'

'Of course I will, darling.'

She didn't look well, he thought. There were several insect bites on her face, arms and legs, which she kept scratching. Her complexion was grey and there were dark shadows under her eyes. She claimed to be sleeping well but he didn't believe her.

'Will you visit tomorrow?' she asked. 'I can't wait to hear about your meeting. You must give me your candid opinion of Elizabeth.'

He agreed that of course he would. It was always hard to leave Diana, but at least this time he had something to fill the long evening.

A uniformed chauffeur arrived to collect him at the appointed time and he was driven up to the Via Appia Antica, the old Roman road that led south out of the city all the way down to Brindisi in the heel of Italy. Trevor mused that it had been named after Appius Claudius Caecus, the man who built the first section of it. He went blind in later life – according to Livy, it was because of a curse that had been placed on him. Livy was a great believer in curses.

There were high walls around the villa and security guards at the gates, who insisted on patting Trevor's pockets and trouser legs to ensure he wasn't carrying any weapons. Trevor looked at the formal gardens stretching in all directions and admired the handiwork of the gardeners, who must have had to water the lawns and flowerbeds every day in summer.

At the front door he was met by a butler, who led him

through a cool atrium to a sitting room from where he could see a swimming pool in which three young children were screeching and splashing. A Pekingese dog ran up to sniff his trouser leg.

'May I offer you a drink?' the butler asked, and Trevor requested a glass of water. He sank into a comfortable armchair and looked around the room. Colourful rugs were arranged on the marble-tiled floors, a glass coffee table held a large bouquet of white roses, and there were shelves of books covering one wall. In a corner, there was a record player and stacks of gramophone records. Floor-to-ceiling windows on two sides meant there was plenty of light, but they were covered in floating net curtains that billowed in the breeze from open windows. The butler brought his water, then left him on his own.

After a while, Trevor got up to examine the books, and found a wide selection: lots of novels, including *Gone with the Wind* and works by Hemingway, Faulkner and Saul Bellow. There were non-fiction books on Judaism, a biography of Tennessee Williams and some art monographs. Suddenly he heard a movement behind him and turned to see Elizabeth Taylor walking down a staircase, wearing a floaty lime-green gown and looking tanned and very beautiful.

'I only have a few books here in Rome. I've got lots more back home.' She held out her hand and smiled warmly. 'Hello, I'm Elizabeth.'

'Trevor,' he said, feeling stupidly nervous. It was hard to look at her directly; perhaps it could make you blind, like looking too long at the sun.

'I have some books of Diana's here. She lent them to me a while ago. Perhaps you will return them for me?' She indicated a pile stacked to one side. Trevor picked them up and said that of course he would, if she was sure she had finished with them. Although she was wearing vertiginous high heels, Elizabeth's head only came up to his chest.

'I'm ever such a fast reader,' she said, sitting in a chair opposite his. 'Now tell me, how *is* Diana?'

'She's bearing up,' he said: his stock phrase for anyone who asked. In fact, it appeared to be true that she was coping but what choice did she have? 'We're doing all we can to get her out.'

The butler brought her a drink on a tray, and she glanced at Trevor's glass of water. 'Won't you have a proper drink? I hate to drink alone.'

'Alright. Do you have gin?' he asked.

'Does the Pope have Bibles?' she cackled. 'Yes, of course I have gin. I drink mine with Coke but we also have lemonade or orange juice.'

'Lemonade, please.'

The butler went to prepare his drink and Elizabeth slipped off her shoes and curled her feet beneath her, drink in hand.

'Now tell me exactly what has happened to Diana. I've only heard the sketchiest outline.' She listened carefully as Trevor ran through the story. He managed to talk about Ernesto without any emotion creeping into his voice, but he avoided using his name, calling him 'Diana's Italian boyfriend'. Elizabeth didn't express any surprise, which led him to wonder if she already knew about the affair.

'Are you happy with her lawyer? Would it be useful to get a second opinion from one of my guys? I've got loads on the payroll.'

'Thank you, but we are happy for now.' He imagined her

lawyers would specialise in contracts and finance rather than Italian criminal law.

'Do you need money? I'd be happy to contribute.'

'No, gosh . . .' Trevor was embarrassed. 'Nothing like that.' He explained that the British Consul had suggested he got high-profile people to provide testimonials, so as to help turn around Italian public opinion, and that he had written to her because she was the highest-profile person Diana knew.

Elizabeth sighed. 'I don't know if you've heard but I'm considered an "erotic vagrant" here in Italy. I'm afraid my support might be counter-productive in the eyes of devout Catholics. She could get tarred with the same brush.' She waved her arm dramatically, indicating a paintbrush coating her. 'But I'll make sure that Walter, Joe and Spyros provide references. And Irene Sharaff. Who else could I try? Perhaps Fellini would be good. Or Marcello Mastroianni? And I think Audrey Hepburn is in town.' She paused to slurp her drink and consider her acquaintances in Rome.

Trevor was bemused. 'Maybe it should just be people who know Diana personally. I'd be most grateful for any pressure you can apply.'

'Give your lawyer's address to my secretary, Dick Hanley, and he'll make sure it happens. I'll introduce you before you go.'

Trevor took a sip of the drink that had been discreetly placed by his elbow, and almost choked at the strength of it. He coughed delicately into his hand.

'We only have another month of filming left but I hope Diana is around to advise. Walter and Joe are producing a Hollywood extravaganza but I know your wife has managed to make several very important changes. Richard and I are impressed by her erudition.' Her voice softened as she said her lover's name, and she shifted her legs beneath her.

'I wasn't aware that Diana knew him personally.'

'We've often talked about her and the advice she's given. He read one of the books Diana lent me because he wanted more guidance on why Mark Antony cracks up in the end. Have you seen him act?'

Trevor nodded. 'He's a brilliant actor.'

She was pleased. 'He likes to understand the psychological profile of his characters and really get under their skin.'

'Mark Antony is a difficult one to work out: he was such a tough man throughout his life, but weak in death. Most commentators are hard on him but I have some sympathy.'

'Don't you think he was destroyed by love? He fell apart when he realised Cleopatra had turned her back on him?'

'I think he was destroyed by his own debauchery, which meant that when the chips were down his own men didn't trust him. The reports mostly come from Cicero, who said "We ought not to think of him as a human being but as a most outrageous beast."' He smiled. 'When Cicero took against you, he didn't moderate his criticisms.'

Elizabeth seemed entranced. 'But this is perfect. I must pass this on to Richard.'

'I assume he'll have read Plutarch's *Life of Antony*. It's kinder to the man than Cicero's diatribes, but still critical. There are many good modern biographies but I always like to go back to primary sources where possible.'

'Are you an Egyptologist, like Diana?'

'I'm a classicist. I've written a book on Plutarch, so our interests are different but complementary.'

'How fascinating!' Elizabeth breathed. 'I bet you have

wonderful conversations at the dinner table.' She glanced at a clock on a side table. 'Talking of which, I'd better get ready for dinner soon. Richard gets so grumpy when I'm late.' She uncurled herself from the chair, moving languorously, her thoughts already with her lover. 'It's been fascinating meeting you. I'll send Dick Hanley down and you can give him the address of Diana's lawyer. And good luck, Trevor. Tell Diana that Richard and I are behind her all the way.'

She stood close to him as they shook hands and he could smell her scent. It was probably very expensive but somehow it reminded him of a type of laundry detergent Diana used to buy: 'Ajax: Stronger than Dirt', the advertisement said.

She wafted up the stairs, turning to wave from the top. Dick Hanley appeared a few minutes later and noted down Signor Esposito's office address before guiding Trevor out to the car that had brought him.

As they pulled out of the gates of Villa Papa, Trevor began to cry. He didn't know why. Perhaps he was touched by Elizabeth's kindness. It was such an extraordinary situation.

The chauffeur opened the glove compartment, pulled out a white silk handkerchief and passed it back to him without a word, as if he was used to grown men crying in the back seat of his car.

Chapter Sixty-Three

At visiting hour the next day Diana forced a smile when Trevor described Elizabeth Taylor offering to get a testimonial from Audrey Hepburn.

'Maybe she could get John Wayne or Marilyn Monroe?' he suggested. 'She made it sound as though the famous belong to some exclusive club in which they can ask each other for favours, even if they've never met.' He'd planned this speech on the way there, hoping to cheer Diana up.

'Something like the Masons, you mean?' She cocked her head on one side. 'Perhaps it's true.'

'Hilary sends her love,' Trevor told her. 'And the letters of support will soon start pouring in. I wrote to everyone I could think of.'

'I'm sure that will make a huge difference,' Diana said. 'Thank you.' But in her heart of hearts she didn't believe it would influence the prosecuting authorities, who were convinced she was a murderer. Why would they release her just because her friends said she was a decent person? Most murderers probably have friends who believe they are innocent.

'I rang that journalist, Scott Morgan, this morning and he is asking around town, trying to find Mr Balboni's home address. He thinks he'll get hold of it soon.'

Diana looked down at her hands. She felt awful every time Trevor was forced to mention his name. Ernesto was such a proficient liar she couldn't imagine the journalist would be able to winkle much information from him, but she supposed he might as well try.

Trevor carried on: 'I went to Termini station on my way here to try and work out whether Helen might have taken the train to Torre Astura. She was seen leaving Cinecittà at around four in the afternoon, so the earliest she could have caught a train would be four-thirty or five. According to the timetable, there are trains from Rome to Anzio on weekdays at five-fifteen p.m., then another at seven-fifteen, and the last one is at nine-fifteen. The journey takes an hour and a half, with several stops along the way.'

'She never had any money,' Diana told him. 'She would probably have bought the cheapest possible ticket, in a third-class carriage.'

'I watched an Anzio train leaving this morning and the cheaper carriages were packed full of farm workers with bicycles, crates of chickens and boxes of fruit. It occurred to me Helen must have stood out if she was wearing that red dress you described. It was an evening dress, wasn't it?' Diana nodded. 'She must have gone home and changed after work. Maybe she caught the nine-fifteen, which got in at ten-forty-five. I wonder if the police are trying to find witnesses who saw her on the journey?'

'It doesn't seem to me as if the police are doing anything at all. They've got their culprit and a couple of so-called witnesses and are simply waiting for the trial.'

'I hope that's not the case,' Trevor frowned. 'But that's why I thought you and I should try and piece together

Helen's final journey to see if we can come up with anything ourselves.'

Suddenly Diana had a flash of inspiration. 'Hang on a minute. Where is her handbag? She would never have gone anywhere without her bag. It was white patent with a gold chain-link shoulder strap. I wonder what happened to it?'

They looked at each other, filled with hope for a second. 'Perhaps Luigi stole it. If only they could find it at his apartment . . . But he's not that stupid.'

'Either that or it was thrown into the water with her and has drifted off somewhere on the current. Which doesn't help us much.'

They sat in silence for a few minutes, mulling this over, then both started to speak at once. 'You first,' Trevor said.

'I was going to say that there might be something inside that would give us a clue about her state of mind. Did she buy a return train ticket? Did she have things for an overnight stay? . . . What were you going to say?'

'I'm not sure she caught the train. I think Luigi might have driven her down. Maybe she owed him money and he was bringing her to you so you could lend her some. You were her last hope.'

'Of course I'd have given her money!'

'But something went wrong when they arrived. Perhaps Helen threatened to expose him and he killed her before they reached you.'

'I'm afraid that's what must have happened. But how can we ever prove it?'

Trevor sighed. 'It worries me that the police aren't even looking for evidence of a third person. Maybe it's there, staring them in the face.' At that moment, he made up his mind. 'I think I'll go to Torre Astura myself and have a look around.'

'Are you sure, Trevor? It might be dangerous. I don't want you getting in any trouble.'

He carried on as if she hadn't spoken, thinking out loud. 'I'll ask Hilary to arrange permission for me to look around the set and talk to the workers. Someone must have seen something. I'll go tomorrow.'

Diana closed her eyes. 'Thank you,' she whispered. At least something was happening.

'It means I won't be able to visit you tomorrow,' he explained, 'but with any luck I'll be back the following day with good news.'

'Thank you for doing this.' She forced another smile. 'I knew I could count on you.'

Her words were slow and her expression weary. Trevor couldn't bear to leave her looking so miserable but the guards were calling time.

'We should have a holiday when you get out,' he suggested. 'Where would you like to go? How about Athens?'

'Maybe,' Diana hedged. 'Athens would be nice.' But he noticed that she couldn't meet his eyes.

Chapter Sixty-Four

Hilary was happy to let Trevor visit Torre Astura, and even arranged a studio car to pick him up and drive him there. On the road west, he kept his eyes peeled, trying to imagine Helen's thoughts on her final journey as she gazed out at the tilled fields, terracotta farmhouses and rows of cypress trees. Was it still daylight or had darkness fallen? The driver spoke English so Trevor asked him how Helen might have travelled from the station in Anzio to the film set. He needed to keep an open mind about events that evening. There was a local bus, the driver told him, but they would have run infrequently at that time of night.

The car stopped at the gates of the Torre Astura set, where a security guard was sitting in a roadside office. Fortunately he spoke English. Trevor got out to chat.

The guard remembered Diana well, and they talked through her movements on the day in question, but he said he hadn't seen her after six that afternoon, when she picked up her bag from the gatehouse, until the following morning when Helen's body was found. He hadn't seen Helen at all, because another guard had been on duty from seven in the evening through to seven in the morning. They worked twelve-hour shifts – night and day. His wife hated him doing this work, he said. She thought the hours were too long, but he was looking forward to seeing all the stars when they came to shoot the outdoor Alexandria scenes.

Since he didn't know what Helen had done when she reached the set, Trevor decided to retrace Diana's movements. The guard told him that she went straight onto the jetty and began making notes, so he walked down that way, past a gaudy imitation of the Serapeum and various other buildings and sculptures, to the waterside. Coils of rope and huge sails lay on the ground, alongside a pile of incense burners and some gold and blue statues cast in resin. A large oared battleship was moored at the end of the jetty and, as he drew closer, Trevor could see that it had been converted from a fishing boat, with a turret added in the centre of the deck. He turned at the end of the jetty and looked back at the miniature Egyptian city built along the shoreline. From a distance it was rather impressive.

He walked back along the jetty and had a quick look around the sets, discovering they were mere façades propped up by metal scaffolding. There was a black structure with ropes dangling down the front that he assumed must be Cleopatra's mausoleum. Whoever had decided it should be black? It seemed unlikely. He explored all the other structures along the front, trying to work out what they were meant to be: Cleopatra's Needle, Ptolemy's Needle, the Palace, the famous Library of Alexandria. There was no lighthouse in the bay, though. Having gone to so much trouble, he wondered why they hadn't made a copy of that wonder of the ancient world, which could reputedly be seen from right across the Mediterranean.

Diana had told him she went to the *trattoria* for lunch around two, so he did the same and found it packed full of workmen in dusty overalls. He ate some pasta and drank a beer but couldn't follow any of the conversations in rapid-fire Italian that took place around him. A couple of times he sensed they might be talking about him but when he turned to look, their gazes were quickly averted.

He'd brought a photograph of Helen, cut from the newspaper, and when he finished eating he leaned over to the men at the nearest table and asked, 'Did you see this girl on the 10th of May?' He spoke slowly and held up ten fingers to try and make them understand. They shook their heads. 'Pass it around,' Trevor motioned. Each table in turn looked at the picture and glanced at Trevor but no one admitted to seeing Helen. He wished he spoke Italian and could question them individually about where they had been that night. Did any of them know the witness who claimed to have seen Diana and Helen fighting? What could he hope to discover without speaking the language? It was hopeless.

After lunch, he walked down to the coast and worked out the path Diana must have taken when she went to bathe in the sea. The heat was intense now. He rolled up his shirt sleeves and carried his jacket over his arm but still he was roasting. He could feel the patch on the top of his head burning where the hair was thinnest. He bent, peering at the shingle, trying to spot anything out of the ordinary.

Who am I fooling? he thought. *The police will have done this. What chance do I have of finding something they have missed?*

After half an hour of walking south, directly into the sun, the shore became rocky and he would have had to clamber across some large boulders to continue. Diana hadn't mentioned rock climbing, so he turned to walk back towards the set again. He couldn't work out where she must have stopped, or which field she crossed to return to the road. No matter. He decided to look in the opposite direction and cross into the army camp to see where the soldier had been when he spotted Helen's body in the water.

Behind the model of the Serapeum, there were piles of scaffolding poles on the ground, along with some tarpaulin sheets, paint pots and stacks of plywood, then a fence separating film-set land from army land. He walked down to the waterfront and found he could easily cross into the army camp. Tents were erected further up a gentle slope but there was no one about. Tentatively he walked towards them, and when he turned to look back at the wide expanse of the bay he could imagine where the soldier must have been standing when he saw Helen's body in the water. He would have spotted the red of her dress first.

'*Signore, questi sono terreni privati.*' A soldier appeared carrying a black assault rifle, the muzzle pointing at the ground.

Instinctively, Trevor raised his hands. 'Sorry. Just looking.' He backed off.

The soldier didn't seem unfriendly but watched until Trevor had stepped back across the boundary onto film-set land. Next, he walked behind the Serapeum, across a field, to the *pensione* where Diana had stayed. He could see a little patio on the ground floor at the back of the building and assumed that must have been hers. It was the only room with a patio. He peered through a gap in the shutters but it didn't look as though anyone else was occupying the room because he couldn't see any personal possessions – just a bed and a chair.

There was an old wooden bench on the patio. It was in the shade, so he sat down, trying to imagine his wife sitting there the evening Helen died. The air was full of the noisy chirping of crickets, the buzzing of bees around a purply-pink bougain-villea and the distant rhythm of the waves. Trevor was overcome by weariness and despair. He'd come all this way and got no closer to understanding what had happened. Meanwhile, Diana was stuck in jail with common criminals. He couldn't think what else to do, though.

I'm impotent, he thought, and the word seemed to sum up all that was wrong with him: his lack of manliness, his inability to deal with things of a practical nature, and his many sexual failures. No wonder Diana took a lover. It was a miracle she hadn't taken many more during the course of their marriage.

Trevor decided he would stay in Torre Astura until seven o'clock and try to talk to the night guard. He wasn't sure if Helen had made it to the entrance of the set, but if she had, surely she must have spoken with him. That gave him three hours to kill in the meantime. He closed his eyes and slipped into a wakeful doze. He could still hear the crickets and feel a slight breeze coming up from the shore but his eyelids were heavy and his limbs melted into the bench. Gradually the doze got deeper, and the external noises drifted further away, until he was sound asleep.

Chapter Sixty-Five

Trevor woke with a start. The sun was setting over the ocean and when he looked at his watch he saw it was almost eight o'clock. Four hours had gone by. He wasn't sure whether the studio driver had waited for him. If not, he would have to find his own way back to Rome.

As soon as he leaned forward, he felt a jabbing pain in his lower back. He must have slept in an awkward position and it had triggered his old trouble. He clutched the arm of the bench and rose carefully, leaning his weight into his arms, before straightening up slowly. He rubbed the painful spot, trying to relax the tense muscles, before he started hobbling across the field towards the film set.

He made his way to the gatehouse and, as he drew near, he saw that the night guard was sitting reading a newspaper.

'Hello, do you speak English?' Trevor asked.

'A *leettle*.' The guard put down his paper.

'I'm Diana Bailey's husband.'

'Ah, yes, yes.' The guard seemed to understand.

'Can I ask you some questions about what happened here?'

'Of course.' He pulled out a chair for Trevor to sit down, wiping the seat with his sleeve.

Trevor retrieved the photograph of Helen from his jacket

pocket. It was becoming rather dog-eared. 'Did you see this girl?'

'Yes, yes.'

Trevor wasn't sure if he had understood the question. 'This is the girl who died in the water.' He pointed towards the Mediterranean. 'Did you see her before she died?'

'Yes, before.'

Trevor felt the stirrings of hope. '*When* did you see her?'

'Almost twelve at night. *Mezzanotte.* She come here. She ask for Diana.'

'What did you tell her?'

'I tell her Diana is in the *pensione*.' He pointed.

'Was Helen alone?'

'Yes, alone.'

So Luigi wasn't with her at that stage. 'How did she look?'

The guard shook his head. 'She look sad.' He waggled his fingers under his eyes to indicate crying. 'Not good.'

'And did she go to the *pensione*?'

'Yes, I see her.' He pointed at the door of the *pensione*.

'Did you see her after that?'

The guard shook his head. 'No. Not until the morning, when she is dead.'

'You didn't see her with my wife, with Diana?'

'No.' He shook his head emphatically.

So this guard wasn't the witness. Who on earth could it have been?

The guard spoke, obviously keen to communicate something. '*Non credo che sia vero che qualcuno ha visto loro due lottare. È così tranquillo qui che avrei sentito. Credo che qualcuno stia mentendo.*'

Trevor couldn't understand what he meant. The guard

398

repeated himself and Trevor tried to pick out a few individual words but it was beyond him. Damn and blast it that he had never been any good at languages.

'Is my driver here?' he asked, miming a steering wheel. Perhaps he could translate.

'He go to *Roma*,' the guard said. 'I call taxi for you?' He mimed a telephone.

Trevor considered his options. He was reluctant to leave with nothing to show for the trip. Perhaps he could find someone to translate while he asked the night guard more questions, since he seemed to be the last person to admit to seeing Helen alive.

'Could I stay here tonight?' he asked, then mimed sleeping and pointed to the *pensione*. 'Maybe I could stay in Diana's room?'

'OK,' the guard said. 'Room number eleven.'

Trevor rose from the chair, wincing and clutching his back, then shook the guard's hand. 'Thank you, sir. Thank you for your help.'

The guard nodded and watched him walk slowly up the road.

There was no bell on the outside of the lodging house but the door was ajar so Trevor walked into a hallway. A radio was playing a song he recognised called '*Volare*'. Dean Martin had sung it, he was pretty sure, but this sounded like an Italian version. He couldn't imagine where he'd absorbed this information, but occasionally he was called upon to supervise parties at the students' union so it might have been there.

'Hello?' he called. No one appeared so he shouted louder. 'Hello?'

A teenage girl emerged from an adjoining room but it soon

became evident that she spoke no English at all. He saw some keys hanging on the wall behind a chair, so he pointed at them and held up his ten fingers and then his thumb to indicate number eleven. Without questioning, the girl handed him the key for number eleven, then gestured down a dim hallway.

He reached the door that had a number eleven on it, although he hesitated for a moment because the second figure had come loose and hung sideways, like the stem of a seven. When he put the key in the lock, it turned and the door opened. He switched on the light and looked in and straight away he could see the room was grim. The bed hadn't been made up, so there was just a grey blanket over a bare mattress. There was a rotten smell he soon tracked down to some rubbish in a wastepaper basket. Everything was musty.

He went to pull back the curtains and was surprised to see they covered just a window. Where was the patio looking down towards the sea? For a few moments he stood, puzzled, then it dawned on him that this must be the wrong room. He went back to examine the number eleven on the door with its loose figure. The next room along was numbered twelve, though, so this must be eleven. How strange!

He had started to pull the door closed when he heard a rustling sound and realised a piece of paper was stuck underneath it. He retrieved the paper and saw that it was a sheet torn from a diary that had been folded in half so it was maybe three inches long by two across. It was an English diary, with the days 'Monday 4th, Tuesday 5th'. He opened the paper and what he saw made goosebumps stand out on his skin. The page was covered with scrawled handwriting, much of it virtually illegible, but at the top it said 'Dear Diana' and at the bottom it read 'Love, Helen' with three

X's. Why hadn't the police found this? It must have been there since the night Helen died.

He sat down on the bed to decipher the note:

Where are you? I need you so much. I've made such a mess of everything and there's no one else I can turn to. I pray you are still here. They said you would be. I don't have a room and I don't even have enough money to get back to town. I want to go home, Diana. I've got mixed up with some really bad people and I can't cope any more, but I don't have enough money for a plane ticket. I went out looking for my friend Scott in Via Veneto tonight to ask if I could borrow it from him but he wasn't there. Then I asked Ernesto but he refused to lend me a penny and none of the American girls have any cash. So that's when I thought of you. I know we argued but you're so nice, I'm sure you'll help. I suppose I'll sneak onto the set and find some shelter until you come and find me. Please hurry. You're my only hope.

Helen had scribbled this the night she died. Someone must have told her that Diana was in room eleven.

He walked back out to the reception area and, using sign language, communicated to the teenage girl that it was the wrong room. She disappeared and returned with an older woman, the *padrona*, who fortunately spoke English. Trevor explained who he was and showed her the note he had found.

'*Madre mia*,' the *padrona* exclaimed. 'I didn't see her.' She asked the teenager, who claimed she hadn't seen her either. 'She must have crept in while we were upstairs. We didn't hear a thing, not so much as a raised voice. There was no argument. I told the police your wife is innocent.'

Trevor's first instinct was to ask them to call the police.

They should see this note. But then he realised that it only proved Helen had been looking for Diana; it didn't prove she hadn't found her. Where could Helen have gone after slipping that note under the door? She must have crossed the field at the back of the boarding house and sneaked onto the set without being seen by the night guard. She'd be looking for somewhere to shelter. He cast his mind round the set, with all the two-dimensional structures, and suddenly it came to him: the only place where she'd be under cover was on the converted fishing boat.

Holding the note, he hurried back down the road to the night guard. He showed him the piece of paper and explained what he thought might have happened, and he kept repeating, 'The boat. Can we look?' and pointing out towards the jetty.

He wasn't sure how much the guard understood, but he picked up a torch and shone a light to illuminate the way as he accompanied Trevor to the barge. It was tethered to the end of the jetty but bobbing in the water and there was a gap of about a foot to leap across to get on board. As Trevor landed on deck, he jarred his back and he yelped in pain. The guard crossed nimbly behind him.

The little turreted area in the centre of the deck turned out to be the wheelroom; there was no space where Helen could have slept. In the ship's hold, mechanisms to operate the oars had been installed. It may have been converted to a warship but it still stunk of the fish that had been flung there over the years. The guard shone the torch into every nook and cranny but there was no sign that Helen had been there. Trevor had hoped to find her handbag, perhaps, or her shoes – she had been barefoot when found, Diana said – but there was nothing.

He went out on deck again and walked towards the prow. The boat was swaying with the movements of the waves and he had to clutch the rail around the edge for balance. How had Helen managed, especially if she'd been high on drugs at the time?

'Where was her body found?' he asked, and the guard pointed to an area a couple of hundred yards across the bay.

Trevor walked right up to the prow and stood looking out at the spot. It was too dark to see which way the current was flowing. He clutched the rail and under his fist he felt an uneven edge. One section didn't fit snugly against the next. When he pushed against it, it gave way and he realised it was broken. He called the guard across.

'Look!'

'*È rotto. Lei sarebbe potuta cadere là,*' the guard said. He wiggled the loose section and it came away entirely in his hand.

They both stared down into the black water ten feet below.

'I call the police,' the guard said, and Trevor agreed. His heart was thumping with excitement. Helen could have fallen against the broken rail and tumbled into the water. If so, that meant Diana was in the clear. But what if the police claimed Diana pushed her?

They rang the state police first of all, but no one answered. By this time it was ten at night. 'Is closed,' the guard said. Then he rang the *carabinieri* and spoke to them, explaining the circumstances. Trevor heard Diana's and Helen's names being repeated several times, and the tone was insistent, but when the guard hung up he said apologetically, 'They come tomorrow morning.'

Trevor was disappointed but he supposed they wouldn't

have been able to see anything at night. He'd have to be patient. He shook hands with the guard, agreed to come back first thing in the morning, then hurried down to the *trattoria* for a meal before they closed the kitchen. If only he could telephone Diana to tell her. It was excruciating not to be able to share this new information, but inmates couldn't receive incoming calls.

After eating, he went back to the *pensione*, and the *padrona* showed him to the room Diana had occupied, the one with the patio terrace.

'Your wife was a nice lady. I hope they will release her soon.' She noticed that Trevor was clutching his back as he stood. 'But look at you. You have a pain in the back. Let me bring you some *aspirina*.'

Trevor gratefully accepted the pills and a glass of water and swallowed them before easing himself down onto the bed and arranging a pillow to support the side that was especially fragile.

The room was dark and airless and he lay sweating, his mind working overtime. Surely Diana must be released after his discoveries? Her affair was over and her work on the film was almost done. Would that mean she would come back to him? Would they fly home together? He knew things could never be the same but surely they could move on. Perhaps this trauma would even strengthen their bond.

He imagined them at their Primrose Hill flat, sitting in the kitchen with a cup of tea, but the vision still felt far away, more pipe dream than reality. *He was too old, too impotent. It wasn't fair of him to hold her back. He truly loved her . . . and perhaps in the end that meant he would have to let her go.*

Chapter Sixty-Six

When Diana came into the visiting room the following day, she was surprised to find Signor Esposito sitting there.

'Where's my husband?' she demanded immediately, panicked that something had happened to Trevor.

'He's still down in Torre Astura,' the lawyer reported, 'but he telephoned and asked me to let you know that they appear to have discovered what happened to your friend Helen.'

Diana's heart skipped a beat. She sat down hard on the wooden chair.

'It seems she came to find you in the *pensione* but knocked on the door of the wrong room. She left you a note then went to shelter on a boat on the film set, where she fell overboard, striking her head. This morning the police found one of her earrings caught in the rigging, and her handbag was underneath the boat, tangled in the anchor chain.'

'Oh no!' Diana began to cry. How stupid and tragic that her death should have been accidental. Had she perhaps been on drugs? Though Diana supposed it made no difference. Either way she was gone. And then she remembered the change of rooms: if only the maid had cleaned number eleven on time, Diana would have been there and Helen would have found her.

'The note says she wanted to go home to England and was planning to ask you for her aeroplane fare.'

Diana cried even harder, and the lawyer pulled an immaculate handkerchief from his pocket and passed it to her. He seemed unconcerned by the emotion, as if this was an everyday occurrence in his line of work.

'Of course, the prosecution could still argue that you were responsible for pushing your friend off the boat, but your husband spoke to the night guard at Torre Astura, who assures him it is impossible that two women could have been fighting nearby without him hearing. This afternoon the police are bringing their witness – a local woman – to question her story. Trevor is waiting to hear what she has to say, then he'll telephone me. Once we know the facts, I'll put them in front of a judge and ask him to release you.'

Diana wiped her eyes and blew her nose loudly, struggling for control. 'Do you think it's likely he will?'

Signor Esposito shrugged. 'It depends on the witness. If she is credible, we still have a problem. But things are looking a lot better for you than they were yesterday. Your husband has done a remarkable job.'

Diana looked down at her lap. 'He's a remarkable man,' she said quietly.

Back in her cell afterwards, she decided not to tell Donatella the news. Relations between them had cooled. That morning Diana had wanted to telephone Hilary but when she opened her purse she found that all her *gettoni* were missing. She'd been robbed. Donatella must have taken them, unless one of the other women had slipped into her cell while she was bathing. There was no point complaining, but the theft left her totally isolated. She needed someone to visit and bring her more *gettoni* before she could make any contact with the outside world.

Her heart was fluttering but she sat on her bed and forced herself to work, looking up tiny details in her books and writing more and more notes. No one would ever read them, but she needed a way of filling her time. She couldn't bear to think about Helen, alone and desperate – so close to finding her, but just not close enough.

Chapter Sixty-Seven

Trevor spent the morning waiting in the gatehouse for the police to bring their witness. He was concerned that the night guard hadn't slept for almost twenty-four hours, so he treated both him and the day guard to an early lunch from the *trattoria*, which was carried up the road on trays so that they didn't have to leave their post.

Shortly after two o'clock, a police car drew up and some Anzio policemen got out, along with a middle-aged Italian woman. She had a long, thin face, and was wearing a widow's black dress, with grey hair pinned up in a bun. When she sensed them watching, she turned and glared.

Trevor and the guards watched as the police asked the woman to identify the precise spot where she had seen the girls fighting. Immediately she became flustered as she looked up and down the road trying to think of a convincing location. The day guard gave Trevor a running commentary on what was being said.

'Were you in a car?' the police officer asked, and she said yes, she was. 'What time?' Just after midnight.

'Where were you travelling from?' the officer asked, and she mentioned a village some miles down the road.

'Where did you see the women?' She glanced around, obviously realising it had to be somewhere out of sight of the night guard's gatehouse. She gestured in the direction of the *trattoria*, which was just out of view round the bend. 'Down there.'

The night guard interjected: 'But I saw Helen walk up to the *pensione*, that way, just after midnight. I would have seen her if she walked past me again.'

The woman turned first one way and then the other, tutting and sighing heavily as if to communicate that they were causing her an immense amount of trouble. 'It was very dark,' she said at last. 'I can't tell you the exact spot.'

'But if it was dark, how can you be sure it was those women? Did you see their faces closely enough to swear in court it was them?'

'I saw their hair. One was blonde and the other brown-haired. They weren't Italian. I could tell that. They looked English.'

The police officer was stern. 'So you didn't see their faces. You just saw two foreign-looking women as you passed in a car. You don't even know *where* you saw them.'

She was defensive now. 'Don't blame me. I simply told you what I saw.'

'You volunteered this testimony, making it sound convincing, but now you are changing your evidence. There will be repercussions, you can be sure of that.'

The officer turned to Trevor and the guards. 'I think we've heard enough.'

Trevor wondered why the woman had contacted the police when she was so unsure of the details. He guessed she might be one of those self-important busybodies who believe all foreigners are immoral, especially if they work on film sets. Some people just liked to stick their noses into other people's

409

business. And there was a strange kind of kudos that comes from being a witness to murder; perhaps that was another motive.

He called Signor Esposito but was told that he was out at lunch, so he left a message with his secretary.

The day guard called him a taxi to take him to Anzio station and Trevor shook hands with both men, thanking them warmly for all their assistance. The night guard would get only four hours' sleep before he had to go back on duty again but he seemed a good man, who was simply pleased that the truth had emerged.

On the train back to Rome, all Trevor could think of was the moment when he would see his wife again and hold her in his arms. He hoped it would be in a few hours' time. Perhaps they could go somewhere special for dinner that night. His stomach was tight with nerves at the thought that something could still go wrong.

As soon as he arrived at Termini station, he called Signor Esposito from a telephone kiosk to be told that a judge would consider the new evidence at a special hearing at seven that evening. It seemed inevitable that he would order Diana's release but the lawyer warned that it might be too late to complete all the paperwork that day. He'd contacted the prison authorities to warn them to be on standby.

'Can I come to the hearing?' Trevor asked, wondering if his husbandly loyalty could somehow influence proceedings.

'No. Diana won't even be there. It's just me, a judge and the prosecutor. I'll come by Pensione Splendid to tell you the result as soon as we're done, so make sure you're there from seven-thirty onwards. I won't send word to your wife yet, just in case it goes wrong, but I think there is reason for optimism.'

It was only five o'clock in the afternoon. Trevor had two and a half hours to fill. He wasn't usually a superstitious man but he decided he didn't want to call Hilary and tell her about the new hearing in case he somehow jinxed the outcome. The judge might still decide the case had to go to trial. Instead he decided to get something to eat and he caught a bus over to the back streets behind Piazza Navona, where he and Diana had found a decent little restaurant when he was there at Easter.

He ate some veal and sat on a shady terrace nursing a coffee and watching the passers-by. Suddenly a Vespa drew up alongside him and he saw that the driver was the journalist, Scott Morgan.

'Howdy, pardner, mind if I join you?' Scott asked. 'I've just been to see Mr Balboni.'

Trevor pulled out a chair for him and summoned a waiter. 'What can I get you?'

They ordered beers and Scott told his news. 'I don't know if it will be of any comfort to find out that Ernesto is a gutless coward who's been hiding away at home, scared of a drug dealer. Christ, he's a nasty piece of work.'

'Why is he scared of a drug dealer?'

'Luigi, the one who supplied drugs to Helen, told Ernesto exactly what to say to the police. It seems he was furious with Diana for pointing the finger at him and decided to incriminate her. That's why he persuaded Ernesto and the other witness to testify against her.'

'Goodness. How on earth did you force him to tell you all this?'

Trevor was astonished. Just when he thought his opinion of Diana's lover couldn't sink any lower . . .

'Money. I paid him. I bet he's broke now that he's not working at Cinecittà. They'll never take him back when they hear what he's done.'

'I'll make sure they don't,' Trevor promised. 'I'll tell Hilary personally.'

'Who was the witness, though? That's what I'd like to know.'

'I met her this afternoon,' Trevor said, and he explained about finding Helen's note and identifying the place where she fell from the boat, as well as the woman's unreliable testimony.

'Was her name Ghianciamina?' Scott asked eagerly.

Trevor shook his head. 'I don't think so. But I can call my friend, the guard at Torre Astura, and ask if he remembers.'

Scott's office was just around the corner, so they agreed to pop up there and phone when they finished their beers.

'Ernesto and Helen weren't really an item, were they?' Trevor asked. 'What did he say about her?'

'He tried to brag that she was chasing him but I reckon it didn't go beyond flirtation. What upset me is that Helen asked him for money for her plane fare the evening she died and he refused point blank to help. If only she had come to me.' *She couldn't, though, because he had never given her his address or telephone number.* He felt awful about that.

'Do you think Diana is going to be in any danger from Luigi once she's out of prison?' Trevor asked. 'Perhaps I should whisk her straight out of the country.'

Scott pondered that. 'It makes me sick to let him get away with it. I wish there was something I could do to incriminate him. The police know he's dealing drugs and don't seem to want to charge him. It was a Saturday night and he must have been loaded with stuff when they took him in for questioning but they chose not to find it. If only there was something else we could get him on – like the way they finally got Al Capone for tax evasion. I bet Luigi doesn't pay his taxes!'

'Why does it have to be so complicated? Why not tell the police what you know about him?' *In any decent justice system, that would be taken seriously*, Trevor thought. *They'd have to. Even the ancient Romans had laws against falsely accusing someone.*

'It would help if I could find a link between Luigi and the witness. Wouldn't it be handy if it turned out to be his aunt or something?'

'Do you really think he'd be so stupid?'

'I dunno. But it would be good news.'

Back at the office, they telephoned the day guard at Torre Astura, who supplied Trevor not only with the name of the woman – Cecilia Tessero – but also with an address. She worked as the housekeeper at a villa two miles up the coast towards Anzio, he said. A house called Villa Armonioso.

'That's owned by Luigi's boss!' Scott exclaimed. 'He's not going to be very happy if his housekeeper is charged with perjury. Holy shit, I wouldn't like to be in Luigi's shoes.'

'Will you call the police or will I?'

'Let me,' Scott said. 'I know a little more about who I'm dealing with. You and Diana need to walk away and forget you ever heard any of this. Get your wife out of jail and go and enjoy your lives!'

Oh God, I hope so, Trevor thought. He glanced at his watch. Time to rush back to the *pensione* and wait for news from the lawyer. He was so nervous he kept forgetting to breathe.

Chapter Sixty-Eight

After Trevor left, Scott considered calling the police about Luigi's links to the Ghianciaminas, but he could predict the reaction. Any charges against the housekeeper would be dropped as soon as they found out who she worked for. Ernesto would never admit to the police that Luigi had manufactured evidence against Diana. And whoever had given Luigi an alibi would stick to their story. No, there was no point. He would have to wait until his drugs story was published and present the truth about Luigi there. He still needed some incontrovertible evidence against the Ghianciamina family, something so big that the police couldn't ignore it. He decided to take another trip down to the Villa Armonioso, but this time by night. It had been late evening when Helen was taken there. Maybe that's when most of their business took place.

Before leaving Rome, Scott headed back to his *pensione* and picked up the binoculars and his camera. He bought some sandwiches and a bottle of water from a bar, and took his leather jacket in case it got chilly later. He wasn't sure how long this would take.

It was almost nine by the time he reached Anzio and headed south past the port and down along the coast road. Dusk was on the verge of turning to night and illuminated signs were switched on outside bars and *trattorie*: Coca-Cola, Peroni,

Buona Cucina. At first he overshot the turn-off but soon realised his mistake and headed back. He hid his bike in the same old shed then made his way by foot across the dunes, aware that it was going to be harder to justify his presence if he were caught this time. He couldn't use birdwatching as an excuse now that it was dark.

A car pulled up at around nine-thirty and, using the binoculars, Scott managed to note down the number plate as it swept through the gates, but he couldn't see who got out because they drove round to the other side of the house. He ate two of his sandwiches and drank some water, then settled in to wait as the night drew in. Two more cars came at eleven but it was too dark to make out their number plates. One left again half an hour later. Another arrived. He lay back against a sand dune to wait, and must have dozed off for a while because he awakened around two a.m. to the sound of a motorboat.

The moon had come out and it cast a surreal white glow over the ocean, almost like the unnatural light cast by the *paparazzis'* flashbulbs in Via Veneto. Through the binoculars, Scott saw a boat pulling out from a mooring behind the villa and heading out to sea. He swept the binoculars round to the horizon and there, lit up in the moonlight, was a huge ship looming out of the blackness like a mountain in the mist. It gave him a start. It was exactly as Bradley Wyndham had predicted: a shipment of drugs was being smuggled out to sea and there wasn't a coastguard in sight.

Scott adjusted the binoculars, trying to make out the name of the vessel, but all he could see was that there were two words, of which the first might begin with *RE* and the second might end in *A*. He took a series of photographs as pallets were hauled up the side of the ship on ropes. If they were packed with drugs, they would be worth thousands and thousands of dollars. One thing he was sure of: this cargo would not have been registered for export, and no duties would have been paid. He'd bet his bottom dollar on it.

The motor launch turned and headed back to shore. Scott took a few more photos until he'd finished the roll, praying that enough would come out to show the villa, the launch and the ship accepting illicit cargo. He didn't have any illusions that he could change the world in a day, but he was more and more determined to nail these people who had caused the death of Helen and goodness knows how many other vulnerable people. The police wouldn't do anything, but *he* would. He was ready to write his article now.

Chapter Sixty-Nine

At nine that evening, a guard came to the cell door and asked Diana not to change for bed because the supervisor was coming for a word.

'Have you been complaining about anything?' Donatella asked sharply. Guilt was written all over her face, and Diana guessed she thought it was about the theft of the *gettoni*.

'No, I haven't. Perhaps it's about my request for us to get extra food. Trevor has paid the money.'

They waited in silence, sitting on their beds, until the supervisor appeared in the doorway. 'Signora Bailey? Pack your things. You're going home tomorrow morning.'

There was no preamble and Diana couldn't absorb the words at first.

'Lucky bitch!' Donatella commented. 'Can I come too?'

'They've dropped the charges against you,' the supervisor explained to Diana. 'You'll be released at eight in the morning.'

'Are you sure?' Diana asked. She didn't want to get her hopes up for nothing. But the supervisor insisted it was true, then turned and left and they were locked in for the night. She stared after her, feeling stunned at the news.

'Your fancy lawyer must have found a loophole in the law,' Donatella speculated. 'I don't suppose you could ask him to look into my case now?'

But you're guilty, Diana thought. 'I'll ask him,' she said out loud.

'You should sue the police for wrongful imprisonment. You deserve compensation for all the hardship you've had to endure, and the damage to your good name. Get the bastards to grovel.'

'I don't want any money. I'll just be happy to be free.'

The witness's story must have fallen apart. She wondered who it was? It didn't matter now, but she'd like to know. She tried to decide what she would do when she was released, but beyond seeing Trevor and hearing what had happened, she couldn't think. She would only have spent eight days in jail but it seemed like weeks. She'd already got used to the routine of meals being brought on trays, lights being switched off at the appointed time, and baths being taken when the guards took you to the bathroom. The only thing she hadn't got used to was the boredom. Even with her books to read, each hour was interminable.

There was no chance of sleep that night. She listened to Donatella's mumbling and wondered what everyone at Cinecittà would say about her ordeal. Would she be allowed to complete her work on the film? Would Ernesto still be there? Had Helen's funeral been held yet and, if not, would she be able to go? And beyond that, she wondered what would happen to her and Trevor. There were no answers, only endless questions.

Breakfast was brought to them at seven and, as they ate, Donatella kept giving Diana odd, slightly aggressive looks.

'You've got money, haven't you? I mean, you've got a house back home and all that?'

'We rent a flat in London. We're not rich,' Diana replied, wondering where this was heading.

418

'Oh.' There was a pause while they both ate. Still Donatella kept glancing across. 'It's just I've written a letter for my children and I wondered if you could see it gets there? You'd have to give it to my sister, because her husband would destroy it if he saw it first.'

'Have you put the address on it?' Diana asked. 'Of course I'll make sure it gets there.' She glanced at it but didn't recognise the area.

'Could you give them some money as well?' She gave Diana a defiant look. 'After all, I've looked after you in here. You could have been in all kinds of bother without me.'

'Yes, I'll give them some money. I'll give it to your sister and ask her to spend it on them.'

'Tell her to get them new clothes, will you?'

'I will.'

Donatella nodded but didn't say thanks, and she just grunted her goodbyes when a warden came to collect Diana at seven-thirty. *She's jealous, poor thing. She'd give anything to be leaving this morning.*

Diana was led down to reception. She hadn't had a chance to wash or brush her teeth. She must look a fright, and God knows what she smelled like. There were various forms to sign then she sat on a bench watching as the minute hand jerked round on a clock face. She wasn't to be released a second before eight o'clock: rules were rules. She wondered if Trevor knew she was being released. Would he be there to meet her? Or would she have to catch a bus back to Pensione Splendid? She had no idea what to expect.

At eight o'clock, there was no ceremony, no shaking of hands, no formal apology. A guard simply stood up, opened a large wooden door and gestured for Diana to walk through.

Bright white sunshine blinded her after the gloom of the prison interior. The air smelled fresh and she could feel a breeze on her skin.

'Diana!' Trevor's voice said, and his arms were round her, which was just as well because her knees felt wobbly. 'I came by bus but I've got a taxi driver waiting to take us back. I thought that was better.' He was gabbling. 'Can I carry your bag?'

She handed it to him, so overcome with emotion she couldn't speak. 'Let's go,' he said. 'No point hanging around.'

They held hands in the taxi and he explained to her what had happened and why she had been freed. She started to cry when he told her the wording of the note from Helen. If only the *padrona* hadn't put her in a different room. That one simple thing had made all the difference between life and death.

She was alarmed to hear about Luigi threatening Ernesto and forcing the witness to testify against her. What if he was still looking for her?

'I think we should fly home, darling,' Trevor said. 'We can't take the risk of him coming after you. If we pack quickly, I expect we could even catch a flight to London this afternoon.'

She considered it for a brief moment, but knew instinctively it felt wrong. 'No, I don't want to leave Rome like that.'

'What *do* you want to do?'

'Truthfully? All I can think of right now is having a bath. And perhaps an espresso with a *cornetto*.'

Trevor squeezed her hand. 'You have that bath. I'll bring you an espresso and buy you as many *cornetti* as you can eat.

If I could afford it, I'd buy you a *cornetti* factory. I'm so glad to see you, darling.'

He leant over and buried his face in her shoulder and she could tell from slight shaking movements that he was sobbing, but he didn't make a sound.

Chapter Seventy

Scott was disappointed to read in the Italian press that police had traced the letter threatening Elizabeth Taylor to a Canadian man with mental health problems. Why had he written in Italian? That's what had raised Scott's hopes that it would turn out to involve an Italian crime family – maybe even the Ghianciaminas – but no such luck. The letter-writer was just another of the many lunatics who sought fame – or at least notoriety – by association with a public figure they had built up in their heads to be a symbol of all that they needed to make their own lives work out.

The day after his night visit to Anzio, he continued his research. First he went to the customs office in Rome to check the register of shipping, but there were dozens of ships whose names began with *RE* and ended with *A*: *Regina Carolina*, *Regina Aurora* . . . he'd never be able to identify the one he had seen. Next he made enquiries about tracking car number plates, but struck a blank there as well. If he'd had a contact high up in the police force, maybe they would have been able to help, but Scott's most valuable contact in Rome was Gianni, and he knew without asking that this was way beyond his photographer's sphere of influence.

Nevertheless, Scott began writing his article. He framed it around H****, a pretty, naïve young girl in Rome, who was sucked into the murky world of drugs. He wrote about a dealer called L****, who deliberately targeted her, bled her dry of money then demanded sexual favours in return for further supplies. He wrote about the young men who drove drugs up from the south in cars with secret hiding places, and left them in a garage to be stripped of their cargo. And he wrote about a crime family called the G*****s, who were untouchable because of their political influence and the bribes they paid to the police force and customs officials, so that no one intervened when motorboats carried unregistered cargo out to huge ships off the coast of Anzio in the middle of the night. What's more, no one investigated when an American journalist was kicked half to death in the street.

He widened out the article to explain Rome's current position as a world centre of drug trafficking, with money laundered through the booming construction industry and every bay and outcrop of the long Italian peninsula providing possible locations for smugglers to load international shipments. He used information from Bradley Wyndham's research about bribes paid to politicians in return for clauses in shipping bills that relaxed regulations. And he finished by writing about H****'s lonely death when, distraught and fleeing from the people who had destroyed her, she slipped, hit her head and drowned.

The first draft of his article was much longer than the *Midwest Daily* normally ran, so he began to hone it, tightening sentences and slashing unnecessary words. He typed it up himself in the evenings, once his secretary had left, and always hid it afterwards in the secret compartment by the shutters.

When he left the office he felt nervous, as if someone might guess what he was up to and seek to put a stop to it. He even considered asking Gianni where he could purchase a gun for self-protection. He'd briefly been a member of a rifle-shooting club at Harvard and, although he'd never fired a handgun, he reckoned he would know what to do. Perhaps he should get one before the article's publication. He felt excited and nervous all at once.

Most evenings he went to the Via Veneto or Piazza di Spagna to have a beer with Gianni and catch up on news of what the stars were doing and where the best photographs might be taken. He looked forward to these chats. Gianni had fast become his best friend in Rome, but Scott didn't confide in him about the article. Gianni sensed there was a secret project and assumed it was to do with the death of the makeup girl in Torre Astura, but he didn't ask questions.

Everywhere they went, Scott kept a wary eye out for Luigi. It seemed unlikely but, if Ernesto had reported their conversation and Luigi asked around, he might realise that Scott was a reporter and, what's more, that he was investigating him. He was several inches taller than the dealer, and probably much fitter, so he reckoned he could beat him in a straight fistfight but what if he had a knuckleduster, like Alessandro Ghianciamina? Or a knife? Or friends nearby who would pitch in?

Fortunately, there was no sign of Luigi that entire week. He must be lying low somewhere.

One evening, after a couple of beers with Gianni, Scott slipped back to the office to take some papers out of the cubbyhole, planning to read them before going to bed. While he was there, the telephone rang and he picked it up automatically.

'Scott!' his editor yelled down the line. 'Knock me down with a feather. Is it really you? I haven't heard from you in such a long time I reckoned you had resigned from the job and just forgot to tell me.'

'Sorry, boss, I've been working on something really big. I'll be ready to send it to you in a few days.'

'I don't want something in a few days! I want something for tomorrow's paper. What's happening on the *Cleopatra* set? Which stars are in Rome? What's the latest on Taylor and Burton? You've got two hours to knock out a story before I slash your name from the payroll. Understand?'

Scott grimaced. He wasn't ready to send the drugs piece yet, and he didn't think readers in the Midwest would be interested in the story of Diana's imprisonment and release.

Suddenly he remembered something Gianni had mentioned earlier. Seemingly there was a scene in the film in which Cleopatra slaps Mark Antony and he hits her back, knocking her flying to the floor. Elizabeth had refused to use a stand-in for the action, despite the fact that she suffered from a back problem, which could be exacerbated by the fall. Anyway, the shots of the scene were sent out to Hollywood for processing, which was necessary with all the film they shot. At Elizabeth Taylor's insistence they were using a type of film called Todd-AO, which had been pioneered by her late husband Mike Todd, and it couldn't be processed in Rome. While in transit, this particular roll of film got damaged, so they were going to have to reshoot the scene and take the risk of injuring Elizabeth's back one more time.

'Perhaps Elizabeth and Richard enjoy hitting each other,' Scott wrote. 'There's nothing like a spot of fisticuffs to stoke the flames of passion. Although it seems that in their case there's already a blazing conflagration.'

He cringed at the cliché. It wasn't his best piece ever but it would do. He filed the copy and headed home.

Chapter Seventy-One

During the afternoon of her first day of freedom, Signor Esposito called round with some papers for Diana to sign, and he brought with him a large bundle of letters he had received in support of her, from colleagues in England and in Rome. She was staggered to read the wonderful things they said: 'a genuinely good person', 'utterly trustworthy', 'generous to a fault', 'I would trust her with my children'.

She was amazed to see that John De Cuir, the set designer, had written a letter, as they hadn't entirely seen eye to eye over the sets. There was even one from Rex Harrison, despite the fact that the most she'd ever said to him was 'Good morning'. She wondered if someone had told him that she rescued Rachel Roberts from an Italian lothario at the Christmas party? They were married now and back in England, as he'd finished shooting all his scenes.

Perhaps the biggest surprise of all was a letter from Sybil Burton, saying that she was convinced of Diana's innocence. How touching that she would write in support of someone she'd only spoken to once in person. Perhaps it would have been influential to receive support from the 'wronged woman'.

Throughout that first day of freedom, Trevor urged Diana to pack her belongings and fly home with him, saying it might be dangerous for her to remain in Rome. Diana listened to his arguments but responded that she didn't think Luigi would pursue her personally. He'd had his revenge and must be aware that the finger would point directly at him if she came to any harm. She promised she wouldn't go out on her own in the city and she'd use studio drivers when she had to travel anywhere outside the film set. She desperately wanted to stay. It would feel like a huge failure to leave the film now, with the climactic scenes still to be shot over the next few weeks.

'Alright,' Trevor finally conceded, over a bottle of Valpolicella at the local *trattoria* that evening. 'But if you stay, I will stay as well. I'll take leave of absence from work. Term has almost finished and perhaps they will agree to send out the students' exam papers for marking. There's no reason why I can't deal with them here.'

Diana felt a surge of gratitude. 'You'd do that? It would be wonderful to have you here.'

'I'll call in the morning and see what I can negotiate.'

Diana had already phoned Hilary to say she would be back at Cinecittà the following day, so a studio car was waiting for her at eight.

'Good to have you back, Signora Bailey,' her driver grinned, and she introduced him to her husband, who was accompanying her.

She felt tentative coming through the gates of the studio in case anyone might blame her for Helen's death. It was reassuring to have Trevor by her side. The guard greeted her and a few people waved across the lawn but when she reached the production office, Hilary and Candy were effusive in their welcome.

'How are you? Was it simply frightful?' Hilary asked, hugging her. 'The whole idea of being in a Roman jail gives me the screaming abdabs.'

'It wasn't so bad.' She turned to hug Candy.

'You've lost weight,' Candy said. 'You look very "Audrey Hepburn". Being skinny is all the rage, according to *Vogue*.'

Hilary rolled her eyes at her. 'There are easier ways to slim, Candy. Try and show some tact for once in your life.'

Diana sat at her desk and pulled up a chair for Trevor. She showed him how to use the phone and they carried on talking while he waited for the international operator to connect him to his head of department at the university in London.

'Ernesto's gone, you know,' Hilary told her. 'His contract's been terminated.'

Diana nodded. That was welcome news. She'd been dreading bumping into him.

'And they held Helen's funeral yesterday, back in Leamington Spa. They wanted just a small affair for family and a few friends, but the studio sent a wreath and a card from all of us.'

'I wish I could have been there.' Diana decided she would write to Helen's parents, offering apologies for her own inadvertent part in the tragedy, and explaining some aspects of the story they might not have been told by the police. It was the very least she could do. They deserved the truth.

'And the only other news from the set is that we're on yet another economy drive. They're trying to get Elizabeth's scenes finished as soon as they can so they can stop paying her overtime. And no more deliveries from Chasen's!' Hilary waggled her finger sternly, mocking the ludicrousness of these pronouncements. 'The film's budget has topped thirty million dollars but they won't stump up a dollar for a bowl of chilli.'

Diana smiled. 'Is Elizabeth upset about that?'

'Not at all. I think she knew she was pushing her luck. She's far more concerned about what will happen to her precious affair once filming finishes, because Sybil will be expecting Richard back in the family home.'

'Gosh, yes. That's going to be traumatic for both of them.'

'*If* he goes. It remains to be seen. Now, are you coming to the script meeting this morning? Here's a copy of the current shooting schedule.' She passed over the typed sheet. 'It's changing hourly, though. I think they're planning to shoot the death scene with the asp today. I saw the asp trainer earlier.'

'You're using a real snake?' Diana shuddered inadvertently. She wasn't keen on snakes.

'Yes, we'll get some footage of it but obviously we won't let a real one anywhere near the stars. We can't risk any more disasters on this film.'

Walter, Joe and everyone else at the script meeting came over to shake Diana's hand and welcome her back to the set, but thereafter it was down to business. Walter announced that he'd been ordered to get all Elizabeth's remaining scenes shot by the 9th of June so she could be taken off the payroll on that date, and that all photography was to be completed by the 30th of June, at which point everyone's expenses would be stopped – rents, studio cars, free meals, the lot. The gravy train was finally pulling into the terminus. As soon as the asp scenes had been shot, two hundred and thirty-five crew plus actors would decamp to Torre Astura, and then to Ischia.

There was a lot of grumbling, and expressions of incredulity. No one thought it remotely possible that they'd be finished with Elizabeth by the 9th because she was needed for a couple of the Ischia scenes. They could use a stand-in for pick-up shots of her back view but no one else could pass for her from the front.

'Diana, I don't think we need take you to Torre Astura.' Walter patted her arm. 'It would be more useful if you could head down to Ischia and do your final checks there before we all arrive.'

Diana was relieved. She would have found it difficult to go back to Torre Astura with all her dreadful memories of the place, and appreciated Walter's thoughtfulness in sparing her that.

On the way back from the script meeting, as she passed Elizabeth Taylor's dressing-room suite, she decided to knock on the door to thank her for her support. An assistant answered and she could see Elizabeth sitting inside, wearing a white bathrobe and no makeup, her hair pushed back behind a thick baby-pink stretch hairband. If anything, she was even more beautiful without makeup.

'Diana!' she called and leapt to her feet to rush over and embrace her. 'I wasn't sure if you would come to work. It's great to see you. Come in and tell me all about it. How was life behind bars?'

Diana laughed. 'I only had eight days of it so I'm hardly the expert, but it wasn't so bad. I even made a friend.' She told Elizabeth about Donatella, the thief, and finished by saying that she was going to get the studio car to take her to Donatella's sister's house that evening to drop off some money for the children. 'A promise is a promise, after all.'

'She sounds like a card. How funny that she hit you for money! I must tell Richard.'

'How is Richard?' Diana asked carefully. Like everyone else, she was curious about their relationship, but didn't want Elizabeth to think she was prying.

Elizabeth reached for her cigarettes and lit one, holding it delicately between finger and thumb, and pursing her lips to exhale. She was an elegant smoker. 'We're both under pressure from all sides. Christ, did you hear that a Congresswoman is trying to pass a motion banning me from returning to America?'

'How can she do that? You're an American citizen!'

'Yes, but I was born in London. This woman' – she frowned – 'Iris Blitch is the name. She claims I am morally degenerate and dragging the morality of all Americans into the gutter. Richard quipped in that case they should expel the whole of Hollywood and half of Congress as well.' She searched a shelf behind her and found a half-full glass, from which she took a swig.

'She can't really have you banned from America, can she?'

'Of course not. I have an American passport. The lawyers say it's totally unenforceable even if she does pass a motion. Jeez, if the Pope can't have me thrown out of Italy, she's hardly going to manage it in the US. I should send her a card, don't you think? Something sweet. Perhaps I'll ask her to pray for me.' She guffawed, making a most unladylike snorting sound.

Diana laughed. 'She'd love that. I bet she'd hold prayer meetings for you.'

'I could use all the prayers I can get, believe me. Now where's that delightful husband of yours?' Elizabeth twinkled. 'Have you packed him off home to London again?'

'No, he's going to stay with me for the rest of the filming. It will be good for us to spend some time together.'

'The two of you must come over for cocktails. How about tomorrow? No, wait a moment, not tomorrow – we're having dinner with the King of Spain . . . Saturday. Can you both

432

come on Saturday? At seven? Richard has been dying to meet you.'

Diana blushed. *Richard Burton dying to meet her? Surely not.* 'Saturday should be fine. I know Trevor would love to meet Richard. He's often said to me he considers him the finest actor of his generation.'

'Does he really?' She was girlishly pleased. 'I liked Trevor a lot. I sure can see why you married him.' She gave a lascivious wink. 'I never could resist a man with a big brain.'

Diana chuckled. It seemed odd that Elizabeth would hit it off with her husband when they couldn't have been more dissimilar: the adulterous diva, who'd been famous since the age of twelve for her populist movies, and the serious-minded classicist who wouldn't even consider buying a television set because he considered it low culture. The door opened and Elizabeth's makeup artist came in, carrying a huge case that rattled as she walked.

'You'll have to excuse me,' Elizabeth said, stubbing out her cigarette, 'I must get ready to deliver my final words of the film to a rubber snake.'

Diana chuckled to herself as she continued on down the drive towards the production office, where her big-brained husband was waiting.

Chapter Seventy-Two

Scott read and reread his article dozens of time, substituting more potent adjectives, until at last he could do no more. It was still much longer than his editor normally printed but he thought that perhaps they might serialise it across two or three issues. It was written in scenes and dialogue, like the new journalism he so much admired, and he'd tried to capture the poignant details that established character: Helen's sinuous style of dancing, with skinny hips keeping perfect time and backcombed blonde hair swaying from side to side; the black stubble on the backs of Luigi's hands where he shaved them, and his shiny black shoes; the harsh barking of the Alsatians at Don Ghianciamina's villa, which reminded him of the chanting he'd heard in a recording of Hitler's Nuremberg Rally.

Instead of calling and dictating it to a copy-taker, he sent it by special courier addressed to the editor. The paper's copy-takers were notoriously sloppy and he didn't want to risk a single error creeping in. After the package had gone, he sat back to wait, jumping every time the phone rang. This could be his big break in journalism; the piece that would get him noticed. He'd discuss his personal security with his editor once they agreed on a publication date. Maybe the paper would pay for him to have a bodyguard. Taylor and Burton had body-guards – why shouldn't he? In the meantime, he kept to public places and parked his bike as close to the front door as he could manage. When he went to bars, he kept his eyes peeled for Luigi, but there was no sign of him.

One night, just over a week after Diana's release from prison, Scott was sitting in a piano bar off the Via Veneto when he saw an Italian man emerge from the ladies' toilet, folding some bills into his wallet. Shortly afterwards, one of the American girls from the *Cleopatra* set emerged, wiping her nostrils with a finger. It was blindingly obvious to Scott that drugs had just changed hands but it surprised him that another dealer had the nerve to move into an area that had been exclusively Luigi's.

The man stood by the bar just a few feet from him, stirring sugar into an espresso.

Scott sidled up. 'Hi, how are you doing?' he said in English.

'OK.'

'I don't suppose you know where Luigi is?'

'How do you know Luigi?'

Scott lowered his voice. 'He used to bring packages for me.'

The man looked at him sharply. 'What kind of packages?'

'Cocaine,' Scott whispered, hoping he wasn't making a huge mistake. Could this be an undercover police officer? A friend of Luigi's out to entrap him?

'Maybe I can help,' the man said, and Scott breathed a sigh of relief.

'Would Luigi mind if I buy from you? This is usually his patch.'

'Luigi has gone.'

Scott stared. 'Gone where? Does he work in another area now?'

'No, gone. Disappeared. You won't see him again.' The tone was matter-of-fact, and that's what made it so chilling.

Scott gave a low whistle. 'What the fuck happened? Did he do something to upset the big boys?'

'Who knows, my friend?' His gaze was level and steely, and Scott got the impression that the man knew exactly what had happened. Perhaps he had even killed Luigi himself and been rewarded with permission to take over the lucrative Via Veneto area. 'So, do you want to buy?'

Scott felt obliged to purchase a small packet of cocaine so they reconvened in the gents', where the exchange took place.

'I wonder if it was anything to do with that English girl who drowned near Anzio?' Scott speculated, watching the face of the new dealer carefully. 'I heard that Luigi tried to implicate a friend of hers who'd made him mad. Maybe he shouldn't have gotten involved.'

The dealer's expression was chilling, his face mask-like but the eyes glittering with suspicion. 'Who are you?'

'Nobody. A customer. That's all.' Scott backed off. 'It's good to meet you. Hey, what should I call you?'

'Call me Luigi. It's a lucky name, don't you think? And watch your step, my friend.'

Scott was shaking when he got outside onto the street. He jumped straight on his bike and rode off at top speed, suddenly nervous that the new dealer might follow him. The reaction when he'd asked about Luigi incriminating Diana had been instant. There was no doubt the dealer knew all about it because he hadn't asked, 'What do you mean?' He knew.

The Ghianciaminas can't have been best pleased at Luigi involving their housekeeper in his petty revenge against Diana. It drew attention to them. Someone had decided Luigi should be eliminated. *Jesus!* Scott regretted letting slip to the dealer that he knew about it. What had he been thinking of?

He zigzagged round the streets until he was sure there was no one following and then he stopped at the office to put the pack of cocaine into the cubbyhole. He considered snorting some because his nerves were shot, but thought better of it. He needed to keep his wits about him at all times now. He couldn't be sure who might be looking for him.

Chapter Seventy-Three

Diana returned to Rinascente department store to buy a new dress for their cocktails with Elizabeth and Richard. She was keen to make a good impression. It was ridiculous, of course, because she couldn't begin to compete with Elizabeth when it came to looks, but it wasn't about competition. She wanted to appear chic, to display another aspect of her personality, so that they didn't pigeonhole her as a dowdy academic.

She browsed the rails for two hours and tried on several outfits but couldn't make up her mind, and it made her miss Helen terribly. Helen was instinctively stylish, one of her many talents.

A shop assistant took pity on Diana as she stood dithering between four different dresses – leopard print, polka-dot, jewelled chiffon, harlequin diamonds – none of which were quite right.

'Is it for a party?' the woman asked.

'For cocktails with friends.'

The woman disappeared and came back with a simple forest-green shot-silk dress, in the new A-line style, which stopped just above the knee. She held it up in front of Diana and instantly it was obvious that it was the right thing: simple and understated. She could wear her pearls with it. How ridiculous that it had taken her so long.

The following Saturday, she dressed an hour before they were due to be picked up and began to apply her makeup, trying to draw fine black lines round the rims of her eyelashes as Helen had done. She smudged them with her finger, then unthinkingly wiped her fingers on her lap – and looked down to see a smear of pancake foundation on the fabric, which she had to sponge off, leaving a round damp patch. What a ditz I am! she thought.

'Why are you nervous?' Trevor asked, as she stood flapping the hem of her dress by the window, trying to make the evening sun dry it and praying there wouldn't be a watermark. 'They're only people.'

'I know. Of course I know that.' She giggled. 'But I notice you're wearing your best jacket, and you've even put on a tie, despite the heat. I've never seen Richard in a tie.'

'Haven't you? In that case I'll take it off.' He loosened the tie and slipped it off then unfastened his top button. 'You look lovely, by the way. That dress brings out the green of your eyes.'

'Thank you, darling.'

They were both ready at least half an hour early and sat self-consciously by the window drinking cups of tea until it was time to hail a taxi.

When they climbed out at the Villa Papa, security staff asked apologetically if they could look inside Diana's handbag and they patted down Trevor's jacket and trouser pockets before the butler led them through to the sunny lounge, the one Trevor had been in before. Everything looked much the same, except that the roses on the coffee table were deep red now, and a child's pull-along train was abandoned in the middle of the rug.

They sat down self-consciously on a sofa, then seconds later Richard Burton swept into the room and they both rose to shake his hand.

'Diana, Trevor, how good to meet you,' he said, his penetrating blue eyes moving from one to the other. 'How are you, Diana? I hope there are no ill effects from your incarceration?'

'I'm fine. Thank you. I was very well treated. Everything was perfectly civilised. If you ever have to go to jail, I can recommend Regina Coeli.' She was gabbling. There was something about him that made her nervous. Perhaps it was the magnificent voice, or the fact that the only other time she'd seen him up close he had been shouting at Candy.

'I don't think being imprisoned for something you didn't do counts as civilised treatment. It seems outrageous that in one visit to Torre Astura, Trevor was able to uncover evidence the police had completely overlooked. But if you are sure no lasting harm has been done, I suppose that's the main thing.' The butler stood, waiting for his orders. 'Do you both like champagne?'

They nodded in unison, although as far as Diana knew Trevor had never tried it.

'A bottle of Bollinger, please,' he asked the butler. 'Let's celebrate! Elizabeth will join us but not for at least another hour by my reckoning because she hasn't yet started to do her hair and it takes an unconscionably long time to arrange.'

'According to Martin Luther, "The hair is the richest ornament of women",' Trevor quoted.

Richard responded: '"Attired to please herself: no gems of any kind/She wore, nor aught of borrowed gloss in Nature's stead;/And then, her long, loose hair flung around her head/ Fell carelessly behind."'

Diana was mesmerised. People paid top dollar to hear this man in the theatre and she could see why because he transformed himself in a way that was magical to watch and listen to. His words took you out of your immediate surroundings so that you felt you could see the woman with careless long hair.

'Terence, *Heauton Timorumenos*,' Trevor recognised. 'Is it Bacchis praising Antiphila? How did you come across such a little-known piece?'

'My drama teacher was very thorough. He recommended Terence for the simplicity and elegance of the language, but I have yet to persuade any director to revive his work.'

'No, it would hardly stand the test of time. And of course, there is the controversy over whether he wrote the plays himself. Cicero and Quintillian thought not.'

The champagne cork was popped and Diana was handed a glass.

'To your freedom,' Richard toasted, smiling. 'May you never be imprisoned again . . .'

'I'll certainly drink to that,' she agreed, and they all clinked glasses before taking a sip. It was divine. Diana decided she even preferred it to the Dom Pérignon she'd drunk at Elizabeth's thirtieth birthday party many moons ago. Before prison. Her life seemed divided into before prison and after prison. It was too early to tell whether the experience had changed her but she felt different, in a way that she couldn't quite put her finger on. Perhaps it was the knowledge that she had been at rock bottom and survived. If she could cope with being falsely imprisoned for murder without falling apart, she could cope with anything. It was a good thing to know about yourself.

Richard and Trevor were talking about W.H. Auden, with whom they both had a slight acquaintance, and quoting poetry at each other, back and forwards like a tennis match. She smiled. They would never admit it but each was trying to impress. It was entertaining to watch.

Suddenly they heard a movement on the stairs and all turned to see Elizabeth descending. She was wearing white trousers, so tight they looked as though they had been painted onto her legs, and a shocking pink kaftan in floaty chiffon. Diana immediately felt overdressed in her smart green frock and pearls. Tony went to greet her and realised Richard wasn't getting up and sat down again.

'Am I late? I see you started without me.' She picked up a spare glass the butler had left on the tray and filled it from the bottle, which was in a wine cooler.

'Your lateness is part of your charm, my love. One always knows one can depend on it.'

Diana turned to look at Richard and was stunned by the alteration in his expression. He was gazing at Elizabeth like a little boy: vulnerable, awe-struck, unable to believe his own luck that he had snared such a knock-out woman. As she sashayed past him to greet Diana and Trevor, he couldn't help reaching out to touch the fabric of her trousers, as if to re-assure himself she were real. His eyes never left her as she shook hands with Trevor and gave Diana a hug, then kicked off her high-heeled gold sandals and curled her legs beneath her in an armchair.

'We were discussing Auden,' Richard told her. 'Do you remember? "I'll love you, dear, I'll love you/Till China and Africa meet,/And the river jumps over the mountain/And the salmon sing in the street."'

442

'Isn't that beautiful?' she drawled. 'You know him, don't you? You must introduce me some time. He sounds like quite a fellow.' The way she said 'fell-ow' sounded very English and Diana realised she was picking up Richard's classical Shakespearean diction and becoming less American.

'He's a very shy man. He'd be struck dumb if he met you. But that wouldn't matter because you can talk forever.' He dragged his gaze away from her to address Diana and Trevor. 'There are no awkward silences at any gathering Elizabeth attends, because there are never any silences, full stop.'

'And yet,' she trilled, 'you're the one doing all the talking tonight, baby.'

Diana could see they were utterly enthralled by each other. They hung on every word the other spoke, sparking off one another's thoughts, constantly watching the tiniest movements of a hand, or the recrossing of a leg, or the scratching of a minor itch. There was a current of electricity running between them that made them seem alert to the other's every breath and heartbeat.

They're trying to learn all they can about each other, Diana thought. *They're hopelessly addicted.* She knew about sexual addiction, because she'd had that with Ernesto; and she knew about love, because when she watched Trevor wincing with his back pain, it made her heart ache. But Elizabeth and Richard seemed to have it all: the emotional and the physical, plus a meeting of the minds. They were well and truly hooked.

And then she thought about Sybil and the children, and realised just how tortured Richard's position must be. Trevor was right; no matter which decision he made, he would lose.

They were talking about Mark Antony now, and Diana knew she should join in the conversation but she enjoyed being a spectator as her husband explained what was known of the debauched, difficult character and Elizabeth and Richard discussed scenes and lines of dialogue from Joe's script. A couple of times Richard referred a question to Elizabeth and she positively glowed with pride.

She's not used to being taken seriously for her intellect, Diana guessed. *She's beguiled by his brain, and flattered that he treats her as an equal.* She remembered Elizabeth saying that Richard called her 'Ocean' and could see that for someone accustomed to being praised for her surface beauty, it would be irresistible to be referred to by implication as 'deep'.

They talked about meeting the King of Spain and his new wife at dinner the previous evening. 'She's a timid little thing. I don't think there's any doubt he bagged a virgin,' Richard quipped.

'I've got a joke for you,' Elizabeth responded. 'A man asks a young woman he's just slept with "Am I the first man who ever made love to you?" She says "Yes, dear, you might be. Your face looks familiar."'

Richard laughed loudest of all, and Elizabeth beamed with pleasure. Diana began to worry that she was being too quiet. She'd hardly spoken since Elizabeth joined them, but she could tell those two liked an audience. It fuelled their exchanges, ratcheting them up a gear. They wanted people to see how happy they were, and that was easier in public because in private they would be inevitably drawn to no-go areas – such as his wife and children. In company, they could be a proper couple in love rather than a pair of guilty adulterers.

Two bottles of champagne were drained and Diana was beginning to feel tipsy although she knew she hadn't drunk as much as half a bottle herself. Trevor was looking flushed but happy. She realised it was the first time she'd seen him properly happy since she told him that Walter Wanger wanted her to come and work in Rome.

'Shall we go for dinner?' Richard suggested. '*Fettuccine* at Alfredo's? I'll get Dick Hanley to reserve a table.'

'We'd better warn Diana and Trevor what it's like out there.' Elizabeth caught Richard's eye for a second then turned to them. 'Since the beginning of what Richard and I call *Le Scandale*, the press attention has been somewhat terrifying. When the car pulls up, you need to get out quickly and walk straight for the entrance with your head down. Don't look at the photographers and, whatever you do, don't respond to anything they say. They can be vile and it's best not to listen.'

'Oh yes, *Le Scandale* could have turned us into hermits if we'd let it.' Richard stood up. 'But when in Rome, we do as the Romans do and eat at Alfredo's.'

Trevor chuckled. 'You know that quotation dates back to a letter by St Augustine saying that Romans fast on Saturdays and you should do the same when you're there? But it's a Saturday today and I'm starving, so *fettuccine* it is.'

Richard put his arm around Elizabeth's shoulder. 'I think this man might possibly know everything. We should keep him around. It could be handy for settling arguments.'

'Don't say that, darling. We *never* argue.' This was obviously a private joke, as she raised her eyebrows dramatically and he laughed.

Trevor sat in the front seat of Elizabeth's car, alongside the same driver who had given him a silk handkerchief after his previous visit, while Diana slipped into the back seat with the two stars. Her leg was pressed against Richard's but far from being embarrassed the champagne had relaxed her so she enjoyed the moment. She'd totally revised her opinion of Richard now she had seen his emotional side and heard him reciting poetry. She felt special, honoured to be in their presence and witnessing the great love affair close up.

The car pulled up outside Alfredo's and Diana climbed out, realising belatedly that she was on the road side rather than the pavement side and would have to push her way through a horde of photographers to get to the restaurant entrance. The noise level was extraordinary, like a steam train whistling right by your ear, and the assault of the flashbulbs disorientated her. For a second she couldn't decide which direction to walk in and stood, dazzled, as if snow-blind.

'Come on.' Richard's voice was right next to her and he grasped her elbow, pulling her behind him as he elbowed his way through the crowd. She couldn't see anything for the flashbulbs, but she did hear someone shout, 'Is she your new tart, Richard?' and realised with a shock they were talking about her.

They pushed inside the restaurant door and instantly the noise level dropped. Elizabeth and Trevor were already there, waiting for them, and she noticed that Trevor looked a bit dazed. How could Elizabeth and Richard put up with that cacophony every time they went out? It seemed to Diana a high price to pay for fame.

'Thank you for rescuing me,' she said to Richard.

He grinned. 'Welcome to our lives. That's your baptism of fire.'

The eponymous Alfredo himself came to lead them to a quiet table near the back. Diana kept her eyes forwards but all the same she was conscious of every single head turning as they crossed the room.

'I think we all want *fettucine*,' Richard ordered, looking round the three of them.

'Oh, definitely,' Elizabeth agreed. 'Do you know the story? It's so romantic. Alfredo's wife lost her appetite while she was pregnant with their first child. She couldn't face food, and he was worried about her, so he went into the kitchen to create a dish he knew she wouldn't be able to resist. And the result was *fettuccine alfredo*, which is now served all over the world. I think that's charming. Will you invent a dish for me one day, Richard?'

'If a miracle ever happens and you lose your capacious appetite then I'll give it some consideration.'

They sat on a banquette pressed close together. Elizabeth took out a cigarette and Richard leapt to light it. He filled her glass, spread the napkin on her lap, was attentive to her every need, and she glowed with the attention.

Some red wine was brought and Diana accepted a glass. She knew she was getting properly drunk but for once decided not to stop herself. It made her more talkative and she began to tell them some gossip from the set: her suspicion that Joe Mankiewicz and his assistant, Rosemary Matthews, were becoming more than just work colleagues.

'He's a dark horse, old Joe,' Richard commented. 'Good for him.'

I'm turning into Helen, Diana thought with a twinge of guilt. But then the whole of Cinecittà was rife with gossip and neither was married so there was no harm done.

The conversation became increasingly silly as they proposed toasts to their forthcoming trip to Ischia, to the asp that bit Cleopatra's breast, and to poor silly Antony. Richard kept reaching for the pepper mill or the wine just so that he could accidentally-on-purpose brush his hand past Elizabeth's magnificent breasts, and she smiled indulgently. In retaliation for a cheeky retort she turned and kissed his cheek, leaving a perfect lipstick outline of her mouth, then hooted with laughter. It was obvious they truly enjoyed being with each other.

Trevor offered to pay half the bill but Richard wouldn't hear of it. They then had to run the gauntlet of the photographers on the way back out to the car. This time the nearside car door was open and Diana scurried with her head down and leapt in, but she turned to see Richard with his arm around Elizabeth, both of them standing with heads held high as twenty or thirty flashbulbs fired at once, illuminating them with an eerie halo. It was a glorious yet unnerving sight.

The driver dropped Diana and Trevor at Diana's *pensione* and they all kissed goodnight – Richard even kissed Trevor on the lips, which seemed uproariously funny at the time – then they clambered upstairs and fell into bed.

Diana slept for an hour or two but opened her eyes at four a.m., suddenly wide awake. She reran all the wonderful memories of the evening, particularly the life-affirming happiness that Elizabeth and Richard felt in each other's presence, and knew that she had never experienced that. Her relationship with Trevor had been about comfort and support, intellectual stimulation and practicality. They cared deeply about each other, but there had never been that fiery passion. They'd never truly had that exhilaration at the sheer fact of being together. And now that Helen's death had underlined the fragility of existence, Diana wondered whether that was enough. She could get knocked down by a car, or be in a plane crash or fall off a boat at any moment.

Was life too short to stick with the loving companionship they had rather than pursuing the 'great love' Elizabeth and Richard shared? She certainly didn't want to hurt Trevor any more. She just wasn't sure that going back to the life they'd had before was an option.

Chapter Seventy-Four

Several days went by and still Scott hadn't heard from the editor about his article. He was surprised because he knew it was good writing and he believed it was a compelling story that would concern American readers, because a lot of the drugs that ended up on their city streets were coming via Italy. So why the delay? Could his editor be on holiday perhaps? But he never took holidays. Were they debating the best way to break the story for maximum impact?

The call came on a Monday evening, just as Scott was about to leave the office.

'It's a brilliant piece of writing, Scott. And you've obviously been very brave – some would say foolhardy – in your research. But unfortunately we can't print it.'

Scott sat down hard in his chair, the wind knocked out of him. 'You're kidding! Why not?'

'First of all, the legal team have been through it with a red pen and there's very little left. You can change the names and disguise them with asterisks but anyone who ever reads a newspaper in Rome would know who you were talking about and that makes it libellous – unless you can prove your allegations, which you obviously can't.'

'I've just found out that Luigi's dead, so he's not going to sue,' Scott argued.

'Yes, but the meat of the story is at the top of the tree where the Ghianciaminas are bribing government ministers and you simply can't say that, can you? They'll either kill you or they'll sue you or both.'

'They might try to kill me but they wouldn't sue because that would be like putting their hands up and admitting "Yes, it's us, we're the crime family he's talking about." Don't you see? That's the beauty of it.'

There was a hoarse laugh. 'You've given me a few headaches over the months you've been in the post, but believe it or not I'd rather keep you alive. I don't want any of my reporters being gunned down if I can possibly help it.'

Scott cast round desperately for arguments. 'You have to print it. I'll resign if you don't. I'll walk out, just as Bradley did.'

'If you walked out I would simply appoint a new correspondent in your place and nothing would have been achieved. Look, Scott, don't throw your piece away. Save it. Turn it into a book about the Mafia one day. Widen your research while you're there, and send it out to publishers once you've left Italy and are safely ensconced elsewhere. Meanwhile, my Berlin correspondent is moving on this autumn and the job's yours if you fancy covering the front line of the Cold War.'

That stopped Scott in his tracks. He'd love to be in Berlin, where the government of the German Democratic Republic had started building a second wall several yards from the first, creating a no-man's land in the middle. But still he wanted his story published. 'If I can get more evidence against the Ghianciaminas would you print it then?'

'No.'

'What if I offer it elsewhere, to a magazine?'

'I suppose I wouldn't stop you, even though it's in breach of your contract. But wait till the autumn and let me get you out of Rome before it's in print. Is that a deal?'

Scott agreed that it was, but he decided to start looking into a magazine publishing deal straight away because it might take several months to come to fruition. He didn't have any contacts in that world and was reluctant to ask his father for help. Instead, he decided to go to the Eden Hotel bar and ask among the foreign press hacks to see if anyone could give him a lead. He hoped they still drank there. It had been weeks since he bothered to look them up, but he guessed they were creatures of habit.

There was a surprise waiting for him as he walked out onto the rooftop terrace and called 'Hi guys!' to the assembled crowd.

A short, baby-faced man wearing round black glasses turned and looked at him quizzically. 'Well, he's a handsome one. Who's going to introduce me?'

Joe stepped forward. 'Truman, this is Scott Morgan of the *Midwest Daily*. Scott, meet Truman Capote.'

And that was unmistakably who it was, all five foot three of him, with his high-pitched, effeminate Southern accent and his pinstriped suit with a silk kerchief spilling from the pocket. Scott was stunned. So Joe had been telling the truth about their friendship after all!

'Enchanted to meet you, Scott Morgan,' he proclaimed, holding Scott's hand for much longer than was comfortable.

Truman continued relating an anecdote he had been in the midst of before Scott arrived. 'Poor Elizabeth is simply beside herself with this pesky woman who simply won't let go. She does a wicked imitation of her, by the way. "Rich-*ard*, come and take the trash out, Rich-*ard*."' He adopted a falsetto that came out as a squeak. 'She called me and said, "Come to Rome, darling, and we can do some witchy spells to make Sybil slither back to the rain-soaked mountains of Wales." So that's what we're doing – making spells!' He gulped the remainder of his drink and called the bartender across. 'I'll have a Justerini & Brooks, darling. Make it a big one.'

'That's a J & B whisky,' Joe whispered to Scott. 'He gets mad if bartenders don't know it. Luckily this one has served him before.'

'So what's the news with you, Spike?' one of the other hacks asked, and Scott's nickname was explained to Truman Capote.

'Have you been spiked recently?' he asked, with a lascivious twinkle.

'Actually, I have,' Scott began, before cottoning on to the innuendo. 'Yeah, yeah, have a good laugh, boys.' He waited till they had stopped chortling before he carried on. 'I was going to ask if you guys know any magazine editors who might be interested in a new journalism piece about the drugs trade in Italy? My editor won't touch it.'

'Drugs? Naughty, naughty. Have you been doing personal research?' someone asked.

'I don't suppose you could get me a little something, could you?' Truman Capote asked. 'Some *co-ca* maybe?'

'Sure,' Scott agreed. 'I've got some in my office. We could stop there afterwards if you want.'

'Isn't he charming?' Truman addressed the group. 'Someone's mummy taught him how to share. I like this boy a lot.' He put an arm round Scott's waist, having to stretch up to reach it. With his other hand, he beckoned Scott to bend down so that he could whisper in his ear. 'Why not let me read your story, Scott, and if I like it I'll show it to my publishers? They never consider anything without an introduction but I could press your case for you.'

Scott was delighted. This was the man who had written *Breakfast at Tiffany's*, and was generally considered one of the wittiest writers in New York. Having him on his side was bound to help. 'That would be wonderful!' he exclaimed. 'The next Justerini & Brooks is on me.'

Soon the drinks were flowing fast and freely and an argument flared up about President Kennedy's policy of spraying Agent Orange over the forests of Vietnam, in an attempt to deprive the Viet Cong of cover from which to attack the Southern Vietnamese. One of the hacks argued that it was against the Geneva Convention to fly over someone else's country and destroy their crops, but Truman Capote was fiercely in support of it. Scott got the impression he had a crush on President Kennedy as he seemed to believe the man could walk on water.

'Remember Bay of Pigs,' someone cautioned.

'Dear boy, the CIA set him up. It was an inside job. Everyone who's anyone knows that.'

There was no arguing with someone quite so adamant. Truman could quote all kinds of authority, from his friend Norman Mailer to his *great* friend Dashiell Hammett. He dropped a name in virtually every sentence.

Scott was only drinking beer but he had an empty stomach and somewhere around the fifth round he began to feel sick. He went to the men's room to throw up and when he came out of the cubicle, Truman was waiting for him.

'Shall we head off now? I told Elizabeth I wouldn't be late, but I'd *very* much like to accompany you to your office first.'

'Sure. I'll take you there.'

'Let's slip off and leave those deadweights with the bill, shall we? I have a feeling the evening is going to get rather tedious from here on in.'

Scott grinned. 'Sure thing. Have you got your own car or would you like a lift on the back of my Vespa?'

'Ah, the Vespa! Symbol of *la dolce vita*. What an enticing offer!'

As they drove to the office, he clung tightly around Scott's hips, his hands uncomfortably close to his privates, and Scott was glad they didn't have far to go. Up in the office, Truman exclaimed over the ingenious design of the cubbyhole, and when he saw the three packs of pristine cocaine, nothing would do but for him to try a couple of lines straight away. Scott refused to join him. Helen's experiences had put him off.

'Here's a copy of my article,' he said, pulling it out of the cubbyhole. He had made three carbons and sent the top copy to the editor so he still had a couple left. 'And I'll write my telephone numbers on it so you can tell me how it goes. How should I get in touch with you?'

Truman held out a white business card that simply had his name and a Manhattan phone number. 'You're honoured. I don't give these cards to many but I believe you have potential, young Scott. I think we should keep in touch. We may be able to work together in future.'

'How soon do you think there will be any news about my article?'

'I'm flying back to New York on Thursday and I'll see my publisher within a week. He can be a little slow but you will definitely hear within the month.' Truman wiped his nostrils with a finger.

Scott was disappointed. He'd hoped things would move faster. But then, he couldn't have the piece published while he was living in Rome anyway, so maybe it was all for the best.

'Don't worry, darling. You have me as your champion. If you are any good at all I'll get you into print. Now, if you don't mind, I think I'll take a taxi back to Elizabeth's. Thrilling as it was to ride on your Vespa, I don't believe my nerves could stand any more of it. Goodnight, my very charming friend.'

It was only after he left that Scott remembered he hadn't offered any money for the three packs of cocaine he'd pocketed. Oh well. It was a small price to pay in the grand scheme of things.

Chapter Seventy-Five

Two days after their dinner with Elizabeth and Richard, just long enough for Diana's hangover to subside, she and Trevor set off for Ischia. They took a *Rapido* down to Naples, then caught the hydrofoil boat across the bay. Diana felt a twinge of guilt as she identified the islands on the horizon for Trevor, remembering an evening when Ernesto showed them to her, long before anything had happened between them. That had been the beginning of the seduction, she realised. He had been playing a long game, prepared to wait for the right moment rather than leaping on her during their stay on the island.

It was a bright, sunny June day. The Mediterranean was an extraordinary cerulean shade of blue, while the sky was more of an azure, but on the horizon they blurred together in a misty haze. The sea breeze made the temperature comfortable. Everything would have been perfect, if only Helen hadn't died and the future of Diana's marriage wasn't up in the air.

'Let's just enjoy this,' Trevor said, and she got a spooky sense that he'd read her mind. He must know she was no longer interested in him sexually. He didn't seem interested in her either. They hugged in bed, but that was all.

'Yes, let's,' she said, and meant it.

Most of the cast and crew were to be billeted at the purpose-built Pensione Cleopatra, but the production staff were based in the nearby Jolly Hotel. Its ballroom had been converted into an office with desks, typewriters and telephones, and through the glass doors Diana could see the glint of a swimming pool. They left their luggage in their room, but Diana was impatient to get down to the harbour and inspect the boats, and Cleopatra's and Antony's in particular. How had the master boatbuilders realised all the final details?

As their taxi wove down into the little cove, she could see Cleopatra's barge, the *Antonia*, from afar, the gold-painted hull resplendent in the sunlight. The *Antonia* was huge and ornate, with purple sails furled round the masts, and numerous statues and urns at prow and stern. It was moored in deep water but connected to the jetty by a series of floating planks with a rope running along as a handrail. It all looked rather precarious, but they got out of their taxi and made their way towards it.

One of the boatbuilders recognised her as she walked along the jetty.

'*Signora Bailey, cosa pensi della nostra creazione?*' – 'What do you think of our creation?' He gestured with a sweep of his arm.

'*Magnifico,*' she proclaimed. 'Better than the real thing.'

He told her that after she had looked round Cleopatra's barge, he would take her out in a motorboat to Antony's ship, which was moored further round the bay.

She and Trevor stepped onto the slippery planks, which tilted under their weight, threatening to tip them into the sea. She clung to the rope, stepping carefully over gaps between planks. Some large silver fish circled below as if expecting to be fed. When she reached the gold-painted side of the barge, there was a rope ladder to climb up to the deck.

'Are they seriously expecting Elizabeth to do this in full Cleopatra costume?' she called over her shoulder. 'That's one sight I absolutely have to see.'

When they got on deck they saw that every single surface that could possibly be decorated had curlicues, incense burners or carvings of Egyptian gods. It wasn't historically accurate but it was spectacular – like the eighth wonder of the world, Trevor said, with only a hint of irony. The local boatbuilders had been working on it for six months since she last saw the basic shape and advised on the masts, and it had been transformed into a floating palace worthy of any queen, whether from ancient Egypt or modern Hollywood.

There was no point in criticising anything because there was no time to change it. Diana made a few notes about where the different scenes would be filmed and highlighted some issues that the continuity staff would have to look out for, but she could see this was going to be the *pièce de résistance* of the whole movie. It was the physical manifestation of the budget over-spend.

They clambered down the rope ladder and into the boat-builders' launch to travel out to Antony's more utilitarian battleship, with huge steel spikes protruding from the front. Everything was just as she had envisioned it, and she was delighted. They toured the other boats that would take part in the sea battle of Actium, and Diana pronounced them perfect.

'That's it!' she announced. 'My work is done. Now all I have to do is relax for a week until the cast and crew arrive.'

They spent the week walking, swimming in secluded bays, eating and drinking in local restaurants and bars, and Diana felt the tension in her muscles slowly dissolve away. With the combination of warm sun and gentle exercise Trevor's back stopped bothering him, and his skin tanned, making him look healthier. The island got busier as the week progressed. Foremost among the new arrivals were some young men on motor scooters wielding huge cameras.

'Here we go,' Trevor sighed. 'They're gearing up for the Liz and Dick Show.'

'They'll have no privacy here, except within the walls of their hotel room – if there. Someone told me that a new chambermaid at the Regina Isabella Hotel, where Richard and Elizabeth have suites, was discovered to be a journalist from *Novella* magazine.'

However, it seemed the couple had given up any hope of privacy because, instead of sailing to the island on a private boat, their arrival was heralded by the whirring of a helicopter resounding through the skies. The noise became deafening as it got closer then dropped down to land at the island's only heliport, five minutes from their hotel. Every *paparazzo* on Ischia was there with cameras primed before the helicopter doors opened and all got plenty of shots of the world's most famous couple.

The filming of the sea battle went according to plan, and on 23rd June they were to film the *Antonia* arriving at Tarsus – an event that had marked the beginning of Cleopatra's affair with Antony. Of course, like every outdoor scene, it was split into panoramic shots, long shots and close-ups, and there was stopping and restarting whenever the camera angle changed. The gold barge should have proceeded slowly into port, its purple sails fluttering and palm trees swaying on deck, to the sound of fifes, harps and flutes, but there was no music. Instead spectators heard the sounds of aeroplanes flying overhead, and the chatter of the watching crowd. Still, it was exciting. Coloured smoke spiralled from incense burners. Cleopatra stood under a golden canopy flanked by two silver cat gods and surrounded by dozens of beautiful young girls. The silver oars flashed through the water, even though the boat was actually powered by a motor.

There were hundreds of tiny craft in the water. Cleopatra's handmaidens threw coins from the deck of the *Antonia*, and seventy-five swimmers from the Italian Olympic team dived to retrieve them. The air was thick with the honeyed scent of hundreds of dollars-worth of flowers wilting in the heat of the midday sun.

It was Elizabeth's last official day of filming, and it seemed very apt that this should be her final scene. She was regal, indomitable, the queen of all she surveyed. Weighed down with gold and jewels, she must have been sweltering in the June heat but not a bead of sweat marked her flawless brow. Diana wondered how she was feeling inside, though. The day was drawing near when Richard would have to make the momentous decision: Sybil, his friends and family and the English theatrical establishment – or Elizabeth and Hollywood superstardom.

Elizabeth was throwing a party in her suite that evening, to which Diana and Trevor were invited, and she expected that the actress would be rather emotional. Hilary told her that Walter had arranged for an ambulance to be on standby in case she did anything silly, but that seemed unduly melodramatic.

Still, one never knew with Elizabeth.

Diana wore her lilac dress, the one Helen had helped her to choose, and when they arrived Elizabeth admired it effusively.

'You're so skinny. I can't wear styles like that with my big momma hips.' She patted them, with a conspiratorial smile.

They were handed bright turquoise cocktails to drink, and Trevor grumbled in Diana's ear that he would rather have had a beer. The suite was overflowing with people crowded onto the balconies to admire the sunset, lounging on Elizabeth's giant bed, or dancing to some 45 rpms playing on a record player. 'I Can't Stop Loving You', sang Ray Charles and all heads turned to look at Elizabeth, who pretended not to notice.

Diana had brought a notebook and she took the opportunity to swap telephone numbers and addresses with cast and crew who were leaving the next morning. Everyone was pledging eternal friendship but Diana wondered how many would keep in touch once they were back in California or New York or London. She had known these people for eight months now and some had been working together for over a year. The intensity of the film-making experience made you feel like close friends but it wasn't the genuine kind of friendship that grew from common interests and long-term loyalty. It was artificial and forced by circumstances.

Trevor was pulled into the circle around Richard Burton, where they were discussing the British writers known as 'Angry Young Men' – John Osborne, Arnold Wesker, Edward Bond and Harold Pinter. Would their works still be read in twenty years' time? Trevor argued that they were of the moment and wouldn't age well but Richard disagreed.

Momentarily alone, Diana decided to sneak out for a look round the hotel, which was considerably swankier than theirs.

She toured the grand public rooms then walked through a glass door into a lush landscaped garden, and there, by the swimming pool, was Elizabeth, all on her own.

'Are you alright?' Diana called, and Elizabeth turned.

'Sure. I just wanted a moment's peace. It's so beautiful here, don't you think?'

'Shall I leave you alone to enjoy the peace?'

'No, come and talk. Want a cigarette?'

She offered her pack, but Diana shook her head.

'How are things with you and Trevor? Do you reckon you two are gonna make it?'

Diana was taken aback by the directness of the question and didn't know what to say.

Elizabeth smiled. 'No, don't answer. I think I know. He's a fascinating man, and great company, but he's not your lover. So you have to decide whether you are going to settle for that. People do a lot worse. Some make such a mess of everything . . .'

She took a deep drag of her cigarette and blew out the smoke in a long puff. 'Richard and I sneaked down to the bay this morning to watch the dawn and it was glorious. There were no photographers around, just us – at least, so I thought. Richard went back to bed and I stayed to watch the sunrise and then suddenly I realised there was an old fisherman sitting there mending a net. He looked about a hundred years old.'

She fingered a chunky diamond bracelet on her wrist. 'I lost this bracelet somewhere last night and I think it must have been on the beach. Then this afternoon the hotel reception called to say it had been handed in and from their description, I'm sure it was that fisherman. But I don't understand why he didn't sell it? Money like that could have turned his life around. Or if he had asked for a reward I'd gladly have paid.'

She gazed out across the pool towards the bay. 'I suppose he must be content with the life he has. There was a kind of stillness and wisdom about him that made me want to ask his advice. I wanted to ask him what I should do with the rest of my life.' She gave a hoarse little laugh. 'Of course, then I remembered that I don't speak any Italian so I couldn't.'

'What do you think he would have said?'

'Well, he's probably Catholic so he no doubt believes I'm an erotic vagrant!' She shivered in her off-the-shoulder décolleté dress. 'But I think what I would have wanted him to say was "Follow your heart". Because no matter what anyone thinks of me, that's what I intend to do. I have no choice. It's the way I'm made.'

She dropped her cigarette only three-quarters smoked and ground it out under one of her pin-sharp heels. 'Come on, let's get back to the party. I need another cocktail.'

Diana followed her back into the hotel building, trying to think of something wise to say in response to the confession, but then she realised it wasn't necessary. Everything had already been said.

Epilogue

In mid-July Scott bought a copy of the *International Herald Tribune* and was stunned to find a piece entitled 'La Dolce Vita' with Truman Capote's byline which was almost word-for-word the same as his. The bastard had stolen everything, from his description of Helen's dancing style through to Luigi's shaved hands, and the only difference was that the Ghianciaminas' name wasn't even hinted at and the villa in Anzio and the attack on Scott weren't mentioned. In a rage, he called the paper's editor but he had no way of proving the piece had originally been his, after Truman claimed he'd hired Scott as a researcher. Scott felt defeated and depressed. His sole achievements after a year in Rome had been some silly stories about movie stars having an affair and a hopelessly mismanaged film running over budget. Big deal!

In early August, *Corriere della Sera* reported that Alessandro Ghianciamina had been killed by a hit-and-run driver. From the details, Scott sensed it was a professional killing. New Mafia bosses were muscling in on the Rome drugs trade and eliminating the competition. It didn't make him happy or triumphant that the man who had broken his nose was dead. He felt sorry for poor Gina to be losing a brother. But most of all he felt relief that he had one less thing to worry about.

At the end of September, Scott was transferred to Berlin just as the Cuban missile crisis led the world to the brink of nuclear war. At last he could write serious stories and over the next few years his reputation grew as he moved from *Midwest Daily* to *The New York Times*. He married an enigmatic East German girl called Suse, who had escaped from East Germany across no-man's land and had a bullet scar on her calf to prove it.

In the late 1960s, Scott finally wrote his book about Helen's death in Torre Astura, drug dealing in Rome and corruption at the heart of Italian government. It was well reviewed but had the misfortune to come out in 1969, the same year as Mario Puzo wrote *The Godfather*, which massively outstripped him in sales. In 1971, Scott's book about the Cold War was published and won the Pulitzer Prize. It was this, alongside his incisive reporting from the front line in Berlin, that made him a household name.

His father died suddenly in 1973 without ever telling Scott that he was proud of him; but by that time it didn't matter anyway.

* * *

On the 15th of July 1962, Trevor went back to London and Diana flew to Alexandria with a skeleton crew and a few members of the cast. Richard was there but Elizabeth couldn't join him in Egypt; it was thought she might become a target for protests because of her prominent support of Israeli causes.

It was a difficult shoot, at a small village in the desert called Edkou. The chaos was worse than in Rome, with missing shipments of wigs and makeup, mutinies by the extras, and everyone exhausted and debilitated by the dry, unforgiving heat, but by the 24th of the month their work was done. Diana said her final goodbyes to Richard, Joe, Walter and Hilary, then flew back to London.

On her return she began sending out letters of application to film and television companies, asking if any of them needed historical advisors and, to her delight, she received a reply from a BBC producer asking if she would help on a series they were shooting that autumn. It was about Richard the Lionheart and the Crusades, not Cleopatra, but she reckoned she could help, and her career change was effected rather smoothly and easily.

In the newspapers, she read that Elizabeth and Richard had holidayed together after shooting finished then attempted to go their separate ways. He returned to Sybil and the girls – but only temporarily. Within a couple of months he was being photographed with Elizabeth again. They just couldn't stay apart.

Diana and Trevor spent the autumn rubbing along together in their Primrose Hill flat. Neither raised the topic of their marriage but neither attempted to initiate marital relations either. They weren't unhappy and there was no one else in the picture so there seemed no urgent necessity to clarify or re-define their marriage in words. In January 1963, a flat came up for rent just two doors along and Diana tentatively suggested that she might take it. She could afford the rent with her new BBC salary, and they needed more space. Neither admitted it was a step closer to the end for their marriage. It didn't need to be said.

In June 1963, Diana and Trevor travelled together to New York for the premiere of *Cleopatra* at the Rivoli Theatre on

Broadway. Their expectations weren't high and Diana was disappointed to hear that Elizabeth and Richard weren't attending, but realised it was unlikely Elizabeth would have had time for a cosy chat. They had moved into an entirely different stratosphere, one in which they had little room for a couple of historians who once dined with them in Rome.

Diana bought an extravagant new dress for the premiere and was glad she had because the photographers were out in force. Joe was giving press interviews at the entrance to the theatre with Rosemary Matthews by his side and Diana was able to have a quick word congratulating them on their recent marriage. They looked very comfortable together. After all the chaos, the astronomical budget, the backstabbing and betrayals, at least one *Cleopatra* love story had ended happily.

Making Cleopatra

It wasn't the first film in the world to overspend and it wouldn't be the last, but it was certainly the most memorable – and entertaining.

'*Conceived in a state of emergency, shot in confusion, and wound up in blind panic.*' That's the director's famous verdict on the filming of the 1963 *Cleopatra*. What began as a two-million dollar potboiler designed to hoist Twentieth Century Fox out of a financial black hole, ended up as one of the most expensive films ever made even by 21st Century standards. Back then it nearly bankrupted one of Hollywood's most famous studios.

They tried to pin the blame on Elizabeth Taylor and Richard Burton, saying their antics had brought the film into disrepute and suing them for fifty million dollars. Taylor counter-sued and they settled out of court. But when you look at the facts, it's clear she bore some of the responsibility for the budget chaos.

Miss Taylor always claimed she was joking when she told producer Walter Wanger that she'd play Cleopatra for a million dollars – an unprecedented amount for any actor at the time. Wanger took her at her word though, and even caved in to her other demands, such as ten per cent of gross, massive overtime payments, and the promise to use a type of film – Todd AO – pioneered by her late husband Mike Todd on which she held copyright. At the age of twenty-eight she was already wealthy but she was about to get a lot more so – and the pattern was established that what Miss Taylor wanted, Miss Taylor got.

The plan had been to film on a Hollywood back lot, but

she insisted they shot overseas because it suited her for tax reasons. Extravagant sets were constructed at Pinewood Studios outside London and real palm trees flown in from LA. Rouben Mamoulian was hired as director and shooting began on 28 September 1960 – only to stop three days later when Elizabeth Taylor caught a cold.

Everyone waited as gusty rain destroyed the gold leaf on the outdoor sets and lashed the poor trees. Then it was rumoured that Miss Taylor didn't much like the script. There was a change of director to Joe Mankiewicz, with whom she had worked on *Suddenly Last Summer*, and shooting resumed after Christmas.

But before long Elizabeth developed pneumonia and on 4 March she collapsed in her suite at the Dorchester. An emergency tracheotomy was performed, and she had to be resuscitated four times after her heart stopped. A month later she flew home to recuperate in LA and the film appeared to be completely on the rocks.

La Dolce Vita

Walter Wanger would not give up on his star though. He had new sets built in Cinecittá studios on the outskirts of Rome, found an almost entirely new cast and crew, and once again filming started on 25 September 1961. The original Caesar and Anthony (Peter Finch and Stephen Boyd) were replaced by Rex Harrison and up-and-coming theatre star Richard Burton, and Joe Mankiewicz was rewriting the script.

But Mankiewicz hadn't finished his rewrite by the time filming started. Every night he sat up till the early hours, sometimes scribbling scenes that would be shot the

471

next afternoon. This meant they were shooting more or less chronologically and couldn't plan ahead – so all cast and crew had to be kept in Rome on full salary, all expenses paid, for a shoot that was originally envisioned to be sixty-four days but which eventually took almost two years. As just one example, Richard and Sybil Burton arrived in Rome on 19 September 1961 and he didn't shoot his first scene until January 1962. You can see where the budget was being spent!

There were dramas on set even before Taylor and Burton started sneaking off for secret assignations in each other's trailers or her private secretary's office. Problems with elephants, problems with an army range next to the Alexandria set, World War Two land mines were found on the beach – and the special film stock Miss Taylor insisted they use had to be flown back to Hollywood for processing so the director couldn't see the 'dailies' until about two weeks after they'd been shot. Meanwhile the star's weight fluctuated, making her sixty-five costume changes fraught with difficulty.

Once word leaked out that Anthony and Cleopatra were having an affair in real life, the press went crazy. The term 'paparazzi' had been coined by Fellini in his 1960 film *La Dolce Vita* but the Vespa-riding photographers in Rome in 1962 went much further than the ones he'd portrayed. They would jump in front of Taylor and Burton setting off flashbulbs in their faces, ran their car off the road, yelled lewd insults, and besieged them when they went to the island of Santo Stefano for an Easter break. (Burton gave her a black eye on that occasion and filming was delayed for three weeks while her bruises healed.)

The movie lurched from crisis to crisis, the budget escalating every day, and by June when they decamped to Ischia to shoot the sea battle of Actium (staged with real boats, some 200 feet long), Walter Wanger had been sacked as producer – but told to stay on and finish the film anyway. The president of Twentieth Century Fox, Spyros Skouras, was forced to resign and Darryl F. Zanuck was appointed in his place. He in turn sacked Joe Mankiewicz then realised he needed him to make sense of the hours and hours of footage, so bribed him to come back and help with the edit.

The New York première

Mankiewicz had always seen it as two films – *Caesar and Cleopatra*, followed by a sequel, *Anthony and Cleopatra* – but Zanuck wanted it cut down to one. It scraped in at just over four hours long, but a huge number of scenes were left on the cutting room floor, including many of Burton's best ones. Taylor and Burton declined to come to the New York première in June 1963 citing 'other commitments', but she claimed when she saw the film in London she was physically sick. The critics were generally scathing, and particularly cruel to Elizabeth – 'Miss Taylor is monotony in a slit skirt' – while Richard was described as 'looking like a drunken sot on a campus'.

Joe Mankiewicz married Rosemary Matthews, his assistant, so that at least brought him a happy conclusion on the domestic front, but his career never recovered. Walter Wanger never made another film. Richard Burton slowly, painfully extricated himself from his marriage to Sybil and married Elizabeth on 15 March 1964. They divorced ten years later and remarried in 1975 but only for nine months.

Despite a final cost of forty-four million dollars, Cleopatra went into profit in 1966 and it won four Oscars (although none were for acting or direction). It's worth watching, but it's very, *very* long.

Did Walter Wanger ever reflect on Spyros Skouras's advice when he first suggested casting Elizabeth Taylor?

'*Don't do it,*' the studio president urged. '*She'll be too much trouble.*'

But for those cast and crew who didn't have to shoulder the financial blame, the consensus was that their ten months in Italy was the holiday of a lifetime.

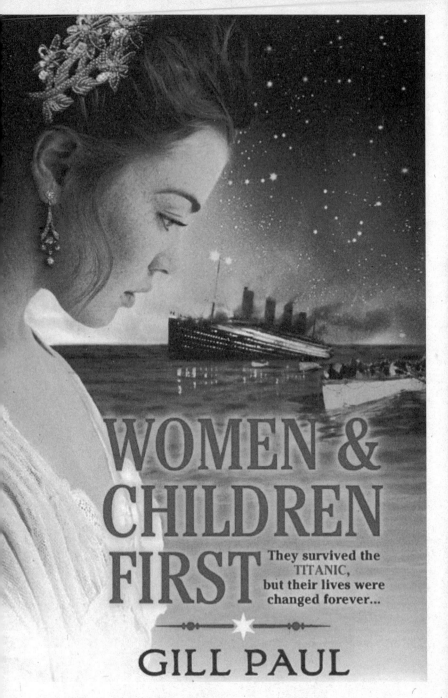

WOMEN & CHILDREN FIRST

They survived the
TITANIC,
but their lives were
changed forever...

GILL PAUL

They survived the Titanic, but their lives were changed forever . . .

Acknowledgments

I couldn't have written this book without the help of John Gayford, an actor who played a centurion in the 1963 *Cleopatra* and is frequently seen standing behind Richard Burton in the finished movie. He has been unbelievably generous with his time, answering my questions by telephone and email and going through the text in minute detail. His knowledge of the making of the film and life in Rome in the early 1960s have been invaluable, while his witty emails brought colour to the working day! I'm incredibly grateful.

Thanks also to Francesca Annis, who played one of Elizabeth Taylor's handmaidens in the film, and who answered my questions about life on the set. And my gratitude to Aurelio Cappozzo and Laura Ronchetti for information on legal processes in Rome at the time.

For those interested in learning more about the making of the film, I recommend Walter Wanger's book *My Life with Cleopatra* and Jack Brodsky and Nathan Weiss's *The Cleopatra Papers*, both published in 1963, as well as the documentary *Cleopatra: The Film that Changed Hollywood*. And do watch the film: it's enjoyable, and certainly much better than the critics said at the time.

Huge thanks as always to Karen Sullivan, my number one reader, who has extraordinarily good instincts for story and character. Anne Nicholson also had some very wise advice. Thanks to Karel Bata for his wisdom on technical aspects of filming and to Luke Sullivan for help with Italian dialogue. And grateful thanks to all the team at Avon: Caroline Ridding, Sammia Rafique, Helen Bolton, Lydia Newhouse, Becke Parker, Claire Power, Cleo Little, Tom Dunstand and Cicely Aspinall, as well as the amazing Claire Bord, whose editing is always spot-on.

Finally, special thanks to Vivien Green, the best agent anyone could wish for. She is wise, fun, fiercely protective of her authors, and a canny deal-maker. Having her on my side has made all the difference, and I'll always owe her a huge debt of gratitude.